SHOW ME
THE
DEADLY
DEER

Previously published Worldwide Mystery title by
CAROLYN MULFORD

SHOW ME THE MURDER

SHOW ME THE
DEADLY
DEER

CAROLYN MULFORD

WORLDWIDE®

TORONTO • NEW YORK • LONDON
AMSTERDAM • PARIS • SYDNEY • HAMBURG
STOCKHOLM • ATHENS • TOKYO • MILAN
MADRID • WARSAW • BUDAPEST • AUCKLAND

Recycling programs
for this product may
not exist in your area.

Show Me the Deadly Deer

A Worldwide Mystery/June 2016

First published by Five Star Publishing.

ISBN-13: 978-0-373-26997-6

Acknowledgments

Writers learn from their readers, and the best possible readers of first drafts are other writers working in the same genre. For years, members of my Mid-Atlantic critique group—Maya Corrigan, Mary Nelson, Helen Schwartz, and Sylvia Straub—have sustained me with feedback and encouragement. Devoted mystery readers Blenda Marquardt and Maxine Glenn read late drafts and advised me on both the writing and central Missouri's subculture. As usual, old friend Joyce Campbell gave valuable comments on early and late drafts. Assistance in portraying police work and private investigation came from multiple sources, including the Columbia Police Department and workshops sponsored by Mystery Writers of America and Sisters in Crime. Numerous members of the SinC Guppies online chapter have aided and abetted through exchanges of information and experiences. My sincere thanks to all.

ONE

Tires skidding around the corner violated the June evening's quiet. I dropped my trowel and reached for the Glock 27 stashed among the unplanted petunias.

Annalynn's black SUV braked as it passed me and then careened into her driveway.

Not like my lifelong friend to race down the quiet residential street. Even so, I'd overreacted. Tamping down the paranoia developed during three decades in Eastern Europe—and reinforced during five weeks back in my Missouri hometown—I tucked the gun into the back waistband of my shorts.

Annalynn jumped out and strode across our adjoining driveways, the setting sun's beam bouncing off her bronze sheriff's star. "Thank goodness you're home, Phoenix. I need your help."

I rose to meet her. "What's wrong?"

"A farm woman called to report her husband didn't come home. He left Laycock, or at least Harry's place, at three o'clock. That gave him plenty of time to drive home to milk the cows at four. Would you please go with me to find him?"

Relief gave way to annoyance. Why should we run around in this heat looking for a tardy husband? "You're *acting* sheriff, remember? You assign cases, not work on them."

Annalynn threw up her hands. "I have *no one* to

assign. The regional major case squad borrowed my deputies to help investigate the killing of that Highway Patrol officer." She took a deep breath. "Besides, the man hasn't been missing long enough for an official search. He probably ran out of gas or hit a deer."

So why the rush? "Let's wait a little while. Someone will spot him."

"I can't wait. It will be dark in an hour." She squared her shoulders. "I'll go alone if need be."

Light dawned. Her husband's shocking death six weeks ago compelled her to answer another wife's call for help. "Okay, I'll go with you." I pushed back the short black hair sticking to my forehead and glanced down at my sweat-and dirt-stained green tank top. My grimy appearance contrasted with her pristine beige uniform, the flawless makeup obscuring her fifty-plus years, and the perfect French roll of her brown, chestnut-highlighted hair. "I need to run through the shower first. Could you feed and water Achilles? He's out back guarding the hummingbirds from stray cats."

"Of course." Her shoulders relaxed as we hurried toward her house, my temporary home. "We'll take him along in case we need to do any tracking."

Tracking? She expected trouble. "Do I know the missing man?"

"No, the Tornells moved to Vandiver County years after you left. I know their names but not their faces."

She cut left to go to her backyard. "Please carry your reserve officer ID." She glanced back over her shoulder. "And Phoenix, if you can't bring yourself to leave the house without that gun, for Pete's sake, carry it in a holster."

ANNALYNN TURNED ON her giant cop flashlight to check the county map. "The Tornells live just past this crossroads."

Three white-tailed deer bounded across the blacktop road a few yards in front of her SUV. I braked to a stop. "When did northern Missouri become a deer preserve?"

"At least twenty years ago. When my kids were little, seeing deer was a treat. Now they're a road hazard. They may even come into Laycock and eat your petunias."

The deer hopped over a shoulder-high barbed-wire fence into a cornfield. I drove on until we spotted a white mailbox. I turned left into the gravel driveway running between the lawn and an unpainted board fence and stopped near the back door of a two-story white house. An outdoor light illuminated a crumbling cement walk-way and three steps.

A sturdy woman in a red T-shirt and cut-off jeans stepped through the screen door of an enclosed porch. A shadow fell on her face, but her rigid posture indicated tension.

Annalynn got out. "Dorothy Tornell? I'm Annalynn Carr Keyser, the acting sheriff. Any word from your husband?"

"No. I'm real worried," the woman said in a low-pitched voice. She pushed back a strand of short ash-blond hair. "Jesse's never late for milkin'. It's hard on the cows."

I climbed out of the SUV. "Hi. I'm Phoenix Smith."

The woman shifted her attention to me. "Mary Smith's daughter?"

"Yes." I'd never seen this woman. "You knew my mother?"

"No, but I know Bessie Hamilton. She told us how

you invited her to live in your house for free after your mother died." Dorothy Tornell pointed at Achilles, whose dark head with its drooping right ear stuck out the back window. "A police dog?"

"No, a pet." I stroked his head.

"He's not a German shepherd, even though he looks a lot like one," Annalynn added. "He's a Belgian shepherd, a Malinois."

Damn. I'd forgotten Missourians call German shepherds police dogs. I opened the door for Achilles, and two white cats dashed off the porch steps.

The woman peered at him. "In this light, you could mistake him for a fawn." She motioned for us to come in. "I'll get you that photo you asked for, Sheriff Keyser."

I hesitated. Gramma had never permitted animals in her farmhouse. "I'm afraid Achilles might play rough with your cats. Is it okay for me to bring him inside?"

"Sure." The woman led us into the large kitchen typical of old farmhouses.

An outdated fluorescent light revealed rough, red-stained hands and a deeply tanned face. She looked older than her forty-six years and stood a bit taller than my five six but shorter than Annalynn's five nine. Four hand-baskets of strawberries (the source of the stains?) and a transistor radio rested on a polished round oak table in the middle of the room. Three past-prime white refrigerators lined a wall.

She went toward a door to our left. "Help yourself to the lemonade in that middle fridge while I dig out a photo." A moment later stairs creaked.

Annalynn took glasses from a drainer by the double sink.

I scanned the room for insight into the Tornells' life.

Worn but waxed beige linoleum. Oak cabinets. A spotless white but aging electric stove. A beige Formica counter with a set of red, white, and blue metal canisters. More elbow grease than money here. A shotgun hung on spike nails driven deep into the top of the doorframe the woman had gone through. So where was the rifle? I checked above the door leading to the porch. The nails were there, but no rifle. When Annalynn handed me a glass of lemonade, I pointed to the shotgun and then to the empty nails.

"You ask her about it," Annalynn whispered. "You're much sneakier than I am."

True. Hearing footsteps on the stairs, I picked up a ripe strawberry. "These berries look delicious, Dorothy. Did you pick them this afternoon?"

"Yes. I raise produce for the farmers' market. You're welcome to take enough for shortcake." She handed a five-by-seven photo in a wood frame to Annalynn. "This is our twenty-fifth wedding anniversary photo. It's two years old."

Annalynn held it so I could see, too. Jesse Tornell was a thin man with dark-blue eyes and curly strawberry-blond hair. His smile, unlike his wife's, looked forced.

I added together the berries, the radio, and the empty nails. "Dorothy, would you have seen or heard your husband if he came home while you were picking strawberries?"

She cocked her head and wrinkled her brow. "Maybe not. The patch is on the far side of the garden, and I had the radio on. What makes you ask that?"

"My grandfather used to keep a rifle over the back door. I gather you do, too. Did your husband take it with him today?"

"No, he didn't." She glanced at the empty nails. Her cheeks turned pink. "He coulda come back and gone after a fox that's been hanging around."

A lie. I waited for her to elaborate on it, something many amateurs can't resist. She didn't. A smart liar. I nudged her to try another: "Or maybe squirrel hunting?"

"No. He hates squirrel meat." Her voice shook. "Got his fill of it as a kid."

Annalynn patted the woman on the shoulder. "I wouldn't worry yet. I'd like for you to call your neighbors to ask if they've seen him. We'll look around the farm. Maybe he stepped in a hole and sprained his ankle."

The woman thought a moment. "We got a dozen black Angus on the back forty. He might've gone over to turn on the water. We got a pond-fed tank there."

Annalynn nodded. "A good place to start. How do we get there?"

"Go on down the road about half a mile. At the second corner you'll see a gate." She looked at Achilles, who sat with his nose twitching and his good ear pointed straight up. "I'll get the T-shirt Jesse wore yesterday. If you find the pickup, your dog can track him from there." She stepped onto the porch and came back in with a gray T-shirt.

Annalynn took a notepad from her shirt pocket. "I'll give you my cell phone number in case you hear anything."

"We ain't got—I mean, you can't get cell service out here."

I suppressed a smile as Annalynn opened the door. People watched their grammar, and their manners, around her just as they had around her father, Judge Carr.

As soon as we were in the SUV, Annalynn said, "I

can guess what Tornell's doing with that rifle: hunting deer. I remember that one of their neighbors claimed he was shooting deer out of season and wanted Boom"— her voice faltered as she said her late husband's nickname—"wanted the sheriff's department to search the Tornells' freezers."

I backed out of the driveway. "Makes sense. A watering hole is ideal for shooting game. She's afraid we'll catch him hunting out of season, but she's so convinced he's hurt that she's willing to risk it."

The edge of our headlights showed low rows of soybeans in the field on our left. "We could be on a wild goose chase. The guy might have had too many beers and fallen asleep somewhere."

"He never has more than one beer. I called Harry's to check." Annalynn cleared her throat. "It's ten past nine, and she's sure something's wrong. I trust her instincts."

At the second corner, the headlights picked up a closed pipe gate.

Annalynn reached over from the passenger seat and turned the SUV's searchlight on it. "The padlock's on the chain. He's not here."

Having relocked doors to hide illicit entries, I wasn't so sure. "We're here. Let's check." I drove the SUV down a slight slope to the tractor-wide gate. Its six rows of rust-red pipe were too close together for me to crawl through. Beyond the gate, a grassy dirt road ran toward the pond.

Annalynn swung the searchlight to the right and held it on red metal behind a large oak tree. "His pickup! We'll have to go back for the padlock key."

I turned off the motor and took my set of keys from the ignition. "No need." I listened and heard nothing but frogs and crickets. I sniffed and smelled nothing but grass and weeds. Nothing stirred as I walked to the gate and, blocking Annalynn's view, opened the lock with a pick concealed in the miniature flashlight on my keychain. Out of habit, I used a tissue to remove the padlock and push the gate back to the barbed-wire fence bordering the dirt road. The hinges creaked all the way. "Drive through and I'll close the gate. We mustn't let any cattle out."

Annalynn scooted into the driver's seat and drove through. "Please get back in. This place is creepy."

When I climbed into the passenger seat, my sixty-pound dog tried to squeeze between the seats to get into my lap.

I rubbed him behind his drooping ear. "Settle down, boy." His unease elevated my own. I drew my gun and lowered the window. "Let's drive up parallel to the pickup."

Annalynn edged her SUV forward and stopped. "Should I draw my gun?"

"Not yet. You operate the searchlight. Do a sweep starting with the pickup."

The first sweep showed the big oak and three baby oaks amid thigh-high grass and weeds to our right, a gently rising grassy pond bank straight ahead, and rows of ankle-high soybeans on the other side of the barbed-wire fence to our left. Annalynn swept the light back. Nothing moved. She focused the light on the pickup. "Now what?"

Achilles' anxiety dictated caution. "Get a round in your chamber and then keep the gun in your holster. I'll check the pickup."

"Something's wrong. I'm coming with you."

Too risky. "I'd rather you stay here and watch my back." Turning off the overhead light and tucking a hefty flashlight under my arm, I eased out the door. I left it ajar in case I had to make a rapid retreat. Achilles came right after me. "I hope you studied tracking before you flunked out of the canine corps."

His good ear up and his nose extended, he pressed his shoulder against my left leg as we moved the few yards to the pickup.

I switched on the flashlight, holding it out to my far left so the beam wouldn't direct a shooter to my body. The driver's window was down. The keys were in the ignition. The window on the passenger side was also open.

Careful not to touch the pickup, I walked around it—and saw nothing but an old Dodge pickup that had been parked in the shade on a hot June afternoon.

Achilles, still pressed against my leg, barked a question.

"Whatever you're asking, I don't know the answer," I muttered.

"I couldn't hear you," Annalynn said from the SUV. "Did you find anything?"

"Just an empty pickup." I thought aloud: "If he's nearby, he heard us drive in. Either he doesn't want us to find him or he can't call out." But he didn't know who we were, and he had a rifle. I shouted, "Jesse! Dorothy sent us to look for you! Jesse!"

A cow mooed somewhere off to the right. Two others replied.

"We're going to have to look for him," Annalynn said. "All three of us."

"Okay." Definitely something wrong here. Must minimize the risk. "Let's leave the SUV here with the searchlight on and hope Achilles can pick up his scent."

"I'll bring the T-shirt." Annalynn trained the searchlight on the pond bank some fifteen yards away and turned off the motor. "Should I draw my gun now?"

"I feel safer with it holstered."

"Ha. Ha. Ha."

Damn. I'd damaged her confidence. I'd coached her in target shooting, but she had little experience with guns. "Stumbling around in the dark holding a loaded gun is a bad idea." I lowered my voice. "I knew an idiot who stepped in a hole and shot himself in the leg. He almost bled to death."

Annalynn handed me the T-shirt. "One of the informants you smuggled out of Hungary into Austria?"

"I'm an economist, not a human smuggler. You're jumping to conclusions." Correct ones. I held the T-shirt under Achilles' nose. I didn't know the right command. Sure to be short. "Find."

Achilles sneezed and looked up at me.

I knelt by the pickup door and pushed his nose to the ground. "Find."

He sniffed and raised his head to lick my face.

I hated that, as he knew. "Oh, hell! What's the magic word?"

"That's what I used to ask my kids. Find, *please*." Annalynn chuckled as Achilles dropped his nose to the ground. "Good boy."

He licked her hand and trotted toward the dirt road, head low. He followed the road, turning right a few feet from where the pond bank sloped upward.

Now outside the searchlight's beam, we stayed close behind our tracker. My light swept from Achilles to the right and Annalynn's from Achilles to the left. We saw little but tall grass and weeds.

Achilles stopped and raised his head. Hackles up, he

faced the pond. He wheeled and darted to me. Closing his teeth on the hem of my T-shirt, he pulled me toward the SUV. I dropped the flashlight, drew my gun, and grabbed his collar. "Sit, Achilles, sit."

He whined, but he let go of my top and obeyed.

Annalynn had drawn her gun and focused her beam on the bank. "Oh, God! I see sneakers. To the right of that old duck blind. Mr. Tornell? Jesse?"

Gott im Himmel! "Hold Achilles while I take a closer look." I picked up my flashlight and walked along the pond bank until I spotted grass that had been mashed down and not sprung all the way back. Two feet from that rough path, stepping as lightly as I could, I made my way toward the shoes. They were attached to jeans-clad legs. Insects swarmed over dried blood on a blue T-shirt and around a jagged stick protruding from the man's back. His shoulders and head lay just inside a blind made of rotting boards and ragged camouflage cloth. A rifle lay by his outstretched right hand. I sniffed. No hint of gunpowder.

Annalynn didn't need to add this grim tableau to the crime-scene photos of her dead husband that haunted her sleep. "Take Achilles to the car and radio your dispatcher to get the evidence tech and medical examiner out here."

"You mean somebody killed him." Annalynn's voice was flat, matter of fact. "Stay, Achilles, stay." She followed my footsteps until she stood behind me. "I asked to be appointed acting sheriff. I have to do the job." Her beam rested on the dried blood and then moved on up to the strawberry-blond hair. "I have to be sure he's dead."

"I'll do it." I moved close to the head, bent over, and stretched my hand out to touch the carotid artery in his neck. No pulse. Cool skin after a hot day and a warm evening. Keeping my tone businesslike, I said, "He's been dead a while. I don't think we should touch anything."

"No, no. Of course not. What's the weapon?"

I shone my light on the stick in Jesse Tornell's back. But it wasn't wood. Doubting my sharpshooter eyes, I bent down to get a better view. "It's a broken antler."

TWO

"AN ANTLER? ARE you sure, Phoenix?" Annalynn trained her light on the object. "You're right. I can see velvet on it."

The velvet indicated the antler had broken off recently. I studied it, not believing what my eyes saw. The prong had entered the body in line with the heart, but how could Bambi gore a man with enough force to kill him?

"Killed by a deer! Incredible." Annalynn stepped well back, holstered her gun, and sank down on the bank. "And I have to tell his wife." She wrapped her arms around her knees and put her head down on them. "I don't think I can do it."

I restrained my impulse to offer to break the bad news. I couldn't—and shouldn't—protect Annalynn from all the harsh reminders of her husband's violent death. Putting my gun away, I knelt beside her and rubbed her back between the tense shoulders. "No one can tell the poor woman any more gently than you will."

"Thanks, Phoenix," Annalynn said after a minute, her voice shaky. "I'll do it somehow. But I'll radio in first." She focused the flashlight on her wristwatch, causing the diamonds to sparkle. "Twenty-four minutes after nine. We found him about nine fifteen?"

"That's close enough for your report." I rose to study the antler again. It protruded from his back about two inches. "I wouldn't mention the antler on the radio."

"Why not?"

"Because it sounds like a macabre joke—man hunts deer, deer kills man. A human killer may be playing games here." I drew my gun at the thought that a killer might be hiding nearby. No. Long gone. Achilles would have warned us.

"You think someone shot or stabbed him and then jammed an antler into the wound?" Annalynn's tone conveyed doubt.

"That's my best guess."

"But the autopsy will show the true cause of death. Why hide a bullet or a knife wound with an antler?"

Good reasoning. She'd kept her head despite her anguish. "A distraction. Time to get out of the area. Maybe even the hope of getting away with it."

"I'll look like a fool if I announce Jesse Tornell was gored by a deer." Annalynn's voice steadied as she spoke. "I'll say 'cause of death undetermined,' and I'll tell Gillian to come ready to check absolutely everything." Now every inch the sheriff, she strode toward her vehicle. "You stay here to protect the body from animals, please. I'll come back as soon as I can. It may take an hour for anyone to get out here." She paused. "I'm assuming you're not afraid to stay alone."

"Of course not." Guarding a dead body didn't register on my fear meter. "If you'll leave me the department's camera, I'll take pictures before anyone else comes and messes up the area."

"Good. Thanks."

At the SUV, I took the camera, booties, and gloves from the big red cooler that held official equipment and supplies while Annalynn radioed a cautiously worded message to her dispatcher. Then she put the padlock in a brown paper lunch sack, the department's standard evidence bag. I opened the noisy gate for the SUV. When Annalynn, a cautious backer, finally edged out, I closed the gate again.

Being a covert operative had taught me nothing about crime-scene photography or police procedures, but common sense said to photograph the scene in an orderly sequence, moving from wide shots to close-ups. Lighting the shots with flashlight and flash, I retraced our route from the pickup to the victim.

Achilles remained at my side until I ordered him to stay on the road to keep him from contaminating the area around the victim.

Framing the body in the camera's screen, I noticed how symmetrical, almost posed, it appeared. I zoomed in for an extreme close-up of the antler. Could a rabid deer have raced up and gored him before he could turn to defend himself? Not impossible but highly unlikely. Much more likely that a human hand had held the antler. The amount of blood on the T-shirt indicated Jesse Tornell hadn't died instantly, but his heart hadn't pumped long.

"Stop speculating, Phoenix," I muttered. "You have no stake in this stranger's death. Be sensible and keep out of it."

Achilles barked once, a call for my attention.

Engrossed in my photography, I ignored him. Tornell's face wasn't visible. His arms were extended as though to stop a fall. His left hand formed a loose fist. His right hand gripped grass a couple of inches from the rifle stock.

He was armed. He was strong. He was dead.

No one could have come through that creaky gate without Tornell hearing him. Yet he'd turned his back, not his rifle, on the killer. The farmer must have known and trusted whoever wielded that antler.

Achilles barked three times, demanding I respond.

I tucked the camera into the waist pack attached to my holster belt and walked down the bank. "I'm coming, *Schatzi*."

He picked up the victim's T-shirt in his teeth.

"What do you mean, boy? We found the owner."

He dropped the shirt, lowered his nose, and moved purposefully down the road.

"Hmm." I shone the light onto another pipe gate some ten yards away as Achilles, nose to the ground, moved toward it. "So Tornell went somewhere else before he went to the blind. Okay. Find, *please*."

A few seconds later Achilles hesitated near the middle of the gate and then moved on to the padlocked end. He paused and looked back at me.

"Find, please."

He crouched and sniffed his way along the gate, moving to my left. Wheeling around a few feet beyond it, he crept back in the other direction. He stopped a few feet beyond the other end of the gate, repeated the exercise, and sat down near the padlock facing the gate.

"So the trail ends here. That doesn't make sense. Just to be sure, I'll open the gate." I used my pick on the padlock.

Achilles growled a mild but firm warning at something beyond the fence.

Scheisse! I was getting careless. Gun ready, I shone the light on the pasture. A cluster of black cattle stood at the outer edge of the beam, their heads turned toward me. Their calmness convinced me no one hid among them. I holstered my gun and opened the gate wide enough to slip through. "Come. Find, please."

Achilles slipped through and crept back and forth along the gate twice. He went back through the gate to where he had lost the trail and trotted in widening circles.

I stepped back through the gate, locked it, and waited.

After a minute or so he came back to the gate and sat down.

"The nose has it. Tornell's trail ends here. Then how did he get to the blind?" I stroked Achilles' dark head and upbraided myself for not thinking to take some of his treat biscuits from the SUV. "If you're right, I should be able to see something between here and the pond—blood, mashed grass, a groove left by dragging."

But I didn't.

I duckwalked from the pond bank to the gate with my flashlight inches above the ground. Bare patches in the road showed only indistinct foot and tire prints. Five feet short of the gate, leg muscles aching, I searched inch by inch for any sign of a struggle or of blood. Nothing.

Could Achilles have made a mistake? Since I'd found him barely alive by a creek a month ago, I'd learned he had an extraordinary sense of smell and, by dog standards, a high IQ. Later I learned the DEA had dropped him from its canine training program, but I attributed that to his friendly personality. Certainly his primary goal was to please me.

But I hadn't prompted him to continue tracking. He'd insisted on that himself. He knew what he knew. And the trail's end made no more sense than that antler.

"I'm out of my element, Achilles. Annalynn and I better leave this one to the professionals." But I couldn't stop thinking about what I saw and, more puzzling, didn't see. "Let's figure out what could have happened if the trail ends at the gate."

I envisioned the farmer leaning on the gate and studying his cattle as Grampa had done. Someone comes up behind him and—what?—picks up a broken antler and stabs him? Shoots him with his own rifle and then sticks a broken antler into his back to conceal the shot? Knifes him and sticks an antler into the wound? No scenario rang true.

And what happened to the blood? Cleaning blood off the ground would take time, expertise, and special chemicals. And how had the body been moved? Carrying a grown man to the blind would require considerable strength. Or more than one person.

One thing was certain: No vengeful deer moved the body.

Achilles growled and raced along the fence between the cattle and the pond.

I switched off the light and dropped to the ground. I landed on my waist pack. It dug under my rib cage where a bullet had sliced through me three months ago in Istanbul. Faint with pain, I struggled to stay conscious as something rushed along the side of the pond. A dim figure arched over the fence, and then another and another. Three deer.

The pain eased. "Achilles! Come! Let the suspects go."

THREE

My COMMAND CAME too late. Achilles yelped in pain and jumped back from the barbed-wire fence.

"Come here, city slicker." I shone the light on his black nose. The barb hadn't broken the skin. "We better sit here and nurse our wounds until Annalynn gets back."

He settled down close to me with his head on my left knee, a signal that he needed soothing.

"Poor boy. Being out here brings back bad memories for you. No wonder you're upset." Turning off the light, I stroked his back and hummed "Moonlight Sonata." A minute or two later a car went by headed toward the Tornells.

A little later clouds moved across the moon. "*Scheisse*! The last thing we need is rain." We sat listening to the crickets' and frogs' repetitive songs. Mosquitoes swarmed around me, prompting me to get up and become a moving target. With Achilles glued to my left leg, we strolled around the pond through high grass searching for signs someone had walked up the bank elsewhere. A narrow track between the bottom of the bank—about four feet high on this side—and the pasture fence marked a regular route for the deer. When I'd gone halfway around the old round pond, I climbed the bank and shone my flashlight around the inner bank. My light showed no disturbance in the grass and dirt. "Damned if I can figure out how the body got there, Achilles."

The inner bank sloped down about seven feet to a small pool of murky water. Tall grass covered the top yard, and clumps of it grew most of the rest of the way down. The last foot or so was bare dirt. I walked on around on the bank's broad top until I neared the body and then returned to the track and switched off my flashlight to save the battery. Soon car lights moved slowly down the road and stopped near the gate.

A door slammed. "Phoenix? Where are you?" Alarm had raised Annalynn's pitch.

"Here. We're fine." I turned on my light and hurried to open the gate.

"Telling Dorothy Tornell was awful." Annalynn took a deep breath. "Thank God I had her sit down first. She fainted." She came through the gate and walked with me toward the pond. "I'd never seen anyone faint except Mother."

I tried to lighten the mood: "Your mother didn't faint. She swooned."

"You sound just like *your* mother. I still miss her so much." Annalynn reached down to stroke Achilles, who had come to comfort her. "I shamed a neighbor into coming to help Dorothy. I had a tough time persuading her not to come back with me."

I remembered how determined Annalynn had been to learn the truth about her husband's death. That's why she'd wangled the thirteen-week appointment as sheriff.

She shook her shoulders as though shaking off memories. "Find anything?"

"Achilles did. He tracked Tornell to the pasture gate and no farther. He must have been killed there."

Annalynn walked past the pond toward the gate, shining her light on the ground. "No sign of a struggle. No blood spatter. Maybe Achilles is wrong."

"I don't think so." I stroked him as I told her what had happened, ending with, "Your CSI tech should find traces of blood, at least if she gets here before it rains."

"Don't count on it. She has only two weeks of experience. We need the major case squad. Maybe if I suggest a tie to the case they're working on…" She took her cell phone from her belt. "Searching… I have a signal."

My relief that Annalynn was tossing off a hot potato mingled with disappointment that we wouldn't investigate ourselves.

"Captain Gist—Sam—this is Annalynn Carr Keyser. I answered a missing person call and found an apparent murder victim in the field by his beef herd. That makes me wonder if he interrupted rustlers, perhaps those responsible for the trooper's murder Saturday evening. Could your M-squad investigate?"

Rustlers? First I'd heard of that theory, but the police don't tell all any more than the CIA does.

She grimaced. "No, I have no proof. I'm merely pointing out a possibility." She listened at least a minute. "I understand, but since you can't help me with this investigation, I have to ask you to release my deputies from your detail." She rubbed her forehead with her free hand. "No, I don't have anyone else to work on this. That's why I answered the missing person call myself." She motioned to me and put her phone on speaker so I could hear.

"You'll have to do the best you can. I need every man I've got," said a hoarse voice. "Sorry to leave you out on a limb, Mrs.—*Sheriff* Keyser"—he didn't sound sorry at all—"but odds are a family member or neighbor killed your farmer. Here's what you do: First, have your tech do a thorough job at the crime scene. Don't expect him to find all that stuff you see on television shows, but you got to have something to show the jury these days. Send your most experienced officer out to interview the neighbors. Ask folks who had a motive. Then check alibis. Then talk the person without an alibi into confessing. Plain old police work. You can probably do some of it yourself. Goodbye."

The bastard's condescension infuriated me. "Was that personal animosity or professional arrogance?"

"Both. Troopers despise amateurs in local law enforcement," she said calmly. "I expected Sam Gist to turn me down, but it was worth a try. I got what I needed most— official instructions on how *I* should proceed with the investigation."

Clever. She'd received an oral waiver on taking part in the investigation. Her terms as school board president had honed her infighting skills. "Do you really think this murder has anything to do with one fifty miles from here?"

She put her phone away. "It's possible Tornell surprised rustlers."

And I'd thought I lived in the past in Vienna. "I doubt it. The cattle are still here, and you can't even see them from the road. Besides, this is a Missouri farm, not a Wyoming ranch. Surely farmers here don't run big enough herds to attract rustlers."

"Phoenix, rustling has become a major problem in parts of Missouri. After all, a steer sells for around a thousand dollars."

Not much of a motive for murder, but I didn't want to argue the point. "Have you heard how the trooper was killed?"

"Don't repeat this: He was garroted—with a wire. A completely different MO."

"Umm. A sneak attack. Nobody came through that noisy gate and sneaked up on Jesse Tornell. Much as I hate to agree with Captain Gist, I think Tornell knew his killer."

A beige squad car pulled over in front of Annalynn's SUV and the driver got out. My light fell on a short young woman with a dark ponytail. She pulled gloves out of a duffel bag as she approached us. Unlike Annalynn, she wore equipment on every inch of her holster belt and a radio transmitter on her shoulder.

"Thanks for working a double shift," Annalynn said. "Gillian Bartolini, this is Phoenix Smith. And Achilles. Consider everything from the road to the pond and between the fences a crime scene. We have a long, long night ahead of us."

Gillian nodded, her round face eager. "Then it really is a homicide?"

"We'll treat it that way," Annalynn said. "Phoenix, you and Achilles can go home. I'll ride back to Laycock with Gillian."

Disappointed, but aware my open involvement would risk exposure of my secret past and pose a PR problem for Annalynn, I bit back a protest and came up with an alternative: "I'll relieve the neighbor and stay with Dorothy Tornell until her family arrives." Some discreet questions and snooping might allow me to eliminate the usual suspect, the widow.

Annalynn reached out and squeezed my hand. "That's so kind of you. She needs someone to answer the phone and—just be there."

I had learned to take credit for good behavior, especially when I didn't deserve it. "What did you tell her about what we found?"

"That we saw a wound but couldn't tell the cause of death."

"Ain't that the truth!"

A TALL BRUNETTE opened the porch door as I parked the SUV beside a gray Buick in the Tornell driveway.

"Hi. I'm Shelley Bulganov." She hurried down the steps. "Now that you're here, I'll go on home. I have to be up at three to help with the milking."

"Of course." I cheered silently at the opportunity to question the vulnerable widow alone. "Does Dorothy have family coming?"

"Not tonight." She got into the Buick and turned on the motor. "I offered to call a friend, but she just shook her head. She's kinda in shock. Bye."

Apparently Shelley didn't consider herself a friend. "I'm sure your coming over was a big help," I said, careful to sound sincere rather than sarcastic.

Achilles whined from the SUV as Shelley backed out of the driveway.

"Stay, *Schatzi*." Gasping sobs sounded from the kitchen as I climbed the porch steps. Remembering Annalynn's nightly pacing and silent tears, I lost my enthusiasm for my self-assigned task. But it had to be done, and common decency demanded that I offer comfort. I went in.

Dorothy Tornell stood hunched over the sink. Her red-stained right hand gripped a paring knife.

For a nanosecond I thought of blood and attempted suicide. Then the basket of strawberries by the sink registered.

The widow choked back a sob. "Tell me what happened. Please. The sheriff didn't tell me anything but that you found him dead on the pond bank. Did he accidentally shoot himself?"

"No. The rifle hadn't been fired." Compassion could wait. Shock elicited information. "Someone killed him."

The knife slipped from her fingers and clattered onto the floor. She staggered to a straight-backed chair at the table and fell into it. "Why? He couldn't have had more than twenty dollars on him. Are you sure?"

She'd placed the blame on a thief, an outsider. Suspicious. No, natural. "Pretty sure, but that's not official. The medical examiner has to determine how he died. Until then, you should tell everyone—even your family—just what the sheriff told you." I picked up the knife and met her eyes, primed to judge her reaction. "Can you think of anyone who would want to harm your husband?"

Eyes blank, she shook her head. "Nobody."

"Anyone angry enough to attack him even if they didn't mean to kill him?"

"No, no. Jesse never hurt anybody." A shadow crossed her face. "He's had some squabbles with neighbors, but never anything that went beyond a few cuss words."

Until now? I sat down in the chair next to her so we were face to face. "You know how men are. You hurt their pride and they lose all sense of proportion and lash out."

She nodded. "I've worried about the way Jesse and Junior argue." She ducked her head. "Jesse never hit him."

Then she wouldn't have mentioned it. "Where is Junior? Can I call him for you?"

Dorothy raised her head, tears streaming down her cheeks. "He's in Colorado." She wiped away the tears. "He got an internship because of his good grades at Laycock Community College. He took the car. That's why

I couldn't go looking for Jesse myself." She drew in a shuddering breath. "I called Junior. He's starting back at daylight."

Relieved that the son wouldn't be a suspect, I patted her hand. "You'll be a big comfort to one another. Do you have other children?"

"My daughter. She lives in Oregon." Tears brimmed over. "She's eight months along and don't dare travel." She covered her face with her hands. When she regained control, she choked out, "She was real upset 'cause she and her daddy argued last time they talked. I hope this don't hurt the baby. I'm glad I didn't know somebody killed him when I talked to her."

"Maybe she won't have to know until the sheriff's department can find out who did it. Tell me—"

"But aren't you the sheriff's department?"

"Me? Oh, no." I'd worn jeans and a turquoise T-shirt to show my civilian status. "I'm an economist. I work for a venture capital company in Vienna, Austria. I'm staying with Annalynn for a few weeks while I sell my parents' house. I came with her in case she needed the dog. I know nothing about police work."

The widow frowned. "But you're the one who's asked me questions."

Score one for her. "I only mean to help. Anything you tell me is unofficial. Of course, I'll pass on any useful information to Annalynn." Satisfied I'd baited the hook, I stood up. "I'm very sorry if I've made you uncomfortable. Would you like for me to go?"

She grabbed my arm. "Please don't leave. I don't want to be alone tonight."

"I'll stay then. Is there anything I can do for you? Any

calls you'd like for me to make? Could I fix you a cup of tea, Mrs. Tornell?" Just like recruiting a CIA asset.

"Call me Dorothy." She smiled wanly. "You can help me take the stems off the strawberries. These are the last of this year's crop, and I promised to have them ready tomorrow morning for the church ladies. They're making strawberry pies."

"A waste of fine berries in my opinion," I said, joining her in pretending normalcy. "Give me strawberry short-cake or berries over vanilla ice cream any day."

"Amen." Dorothy rose and went to the sink. "I washed them already. We can work at the table." She rinsed the knife she'd dropped and pulled a paring knife from a rack. "I'll get you some gloves so you won't stain your hands." She opened the cabinet under the sink, pulled out light rubber gloves, and handed them to me.

I let the air clear for a minute or so as we began the repetitious work. "You said Jesse had squabbled with some neighbors. Tell me about them."

Dorothy focused on the berries. "I guess telling you wouldn't be like accusing somebody to the police."

"No, of course not. Anything you want me to keep confidential, just say so." I'd decide whether to pass it on.

Dorothy glanced up. "I expect you might tell the sheriff, though."

No fool, this woman. I considered for a moment and opted for the truth: "If I thought it would help find the killer."

She nodded. "You two must be pretty good friends."

"Yes. We grew up next door to each other."

"I was in the Carr castle once. On a house tour to raise money for band uniforms. I'll never forget that pretty staircase in the big hall and all them beautiful antiques."

"I sleep in one of those, the four-poster canopy bed that Annalynn used as a child. We've remained close since I left Laycock—closer than most sisters. Certainly much closer than I am to either of my two brothers."

Dorothy wiped away tears with the back of her hand. "I got no brothers or sisters. Sure wish I had a friend like that. I lost touch with my old friends when Jesse and I moved here from Putnam County. I spent all my spare time—God knows there's never been much of that—on my kids. You got any kids?"

"No." Share personal information to get personal information. "I married right out of college. We saw things differently"—I believed in monogamy—"and went our own ways. I took a doctorate in economics and found a job in Europe."

"Jesse and I didn't always see things alike. He wanted everything done his way, but nobody ever worked harder for his family." She put down her knife. "I'm not accusing anybody, but I can think of two people who might've lost their temper and attacked him." She paused. "I'll tell you if you'll promise to check them out yourself—you know, find out where they were today and stuff like that—before you tell the sheriff."

Progress. "I'll be glad to do that." I waited five seconds. "You realize I may need Annalynn's help to do things like check work and phone records."

Dorothy picked up the paring knife. "Okay. Nobody knows better than she does what I'm going through. I admire the way she took on her late husband's job as sheriff. If I can't trust you two, I can't trust nobody."

A twinge of guilt marred my triumph. "You're both strong women, Dorothy."

Her face contorted, but no tears flowed. "I feel like

I'm in a nightmare. If I couldn't smell these strawberries, I'd swear I'm asleep." She shivered. "I better tell you right now before I think better of it. We've had a lot of trouble with Floyd Vanderhofen, the neighbor whose land adjoins that pasture back of the pond. He moved there about three years ago, and he let his fence get in such bad shape his cattle came through it. He refused to fix it, so Jesse cut down some of Floyd's scrubby trees for posts and put up a good barbed-wire fence. He billed the wire to Floyd. He wouldn't pay, and he filed a suit for the value of his trees in small claims court. We're supposed to go to court next week."

"He certainly sounds worth checking out." Could finding the murderer be so simple? Why not? People who killed someone they knew surely had obvious motives. "What can you tell me about him?"

"Not much," she said, her hands flying through the berries. "He's divorced. In his fifties. He teaches biology at Laycock Community College. Junior says he's a big environmentalist. Loves the deer and all that. He's not a real farmer, that's for sure."

"I'll check his teaching schedule and go from there. Who else?"

"Straw Bulganov. He's been in jail for meth. He lives three miles down the road in a ramshackle house that his father—Vlad Bulganov—owns. Last March Vlad hired Straw and Jesse to fix the inside of a new shed for his new tractor, one that cost two hundred fifty thousand dollars. Straw didn't show, so Jesse told Vlad he and Junior could handle the job. Straw came over to the shed and called Jesse all sorts of names and said he'd be sorry."

"I'll check on the Bulganovs." Who would have

thought I'd be checking out Russians in Missouri? "Is the woman who just left Straw's sister?"

"Sister-in-law. Bob, her husband, is as hardworking as Straw is shiftless, but they're only half-brothers. Bob's mother passed away when he was a little kid."

The brothers Bulganov. "Can you think of anybody else?"

"No. Nobody." She worked in silence as we finished the berries. "You can sleep upstairs in Junior's bedroom tonight, Dr. Smith. The bed is already made up."

"Call me Phoenix." Getting an Eastern European's confidence had never been this easy. I dismissed my duplicity as necessity and planned to search the house for evidence to clear—or to condemn—the prime suspect.

FOUR

I SLEPT FITFULLY in Junior's sagging twin bed, wakened by sobbing, by Achilles licking my foot, by a full-throated thunderstorm. The rain wouldn't leave much evidence for the tech to gather.

An alarm clock in the neighboring bedroom woke me from my deepest sleep. It was still dark. Encumbered by the voluminous cotton gown Dorothy had given me to sleep in, I stepped into the dark hall when I heard her go down the narrow, creaking staircase. "Good morning."

"Go back to sleep," Dorothy said. "I'm going to do the milkin'."

"Can I help you?"

"Thanks, but it's easier to do it myself than tell somebody else what to do."

"Okay, but I'll fix breakfast for you. What time will you finish?"

"Around seven thirty. There's eggs and sausage and coffee in the refrigerator." She hurried on downstairs, and I heard the bathroom door close.

Achilles licked my hand.

"I'll take you out and get some biscuits from the SUV as soon as I'm dressed," I assured him. After Dorothy went to the barn, I put on my clothes and went through the small room. A cheap dresser with nothing but an archery trophy on top held winter clothes. In a plastic wardrobe hung one gray suit, half a dozen polyester ties, and two bright-white dress shirts. Science textbooks lined the back edge of Junior's desk, a piece of plywood resting on sawhorses. A big cardboard box in a corner held an assortment of old sports equipment: a baseball bat and glove, a sports bow, a cloth quiver containing round-tipped wood arrows, an elliptical basketball. Not even a *Playboy.* My search seemed silly, not to mention intrusive, but I always checked everything I could when in alien territory.

I went downstairs to wash the sleep out of my eyes and wish for a toothbrush. I ran my hands through my hair and gave it a shake. It fell into place, but if I didn't get a cut within the next two weeks, I'd look like a shaggy dog. I hadn't brought any makeup with me, but my dark skin showed no purplish smudges under my tired eyes. I'd gained back enough of the twenty pounds lost after being shot that my crow's feet and laugh lines no longer formed ditches.

Achilles whined to remind me he was waiting to go out.

The sun peeked over the red barn and turned the puddles in the driveway into miniature reflecting pools. The wet grass soaked my running shoes by the time I got to the SUV to raid Annalynn's stash of dog biscuits. I perched on the front seat and fed Achilles while I re-evaluated what Dorothy had told me. Her words rang true, and her grief seemed genuine. But she'd lied about Jesse's hunting and hitting his son. We had to consider her a suspect. Motive? Not a woman to take a lover, I judged, but she obviously needed money. Life insurance? The sale of the farm? At last something I knew how to do: assess their finances. Now to find their financial records.

I tied Achilles' long leash to a tree and left my wet

shoes on the porch. Pulling on a pair of gloves from under the sink, I turned on a floor lamp in the living room and did a quick search through the old *Reader's Digest* condensed books and a dozen paperback romances in the board-and-brick bookcases beneath the two front windows. The room contained little else but a wood stove, a maroon vinyl sofa with a fake China-made blue-and-white Wedding Ring quilt tossed over it, and a matching recliner. An old boom box and a stack of CDs rested on the bottom shelf of a stand holding a twenty-six-inch LCD television. High school graduation photos of the son and daughter stood on either side of the TV. The Tornells had no money to spend on decorating.

Neither the bathroom nor the lightly stocked pantry took more than a minute to check. With light streaming in the kitchen windows, I went through all the cabinets. The only papers were old manuals for small kitchen appliances. Then I checked the three refrigerators. No papers, but plenty of venison in the freezing compartments.

I glanced at my watch. After six thirty—broad day by a farmer's reckoning. I'd used more time than I thought, but I was accustomed to searching offices and computer files rather than homes. I hurried upstairs into the bedroom across from Junior's. A double bed with a white chenille bedspread took most of one side of the room. A sewing machine and a dress form occupied the other. I flipped through patterns and scraps of cloth stored in cardboard boxes under the bed.

That left the big bedroom with a window facing the barn. Dorothy had pulled up and smoothed out the faded floral coverlet on the queen-sized bed. Nothing under the mattress. Winter clothing filled four cardboard boxes underneath the bed, underwear and summer clothing the

antique three-drawer oak dresser with a clouded mirror.
Nothing but clippings of recipes, homemade pesticides,
and household hints in the old coal bucket. The draw-
ers of two small bedside oak tables—the most valuable
furniture in the house—held ballpoint pens, small pads
of paper (giveaways from advertisers), udder cream (for
the hands, I concluded), and facial tissues.

I pulled back the closet door, a white shower curtain hanging from a tension rod. A six-foot rod holding
mostly women's clothes ran the length of the closet. The
far end held a man's shirts and trousers plus two suits.
Three rows of shoeboxes occupied the shelf above. Did
I have time to go through all of those? Most papers, and
certainly tax forms, don't fit well in a shoebox.

A small safe sat in the corner behind a row of shoes.
I knelt to examine it and recognized a mass-produced
model that came with several standard combinations,
all of them locked in my number-oriented brain. If the
Tornells hadn't changed the combination, I'd open it in
seconds. It took three tries.

I pulled out the papers—tax forms, business and ma-
nila envelopes, paper from the pads. I looked for insurance policies first—one for the house, one for the car and
pickup, none for life. Dorothy hadn't killed him for life
insurance. To get an overview of their financial state, I
skimmed their last federal tax return. The farm had operated at a $19,000 deficit. Seeds, fertilizer, and interest
on a six-month $75,000 loan to pay for them accounted
for most of the loss. The sale of milk, corn, soybeans,
and beef cattle generated the farm's income. The only
other declared income was $5,042 from a construction
company (on a 1099, not a W-2 form) and $33 in interest
from a Laycock bank.

No way selling strawberries and vegetables at the farmers' market kept them going. They had to have other sources of undeclared income. I checked the two largest and thickest envelopes: first and second mortgages totaling $550,000 for the 400-acre farm. Its market value? A farm this size had been viable in my grandfather's day—before farming had become agribusiness requiring $250,000 tractors.

A checkbook showed a balance of $1,204. A business envelope labeled electricity held fifteen one-hundred-dollar bills. Hmmm. If you weren't declaring income, you might hesitate to put it in the bank. People without much money lacked my expertise in removing income from the taxable column.

Only a dozen small pieces of paper remained. The top one bore a cryptic note: "4/16—V—7 @150." Must be the record of work on Vlad Bulganov's shed at the rate of $150 a day for seven days. The next one followed a similar pattern: "1/14—GR-1@175." GR paid better than V. But HH didn't: "5/16—HH-2@100." And someone else paid even less: "3/10—FB—2@75." I opened a folded piece of brown paper: "6/4-GR." About three weeks ago. Same guy as in January, but no amount given.

A car pulled into the Tornells' drive. I peeked out the window—Annalynn in the squad car. Bloody hell! She'd throw a fit if she caught me doing an illegal search. Taking care to put the papers back as I'd found them, I shoved the safe back in place and straightened up the shoes.

Halfway down the stairs I realized I still had on the kitchen gloves. I stuffed them into my pocket and answered Annalynn's knock. Her hair was perfect and her uniform neat and clean, but makeup no longer could hide her exhaustion and depression.

"You look—like you need some coffee." I glanced at my watch. "I'll put it on and start breakfast. Dorothy will be up from milking in a few minutes."

"Coffee sounds good. I don't think I can eat." Annalynn crossed the porch into the kitchen, sank into a chair at the table, and covered her face with her hands. "I can't do this, Phoenix. I'm going to resign as soon as I get back to Laycock."

Unsure whether she sought confirmation or objection and unsure which I wanted to give, I said nothing. Instead I took out the coffee maker and coffee—located during my search—and filled the pot. Without looking at her, I got out the skillet, eggs, sausage, bread, and toaster.

"Phoenix?"

"I heard you."

"You always have an opinion on everything. I want to hear it."

The rare sarcasm told me how upset she was. I turned on the burner and faced her. "I base my opinions on facts, preferably irrefutable numbers." Not many of those in economics, or anywhere else. "Tell me why you think you should resign."

"Because I don't know what I'm doing. I can't lead a murder investigation." She rubbed her eyes. "We found nothing to back up your theory that he was killed at the gate, and the hospital's chest X-ray showed nothing except the antler."

"An X-ray could miss a knife wound." I put three sausage patties in the skillet, two for Dorothy and one for me to split with Annalynn.

"Face it, Phoenix. We have no idea what happened. You haven't told me not to resign because you don't know any more about how to work a case than I do."

I bit back a defensive reply. Better for her to take out her frustration on me than—much more typical—to hold it inside. "No, but we—not the certified cops—dug out the truth about Boom's death. I see no reason we can't figure out who killed Tornell. We already know two key things: He didn't leave the gate on his own feet, and he knew his killer." I added, "Three things, actually. Dorothy gave me names of two possible suspects last night. I'm going to check their alibis today."

Annalynn jumped up. "No, you're not! You'll leave that to my staff. You had no right to question her. Did you pretend you're a real deputy?"

"No. I made my civilian status clear." I had to calm her down. "Would you set the table, please?" I pointed to the cabinet with the plates.

Her face pale and tense, she opened the cabinet. "You keep out of this. I mean it." She glared at me. "Where's your blankie?"

"My what?"

"Your security blanket. That gun you've been carrying everywhere since you came back to Laycock."

My blankie. That's exactly what the Glock had become. "It's upstairs." And I had to have it. Now. "Watch the sausage, please." I ran up the stairs and strapped on the holster. Since I was there, I made the bed.

When I came back down, Annalynn had set the table and was pouring coffee. She smiled ruefully at me. "We're a fine pair, aren't we? I'm sorry to spoil your fun, but we have to leave the investigation to real detectives."

Dorothy burst through the porch door and into the kitchen. She waved her portable radio at us. "They're saying a deer killed Jesse."

FIVE

ANNALYNN'S LIPS FORMED a word I'd never heard her say, and the coffee she was pouring ran over the edge of the mug.

I grabbed her hand to stop the spill. "Who said it was a deer, Dorothy?"

"KILC news. He said the hospital had 'confirmed the report.'" She tossed the radio onto the table. It slid through the spilled coffee. "You told me *someone* killed him, not a goddam deer." Her chest heaved and she choked back a sob. "I have a right to know the truth."

Annalynn handed me the pot and guided the woman into a chair. "Yes, you do. The problem is, we don't know the truth."

Dorothy rubbed both eyes with grubby hands. "I don't understand this at all."

The phone rang.

Dorothy shook her head wildly. "I can't talk to nobody now."

"Phoenix, please answer that," Annalynn said.

I went into the living room and picked up the phone. "Tornell residence."

"Who is this?" A quavery woman's voice.

"A family friend. Who's calling, please?"

"Dorothy's mother. Tell her Garth Raymo, our neighbor, is bringing us down. We'll be there about nine."

That relieved me of the obligation of babysitting the

widow. "I'll tell her." I went back into the kitchen. "Your parents got a ride with Garth Raymo."

Dorothy nodded, her body shaking with suppressed sobs.

Annalynn patted Dorothy on the back and handed her a mug of coffee. "I understand how horrible it is not to know what happened. It almost drove me crazy when my husband died. I'll tell you what we do know: A broken antler was sticking out of your husband's back."

Dorothy shook her head. "I can see a bull goring him, but a deer?"

I jumped in, afraid Annalynn would tell her about Achilles tracking Tornell to the gate. "We're skeptical, too." Keep Annalynn out of this. "*I'm* skeptical, I should say. *I* think someone killed him and then"—this was delicate—"stabbed him with an antler to hide the true cause of death." I grabbed a dishrag and wiped up the spill.

Dorothy sipped the coffee and looked back and forth between Annalynn and me before settling on Annalynn as the authority figure. "What do *you* think?"

Annalynn closed her eyes a moment. "Dorothy, we have to assume a person did it until evidence proves otherwise. That's why I've authorized an autopsy by a forensic expert in Columbia." She pressed her temples with both hands. "The statement I issued says only that the cause of death remains unknown. You can help the investigation by saying the same thing."

Dorothy pushed the coffee cup away. "How long until you get the results?"

"Tomorrow, I hope. Certainly by day after tomorrow, by Thursday." Annalynn stood up. "I have to get back to Laycock and shut up whoever is talking to the radio station."

"You better eat breakfast first," Dorothy said. "You look like you need it."

"Thanks, but I can't." Annalynn extended her hand. "Phoenix will stay with you until your family comes. I'll ride back with my technician. She should be done by now."

"Take Achilles with you," I said. "He needs his regular rations."

"Will he go with me if you don't?"

"Yes." He'd shown an uncanny sense of when Annalynn needed comforting, unqualified love. Dogs gave that better than people, or at least better than I did. I thought about her intention to resign. Here I could help her. "Promise me you won't burn any bridges before you talk over your plans with me."

She nodded. "I'll wait if I can. I'll talk to you soon, Dorothy."

I went outside with Annalynn and untied Achilles. "Go with Annalynn," I said. In his good ear I whispered, "Guard Annalynn. Guard."

I couldn't tell whether he understood me, but he went with her willingly, and I returned to the kitchen to deal with Dorothy.

She had dished up the sausage, put in toast, and broken eggs in the skillet. "I don't need to be here when the tanker picks up the milk. As soon as we eat, we'll go over to the pond. I gotta get the pickup." She faced me, obviously primed to overcome any objections. "And I gotta see exactly where you found him."

"Of course. You better take a key. The tech would have taken the set in the pickup to check for fingerprints."

We ate in silence, both lost in our thoughts. I enjoyed the meal, except for the pallid coffee. The Viennese are fanatics about their coffee, and I missed the rich flavor. The sausage had an unusual taste, rather gamy. Venison, of course.

When we finished, Dorothy said, "You got a pistol. Should I take the shotgun?"

Jesse's rifle hadn't done him any good. "Guns are dangerous if you don't know how to use them." Especially for the people you're with.

"I couldn't hit the rain barrel with the rifle, but you can't miss with a shotgun."

I had no intention of getting in the SUV with a possible suspect holding a shotgun. "My dad taught me to shoot when I was eight. You won't need to ride shotgun with me."

She didn't argue. She retreated into her own world until I pulled up to the pipe gate. The padlock was gone.

"I'll open it," she said, jumping out. She unknotted the chain holding it closed and pushed the gate open.

No yellow tape warned us off, so I drove through and parked near the pickup. I got out and walked over to it. The windows were rolled up, and the ignition was empty.

Dorothy joined me, her jaw set, her cheeks free of tears. Like Annalynn, she had to see where her husband had died.

"We saw the pickup first. Achilles tracked him from here." I led her to the pond bank, stopping ten feet away. The grass around the blind had been flattened by many feet.

Dorothy stumbled, and I took her elbow to support her. "He was on his stomach, his arms stretched out, his head in the blind."

She retched, and soon her breakfast covered the grass in front of us. She sank to her knees.

I rubbed her hunched shoulders. "I'm so sorry, Dorothy. I shouldn't have brought you here."

She shook her head. "I had to see. I had to. Just give me a minute. By myself."

I walked toward the pasture gate, inspecting the ground and hoping Gillian had checked it for blood before the rain fell. Ignoring the wet grass, I headed around the pond and climbed the low bank to look over the pasture and count the cows. A few yards in front of me a black Angus cow and calf drank from the water tank on the other side of the barbed-wire fence. Pipe fences painted a dull green—invisible the night before—formed the other three sides of a small lot with a feeding trough and an open garden-sized pipe gate at the back. The deer had jumped the barbed-wire fence to the right of the lot. A dozen black cows and five calves grazed on a hill running down from the lot to a small ditch. An idyllic farm scene.

I joined Dorothy, now leaning on the pasture gate.

"Jesse sold off our calves weeks ago," she said. "Looks like Floyd's calves got through the fence again."

"Too bad I don't have Achilles. He'd get them out of there fast." Maybe. Had he ever met a cow before last night?

"I can't deal with this now. Junior can drive them out." She turned around. "Let's go. I wanta clean up before the folks get here with that gentleman farmer. Bringing them down is right nice of him, but I don't like him much. Jesse fixed the fancy staircase in Garth's Victorian last March, and he had the nerve to ask Jesse to take calves instead of cash for payment. I put a stop to that idea." She gulped as her eyes rested on the spot where Jesse's body had been. "I think you're right. I don't believe a deer could've surprised Jesse and gored him."

The widow slid off my suspect list. "It may be easier for us to find out the truth if you don't say that to anyone else."

"I have to tell Junior, but I won't tell nobody else."

A BLACK BMW pulled into the drive as I finished packing the strawberries for delivery. Dorothy was taking a bath, so I went out to meet the visitors.

The driver had gone around the car to help an old man out of the front seat.

An elderly version of Dorothy struggled to climb out of the back seat. She wore her white hair pulled back in a bun and a black dress too heavy for an already warm day. She said, "I'm Leila Lapinski, Dorothy's mother."

I extended my hand to help her. "I'm Phoenix Smith."

She gripped my hand. "Phoenix Smith! The Lord be praised for bringin' Dorothy an angel like you."

Obviously mistaken identity. "Have we met?"

"No, child, but Bessie Hamilton's told me how good you been to her. She loved that patio rosebush you sent her last week." Mrs. Lapinski gestured toward the men. "The old coot's Bert. And this handsome bachelor is our neighbor, Garth Raymo."

A bald Yul Brynner type in pressed beige Dockers and a short-sleeved white shirt that exposed impressive biceps, he smiled at me. "Always pleased to meet an angel."

"Always pleased to meet a bachelor," I said, sure the flirtatious reply would tickle Mrs. Lapinski and please her obliging neighbor. I guessed him to be in his early forties, on the edge of my dating range. More important, at the moment, he had the same initials, GR, that I'd seen on two scraps of paper in the safe.

Bert Lapinski, a once-tall man now bent and clutching

a four-pronged cane, ignored me and stared at the porch steps. "Have to ask you to help me get inside, Garth."

"No problem." The younger man took the older one's elbow. "I want to give Dorothy my condolences before I go."

Dorothy came out in a housecoat. "Phoenix, Sheriff Keyser just called and said for you to head straight home. You got an urgent phone call from your office in Vienna."

SIX

No one from the CIA would call me. The call would be from Adderly International, the venture capital firm where I'd worked both before and after leaving the CIA. I'd been on medical leave for three months and could think of nothing pending that my three assistants couldn't handle. Was Annalynn passing on a real message or warning me to butt out of the investigation? Either way, time to go. I stayed only long enough to get directions to Shelley Bulganov's house to deliver the strawberries.

My good deed gave me an excuse to check out the neighborhood. I drove past the crime scene and an unpainted house that leaned like the Tower of Pisa. That abandoned house symbolized the death of small farms. Then came another crossroads—they fell about every two or three miles—with a sign pointing left to the Family Baptist Church. The low-paying FB on the paper in the safe?

A half mile later a small American flag flew above a big black mailbox labeled "Bulganov Farms," patriarch Vlad's place. Trees blocked my view of the house. The murderer could have driven by unseen. Just beyond that dozens of grazing Holsteins—the distinctive black and white dairy cows—and a big white mailbox identified Shelley and Bob Bulganov's farm. I pulled into a long, two-lane blacktopped driveway running between a sparkling white board fence and the lush lawn of an old but well-kept two-story white-frame house. The Bulganov clan obviously did much better than the Tornells.

Off to the right a rambling white barn bore a big Bulganov Farms sign. So did a white tanker truck. Half a dozen Holstein calves galloped awkwardly across a small pasture to the board fence as I got out of the SUV. They stuck their heads between the boards to be fed or fussed over. Instead I followed the red-brick walkway to a large porch and the front door. No one answered my knock, so I left the berries in the porch swing.

As I turned to leave, a four-door blue Ford pickup pulled into the drive and stopped in front of the SUV. A sign on the driver's door said Bulganov Farms. A tall, solid man in a Cardinal baseball cap, a blue chambray shirt, and jeans wet up to his knees jumped out. He had a smudge of dirt on his chin and a friendly smile on his lips. An attractive guy, but then I'd always had a weakness for outdoor types.

"Hi. I'm Phoenix Smith," I said, extending my hand. "I left Dorothy's strawberries for the church group on the porch."

"Thanks. I'm Bob Bulganov." He wrapped a huge, rough hand around mine. "Shelley's working at Hy-Vee today, so I'll take charge of the berries." He grinned. "I promise to leave enough for the pies." He sobered. "She told me you and the sheriff found Jesse. You really think a riled-up deer gored him?"

His forthright question reminded me rural Missourians tend to go straight to the point. "I know nothing about deer. What do you think?"

"I know a lot more about cows than deer, but it doesn't sound right to me. Deer rarely attack, and when they do, they usually rear up on their hind legs like a horse and pound you with their front hooves, not gore you like a bull. The antler breaking off bothers me, too. An antler is as solid as a cow's horn." He pointed to my holster. "Does that gun mean I need to carry a rifle and shoot any passing buck? Or do I need to lock my doors and make sure my wife and my two teenagers are never alone?"

"I wish I knew, but I don't." His questions drove home how many people this murder affected and how crucial it was to catch the killer. "By the way, how developed are a buck's antlers this time of year?"

"Enough to hurt somebody, especially on the older ones. Bucks around here grow big racks, and a mature buck weighs maybe three hundred fifty pounds." He frowned. "A buck *could* kill a man."

Maybe, but it couldn't move his body. "Would a buck attack to defend a fawn?"

"Only in a Disney movie, at least in June. The bucks don't live with the does and fawns during the summer." He shook his head. "The whole thing just doesn't add up."

Agreed. "Sheriff Keyser has put all the department's resources on the case."

A calf bawled.

He turned. "Stop that. The boys fed you." He grinned. "That one was born hungry."

"How many cattle do you have?"

"Bulganov Farms owns more than three hundred head of Holsteins. We're milking about two hundred fifty right now, most of them at the north barn. That's our high-tech operation. I can tell you exactly what every cow there had for breakfast, how much milk she gave, and what the butterfat content was."

I liked his enthusiasm, but I didn't have time to learn

about dairy farming this morning. "Not like my grand-parents' day. Well, I have to get back to Laycock."

He touched the bill of his cap. "I'd sure appreciate hearing what the sheriff finds out."

DRIVING BACK, I pondered what to say to Annalynn about resigning. My growing fascination with Tornell's death prejudiced me to argue for her—and me—to work on the case. More to the point, Annalynn needed the case to divert her from her grief. She also needed the salary she would earn by serving the remaining eight weeks of her thirteen-week appointment. Good ol' Boom had exhausted her inheritance.

I didn't doubt our competence. Annalynn and I had uncovered the truth about her husband's death, with a little help from Connie Diamante, the third member of our teenage trio. I was known as the brain, Annalynn as the beauty, and Connie as the talent. We'd been harmonious until my junior year, when Connie kept coaxing Annalynn to do things I couldn't afford. Naturally I pretended I didn't care. Annalynn saw through that. She held the three of us together, though Connie and I played a nasty game of insulting each other. That sniping resumed when I returned to Laycock almost forty years later. Connie and I had put old resentments aside to help Annalynn cope with Boom's death.

Now Jesse Tornell's murder had sandpapered Annalynn's raw grief. Why should she subject herself to the pressures of this investigation? Maybe she should resign.

By the time I parked her SUV in the garage, I'd concluded that I should serve as a sounding board, not an adviser, and let Annalynn decide for herself.

She and Achilles had gone, but she'd left a note by the

hall phone saying to play a message from Reginald immediately. I hadn't spoken to my British boss, a partner in the international firm, since I left the hospital in D.C. six weeks ago. I hit Play.

"Phoenix, Reginald Sterling-Jones here. We miss you and hope you've fully recovered. That's partly selfish. SZ-Power wants an analysis of expansion opportunities in Hungary, and the CEO, Janos Szabo, asked specifically for you. Please be so kind as to call me immediately, whatever the hour, and I'll give you the details. I know I don't need to give *you* my numbers. *Auf wiedersehen*."

The name set off alarm bells. Why would Janos Szabo ask for me after no contact for more than twenty-five years? Had he connected me to his defection and his wife's chilling escape from Hungary before the Iron Curtain rusted away?

"Don't invent trouble, Phoenix. Get the facts." I stepped from the hall into the former ladies' parlor. Annalynn had left the front section of the long, narrow room as a sitting area and turned the back third into a home office. I went around the carved Indian wooden screen separating the sections, grabbed paper and a pen from her nineteenth-century rolltop desk, and dialed Reg's home number.

He picked up on the second ring, and we went through five minutes of pleasantries, news of staff members (all of which I knew from emails), and my recovery from an infection following emergency gall bladder surgery.

Then he began his pitch. "Phoenix, I hope you've tired of village life and are ready to return to the music capital of the world. Surely *Wiener Blut* flows in your veins."

I shed the soft Missouri drawl and colloquialisms that

I had rejuvenated and spoke crisp international corporate English. "I love Vienna, but family obligations dictate that I stay here for the foreseeable future." Until Operations knew who had identified me as a CIA courier rather than an American tourist and shot me, my contact, and several bystanders in the Istanbul spice bazaar.

"I'm devastated, as Chloe will be," Reg said. "She delights in your renditions of ragtime. But, my dear, you can complete the analysis without leaving your cottage. Gunther will email everything you need."

I had no interest in the project, a standard study, but I needed to know why Szabo had asked for me. "Rein in your ponies, Reg. Gunther can handle this. I can't fathom why Szabo requested me. Did he say?"

"No, but he'd like for you to call him in Budapest. He was so adamant about talking to you that I assumed he's one of your discarded lovers."

I laughed. I'd fed my gossipy male co-workers' suspicions that my frequent short trips involved discreet dalliances. "All we ever shared were economic statistics." Extremely revealing ones. I'd spent six months coaxing them from Szabo, a minor bureaucrat. Those stats had seemed so important then. Now the thought of them made me yawn. "If you can give me his number, I'll call him tomorrow."

"Thank you. Thank you. Give me a moment to retrieve it."

I doodled the head of a snarling deer as I waited.

He recited the number and added, "Actually, I called to discuss a more important matter with you. Adderly International is opening an office in New York in September. We'd like for you to run our Eastern European division there."

A plum job, one Gunther would give up wine to have. "That's a flattering offer, Reg. I'll give it serious consideration."

"Excellent. Let me know before your Day of Mourning—July Fourth."

Annalynn wasn't the only one facing a major decision. I drew a line through the deer doodle.

SEVEN

I DANCED A victory waltz in the central hall to celebrate my triumph as an economist—and as a covert operative. Reg would never have offered me the power job in New York if he'd had any hint that I'd worked for Adderly while with the CIA.

The phone interrupted my freestyle interpretation of Strauss II's "Wiener Blut." The caller ID showed Connie Diamante. Surely whatever she wanted could wait until I'd taken a shower. No, better not tick her off again. Annalynn had relied on her for emotional support before I came and would need her when I left. I answered the phone.

"Hi, Phoenix. Annalynn asked me to pick up some takeout and give her a lift home. We'll be there in about half an hour." She paused. "I'm worried about her. She's been coping so well, but this farmer's death has rocked her. Do you know why she wants to talk to us together?"

Because Annalynn didn't trust me to help her decide whether to resign. That hurt. "Yes, but she obviously wants your gut reaction. I'll set the table for lunch."

I hung up before she could ask me more. Annalynn would get a second opinion—and Connie always had one—without any input from me. She always chose the songs we performed—a prelude, she thought, for her Broadway musical comedy career. Forget it. I'd lived my adolescent dream. She hadn't. Neither, sadly, had

Annalynn. She'd planned to become the state's first female senator.

I took Annalynn's second-best dishes—Old Country Roses—and the stainless steel flatware from the walnut china closet and set three places at one end of the lovely old matching table. I couldn't resist running my hand down the glowing, unmarred wood. It was the only one of Annalynn's antiques I coveted.

It would be a great start for furnishing a condo in Manhattan, a city where I could indulge my love for opera, orchestra, and all sorts of music and theatre. The biggest musical event in the six weeks I'd been in Laycock had been Connie's piano and voice students' recital at the First Methodist Church.

A new thought sent a current through me. Mario lived in New York now. We'd met in 1991 when he'd come to Vienna to study and sing in the Opera chorus. By the time he got a major role in Milan, we were discussing marriage. The alarm on my biological clock warned me to take a chance, but a perfumed scarf in his luggage stopped me. I wouldn't give up my satisfying double life to worry about another husband cheating on me. I ended it. He left Vienna. My heart mended, lightly scarred.

Enough dwelling on love lost. He now sang second-tier roles at the Met and lived with his young wife and two small children somewhere in Connecticut.

I went upstairs to wash that man out of my hair and change into green shorts and a beige tank top—my standard outfit for the hot, humid weather. Much like in my teens.

When I emerged from the bathroom, Achilles jumped up to try to lick my face. "Sit," I ordered. He obeyed, and

I knelt to give him a hug and a full set of strokes and rubs before going downstairs.

He ran ahead of me, dashing through the dining room into the kitchen to tell Annalynn he was ready for lunch, too. She'd been afraid of him when I brought him home to recover from attempted caninicide. I'd asked her to feed him to help them establish a relationship. Now they relied on each other.

Connie—her short blond hair even curlier than usual—nodded a greeting as she poured iced tea into tall crystal glasses at our places. She favored the colors of the rainbow, and today her scoop-necked sleeveless top hit the hard end of the orange spectrum and her snug peach slacks the soft end. She could pass for early forties rather than mid-fifties. I consoled myself that I looked at least five years younger than when I'd arrived back in Laycock. So did Annalynn—or she had yesterday.

The microwave dinged, and I smelled Chinese food. My digestive system remained sensitive, but I could eat small meals as long as I avoided fatty or spicy foods, both of which I loved. I took my seat.

Connie placed the pitcher on a hot pad and took the seat across from me. "Now that we have another murder case, Phoenix, will you teach me to shoot?"

And put my and others' lives at risk? No way. "Sorry. My boss called about a special assignment today. I won't have the time."

Annalynn, dressed in her blue silk robe, emerged from the kitchen carrying a silver tray loaded with bowls of rice, cashew chicken, and beef with broccoli. She took her place at the end of the table and studied my face a moment before speaking: "I want to talk to you both about whether I should resign."

"I vote no," Connie said. "I don't know why you would even consider it when you've got a smart-ass like Phoenix and a natural detective like me to help you."

Annalynn closed her eyes and took a deep breath. "You and Phoenix are two of the reasons I must consider it. Involving myself in this investigation is one thing. Exposing you to danger—and ridicule—is another."

"Delete those two reasons from your list," I told her. "I don't care about ridicule." I smiled. "And Connie is used to it."

Connie flicked a grain of rice at me. "Annalynn said you got an urgent call from your boss. Are you about to catch a broom back to Vienna?"

Unlike Connie, Annalynn knew I couldn't return to Vienna, but her shoulders grew rigid. "Is something wrong in Vienna, Phoenix?"

"No. A client requested me on a project." She didn't need to know right now that Reg had offered me a job in New York.

Connie stirred rice into a helping of cashew chicken. "Isn't your medical leave about up? Won't you have to go back soon or give up your job?"

I couldn't tell whether she wanted me to leave or to stay. She'd always envied the special bond between Annalynn and me. "Reg knows I can't leave until I sell the house."

Connie heaved an enormous sigh. "Then you'll be here forever. Nobody wants to buy a little brick house next door to a limestone castle."

Annalynn chimed in. "She has a point, Phoenix. Instead of selling your house, why don't you use it as the headquarters of your new foundation?" She reached out to touch my hand. "You know I'd love for you—and Achilles—to live with me."

It was more a plea than an invitation. Thankful I hadn't mentioned New York, I squeezed her hand. "I'll think about it, but let's focus on your problem, not mine. Let's be logical, not emotional. Tell us the pros and cons of resigning."

"I'm not qualified for the job." She sipped her tea. "I don't mean just this homicide. My lack of police training endangers the county."

Connie shook her head so hard her curls bounced. "Nonsense! You've done a great job in a terrible situation."

Annalynn pushed food around on her plate. "*We* did a great job in exposing the truth about Boom's death—my reason for going after the appointment." She speared a piece of broccoli. "I should have quit then instead of trying to run the department. The deputies don't respect me. They're exhausted because I haven't been able to recruit staff. Morale is awful. The leak to the radio station shows I can't control the department."

I couldn't let her continue to whip herself. "The only ones who don't respect you have snouts and curly tails. You're a fine administrator. And most of the deputies are delighted to have the overtime." Their salaries were pitiful, even by Missouri's abysmal standards, because the county lacked a solid tax base. "I'd bet the medical people leaked the information, not your staff."

Annalynn stared at me. "Are you saying I shouldn't quit?"

Careful. "No. Only you can do that. I'm saying you shouldn't walk out on an obligation because you're insecure. For your own peace of mind, you should look at the facts and think this through. Then you can make a decision you won't second-guess."

Connie spooned sugar into her tea. "Phoenix is right. This time. We understand your concern, Annalynn. I thought you were crazy when you pinned on that ugly star, but you proved me wrong. You won't help the county by quitting. The commissioners would just appoint some idiot who thinks a rabid deer killed Jesse Tornell. Don't you think you owe it to his widow to find out what really happened?"

Annalynn smiled bitterly. "The widow, the automatic suspect if the autopsy eliminates a killer deer. This morning two of my staff said it's usually the spouse." She sipped her iced tea. "One thing I *can* do as sheriff is spare Dorothy Tornell the trauma of being a suspect. Fine. I won't resign, at least not yet. If the autopsy results support Phoenix's theory that someone used the antler to hide murder, I'll request the major case squad again—this time in writing." She took her first bite of food.

I suspected she had decided to stay earlier and had sought confirmation from us.

"We may solve the murder by the time you get the autopsy report," Connie said. "The principal always called us the triple threat."

The phone rang two quick rings—the signal that the call came from the sheriff's department. Annalynn hurried through the pocket doors and into the central hall to answer it. Her end of the conversation consisted of short questions: "Who?"

"Where?"

"When?" She ended with, "I'll take care of it." She came back to the table, her face grim. "Two teenage boys brought in the 'mad' deer they shot. I have to stop a deer massacre."

Achilles growled and ran to the old-fashioned over-sized sash window.

I reached for my gun, but I'd left it upstairs.

Connie sidled up to the window to peek out. "A mob of reporters is coming up the front walk."

Damned troublemakers. "Get rid of them, Connie."

She stepped back from the window. "*Moi?* How?"

"I'll talk to them," Annalynn said. "Connie, please ask them to give me ten minutes and offer them a cold drink. I'm going up to put on my uniform."

Connie ran her hands through her curls and went out onto the porch, closing the front door behind her.

As Annalynn headed upstairs, the phone rang again—two quick rings. She came back to answer it. After a few seconds, she said, "Good job, Gillian. Can you tell me anything about the bullet?" Pause. "Then it couldn't have come from Tornell's rifle?" Pause. "I see. Tell no one else. *No one.*" She hung up.

I joined her in the hall. "What's this about a bullet?"

"A large bullet—probably from a hunting rifle—knocked the fatal antler off a deer within the last couple of days. Think about that while I change."

A difficult shot, even using a telescopic sight. Would anyone hunt for a buck with a pointed prong and shoot it off so they could use it as an untraceable weapon? Yes. Every CIA operative I'd known would revel in such a deception.

How hard would it be for an experienced hunter to find a suitable rack? Considering the deer population in northern Missouri, fairly easy. I returned to the empty table and helped myself to cashew chicken.

Connie came back in and frowned at me on her way to the kitchen. Having no intention of giving the press a chance to question me, I ignored her.

Procuring an antler tip took time and planning—premeditation, not impulse. Someone had a major motive. Someone dangerous, clever, determined. Someone Annalynn should not go after alone.

What now? Look for a deer with a missing antler? Knowing its home on the range could help us zero in on the killer. Odds were that he—they?—had hunted in home territory. The two possible suspects Dorothy had mentioned lived near the Tornells' farm. Surely a buck didn't range far in hot weather with food plentiful. Achilles and I would take a few walks in the woods.

"What's with you?" Connie went by me with a tray holding four glasses for the so-called mob. "You avoid reporters like someone in a witness protection program."

Annalynn came down the stairs as Connie went out the front door.

"We need to find that deer," I said.

The phone rang again—two quick rings. Annalynn answered it. After a few moments, she said, "They're on my porch right now." Pause. "Oh, Lord. Tell anyone who shoots a buck with part of an antler missing to bring it in. Otherwise send any deer not foaming at the mouth to Wild Man's Butcher to be dressed and donated to the food bank. I'll be back to the office shortly." She hung up. "Some city slicker shot a Jersey heifer. I have to stop this nonsense." She polished her star with a tissue. "Do I look ready?"

I smiled. "Always. The camera loves you, and you handle the press like a veteran politician."

She took a deep breath and stepped outside, leaving

the door open a couple of inches. The porch, ten-feet wide and running the width of the house, offered shade and comfortable seating for the reporters.

"Good afternoon," the sheriff said, her voice serene but solemn. "Thank you for coming. I don't have a formal statement, but I'll tell you what I can. I'll stand at the north end of the porch, if that suits you." She led the mob—a female student from the University of Missouri's KOMU-TV, a young man from northeast Missouri's KTVO, a lanky kid from Laycock's KILC Radio, and silver-haired Vernon Kann, the retired editor and owner of the *Laycock Daily Advertiser.*

Achilles nudged me. I let him out, leaving the door open far enough that I could watch. He circled the reporters to stand by Annalynn's side. He didn't growl or bare his teeth, but his stance warned them to keep a respectful distance.

Annalynn stroked his head. "Last night—Monday night—the sheriff's department responded to a call from northeastern Vandiver County: Jesse Tornell had not come home. About nine fifteen p.m. we found his body on his farm. I sent it to a forensic specialist to determine the exact cause of death. I expect to receive the findings Thursday."

A young woman in a red dress edged forward with her video camera. "Ronnie Walters, KOMU-TV. Sheriff Keyser, the Vandiver County Hospital has confirmed that an antler pierced Jesse Tornell's heart. The Missouri Conservation Department says deer rarely gore people. Have you classified his death as an accident or a homicide?"

Face neutral, Annalynn said, "It's too soon to classify it as either. Until we receive the autopsy, all I can tell you is that the death was not from natural causes."

All the reporters spoke at once.

She held up a hand for quiet. "We don't *know* how he died, and I will not speculate."

Vernon Kann's penetrating tenor rose above the other voices. "A rumor is going around that a rabid deer gored Mr. Tornell. Can you confirm that rumor?"

Annalynn shook her head. "No, Vernon, I can't. We deal with facts."

The KOMU reporter pointed her camera at Achilles. "Did this police dog lead you to the victim?"

Annalynn smiled. "Vandiver County doesn't have a K-9 squad."

"Arlen Jayson, KTVO," said the other TV reporter. "Sheriff Keyser, we've heard reports that you're handling Jesse Tornell's death as a murder. Do you believe the antler was wielded by human hands?"

The group quieted, waiting for Annalynn's reply and, doubtless, hoping for legs for their stories. She'd given them a big story before and they'd come to Laycock expecting another.

Annalynn shook her head. "Please don't report rumors. It's my department's legal and humane obligation to determine the cause of any death not due to natural causes. That's what we intend to do."

Another explosion of questions.

She held up both hands for quiet. "I can't give you answers I don't have. But I have another concern. Since that rumor of a rabid buck spread this morning, inexperienced hunters have shot a doe and a milk cow. The sheriff's department cannot overlook illegal slaughter of animals."

The teenage reporter jockeyed his way forward. He was using his cell phone as a mike. "M. L. Moniteau, KILC. Don't people have a right to defend themselves?"

"Of course." Annalynn's exhaustion sounded in her voice. "Almost any wild animal will attack when cornered, but all of us know deer prefer flight to fight. I'm asking citizens not to corner deer and not to shoot except in self-defense."

"But—"

Annalynn interrupted. "I know the thought of a killer deer is frightening. To protect the public, we've established a volunteer force of experienced hunters to respond to calls about deer behaving—umm—strangely. We also urge citizens to report immediately any sightings of a buck with a broken antler. That's all today."

With Achilles breaking a path, she walked through the reporters and back inside, closing the door behind her.

"What volunteer force?" I whispered.

She smiled. "You."

EIGHT

I COULDN'T BELIEVE her words. "You're appointing me the county deer hunter?"

"No, you volunteered." Annalynn's lips twitched as she walked past me to the table. "You said we must find the deer the antler came from." She picked up her plate. "I'll take my food to the office." She paused at the kitchen door, her back to me. "If you can't help with the investigation, Phoenix, this is the time to say so."

She knew I couldn't resist the challenge. "If you're in, I'm in."

"As you said, I can't walk away from an obligation." She went into the kitchen.

A-hunting I would go. I glanced out the dining room window. Connie and Vernon, a ramrod-straight man in a short-sleeved white shirt and red bow tie, stood at the foot of the porch steps with their heads together. Who was pumping whom?

Connie ran up the steps and practically skipped into the dining room. "The KTVO reporter overheard a couple of Highway Patrol officers talking. One said the death was a freak accident. The other said it was probably someone with such an obvious motive that even an accidental sheriff could solve the case."

Annalynn shot out of the kitchen, a plastic container in her hands. "Where did Arlen hear this?"

"A fast-food place in Macon. Vernon was furious. He said that kind of leak is no accident."

The disparaging comments didn't surprise me, but the newspaperman passing them on did. "He's after the inside track on the story."

"Of course," Annalynn said. "But I trust him to get it right. He does a good job on local news. He always called me himself for a comment when anyone attacked my positions as school board president." She frowned. "He didn't endorse Boom when he ran for sheriff, but he didn't endorse his opponent either."

The veteran newsman showed good judgment. Boom's lackluster careers as a pro football player and a car dealer hadn't qualified him to be sheriff. On the other hand, the incumbent he challenged had failed to stop the devastating spread of meth in the county.

Connie glanced at her watch. "I have an hour free before piano lessons and some time this evening. Anything I can do?"

Annalynn hurried toward the door. "Phoenix, please fill Connie in on what we need to know. I've got to get to the office."

As Annalynn left, I put our plates on the tray.

"Phoenix! I'm not through eating!"

"Relax. I'm just going to warm up our food. Fetch a notebook and pen. Please."

"Sure, boss. Anything you say, boss."

If only I could fire her.

"Sorry, Phoenix." She slumped in her chair. "I'm worried about encouraging Annalynn to stick it out. I got a call from Cincinnati Sunday night."

"From Gracie." Annalynn's daughter worked there as a prosecuting attorney.

"She and her brother talked. They want us to persuade Annalynn to resign."

Neither Gracie nor Walt knew Annalynn was deep in debt. "And do what? Shuttle back and forth between Cincinnati and Omaha to read picture books to the grandkids?"

"Sounds good to me right now. I wish I could afford to spend a couple of weeks in Oregon with my two girls and their little ones." She threw down her napkin. "Gracie suggested Annalynn go back to Vienna with you, spend time in a 'different ambiance.'"

Stupid kids. Had I been that oblivious to my mother's feelings when Dad died? I hoped not. I carried the tray into the kitchen. "I'm not going back to Vienna, and I'm certainly not suggesting Annalynn leave her home. It's the rock she stands on."

"Thank God. For once we're humming the same tune." Connie joined me in the kitchen and watched me set the microwave timer. "Awful as this murder is, it has energized Annalynn, given her something important to focus on. You can see a difference in her body language." Connie took the grocery list pad from the island. "So what's my assignment this time?"

"Let me think a minute." I didn't trust her to handle anything crucial, but she had a knack for getting people to prattle on and, perhaps because of her stage experience, could regurgitate what she learned. "You know your way around LCC. See what you can pick up about a teacher named Floyd Vanderhofen. He's suing the Tornells over a fence dispute." Seeing her mouth move toward a pout, I added, "He's a possible suspect. I can check his teaching schedule online, but we need to construct a profile."

She brightened. "Temperament. Relationships. Sex life. I'm on it. What else?"

The microwave dinged, and we took our lunch back to the table.

"Background on the victim. He did carpentry to supplement the farm income. About all I know so far is that he never drank more than one beer at Harry's Hideaway. We need to know his reputation—reliability, honesty, competence. Was he likeable or contentious? Did he have enemies? We'll be checking all his other neighbors, too, particularly the Bulganovs. Do you know anybody in that corner of the county?"

"No. After all, I moved back only a couple of years ago. Between recovering from my divorce and taking care of Mama that first year, I didn't get around all that much. And I don't usually run into anyone from out there anyway."

"What about your cousin Trudy, the gossip queen?" I avoided her because I didn't want to compare stories of gall bladder surgery. And because, as our teenage baby-sitter, she'd made us go to bed and then snooped in our mothers' closets. A certified busybody.

"Trudy may know some of the farmers out there. If she doesn't, she'll know people who do. I'll go borrow a cup of sugar after my lessons today."

"Thanks." I stood up. "If you'll excuse me, I need to let Achilles out and start searching on the Web." Play nice, Phoenix. "Can you come over tonight to share notes?"

"Sure." She stirred rice into her beef and broccoli. "You're much stronger than you were a month ago, Phoenix, but Annalynn isn't. Grieving takes a long time.

Please think about that before you make plans to escape boring old Laycock again."

Had she somehow picked up on my new job offer? I'd never respected her intellect, but her insights impressed me. "Of course. See you later."

I turned Achilles out to race around Annalynn's backyard, which extended all the way to the street a block behind the house and included a small orchard. Then I went upstairs to my room, plugged in my laptop, and settled down on the bed. I started by googling Floyd Vanderhofen. He had only one entry: He'd moderated a panel on preserving native species at a local conference. Google hadn't spied even one credit in a professional journal. An academic lightweight.

I went to the LCC site and clicked on faculty. His entire entry didn't fill one screen. A mug shot showed a post-prime lean runner's face with an ineffective combover of bottle-black hair. A former high school biology teacher in Wyoming, he had taught environmental sciences at LCC for three years. His only summer session course met at eight a.m. Tuesdays and Thursdays. So he hadn't been in class yesterday afternoon. Using an antler might appeal to someone angry that Tornell shot deer out of season.

Back to Google to look for the Bulganovs. The younger brother had five entries, all articles in the *Laycock Daily Advertiser.* I clicked on the oldest: "William Wallace (Straw) Bulganov, 19, pled guilty to driving while intoxicated and…" The page was no longer up. I clicked on each of the other pages in turn. The *Advertiser* didn't archive articles online for more than three months, but the headlines on Google told me Straw had been arrested for distributing meth and had gone into and come out of a rehabilitation program. Annalynn would have full access to his files. I sent her a quick email.

That done, I turned to my own most pressing problem: updating my information on SZ-Power and Janos Szabo. I'd kept track of his rise from refugee to entrepreneur. He didn't know it, but my recommendations—filtered through my private contacts—had landed him his first job in the States. After that he'd needed no help. The difficulty in helping him without leaving tracks had prompted me to establish an offshore foundation to assist the few idealistic assets whose lives my CIA work had disrupted. My CIA salary didn't give me money for such largesse, but my investments did.

Google had hundreds of entries on Szabo. I reduced that to a dozen on SZ-Power's investments in Hungary. His company had the infrastructure, the expertise, and the capital to expand. His request to my employer made sense. Asking for me didn't.

I skimmed a profile on Szabo from a national business magazine. His wife, Klara, played cello with the Cleveland Orchestra. Their twin son and daughter studied at MIT. The Szabos had donated big bucks to various local charities and state political candidates. The unhappy Hungarian who'd sold me classified economic data "for my doctoral dissertation" had become a model American.

I remembered the months of painstaking preparation required to identify and recruit him in the pre-Web 1980s. The information I'd found in an hour would have taken me days to find then, but that kind of information couldn't replace the face-to-face, and phone-to-phone, legwork I'd done over the years among my many academic, nongovernmental, and corporate contacts.

The telephone rang the double ring. "Phoenix Smith speaking."

"Hi, Phoenix. This is Diana. Sheriff Keyser would like for you to check out a report of a rabid deer at Star Corner."

Odds favored a hoax, somebody's idea of a joke. "Who made the report?"

"He didn't leave a name, and our equipment can't get a phone number or location. He said a rabid deer charged his car at a stop sign by the creek and chased it up a hill. Hold on just a sec."

I'd have to go to show the sheriff's office was doing something. Where in hell was Star Corner? I needed a county map.

Diana came back on. "Vernon Kann came by to sign up for the deer squad. He'll pick up his Winchester and come by for you in Annalynn's SUV—she wants you to be able to contact us by radio. Should be there in about fifteen minutes. Okay?"

Just my luck that I'd have to go out on a wild goose chase with a reporter. "Okay. Have him bring a county map."

With the press along, I needed to look like a deer hunter. Camouflage pants and shirt weren't part of my sparse wardrobe. Besides I wanted to be seen, not become a target of some trigger-happy kid using the rabid deer report as an excuse to shoot anything beige. I settled for jeans and a short-sleeved purple-red top that resembled nothing in nature and emphasized my curves without being immodest. I whistled to Achilles from the window as I strapped on my holster and waist pack.

Another reason for the call occurred to me: Tornell's killer sought to establish the idea that a rabid deer gored the victim. Star Corner must be near the Tornell farm.

Vernon pulled into the driveway as I gave Achilles a drink for the road. I grabbed his leash on my way out the door.

"Hi, Vernon," I said, opening the SUV's back door for Achilles. I'd met the man once when Annalynn and I had gone to the country club for dinner. "Is Star Corner near the Tornell place?"

"No," he said, his high-pitched voice a little too loud. "The opposite side of the county. About twenty-five minutes away, if you don't mind breaking the speed limit."

"I don't mind." I upped my volume a bit to make sure he heard me. "And since I'm a reserve officer, I'll drive." I prepared to overcome objections, but he immediately got out and walked around the SUV.

"I've heard about your driving. Guess I better buckle my seatbelt." He cast an appreciative glance at me as he put on a green John Deere cap. He'd shed his white shirt and bow tie for a yellow polo shirt. Apparently he didn't want to be a target either.

I observed the speed limit until we left the town. Then I drove as fast as the two-lane blacktop road and the SUV's stability would allow.

He held on to the handgrip and grinned like a kid going to the circus. "Takes me back to my days as a real reporter. I worked the police beat in Kansas City for three years. You really expect to find a rabid deer up there?"

Why lie? "No, but I'm expecting you to report that the deer squad looked."

He chuckled. "I'll do that. Your dad used to brag what a great shot you are."

"You knew my father?" He'd been dead almost twenty years.

"Played poker with him at the VFW hall. The judge—Annalynn's dad—said Jack Smith was the bravest man he ever knew. I remember the first time I met him. He came in wearing a black armband. He was mourning the day Eisenhower betrayed the Hungarian freedom fighters—when the Russians invaded in nineteen fifty-six. That was about nineteen eighty-one. He and the judge went on about it all night."

"They marked every anniversary. Dad talked me into writing a term paper about American responsibility for the disaster in college. That gave me the idea to study Eastern European economics as a graduate student." And prompted me to listen to a professor who urged me to consider working for the CIA.

For ten minutes Vernon shared recollections of my father—his skill in counting cards, his quiet assistance to young veterans adjusting after serving in the unpopular war in Vietnam, his interest in international news. The newsman told a good story.

I speculated about his motives for sharing memories of my father. A form of flirting? A widower, Vernon had given me the subtle scan of a man who appreciated women, but he'd done nothing to indicate an attraction. Building trust? If he was playing me to get the inside story of Tornell's death, he was too smart to ask direct questions.

"When we top this hill," Vernon said, "you'll see Star Corner below us about a quarter of a mile."

Pastures lined both sides of the road on the long incline. The land was rough, cut by glaciers, and most of it too steep to cultivate or even to mow. Clusters of black Angus rested in the shade of lone trees on the few level spots—natural terraces.

I slowed to forty-five as we topped the hill and started down a long slope. Two narrow gravel roads came out of the rolling hills at angles to intersect our road a little before a small creek. Both had stop signs. Near the top of the next long hill narrow roads angled off to the left and right, completing the top of a rough six-point star. Nothing moved in the pastures. Some young cottonwoods along the creek provided limited shade.

The hair rose on the back of my neck, a surprisingly reliable sign of danger. "This doesn't look like a place Bambi would hang out at four thirty on a ninety-degree day. I smell trouble." I drove over the creek and up the hill to pull off by a small three-sided wood hut, a school bus stop, near the side road to the right.

"You smell a trap?" A smile played at the corners of his mouth. Then he sobered. "If I'd come to a crossroads like that with no protection and high points all around in Nam, I'd have been damn cautious. But you never served in the military. What makes you suspicious?"

Nothing. Experience. Excessive caution after being ambushed in a busy bazaar. "Probably Dad's war stories." I visualized what we'd just passed. "If I keep my head low, the roadside ditch will give me cover. I'll walk down to the creek to check for signs of deer. Achilles will tell me if anybody or anything is lurking. May I borrow your rifle?"

"Hell, no. I'm coming with you." He rolled out of the SUV. "Please open the back so I can get it."

I didn't want company, but I knew his male ego demanded he "protect" me. I let Achilles out and held on to his collar. "Quiet, boy. Quiet." I wished I knew what commands he'd learned in K-9 training before he flunked out. "Stay with me."

Vernon took an old Winchester 30-30 out of the back. "Don't worry. I'm not going to stumble and shoot you. I went on too many patrols to do that."

We crossed the road and walked at an angle into the narrow roadside ditch that ran about three feet below the shoulderless road and six feet below a barbed-wire fence. Achilles' good ear went up, and he moved into the ditch two feet ahead of me. I paused to listen. Achilles put his nose in the air and then to the ground, but he registered no reaction. A soft wind blew from behind our left shoulders, stirring but not cooling the hot air. Sweat trickled down my face. The sooner I got out of the heat, the better.

I hadn't approached an area so cautiously for years—perhaps not since the harrowing night I substituted for a trapped operative and smuggled Klara Szabo into Austria. Was that newly evoked memory making me over-react? No matter. Always safer to be paranoid.

In silence we walked down the hill.

"If deer hang out here," Vernon said softly as we neared the creek, "we should see tracks by the water, most likely near the broadest part of the creek."

Not wanting to raise my voice, I turned so he could read my lips. "Would you come here to hunt?"

"No. I wouldn't expect to find deer here."

The ditch bank was lower now. I crouched down, dreading to walk out of its shelter to the creek.

Achilles edged forward, his nose outstretched. A rabbit darted through the knee-high grass by the creek and toward the trees.

"Stay!" I ordered. "Good boy!" I straightened up to peer over the grass along the top of the ditch at the tree-lined hilltop to my right. A flash of light caught my eye. "Down!"

Achilles dropped. A chunk of soil flew out of the bank above his shoulder as a shot sounded. A second shot sent Vernon's green cap spinning past me.

NINE

"GOD DAMN IT!" Vernon said between clenched teeth. He was sprawled against the bank behind me, but no blood flowed.

Grabbing the rifle from his hands, I skirted him and scurried up the ditch several feet. Calculating where I'd seen the flash of glass or metal, I popped up enough to stick the barrel through the grass at the top of the bank and fired off five fast rounds. I dropped down and listened. Nothing but bird wings. I hadn't expected my bullets to come close to the bastard, but I sure as hell wanted to scare him off.

Achilles pressed against me, his body quivering so violently that he felt electrified. He'd not forgotten the pain of a bullet any more than I had.

I didn't feel all that steady myself. I leaned against the grassy bank. "Vernon?"

"I'm okay," he said, his voice now at countertenor pitch. "I slipped when you yelled to get down. Some fool nearly killed your dog." He tried to regain his feet and fell back against the bank with a moan. "My left ankle hurts like hell."

I'd heard two shots a split second apart. Apparently Vernon hadn't. I glanced at the bank across from him but spotted no entry point for a bullet.

A motor—not a car, maybe a scooter—started on the shooter's hill. We listened to it fade away.

"Don't stick your head out yet," Vernon warned. "Somebody could still be up there." He held out a hand for his rifle.

Ignoring him, I crept down the ditch, stretched out the rifle to reach his cap on the roadside bank, and drew it close enough to pick up. A thin slice about a half-inch long was missing from the tip of the green bill. Four inches to the left and Vernon couldn't have survived. Damned good shooting, considering the second target stood roughly fifteen feet from the first. I said nothing. Vernon didn't need to know what a close call he'd had, at least not until I could get us out of here. Keeping low, I went up the ditch four or five yards, wrestled the biggest weed I could find out of the ground, stuck the cap on the top of it, and held the cap up over the edge of the bank. I counted to five. Nothing. I lowered the cap, counted to twenty, and raised it for a ten count. Nothing. The shooter must be gone.

Achilles, pressed against me, was whining softly.

I tossed the cap to Vernon. "The hat trick always worked for Roy Rogers."

Vernon caught the cap by the bill, stuck it on his head, and tried to get up. He groaned. "I can't put any weight on my left ankle." Sweat streaked down his face.

Now what? I lacked the strength to support him, and the thought of moving into the open gave me the willies. Think like a cop. Call for backup. "Don't move. I'll check your ankle as soon as I call for help." My cell phone couldn't find service. I held out my Glock to Vernon. "This is ready to fire. I'll keep the rifle while I go use the radio. Will you be okay alone until I can bring down the SUV?"

He stared at the Glock a moment before reaching out for it. "I'll be fine." He adjusted his grip. "Be careful."

Achilles at my heels, I walked up the hill in the ditch, keeping my head and shoulders below the top of the bank and pausing frequently to listen. My head said the shooter had fled. The fresh scars on my stomach reminded me to be careful. When we were parallel to the SUV, I steeled myself to rush up the bank and sprint across the road. "Ready, boy? Go!"

We raced across the blacktop and to the far side of the SUV. I opened the passenger door and Achilles leapt into the front seat. The SUV felt like a sanctuary, but I knew bullets could penetrate both windows and doors. Keeping my head low, I wrestled with the radio until I got a connection—a bad one. When the dispatcher answered, I didn't know what to shout. I didn't know the police codes, and I didn't want to tell the world what had happened. "This is the deer squad at Star Corner. Vernon fell and hurt his ankle. I need an officer to help get him to the hospital." So far so good. Now the delicate part. "Tell the sheriff to send Gillian to clean up some dirt, too."

A long pause. "Hold on. I'll contact the sheriff."

I didn't want to talk about this on an open radio frequency. "Gotta go." I turned off the radio. Amazing how "gotta" came so naturally after decades of not saying it.

To my disgust, my palms were clammy. An irrational—maybe not so irrational—fear of being shot again had hounded me since the incident in Istanbul. I was relieved that instinct and experience had outmuscled fear when the bullets hit. I hugged and stroked Achilles, took some deep breaths, and raised my head enough to see out of the SUV.

Nothing moved on any of the roads. I crawled into the

driver's seat, made a U-turn, and drove down the hill to Vernon. Calm but cautious, I took the first-aid kit from the cooler and, rifle in hand, walked down the bank to him. "Help is coming. How are you feeling?"

"Like a clumsy fool." He had taken off his left shoe and sock. "It's a sprain, not a break. If you put on an ACE bandage, I think I can crawl up the bank."

"Relax. We'll wait for help." I took as much care as I could bandaging the swollen ankle, but his face went pearl white.

A car topped the long hill and sped toward us. I relaxed as I recognized a squad car. Too soon for Gillian. A deputy must have been in the area. I handed the rifle to Vernon, took back my pistol, and scooped up the shell casings.

"That's a good idea. Annalynn will take a lot of flak if we find out you blasted away at some kid who mistook your dog for a rabid deer."

Should I end his illusions and tell him how close he came to resting in peace? No. That would be Annalynn's call. "I don't like littering."

The squad car pulled up nose-to-nose with the SUV.

Vernon looked at the fresh dirt kicked up by the bullet intended for Achilles. "The guy aimed too high. Otherwise your dog wouldn't be here."

I nodded. But the shooter hadn't aimed too high. If Achilles hadn't responded instantly to my "down" command, he would be dead.

A tall, burly young deputy called Spike jumped down the bank, a frown on his square-jawed face. "The dispatcher asked me to respond to your call. What happened?"

I wondered if he was still steaming because I'd given

him the slip when he was guarding me from unknown killers three weeks ago. Not the audience I wanted. "Mr. Kann hurt his ankle."

Vernon said nothing for a long moment. Then he winked at me. "I've fallen and I can't get up. Can you help me to the road, please?"

The deputy inspected the bandaged ankle. "Do you mind a fireman's carry?"

"Sounds good to me," Vernon said. He wiped sweat from his face with a white handkerchief.

I couldn't leave a rookie like Gillian alone out here to gather evidence. "Spike, could you drop him off at the hospital emergency room? We were on our way to look for deer tracks along the creek when he fell, and I'd like to do that before I leave."

"Sure," Spike said, preparing to lift Vernon. "He can tell me what happened out here as we drive to town."

He suspected I was holding out. Good for him. "Yes, Vernon can give you the whole story, starting with the report of a rabid deer." By the time Vernon finished, they'd be halfway to Laycock.

Spike went up the bank as though carrying a child. He helped Vernon into the squad car and pulled a red bandana from a back pocket. The deputy wiped sweat from his tanned face and then swiped the bandana over his bristle of brown hair. "Sure you want to stay out here by yourself, ma'am?"

Teeth clenched, Vernon said, "Forget the damned deer, Phoenix."

"Achilles and I will be fine. But I'll keep your rifle, if you don't mind."

"Of course. Call me when you get back to Laycock."

When they drove off, I fished out a bottle of water

and a paper cup so that Achilles could share it with me. I needed it to coax him out of the SUV and down into the ditch to act as my backup. Once there, I spent five minutes stroking and talking to calm him—and me— down. All the while I kept eyeing the roadside bank for some sign of the second bullet. I couldn't tell exactly where Vernon had been when it hit, but he must have been standing upright rather than hunkered down as I'd been. I narrowed the likely area down to a rectangle four feet long and a foot deep at the top of the bank and began searching inch by inch for a hole. I found it beneath grass that Spike had mashed down with his size fourteen shoe. I pulled out the grass but left the digging for Gillian.

Achilles had crawled under the front of the SUV.

This was the second time in a month that he'd nearly died on a creek bank, so I didn't call to him as I approached the shallow, eight-foot-wide creek to look for deer tracks. It narrowed, and the bank became steeper and muddier as I followed it away from the road. No watering hole here. Clearly the call had been a hoax, but no joke. Although my head told me the shooter had fled, I had to force myself to turn my back on the hill where the shooter had perched and start back to the road.

A squad car zoomed down the hill and pulled over in front of the SUV. Annalynn jumped out on the driver's side. "Phoenix! Phoenix!"

"Down here by the creek."

Achilles crawled out from under the SUV to greet her.

She sagged back against the car and covered her eyes with her right hand. Finally she straightened. "Spike told the dispatcher you insisted on staying here alone and didn't even tell him someone had fired at Achilles. What were you thinking?"

She sounded exactly like my mother. Why not? Annalynn had spent half of her childhood in our house and moved back to the castle shortly after her mother died. Mom had served as Gracie and Walt's grandmother. Annalynn had become closer to Mom than I was. They'd sometimes ganged up on me.

Gillian came around the car with her duffel bag. Dark circles ringed her young eyes, but she looked as eager as she had the night before. "What am I looking for?"

"Hi, Gillian," I called. "Come down the bank and I'll show you where to find two bullets—the first aimed at Achilles, and the second at Vernon." Once more I scanned the top of the hill for any sign of the shooter.

Achilles applied his shoulder to Annalynn's leg, nudging her toward her SUV. When she resisted and followed Gillian down the bank, he came along.

I explained what had happened, and Gillian dug for Achilles' bullet.

Annalynn fetched a pair of binoculars from the squad car and, from behind the SUV, focused on the top of the hill. "How far away was the gunman?"

"About three hundred fifty yards. He probably used a good deer rifle with a scope." I didn't like her standing exposed on the road. "Come down and I'll show you where Vernon was."

"I think this bullet hit a rock," Gillian said. "It's damaged." She put a clump of dirt in a paper bag and walked up the ditch to start on Vernon's bullet. "Why didn't Mr. Kann duck down after the first shot?"

"He didn't have time. The shots couldn't have been a second apart."

She whistled. "That's sniper shooting."

Annalynn shuddered. "Hurry, Gillian. It's after seven.

We need to go up on the hill while we can still see. Phoenix, let's have a look at the county map."

We scrambled up the bank, my wound protesting. I hid the pain.

Annalynn took a map from the squad car and spread it out on the hood. "The road that goes up there leads to another crossroads." She pointed to where two roads crossed and went off into the counties on the west and north.

"A lot of options on which way to go. Like at the Tornells'."

Annalynn tapped on the crossroads by the Tornells' farm—at least twenty miles east. "Do you think there's a connection?"

"Probably. My first thought was that the caller wanted to establish the idea of a killer deer." To my great relief, the pain subsided. "But I can't understand why Tornell's murderer—or anyone else—would shoot at Achilles and Vernon."

"I got the bullet," Gillian said.

"Good. You follow us in the squad car," Annalynn said. "Achilles, come." She opened the SUV's back door for him. "You drive, please, Phoenix."

As we pulled out, I said, "Obviously the caller wanted to lure the sheriff's department out here."

"Or the deer squad. The TV and radio stations all mentioned it."

I turned left onto the narrow gravel road that ran toward the shooter's position. "Who knew that Vernon and I are the deer squad?"

Annalynn made a face. "My department, maybe a few others. It was no secret."

Could have been no one or dozens. Move on. "The

shooter obviously knew the area, knew where to place himself for a clear shot and a quick getaway. He probably planned to shoot whoever showed up." I pulled over to the side of the narrow road by a break in a wire fence. Gillian stopped behind us.

Leaving Achilles in the SUV so he wouldn't disturb any evidence, we found the tread of a small tire at the edge of the road. While Gillian worked on capturing that, Annalynn and I followed a path of crushed knee-high grass to a small stand of trees.

"A motorcycle would have left a bigger track," I said. "He must have a moped or scooter." I thought of evasion tactics I'd used. "You can toss one in the back of a truck or van, or even a roomy car trunk. Or abandon it somewhere. Changing vehicles makes it harder for anyone to track you."

We halted by a fallen tree. The crushed grass indicated the shooter hid behind it, probably using the trunk as a resting place for his rifle.

Annalynn lifted the binoculars to her eyes. "With these I'd be able to tell the SUV had two people in it as it came down that long hill. Did Achilles have his nose sticking out of the window behind you?"

"Yes. Could I have the binoculars a moment, please?" I focused on where I'd parked the SUV. The hut's low roof came into view. "He couldn't see Achilles, but he could see Vern and me when we got out of the SUV." A mistake on my part, but who expected a sniper? "He could have hit us at that distance, but we might have survived. He waited until he could shoot to kill."

TEN

"WE DON'T *KNOW* he shot to kill. Maybe he meant to frighten two unknown people and a dog." Annalynn removed a flashlight from her belt and shone the light on the crushed grass by the trunk, now in deep shadow. "He certainly planned well. He staged this near the county line. He left nothing obvious behind. Gillian won't be able to take prints on that rough bark." She shook her head, perplexed. "All this effort, yet he couldn't know who would respond to his nine-one-one call."

I lifted Vernon's rifle to aim at the spot where Achilles had stood, but it was too dark to see. The shooter had fired about ten seconds after Achilles emerged from the ditch's protection. Right after I'd told him to stay. The thought nauseated me. I pushed it away. The second shot targeted Vernon, not Achilles, but the shooter saw the dog drop. Had he expected me to run into the open to Achilles? If I had, would a third bullet have plowed into me? I touched my souvenir of Istanbul.

"Phoenix," Annalynn said, "do you think maybe he just intended to scare you, to taunt my department?"

"No. He missed Achilles because I yelled a warning, not because of bad shooting." I studied the open spot between the creek bed and the roadside ditch. "If he'd waited a few more seconds, all three of us would have been out in the open. The proverbial sitting ducks. He definitely intended to kill Achilles."

"But why?"

"I've no idea." Nothing more to see here tonight. "By the way, Spike got here awfully fast. Was he where he was supposed to be?"

"Yes. He's been patrolling the roads along the county border for the M-squad. Rustlers like to cross county lines." She started back toward the SUV. "Maybe the caller wanted to draw Spike over here."

"The classic diversion tactic—so the rustlers could— uh—stampede a herd thataway?"

Annalynn smiled. "Forget the cowboy films. Today a favorite *modus operandi* is to load a few cattle from a large herd into a stolen truck and take them straight to a sale barn. The farmer may not miss his animals for days." She sobered. "If the shooter was a rustler, the trooper's killer must live near here. I better radio this to Sam Gist."

"The condescending captain? Let's wait until we *know* why the guy shot at us." I kept my voice low. Gillian was walking toward us, her eyes on the vehicle's track.

"Captain Gist and the M-squad need to know about the shooting. Even though he probably will ignore anything I tell him." Annalynn thought a moment. "I'll have to give him just enough information to make him ask for more. He'll believe only the conclusion he reaches on his own."

I smiled. Annalynn had always understood how to get people to do things. She should have had the political career she'd anticipated as class president.

Gillian approached us. "Did he leave us anything?"

"Not that we could see," Annalynn said, moving on toward our vehicles. "Please check around that fallen tree before we go. I'll radio in."

She had as much trouble getting through as I had. "Anything new, Diana?" A burst of static. "Please check for reports of a stolen or abandoned two-wheeler. And tell Captain Gist I'll send him a report of someone firing on our deer squad." More static. She glanced at her watch. "We'll be back by nine."

She signed off. "Sorry, Phoenix, but you'll have to fill out a report. I'll email the form so you can do it at home on my computer."

I didn't like the idea of writing a police report. I'd spent more than twenty years filing reports that gave the required information but not the whole story. Omissions had protected me—and my special assets—from accidental exposure. Neither embassy-based CIA staff nor KGB operatives in Vienna knew who I was. The ultra-suspicious East Germans had checked me out several times but found nothing.

I opened the back door of the SUV to let Achilles out. "Annalynn, you're exhausted. Why don't you stretch out on the back seat while we wait for Gillian. I'm going to take Achilles for a run." I handed her Vernon's rifle.

She took it and climbed into the back seat. "I don't think I can sleep."

"Then just relax." I closed the door. "Let's go, Achilles."

He trotted around to the front passenger door.

"Not yet, boy. It's good to run off a little tension." I walked down the road, too tired to follow my own advice. Achilles glued himself to my left knee until I picked up the pace, managing a gentle jog. Gradually he moved ahead of me, darting back and forth across the road, sniffing, leaving his mark on fence posts, trotting back when I fell more than twelve feet behind. When I turned back toward the SUV, he raced ahead to the front passenger door. We repeated this several times before Gillian returned.

She carried her duffel bag in one hand and a paper evidence bag in the other. "I took samples of the grass and bark, but I don't think I'll be able to tell anything. He put a plastic sheet or tarp down over where he stood and the trunk." She wiped sweat from her forehead with her wrist. "I hope I'm not missing anything."

I smiled. The kid was disarmingly honest. "The guy's a real pro. If we didn't have the bullets, no one would believe someone shot at us. I'd like to hear your take on what happened here."

She wrinkled her brow. "It had to be a setup. The question is who he thought he was setting up."

"Any idea why anyone would shoot at Mr. Kann?"

"He had the rifle. He woulda looked like a bigger threat than you."

Scheisse. I hadn't thought of that. "And why shoot Achilles?"

She shrugged. "Beats me. I've heard lots of criminals are afraid of police dogs." She smiled at Achilles. "He looks kinda scary."

The scary dog licked the hand holding the evidence bag. Then he wheeled, barked at me five times, and trotted around the SUV to the passenger door.

"He has spoken," I said. "It's time to go."

ANNALYNN AND ACHILLES were both asleep when we pulled into Laycock. My stomach growled. I parked in front of the Dogwood Diner on the quiet courthouse square.

The half dozen people in the place stared when I walked in the door. I glanced down at the smudges on my clothes and arms. I guessed that my face also bore the marks of my adventure.

The white-haired owner stuck her head out of the kitchen. "Land, child! What happened to you?"

"I was too hungry to clean up before I came in." No one here I knew. Maybe they didn't know me. "Could you please fix me two of your specials to go?" I thought of Achilles. "And two plain hamburgers, no buns."

"Meatloaf, greens, mashed potatoes, and cornbread okay?"

Comfort food. "Sounds good." I went past the tables and booths and around the corner to the restroom. A streak of dirt marred my left cheek, and a dozen yellow-green hayseeds stood out like glitter in my black hair. I cleaned up as best I could and went out to perch on one of the duct-taped counter stools.

The woman came out of the kitchen, her face screaming curiosity. "Heard you and Vernon went out looking for a rabid deer this afternoon."

I grinned to hide my dismay. "The sheriff gives me the fun jobs. Who told you?"

"An X-ray technician. He said Vernon hurt his ankle but didn't break anything. Said you stayed out there on your lonesome looking for that killer deer." She laughed. "I don't s'pose you found it."

So word of the shooting hadn't gotten out. Vernon probably saved that for an exclusive in tomorrow morning's paper. "Not even tracks. The call was a hoax."

"Kids, most likely."

I fished some bills from my pocket and handed them to her. "If you hear who thinks they pulled a great prank, give me a call. I know where I can find a raccoon to move into his attic—or his car."

A man behind me laughed.

An older man with a cloth chef's hat came out of the kitchen and handed me a paper grocery sack. "You call me next time you want to go out on a wild deer chase. I'm ready to do my civic duty, long as I can do it with a pretty lady."

The woman swatted him on the shoulder with a menu. She smiled as she handed me the change. "I'd take along a much younger man next time, honey. *Much* younger."

I laughed with the rest and waved goodbye to the room. The story of my returning after dark from a wild deer chase would be all over town before noon.

Annalynn sat up when I opened the SUV's back door to store the food where Achilles couldn't reach it. "Vernon called. He wants to talk to us immediately. We have to tell him he was a target, Phoenix."

Not in my world, but I didn't live there anymore. I climbed in and fended off Achilles' doggie kisses. "You can eat in a minute, boy. Where does Vernon live?"

"On Elm in that beautiful sky-blue Victorian with white gingerbread."

"I'm so hungry my stomach hurts, and I don't think you've eaten more than a few bites all day. Can't we eat first?"

"We'll eat there. I told him you were picking up food." After a moment she added, "I'll handle Vern."

Hmm. "You mean I should keep my mouth shut."

"Phoenix, please don't be offended. I just meant—"

I laughed. "You're right. You're the one to talk to the press."

A little after nine, I turned into a circular driveway—built originally for carriages—and parked by the well-lit front porch.

Achilles barked. He didn't sound happy.

"Never fear. I got you a special dinner, and you can have it right now."

"Not in the SUV, please," Annalynn said, getting out with the bag in one hand and the rifle in the other. "Achilles can eat on the porch."

The big white front door opened. "Come in, all three of you," Vernon called from a wheelchair. He wore light green pajamas under a short dark-green robe. A blue medical boot protected the damaged ankle.

Annalynn led the way in and placed the rifle on an old steamer trunk by the door. "How are you? Are you in a lot of pain?"

Vernon wheeled himself backward with some skill. "I'm fine, thanks to the pills, but I'll be off my feet for a few days. You two—pardon me, you three—must be exhausted. Let's go into the kitchen."

He rolled down a wide hallway and maneuvered the wheelchair to turn right into a large kitchen with a table for four in front of a picture window. It was set for two. Pitchers of iced tea and lemonade and a platter of brie and crackers occupied the center. Vernon took the place where his John Deere cap rested on a closed laptop. "Phoenix, you'll find a bowl under the sink for the dog's food."

"You've been very thoughtful. I'm so sorry you were hurt today," Annalynn said. "Would you excuse me? I haven't had a chance to wash my hands." She left without asking where the bathroom was. She obviously knew her way around Vernon's house.

He watched her go. *If we were still in high school, I'd have said he had a crush on her.* I found a plastic bowl for Achilles' hamburgers and put it on the floor by my chair and then dished up our meals on the pretty floral china plates. The meatloaf smelled marvelous. I'd risk the grease.

Annalynn came in and poured lemonade all around.

Vernon touched the laptop. "I had my daughter bring this to the hospital. While I was waiting for the results of the X-ray, I filed a story about a caller perpetuating a hoax and someone shooting at the deer squad's fawn-colored dog."

I expected Annalynn to speak, but she dove into her food instead.

He held up his cap. "When I got home, my grandson said, 'What happened to your new Father's Day cap?'" He glared at me. "What in tarnation happened to my cap?"

I glanced at Annalynn.

"Tell him, Phoenix," she said. "Give him the facts."

But not our speculations. I sipped my lemonade to give my tired brain time to boil it down. "A second bullet hit your cap. We retrieved both bullets."

He glared at me. "Why didn't you tell me I'd almost been killed?"

Not an easy question to answer without revealing my need-to-know philosophy. I countered with a question: "Why did you think I grabbed your rifle and fired back?"

He chewed on his lip. "I underestimated you, thought you were overreacting. Even so, you should have told me."

I didn't have a credible answer, so I apologized. "I'm sorry. I didn't see any point in upsetting you."

He stared at me for several seconds. "The fruit didn't fall far from the tree." His face changed subtly, trans-forming him from a man who'd escaped death to a reporter after a story. "You must have checked where the shots came from. What did you find?"

I nodded to Annalynn. Time for her to take over.

"Nothing except the track of some kind of motorbike," she said. "I need a statement about what happened from the time we told you about the report of a rabid deer until you left Star Corner."

He patted the laptop. "I wrote down every detail I could remember. A big one, at least from my point of view as a target: I didn't tell anybody we were going out there. Did you, Phoenix?"

"No."

Annalynn said, "The shooter couldn't have known who would respond to his call. We don't know who he was or why he fired at you. Our nine-one-one equipment couldn't identify the caller or his location. Vern, I'm completely stumped. I have no leads. And I have no leads on the Tornell case." She paused a moment. "Do you think I should resign?"

"No! Of course not." He slapped the table. "Don't let those idiots run you out!"

Marvelous! She'd played to his desire to protect and received his support.

Annalynn smiled slightly. "Which idiots, Vern?"

Red crept up his neck. "I—uh—I heard that one of our fine citizens asked a county commissioner to rescind your appointment and replace you with Laycock's former police chief. It took me five years to convince the old coot to retire. You may lack training in law enforcement, but you're the best we've got. By far."

My opinion of Vernon rose.

"Thank you for your confidence in me," Annalynn

said. "I'll hold on, at least until I can get a major case squad to take over the Tornell case."

His eyes lit up, and he stroked the laptop. "So a person killed Tornell."

"Off the record, Phoenix and I think so, but I meant it today when I told the press we simply don't have the facts yet."

He nodded, all newsman now. "I've always cooperated with the police. After today, you owe me the first call when you have anything concrete. I can break it on our website and get the story out as fast and twice as accurately as the broadcasters."

"Well," Annalynn drawled, "what do you think, Phoenix?"

She knew how much I distrusted the press. But having the newspaper publisher in her pocket couldn't hurt. "I trust your judgment, Annalynn."

Vernon snorted. "I thought you two were going to play good cop/bad cop."

"No, but we have some questions." Annalynn nodded at me.

I was on. "Were you ducking down or standing straight when the shots were fired?"

"Standing straight. I didn't think we were going to see deer or humans out there." He picked up the cap. "I slipped when you yelled, but I don't know whether that was before or after the bullet hit my cap. The same thing happened in Nam—a bullet scratched my helmet." He put the cap on. "I'll have nightmares tonight."

I said nothing. We all had nightmares.

Annalynn patted his hand. "Vern, since the *Advertiser* has already gone to press, I'd like for you to consider keeping quiet about the second shot. If the shooter is the only one who knows he shot at you and brags about it, it would help us identify him."

He fingered the laptop. "I'll hold off until noon, if you'll give me some answers." He focused on me: "Why didn't you tell the deputy what really happened? Don't you trust him?"

"I trust him." Like I trusted everyone—with deep reservations. "I didn't want to delay getting you to the hospital. Besides, the crime-scene tech was on her way."

He frowned. "You didn't learn to be so secretive in Laycock."

Annalynn laughed. "I've said the same thing. As an executive at a venture capital company, keeping secrets is her job." Her cell phone rang. "Sorry, I have to take this." She went into the hall.

Vernon leaned forward. "She won't get that M-squad for weeks, not until certain people start clamoring for a professional law officer to come in and solve the case." He'd managed to lower his volume and his pitch. "If that second bullet hadn't come so close, I'd think somebody was just trying to make her a laughingstock. Understand this: I'll help her any way I can. And I know how to keep secrets, too."

I reached across the table to shake his hand. He was a valuable ally.

Annalynn returned to the table. "A motorized bicycle disappeared from a yard in Milan sometime between noon and four today."

"Could be it, but Milan's at least forty miles from Star Corner," Vernon said. "Any word on the bullets?"

"From a hunting rifle. We can match one of them to the gun—if we ever find it." Annalynn gave Vernon her business card. "Please email your statement and your article to me. I'd like to read both before the paper comes out tomorrow morning."

"I accidentally misled the public big time." He opened the laptop. "How about giving me a quote for my online update?"

"Okay." Annalynn thought a moment. "Filing a false report is not a joke. It's a serious breach of the law. We will arrest and prosecute."

I took our empty plates and silverware to the sink and rinsed them off. Achilles trotted into the hall, ready to go home. Annalynn and Vernon followed him, exchanging parting courtesies.

Outside, Annalynn went to the driver's seat. As soon as we pulled away, she said, "Those shots at Star Corner must be related to Jesse Tornell's death. I'm going to ask Gillian to see if the bullets came from the same rifle that shot off the antler. That could lead us to Jesse Tornell's killer."

ELEVEN

I HATED TO discourage Annalynn, but Gillian wouldn't be able to check the antler's ragged edge against the bullets. "I don't think she can get anything concrete to connect the two incidents."

Annalynn sighed. "Okay, but we have logic." She turned the SUV toward her office. "In the last five years we've had eight homicides in this county, six by relatives or lovers and two by career criminals. Yesterday we had a homicide that made no sense. Today we had an attempted homicide that made no sense. We can assume they're related. Agreed?"

"It's a statistical probability, not a certainty." The energy from the food was draining away. I longed for sleep. "Okay, a relationship is probable enough that we should make the sniping part of the homicide investigation."

Annalynn came to a complete stop at a stop sign even though no other cars were in sight. "Could you call Connie, please? Tell her to meet us at home in half an hour."

I groaned. "It's ten o'clock. I'm exhausted and I'm dirty and I'm grouchy as hell. Can't we invite her to come for breakfast instead?"

"She told the dispatcher she found a CD you wanted."

"What CD? Oh. That must be her idea of code." I dialed.

Connie answered on the first ring. "Glad you're back

in town. I've been hearing about your trip." The crack of pool balls against each other almost drowned her out.

She had to be at Harry's Hideaway. "Can this wait until breakfast?"

"Definitely not." She spoke with a pronounced drawl. "Hurry on over to Harry's or you'll miss the fun." She hung up.

"*Scheisse!* Connie says to rush over to Harry's."

"We're five minutes from there." Annalynn pulled into the parking lot shared by the sheriff's department, the Laycock police, and the city/county jail. "You can listen to an enhanced tape of the call on the way." She stopped the SUV by Gillian, who handed me a tape recorder and two file folders. Vandiver County couldn't afford high tech.

As Annalynn pulled off, I punched the play button. Three or four seconds of fabricated static. "Hello… Hello… Damn it…" A man's voice came faintly through light static. Heavy static. "I can't hear you, sir. Please speak up." Obviously the 9-1-1 operator. Heavy static. "A dang deer rammed my back fender…" Heavy static. "At the stop sign out at Star Corner." Static. "The crazy thing chased my car right up…" Prolonged heavy static. The call ended.

The static had obscured most of the vocal clues. I played the tape again. His "right" sounded like someone from Alabama, not from Missouri.

"Well, Phoenix? Can you tell anything?"

"He was creating the static and faking the accent. The pitch was too low for someone supposedly so excited. He may have used a device to modify his voice print."

"He knew what he was doing, then. That puts him in the career criminal category, not what I'd expected."

Nor I. "I could be wrong about the voice modifier." I'd used one so often, I expected others to do the same thing. "Anyone can create static."

Annalynn made a rolling stop at our turnoff for the nightspot. "What do we do when we get to Harry's?"

"The sight of your uniform would stop whatever Connie wants us to see. If you take her seriously"—something I rarely did—"then I better go in alone."

"If there's one lesson I've learned, it's never to go anywhere without backup."

"Then I'll go in the front and you and Achilles can slip in the back." I pictured the layout of the old three-bay garage and grocery combination that had been converted into a sports bar. A pool table rested on each of the three car lifts, one of them directly in front of the front door. Beyond the lifts stood a dozen or so four-person tables and, against the far wall, the long bar. On the left was a small stage with a piano. On the right, in the old grocery, was Tequila Junction, a hangout for local Hispanics. "I'll go in and join Connie. It's so dark in there that no one will notice my gun if I keep my top over it. You and Achilles stay in the hall by the restrooms until we see what's happening."

"Okay. Give me time to get in the back door before you go in. We'll coordinate with our cell phones." Annalynn pulled into a dark spot in the large parking lot.

"Pull through and face the road in case we need to leave fast," I advised.

"I know. It's in the department handbook. I don't see Connie's yellow VW Bug. Call her, please, and see if you can find out anything else."

I dialed. "We're outside."

"Perfect. They're heading for the pay phone by the door. Bye."

The pay phone? That would obscure the caller's identity. "I think we're about to get another call about a rabid deer."

We were both too tired for this cops-and-robbers nonsense. I'd fix Connie if she had misled me. I dialed Annalynn's cell. She answered and put the phone back on her belt and a Bluetooth gizmo on her ear.

"Achilles, go with Annalynn."

She let him out on her side, and he trotted beside her toward the back door, sniffing the air—probably smelling the mesquite-grilled hamburgers—and looking back at me.

Sliding my waist pack along my belt until it reached my holster, I strolled behind ten pickups and cars. Out of habit, I noted the license numbers. All were local. None were familiar. I raised the phone to my ear. "Are you inside?"

"Yes. I see three young men by the door. Come on in."

I opened one of the double doors, stepped inside, and surveyed the room as though looking for someone. No Connie. The only woman at the pool tables was a pregnant brunette.

Three young men in baggy jeans and black T-shirts huddled around the pay phone to my right.

"I dare you," a short chubby one said.

A tall skinny kid with hair so blond it was almost white held up a quarter. "You pay for our beers and I'll do it."

I turned to my left to peer into a case full of antique baseball caps. "They should be here any minute," I said into my phone, not bothering to lower my voice.

Chubby shook his head no. "Why should I pay for the beers? You're the ones celebratin'."

"Because after I call, we gotta move it," the tall blond said.

Chubby grabbed a passing waiter and handed him a bill. "That's for our tab. Keep the change."

"All fifteen cents," snickered the third guy, tall with black hair so curly it must be permed.

"Hurry up, then," Chubby said. "I gotta be at work in twenty minutes."

The blond glanced toward me.

I bent over to study a St. Louis Browns' cap.

"Here goes nothin'." He picked up the phone, put in his quarter, and dialed three numbers.

"They just dialed nine-one-one," I whispered into my phone. "Join me in about fifteen seconds."

"Hi," he said in a falsetto voice. "I want to report a rabid deer at Six Six Two West Aldridge." He flailed his free arm at his buddies as they doubled with laughter. "It's foamin' at the mouth and tryin' to mount the dog." He cracked up and slammed down the receiver.

I moved in front of the door a step ahead of the three men. "Got a light, fellas?"

"Outta the way, lady," the caller said, holding out his hand to shove me aside.

Achilles moved between us, growling and baring his teeth.

"Police!" Annalynn shouted. "Hands on your heads! Faces to the wall!" She held out her gun with the two-hand grip. "Deputy, cover them while I call for a squad car."

So she had decided to make a big deal of it. I drew my

gun. "You heard the sheriff. Against the wall." Didn't some movie cowboy's sidekick always say that?

Swearing and protesting and paying more attention to Achilles than my gun, the three stooges lined up by the phone.

Annalynn said, "I'll radio the dispatcher from outside where it's quieter." She stepped through the doors.

Harry, bald head shining, ran from the bar. "What's going on, Phoenix?"

"Your patrons phoned in a false report of a rabid deer. They're going to jail."

The three quieted and turned their heads to watch.

Harry laughed. "Ah, Phoenix, the boys were just fooling around. You know I don't allow any trouble in here. They didn't hurt anybody. Let them go."

"Can't. It's a serious offense." I gave them my best glare. "Put your palms flat against the wall well above your heads, and keep your mouths shut."

They muttered but did as they were told. For the next couple of minutes they squirmed and turned their heads to give Harry and me entreating looks.

Finally Annalynn came back inside. "Gentlemen, you're under arrest. You have the right to remain silent. Anything you say can and will be used against you in a court of law. You have the right to speak to an attorney, and to have an attorney present during any questioning. If you cannot afford a lawyer, one will be provided for you at government expense."

By damn, Annalynn had memorized the whole Miranda warning. I had an uneasy feeling that she didn't need to say it at this stage, but it sounded impressive.

The three stooges heard her out. Then they all protested, drowning out each other's pleas and obscenities.

"Hell, Annalynn," Harry said, "you're letting that star go to your head. Boom would have settled it right here. He never would've—" He stopped. "Sorry. I'm just saying that you're making a mountain out of a molehill."

"Harry, get behind the bar—*now*." The sheriff didn't say please.

Face red and teeth clenched, Harry went.

Curly looked around at Annalynn. "Aren't you gonna pat me down?" He gulped as he saw the negative reply on her face and turned back to the wall.

This jackass gave stupid a bad name. None of the three had the savvy to make the Star Corner call. Surely Annalynn could see that. Was she making an example of them to discourage other prank calls?

Achilles paced back and forth behind the men, growling until a white Laycock police car screeched to a stop outside the door. Handcuffs ready, a skinny young black Layton police officer hurried in. "Three passengers, Sheriff?"

"Yes, Officer Moniteau," Annalynn said loud enough that eager ears could hear. "They're county prisoners. Their offense involves a felony that we're investigating."

I nodded, going along. What in hell script was Annalynn following?

"Happy to house them on the county's dollar," the officer said. He handcuffed them and patted them down.

The three said nothing loud enough to be understood as we watched him load them into the back of his squad car.

"I'll ride with you, Michael," Annalynn said. "Phoenix will follow us."

I motioned for her to walk with me toward the SUV. "Do you know these kids?"

"No, but I recognized the caller from his mug shots. He's one of Dorothy's suspects. Straw Bulganov."

TWELVE

"NOW I HAVE a reason to question him," Annalynn whispered. She opened the SUV door and picked up a folder. "Please ask Connie for a ride home, and thank her for the tip."

"I didn't see her in there."

Annalynn laughed. "She'll love that you didn't recognize her."

I groaned, ashamed that I'd missed her. "The pregnant brunette." Fatigue hovered over me like a vulture. I dialed her cell. "Could you please pick me up at the jail?"

"I'll be home as soon as I get the milk."

She loved to play undercover cop. I had to find a way to discourage that before she got hurt.

"Thank you," Annalynn prompted.

"And thanks. Great catch. Bye."

"Thanking her didn't hurt, did it?" Annalynn shone her flashlight on a sheet. "Hmm. Spike questioned Straw after the meth arrest. I don't think I'll call him in tonight. He's furious that you didn't tell him about the shots fired at Star Corner."

The CIA's need-to-know rule and my well-founded paranoia had led me astray. "Sorry. I made a bad call. Tell him you reprimanded me for it."

She smiled. "I'll do that." She handed me the folder and headed for the city police car. "Please be sure you leave nothing out of your report."

Her parting words held both a reprimand and a warning. I dreaded summoning enough energy to write the report. Three months ago a hectic eighteen-hour day wouldn't have fazed me. This Tuesday had lasted a week. Achilles and I got into the SUV and he stretched out to put his head in my lap. Neither of us had fully recovered from our wounds—physical and mental. I stroked his head and murmured praise as I followed the Laycock police car. It pulled into the steel-gated underground garage that housed the sally port, the prisoner entrance to the jail. When Annalynn and the officer had herded the prisoners inside, I drove into the lot and parked in her space.

I pried the folders out from under Achilles, but Connie's car pulled up alongside before I could look at them. Achilles barked a greeting to Connie, who was back to her blond self. When I let him out, he jumped up to put his paws on her open window.

She stroked his head. "Our hero. Lassie would be proud."

I let him into the back seat. "You did pretty well yourself tonight."

"Thanks. Wasn't Annalynn fantastic? You'd think she's been sheriff for years instead of a month. What took you two so long at Star Corner?"

I fastened my seatbelt. "What have you heard?"

"Damn it, Phoenix. Tell me what's going on. I'm part of the team, too."

"I know, I know. We're a trio, not a duet. Don't get your curls in a knot. Let me hear the gossip before I tell you what actually happened."

She put the car in gear and, ignoring the stop sign, sped out of the parking lot. "Okay. Sorry if I overreacted—this time." She inhaled and exhaled. "Trudy's friend in the emergency room said you and Vernon went to find a rabid deer. He fell down when someone mistook Achilles for a deer and shot at him. When your and Annalynn's cells both went to voice mail, I deduced you were working in an out-of-service area."

Deduced? Shades of Sherlock. Damned drama queen. Not fair, Phoenix. Give credit. "You deduced correctly. Why on earth did you go to Harry's in disguise?"

"People know I'm Annalynn's friend. They speak more freely about Tornell to a stranger." She paused. "Besides, it gave me a chance to suggest to Harry that he'd attract more people with some live music. I have bills, Phoenix. I really need that gig as Earlene, and I can't do it without you as Ma."

Weeks ago we'd risked going undercover at Harry's, Connie as a traveling country singer and me as her accompanist. Harry had offered Earlene a contract, and Connie wanted to take it. A terrible idea. "We can talk about Earlene when I don't have to hold my eyes open to stay awake. What else did you hear about Star Corner?"

"Everyone is laughing about the deer squad 'falling down on the job.' I heard that same lame joke over and over. People think somebody shot a rifle in the air as a punch line. Those three Annalynn busted went on and on about the funny—mostly dirty—things they could say to nine-one-one to draw out the snobby sheriff's stupid deer squad. After the third beer, they were ready to actually do it."

"Do you know any of them?"

"Not by name. I'd never seen the tall blond kid. The fat one stocks shelves at Hy-Vee. The curly-headed kid came to my door last week asking to mow my lawn or clean my gutters. That's all I got. Tell me about the rabid deer."

I summarized the Star Corner incident, a good rehearsal for my official report.

"Geez, Phoenix. You really attract the homicidal maniacs." She pulled into Annalynn's drive and opened her car door. "I'll tell you what else I found out over a glass of chardonnay, or are you still off alcohol?"

May as well listen a little while. My stomach was complaining about the fat-laden meatloaf and I wouldn't be able to sleep yet. "I'll stick with tea."

She opened the front door with her key, turned on the hall light, and punched in the security code. She turned to inspect me. "Are you okay? You're sort of gray everywhere you aren't dirty."

A chance to go right to the tub. "I'm utterly exhausted."

"What are those folders you're carrying?"

How sympathetic. "Something Annalynn wants me to look at."

Connie held out her hand for the folders. "You go get ready for bed. I'll give Achilles some biscuits and water and fix your tea."

"And look in the folders."

She grinned. "Of course. You know Annalynn would let me."

"No, I don't." Why fight it? "You should call and get her permission." Knowing she wouldn't, I dragged myself upstairs, soaked for fifteen blissful minutes, jumped into my pajamas and robe, and went downstairs feeling more human but no less tired.

Connie had both folders open on the dining room table and a glass of wine in her hand. She studied me. "Your color is a little better. I don't understand why you refuse to go to a doctor." She poured me a cup of tea. "What are we looking for on these maps?"

"Crossroads," I guessed. "Annalynn has a theory about crossroads and getaways."

"Listen to her, Phoenix. Hard as it is for you to believe, she's as smart as you are." She sipped her wine. "And better dressed, even when she's in uniform. When are you going to buy some grown-up clothes?"

"When the occasion warrants it." I thought of the custom-made suits, blouses, and evening wear in my closets in Vienna. I stored my trademark collection of one-of-a-kind pieces of gold jewelry in a bank box. If I wore my work and play wardrobe in Laycock, people would say I was putting on airs. New Yorkers, on the other hand, would ask the designer's name. But now I needed to cull what I could from Connie's findings. The quicker the better. "Did you pick up anything about the Tornells' neighbors?"

"Trudy said Vlad Bulganov is one of the wealthiest farmers in the county. He's bought up the smaller farms around him and owns maybe five thousand acres. He and his older son, Bob, own a big dairy herd. Trudy heard they spend a million dollars putting in crops every spring. Vlad's not able to do much of the work himself anymore. His second wife and Bob run the operation. The younger son, the one who made the call, is such a loser that they treat him like a hired hand." She paused, waiting for my reaction.

"Is this gossip or reliable information?"

"Trudy sounded pretty sure of it. She knows Bob's wife. She works at Hy-Vee." Connie leaned forward, eager to share. "I put on my big straw hat from *Carousel* and hung out around the checkout looking at magazines. She told customers Tornell was a hard worker and good neighbor. Faint praise, I'd say."

I knew Connie. She'd barely started act two and was building slowly to act three. To speed her up, I pushed back my chair. "Excuse me. I have to go write a report."

She glared at me. "I spent six hours playing Nancy Drew and you can't listen for fifteen minutes."

"I summarized six hours in two minutes." I yawned. "Please get to the point."

"You're the one who always wants facts, facts, facts." She pouted a moment, just as she had in high school when I put her down. Then her expression softened. "You look like something dragged from the bottom of the pond. Relax. Sip your tea. Criminals won't take over the county if you write that report in the morning."

She just didn't get it. She'd never finished her papers on time in high school. "Annalynn needs it right away to send to that trooper who's being such a jerk."

"And you never let Annalynn down." She reached over and touched my forehead with the back of her hand. "No fever. You'll live. Here's my big score, and I got it wearing that same costume I used at Harry's. Did you recognize my character?"

Damn amateur! "No. You should never risk playing twenty years younger anywhere but in a very dark room." I jerked back as her fingers tightened on her wine glass, afraid she was going to throw its contents at me.

She smiled and raised the glass. "You're jealous. I did just fine." She sipped. "Okay, spoilsport, just for that, I'm not going to tell you the juicy stuff about Vanderhofen until you guess what show inspired my disguise."

I was tempted to violate the Geneva Conventions. "My God, Connie, we're not in high school."

"You're the one acting like a bratty teenager, Dr. Charm. Guess."

She'd rolled back almost forty years. And I still couldn't resist her challenge. Had to be a musical she'd done in summer stock. I flashed on the posters in her house. I pumped my fist. "The pregnant secretary in *Auntie Mame*."

She slammed her glass down. "You're really annoying when you're right." She blotted a splash of wine from the folder with a napkin. "Vanderhofen had to resign from his teaching job in Wyoming and get out of the state."

A clouded past for Dorothy's other suspect. Interesting, if true. "Fact or rumor?"

"Fact-based rumor, I'd say." Her girl-next-door face glowed the way it had when she talked about starring on Broadway. "I went over to the college cafeteria half an hour before night classes began and joined a table of four gabby teachers. One said what a good student the Tornell boy is and how elated he was to get away from the farm this summer. Another one said Vanderhofen accused the Tornells of killing deer out of season." She sipped the wine.

My eyes threatened to close. "I'm sorry if I've been sharp, Connie, but I'm fading out. Get to the resignation, please."

"You're no fun anymore, Phoenix. But then you never were." She took off her hoop earrings and put them on the folder. "Just the facts, ma'am. Dwayne somebody says Vanderhofen belonged to Patriots Primeval, an ecoterrorist group. He—Dwayne—read an article online about the Patriots setting fire to some big houses being built on a mountain." She paused for effect: "Vanderhofen resigned a couple of weeks later."

Intriguing, but not conclusive. I rubbed my eyes and

tried to concentrate. "How does Dwayne know the resignation had anything to do with the fire?"

"A matter of logic." She stared at me defiantly. "It sounds worth following up."

Considering Dorothy's suspicions, I had to agree. "Absolutely. Nice work. Annalynn can contact the police in Wyoming. Anything else—good or bad—about him?"

She shook her head. "Nobody else knew Vanderhofen. He must not be very social." She picked up the Bulganov folder. "For God's sake, Phoenix, go to bed."

Instead I went to Annalynn's computer in the ladies' parlor and downloaded the report form. It asked for some times I didn't know and included some abbreviations I couldn't decipher. The best thing about it was that it limited my account to about a third of a page.

Achilles stretched out beneath the antique desk and put his head on my feet.

As I started my final sentence fifteen minutes later, Connie walked around the ornamental wooden screen that separated the office from the sitting room area and read over my shoulder. I hate that, but I said sweetly, "See any typos?"

"You really cut it down to bare bones." She picked up a writing pad. "That's one mean deer. A rabid one?"

"*Scheisse.*" I emailed the report to Annalynn. "I promised Reg I'd call a client in Budapest tonight." It was nearly midnight. I did a quick calculation "I'll call at six, when I'm fresh."

"Now you're talking sense."

Connie had done a lot of work today, too, and done it well. She'd do anything for Annalynn and, despite our exchange of barbs, she'd treated me okay. I'd maintained relationships with many malicious and avaricious people.

Time to forget adolescent hurts and cozy up to Connie. "You've been a big help today." That sounded condescending. It was. I pushed my tired brain to come up with a way to wipe out my mistake. The second highest form of flattery is asking for help. "Anything strike you in the folders?"

"No, but I'll talk to Trudy again." She patted my shoulder. "Go to bed, smart-ass."

MY ALARM AND the grandfather's clock in my room sounded a discordant duet at six o'clock. I punched off the alarm and used the morning light to find my way to the bathroom. Splashing cold water on my face woke me enough to convince me I didn't *have* to go back to bed. I also didn't have to get dressed before I made my call.

Achilles followed me downstairs and trotted into the entertainment room on his habitual morning circuit of the house. I went to Annalynn's desk to dial Szabo's number.

"SZ-Power," a woman said.

Definitely a Hungarian. "Good afternoon. This is Phoenix Smith of Adderly International. Dr. Szabo asked me to call. Is he available?"

"One moment, please. I will inquire." She put me on hold for a minute. "Dr. Szabo will be with you in one moment, please."

He came on two minutes later. "Frau Doktor Schmidt, what a pleasure to speak to you after all these years. Have you returned to Vienna?"

His mother tongue lurked in his stress on the first syllable of words, but his vowels and rhythm now sounded distinctly American. "I'm still in the States recovering from a post-surgical infection and attending to family matters. I was delighted, and very flattered, to hear you asked for me. I've read about your success the last few years. I applaud you for going back to Budapest to help spur the Eastern European economies."

"My heart leads, my business follows. I need your advice to make sure I don't listen to my heart instead of my head."

He'd never been a man to put sentimentality above economic self-interest. He definitely wanted something else from me. "I understand your caution, and certainly Adderly can give you an excellent objective analysis of investment risks and potential." Achilles put his nose on my knee. I reached down to stroke him. "Normally I'd be more than happy to lead the team. Unfortunately, my obligations in the States preclude that possibility. I would enjoy renewing the stimulating discussions we had—when was it?—twenty years ago?" Too obvious a mistake. "No, longer than that. You helped me locate some data I needed to complete my dissertation."

"Yes, of course. I'd forgotten."

A flat lie. I'd paid him off with a then rare laptop computer. No one from that time and place forgot his first computer. He must suspect my CIA ties. "Getting reliable information was almost impossible in those days."

"And still is, in many cases," he said. "That's why I had hoped to take advantage of your wonderful contacts and your incomparable skills as a researcher and analyst."

A slight increase in his Magyar stress pattern told me the real reason for his call was about to surface. I played the game by responding, as culture demanded, with a compliment. "I wish I had your skills as an entrepreneur."

He laughed. "My old friends here tell me that. I've talked to several of the people who attended that UNIDO conference in Vienna where we met."

"That was an extraordinary group." I'd wheedled information from two other attendees and, when I'd drained them, I'd given their and Szabo's names to local CIA operatives to recruit as assets. The Rumanian had stayed in Bucharest and now held a high government job. The East German had defected a few months after Szabo did. I fished for the name of someone Szabo would know the CIA didn't recruit. "I've run into several people over the years. I had dinner with Violet Bartok occasionally when I visited Budapest, but I haven't seen her since two thousand four." He, and everyone else, knew the Hungarian government had assigned her and another economist to spy on the other Hungarians attending conferences.

Achilles whined for attention, and I rubbed behind his ears. "That's my dog you hear whining, not me. He's waiting for his morning run."

"If you have a dog, you must plan on staying there." He was silent for a moment. "Speaking of old acquaintances, I bumped into Heinrich Mueller in Chicago about a month ago."

The East German defector. Had they made the connection between their contacts with me and their recruitment by the CIA? "Was he the Czech who passed out from too much *heuriger* wine the night we went to Grinzing?"

"No, he worked at the East German Embassy's economic office in Budapest."

"I avoided the East Germans." Surprise him. Bring the CIA thing out in the open. "They thought every American living in Vienna worked for the CIA."

He laughed. "But Frau Doktor, we all thought that. One of my former colleagues here accused me of cooperating with the CIA to get out of Hungary."

Was he afraid of exposure? "I'm not surprised. Many

people must be jealous of your success." I changed the subject to see if he would come back to the CIA. "And of your wife's success as well. I looked you up online yesterday and learned that she plays with the symphony. I doubt that she remembers our being introduced at a cocktail party, but please give her my best regards."

"She remembers you very well. I'm disappointed that you aren't available now, but please keep in touch. The next time you visit Budapest we will take you out for a night of Hungarian food and music. I know you love both."

"I certainly do. I look forward to seeing you again. Goodbye." I hung up and thought over our conversation. *"Gott im Himmel!* He knows!"

THIRTEEN

"WHY ARE YOU UPSET, Phoenix? Who knows what?" Annalynn, still in her robe, handed me a cup of coffee. "What's going on? Remember, you promised not to lie to me."

I'd been ready to. Out of habit. Telling her the truth would be a relief after my years of secrecy. "I just talked to an old acquaintance. He apparently has deduced"—Damn it. I'd used Connie's word—"that I worked for the CIA."

"The man in Budapest who wants you to do the feasibility study." She walked around the screen and sat down on the love seat. "You retired from the CIA years ago. What harm would it do if someone outs you?"

I dropped into the matching chair and put my feet on the hassock. "If my double life comes out, everyone I've known since grad school will come under suspicion of having spied for the CIA. We're not exactly popular in Europe, you know. A Bulgarian friend and I have had season tickets at the Volksoper for years. Her university department chair despises the CIA. If she comes under suspicion, she'll lose her job." I sipped my coffee. "Casual acquaintances may be accused of helping me maintain my cover. Some consultants would lose contracts with international NGOs—nongovernmental organizations." I thought of a Rumanian, my third target at the conference where I'd met Szabo. "One fairly high official could be charged with treason."

"With treason? Surely you're exaggerating."

"Annalynn, when you sell your government's secrets to another country, it's treason. I don't think treason has a statute of limitations." I sighed. "A lot of CIA assets are greedy slimeballs who deserve anything they get. Few are revolutionaries or idealists." Part of my job had been to identify and concoct a way to recruit—usually with bribery or blackmail—people with access to useful economic information. "I've set up an offshore foundation to help the idealists and the naïve." And shelter about five million dollars in investments from taxes. "I can't do anything for dozens of innocent people—including academics with whom I wrote studies—who would suffer if rumors link them to covert work I did years ago."

I sat brooding, something I'd rarely done before being wounded while carrying out a post-retirement CIA mission. Was I losing my edge now that a bullet had proved my vulnerability?

"I worried about physical danger," Annalynn said. "I never thought of the emotional price. It explains why you distance yourself from people."

Her words stunned me. "Have I distanced myself from you?"

"No, but only because I wouldn't let you." She smiled. "And because you're a secret softie. If I hadn't been so desperate for your help when you came back to Laycock, you would have continued to shut me out of the hidden half of your life."

I nodded. She understood me better than anyone. "Talking to you about those covert years helps me cope. I've been pretty desperate myself."

"Two hearts are better than one." She raised her coffee cup to clink it against mine. "And three hearts are even better. I wish you would stop pushing away Connie."

"I can't trust her with the secret of my CIA life. And I don't trust her judgment in these investigations. Besides, her perkiness annoys me."

"Be honest with yourself, Phoenix. You stay detached from everyone."

"My double life enforced caution in relationships."

"That life has ended," Annalynn said. "Which reminds me of this man in Budapest. Are you absolutely certain he knows you were a—what did you call it? It had something to do with knocking."

"I was a NOC, short for non-official cover, meaning no diplomatic immunity." Absolutely certain he knew? In my gut, yes. In my head, no. "My best guess is that he's suspected for a long time. I'll bet his wife figured it out. Women pay so much more attention than men." He was allowed to go abroad with government delegations—as long as she stayed home. We had to smuggle her out of Budapest while he was abroad. I was supposed to help plan the escape, not run it, but a glitch meant I had to do it or we had to abort. My success on that mission added behind-the-lines troubleshooting to my career.

"Why do you think the wife recognized you?"

"She has a musician's ear, and I didn't disguise my voice all the time we were together." Like when we switched vehicles and had to run full out about half a mile to reach the next ride on schedule. "I warned her to never say anything about how we got out to anyone except her husband for all of our sakes, and I think she's honored that."

"Then why would the couple expose you now? What would they gain?"

"I don't know. Maybe they want to be sure I won't expose them and threaten the business deal. Maybe they want to threaten to expose me."

Annalynn tucked her legs up under her. "How would being exposed affect *you?*"

"Adderly International would fire me. I'd never work in my specialty again."

Annalynn smiled. "You're tempting me to expose you myself to keep you here." She grew serious. "I don't think you should worry about being outed. They can't afford to let the CIA link come out any more than you can."

I nodded. "That's logical." But people often don't behave logically. I put the issue aside. "I'll let Achilles out and we'll look at the folders."

When I came back, Annalynn had spread out a rectangular computer-generated map of northern Missouri, southern Iowa, eastern Kansas, southeastern Nebraska, and western Illinois on the coffee table. The map covered an area roughly 350 miles long east to west and 250 miles deep north to south. Our county, Vandiver, fell near the center.

I stared at it, clueless. "Why are we looking at this?"

"This is the map the M-squad is using. Each X— twenty of them—marks a farm or ranch that's lost four to six Angus calves to rustlers over the last few months."

I didn't understand why Annalynn was focusing on the M-squad's case rather than ours. "Do you really see a connection between the trooper's death, Tornell's death, and the shots fired at Star Corner?"

She sighed. "No. I was hoping you would."

I looked for a pattern in the X's. They formed an irregular border on the east, north, and west edges of the map, mostly twenty to fifty miles outside Missouri. The only three in Missouri were in the far northwest and far northeast corners at least a hundred miles from us. "All the out-of-state X's are near roads that lead into Missouri, but none run directly into Vandiver County."

"No, but all the north-south roads connect to U.S. 36. That's where the trooper was garroted."

The highway ran east to west a few miles north of Vandiver County. "So the rustlers may live near that spot. That's why Captain Gist wants your deputies patrolling the back roads. Do you know exactly where the trooper was killed?"

"No. Somewhere northwest of us, between Chillicothe and Laclede. That same day five calves went missing from near Leavenworth." She tapped Kansas. "A thief would expect to see fewer troopers on U.S. 36 than on I-70."

I was skeptical. "How do they know that rustlers killed the trooper?"

"He radioed in that he had pulled over a pickup because it didn't match its license plate, which turned out to be stolen. According to Spike, the trooper said something like 'I smell cattle' after he got out of his car. I understand they have evidence connecting the vehicle to these specific cattle thefts, but the M-squad isn't saying what."

"I take it the trooper didn't videotape the stop."

"No. He either didn't have a camera or it wasn't working. From what I've heard, either a passenger came around the vehicle behind the trooper with the garrote or someone jumped him as he walked back to the patrol car to check the driver's license on the computer."

"A garrote is a fairly unusual murder weapon. That

could mean a Special Forces background, but using one takes more nerve than skill. It could have been anyone."

I studied the map. "Sorry, Annalynn. Other than the proximity of crossroads and a possible military background of the trooper's killer and the Star Corner sniper, I can't see any connections."

She folded up the map. "Do you think the Bulganov boy or his friends knew enough to make the call luring us to Star Corner?"

"Probably not. The caller seemed much more savvy than the three stooges."

"Kids know a lot about this stuff. They could be playing dumb."

"I doubt they were acting. I didn't see any background in electronics or law enforcement in the file. Nor time in the armed services."

"I'm going to have to let them go." She shook her head ruefully. "The prosecuting attorney called me before I left the jail. She'd heard from all three families. She said we have a case against Bulganov, but charging the two 'bystanders' isn't worth the trouble."

So the families had clout and didn't want to confront Sheriff Integrity directly. "A pity. I could see those three as a gang of calf rustlers. What are you going to do with Dorothy's suspect?"

"He's still on probation from a meth conviction. We'll use that as leverage when Spike questions him this morning." She finished her coffee and stood up. "If he has an alibi for Monday afternoon when Tornell died and for yesterday afternoon when the shots were fired, we'll release him but file charges for last night's nine-one-one call."

She needed support from a power in the community.

Like the local newspaper. "Did you tell Vernon about young Bulganov?"

"No. The newspaper calls my office every morning." She smiled. "Why don't you give him an informal call? After all, you owe him."

I groaned. "You want to turn me into an anonymous source?"

"Vern will know where to find eyewitnesses happy to talk about what happened at Harry's Hideaway." She rose. "I'm hungrier this morning than I have been since— in weeks. How would you like oatmeal with blueberries for breakfast?"

"Sounds good." Having others' problems to worry about had distracted Annalynn from her own. I followed her to the kitchen and took the frozen blueberries from the refrigerator. "I want to ask you something: Why have you been talking about resigning when you obviously have no intention of doing that?"

She didn't answer immediately. "I fully intended to yesterday morning."

"But not at lunch with Connie or at dinner with Vernon."

"I admit I asked both of them to help justify my decision." She took the oatmeal from the cupboard. "I thought about it while I drove back to town yesterday morning. I considered the altruistic reasons, the serving-the-community arguments that Connie and Vernon gave. I feel safe telling you they aren't the real reasons I won't resign: I need this job. I need it to pay my bills, and I need it to occupy my mind." She took out bowls and turned to face me. "Are you shocked?"

"Of course not. Annalynn, those are the same reasons most people go to their jobs every day."

"Not your reasons. You chose a dangerous job because you wanted to undermine communism." She smiled. "When that happened, you stayed because you loved the excitement. You can't say Laycock hasn't offered enough challenge even for you since you came back." She took milk out of the refrigerator. "What are you going to do today?"

"The job you gave me: deer hunting." A perfect cover for talking to the Tornells' neighbors. I'd get things out of them they wouldn't tell a cop.

FOURTEEN

AFTER BREAKFAST ANNALYNN left for the sheriff's department to monitor Straw Bulganov's interrogation, and I went to the Web to search for information on the Patriots Primeval.

The group's site had only an "Under Construction" sign on it, but Google listed a dozen newspaper articles. The older ones dealt with the group participating in several better-known environmental organizations' protests and campaigns in Wyoming and Colorado. Five dealt with "ecoterrorists" torching a developer's mountainside homes, the incident Connie had heard about. I guessed that the group had moved from idealism to fanaticism and then died or gone underground. The last article—more than three years old—told of a young Patriot being expelled from high school for destroying fences that blocked a corridor used by pronghorn elks. The article said his biology teacher, Floyd Vanderhofen, served on the Patriots Primeval's board. Connie had scored a point.

I sent Annalynn an email summarizing what I'd found and one to Reg recommending he assign Szabo's work to my team without promising my input.

Then I dressed for my day as a deer hunter, although I expected to spend more time in living rooms than in the woods. In Vienna, my four closets, two of them concealed, held clothes for everything from the Opera Ball to cat burglary. My closet here featured casual clothes for being inconspicuous. I needed to look ready to tramp through fields but in a friendly, unofficial manner. I selected forest-green twill slacks, a light-green cotton top, and a short-sleeved white blouse that covered my holster. Not bad.

I stocked my white Toyota Camry with snack crackers and apples for me, dog food and treats for Achilles, and water for both of us. To make him more physically and psychologically comfortable, I put his old green blanket—his bed since the day I'd rescued him—on the passenger seat and rolled his window halfway down. He gave me a long look before hopping in, and his nose came to rest on my right leg as soon as I fastened my seatbelt. At least he didn't drool. Much.

My car's clock showed nine and the thermometer eighty-three. Add high humidity and the total came to one miserable day. Years of Vienna's relatively cool summers had deprived me of my tolerance for heat. I turned on the air conditioning even though Annalynn's mandated first stop, Vernon's house, was only a few blocks away.

I parked the car in the shade of a big old maple tree and thought of the beautiful elms—dead from Dutch elm disease—that had shaded our house during my early years. My parents lived with window air conditioners in the bedroom and living room until I'd insisted on installing central air as their thirty-fifth wedding anniversary present.

Achilles headed for the maple to leave his mark, and I went toward the wide porch where Vernon sat in his wheelchair, his injured leg up and a laptop balanced on a board on his lap. Despite the heat, he wore a long-sleeved white shirt. He'd turned back the cuffs from his wrists.

"Phoenix! Good morning. You're looking quite fetching despite our little adventure." He motioned toward a white rocker near his wheelchair. "I'm staying home today. My daughter likes it better when I'm not at the paper to second-guess her anyway." He closed a file and opened a new one. "Tell me what happened last night at Harry's."

Talking to the press made me nervous. I stalled. "You've seen the police report?"

"Yes, such as it was. Annalynn promised you'd give me the whole story—if I don't quote you or print the tip-ster's name. Consider this deep background." He smiled and closed his laptop. "Look. No notes."

Big deal. He'd remember everything I told him. But Annalynn needed his influence among community lead-ers. I'd have to cooperate to get cooperation. I started my account with Connie's call and ended it with the arrival of the Laycock police officer.

Vernon said nothing until I finished. "Why is the Bul-ganov boy the only one being charged?"

Not a question to ask me, but answering it gave me a chance to make my point. "That was the prosecutor's de-cision." I hesitated a moment to appear reluctant. "This is strictly off the record. The families called her within minutes. Annalynn's going to receive a lot of flak for keeping all three in jail last night."

"They'll back off a little when they know what really happened at Star Corner." He paused. "Do you think these boys fired those shots?"

"No, but officers will check alibis and phone records." I reached down to stroke Achilles, who had settled at my feet. "That's really all I can tell you. I'm going out to the area around the Tornells' farm to look for a deer with a missing antler tip. Any advice?"

"Bucks are creatures of habit. A good hunter goes out before deer season and learns what trails they follow, where they hang out, where they go for water. I'd ask the farmers where to look."

"I'll do that." Maybe he could guide me. "Anyone in particular I should talk to?"

He stared at me. "The same people I would if I were on my feet. Be careful."

He'd guessed my plan. I stood up. "I wonder if I could borrow your rifle."

"Sit down a minute. I want to ask you something." He grinned. "If you answer, I'll lend you my gun."

Now what? I sat down.

He ran his right hand over the laptop as though impatient to open it. "This time I'll ask *you* to keep the conversation strictly between us."

I nodded.

"I've heard that Annalynn has serious financial problems. Is that true?"

Bloody hell! That bastard at the bank couldn't resist telling tales. I laughed. "You know her father left her a fortune."

"And I know her husband lost it." Vernon pressed his thin lips together. "Boom Keyser was a handsome good old boy with no business sense. The smartest thing he did in his entire life was marry Annalynn."

"Agreed, but he didn't control all the money." Enough of it to leave Annalynn with major debt and few assets beyond her beloved nineteenth-century family home.

He frowned. "If she needs cash to—to tide her over, I would like for you to suggest that she sell me her Mercedes. I could use a better car."

The blue book on it would be at least $30,000. His

generosity touched me. "Thank you. I won't forget your offer, but you needn't worry about her finances."

"I see." He opened his laptop. "I googled you. I couldn't understand your treatises in academic journals, but your series in *The Financial Times* on investing in Eastern Europe made a lot of sense." He raised an eyebrow. "May I assume you followed your own advice?"

"Yes." He wanted to be sure I could afford to help Annalynn.

He nodded. "I'll leave solving her financial problems to you, then. One more thing: Is Annalynn planning to run for sheriff when her appointment expires?"

He'd surprised me. "We've never discussed it. I don't think it's occurred to her." No reason it should. Turning my offshore foundation into a genuinely useful tool—instead of primarily a fancy tax dodge—made a lot more sense than running for sheriff, though I hadn't yet spelled out that possibility to Annalynn.

"She should run. The newspaper will endorse her, and I'll guarantee to raise most of the campaign money myself. If she can solve Tornell's murder, nobody will have a chance against her." He leaned forward. "Finishing out Boom's term will give her time to grieve and to get her affairs in order." He'd dropped his voice. "And lay the groundwork for her to run for the House. Our district's incumbent will announce his retirement soon. Think about sending Annalynn to Washington while you're on your wild deer chase."

I THOUGHT ABOUT it as Achilles and I drove away from Vernon's with his rifle secured in the trunk. Annalynn had dreamed of a political career since seventh grade and had worked toward it in local and state politics since her son and daughter came out of diapers. To get a county commissioner's vote to appoint her sheriff, Annalynn had agreed not to run for the state legislature. Bypassing Jeff City and going to Washington would give her a great lift. And solve her financial problems.

My route took me past the sheriff's department. A van with a Kansas City television station's logo on it stood in the department's parking lot. That station had covered our investigation of Boom's death. Vernon was right. If we solved Tornell's murder, Annalynn would receive invaluable publicity for the campaign. She'd love to go to Washington, and I wouldn't mind an opportunity to influence our foreign affairs budget and domestic economic policies. Not to mention monitor certain CIA activities.

I parked on the street and pulled out my cell phone to dial Annalynn's cell.

She answered on the first ring. "Where are you?"

"Heading out of town. Did you find out anything from the Bulganov kid?"

"Not much. He has the same weak alibi for both Monday and Tuesday. He milks cows every morning from four to nine and was painting his kitchen both afternoons. Unfortunately the officer I sent out to question neighbors yesterday afternoon didn't go into the house. He talked to the wife out in the yard. She said Straw wouldn't talk to the police without a warrant. We'll release him in an hour or so."

With the official questioning done, I didn't have to worry about breaking laws and complicating matters for Annalynn with my unofficial interrogations. "I'll go by his house this morning and check for signs of fresh paint."

"Phoenix, I don't want you checking for paint or looking for that deer alone. Once the autopsy proves we have a homicide, I'll insist on pulling Spike off the M-squad. He can go out with you."

Nothing like an angry young deputy to cramp my style. "That would mean losing a day. I have Achilles, and no one knows we're going to be out there."

"You intend to do more than look for that deer, don't you?"

She'd not believe a denial. "Annalynn, people clam up when they see a cop. They'll prattle on to me, a middle-aged volunteer on an idiotic errand."

Annalynn laughed. "Don't fool yourself. They'll know what you're up to."

Of course. Everyone would remember Achilles and I had been with her when she found the body. "Maybe I should use a disguise."

"No. Definitely not. Just use your charm. The way you did with Dorothy. But don't take chances. Check in with me every hour or so—whenever you can use a phone."

"You don't need to worry about me."

"Promise me, Phoenix. I don't like you being out there with no backup."

Her words and intonation sounded exactly like my mother's and aroused the same wish to rebel. "And if I don't?"

"I'll send Connie out to join you."

She meant it. "I promise. See you later." I hung up and took off before she could change her mind about my going hunting alone.

FIFTEEN

AT THE CROSSROADS near the Tornells' place, I stopped to glance at the county map on which Annalynn had written the names of their neighbors. Straw Bulganov lived on the same road as the Tornells but about three miles east. I checked my watch: a quarter after ten. If I didn't fool around, I could talk to Straw's wife before he got home.

Achilles thrust his head out the window and barked. In a field of freshly baled hay, a meadowlark hopped away dragging its wing—a ploy to draw the threat away from a nest hidden somewhere among the stubble.

"Quiet, boy. You're scaring that poor mother bird."

He whined and shifted around to put his head in my lap.

I stroked him. "I'm sorry to bring you out here. I know the country brings back bad memories."

Driving past the Tornell house, I saw no sign of a car, person, or animal. At the crime scene, yellow police tape held the gate closed. Nothing moved there or at the two Bulganov farms.

Everyone but me had the sense to get in out of the miserable heat. With a mile to go, I closed Achilles' window and turned the air conditioning on high to cool down before I reached the younger son's home. It was on my left just past a gravel road. Maple trees shaded a small gray house. I turned into a short drive that contained more dirt than gravel and parked on bare ground beneath the branches of a towering oak tree. I unfastened my seatbelt and reached into the back seat for the blouse I'd brought to cover my gun.

High-pitched whoops pulled my attention to two naked little boys with wet white-blond hair plastered to their heads. They raced toward me through ankle-high grass.

"*Scheisse.*" I squirmed to get my right arm into the blouse sleeve.

Two curious faces—each a miniature Straw Bulganov with baby fat—peeked in my window. One twin smiled and the other frowned.

"Hi," the smiling one said. "Are you a gramma?"

"Nah," scoffed the other one. He had a scratch on his chin. "She's a goddam cop."

So much for hiding my weapon. I opened the door and the boys—I guessed them to be four—backed away just enough to let me out. "I'm not a grandma or a cop. I'm a deer hunter." I opened the back door to toss my blouse inside and to get Achilles' leash. "My deer-hunting dog is Achilles. Come, boy."

He didn't move except to turn his head to gaze out the passenger window at the trunk of the tree.

"He's shy," I said. And smart enough not to tangle with these two tanned beasties. I turned on the ignition so that I could lower the windows. "My name is Phoenix Smith. What are your names?"

"Guess, you goddam cop," the scratched one said, backing up to be a little beyond my reach.

"That's easy. Rumpelstiltskin and Pinocchio."

The smiler giggled. "Wrong. Guess again."

I walked slowly toward the house. "Peter Piper and Little Jack Horner?"

"Stupid goddam cop," the scratched one said, skipping backwards ahead of me. "Guess some more."

I searched my memory for names my brothers' kids had found funny, or even familiar, figuring I could keep walking as long as I kept talking. "Happy and Sleepy? Pokemon and Ninja? Rudolph and Frosty?" We passed through the lawn sprinkler the boys had been playing under, and now both were giggling. "Hoot and Holler? Up and Down? Here and There?" We were almost to the front steps. "I give up. I'm going to call you Amadeus and Nibelungenlied."

"No, no," the smiler protested. "I'm Willy and he's Wally."

The screen door opened. A chubby brunette—little more than a girl—stared at me. She had flecks of light-blue paint on her tight dark-blue tank top.

"She's a goddam cop," Wally said, "but she's funny."

"She's not a gramma," Willy added.

I laughed and extended my hand. "I'm Phoenix Smith. I'm part of the deer squad, the volunteer group that's trying to find"—I paused, not wanting to scare the boys—"a deer with a broken antler." I lowered my rejected hand.

She closed the door but didn't move back. "I know nothin' about it."

I smiled. "I'm not surprised. I'm asking people who live near the Tornells if they know of any places around here that bucks hang out or go to drink."

Willy ran back under the sprinkler. "She's got a great big dog."

The woman pushed her long hair away from her face and wiped sweat from her forehead with the tail of her top. "You can't go lookin' for deer. That's trespassin'."

"Of course. I'll get permission first. I know everyone

is anxious to help find out what happened to Jesse Tornell." Her round, anxious face looked vaguely familiar.

She slumped against the doorframe. "I can't give you permission. We don't own this place. I can tell you, though, you wouldn't find any deer in that field out back." She closed her eyes and took a deep breath.

I saw an opening. "Are you ill? Do you need some help?"

"She doesn't feel good," Wally volunteered. "She frew up."

The woman turned and ran.

"Play in the water, boys," I said, opening the door and stepping inside. I followed the sound of retching through a living room furnished with Salvation Army discards and into a bathroom littered with old towels.

She knelt in front of a toilet.

The young mother needed a mother. She'd have to settle for a helping hand. I dampened a faded washcloth in the sink and held it to her forehead, supporting her head as she "frew up" again.

When she had finished, I filled a plastic Flintstone glass by the sink with water. "Here, rinse out your mouth."

She obeyed and handed me the glass.

"Do you feel well enough to stand?"

She nodded, and pushed herself up. "It's morning sickness. We painted the bedroom yesterday afternoon and the paint made it worse."

She'd confirmed Straw's alibi for Star Corner. I put an arm around her waist and helped her to a futon covered with a faded blue blanket. "Is there someone I can call to come look after the boys?"

"My husband will be home soon." She positioned herself within range of a rotating floor fan. "I'm Tammy Kay Bulganov. You're the one who was with the sheriff when she found Jesse."

I perched on a recliner covered with a garish beach towel. "That's right."

"You really think a deer killed him?"

"I don't know, but he had an antler in his back."

She gulped and covered her mouth.

Wally hit the screen door with the flat of his hands. "Mama, we're hungry."

Sure handling food would send her back to the toilet, I said, "You rest, Tammy Kay. I'll fix something for them—cereal, scrambled eggs, sandwiches?"

She smiled. "Dorothy said you're real nice. There's peanut butter in the refrigerator and bread on the table. And they can have some apple juice."

I rose and started toward the kitchen, visible through a doorway straight ahead of me. "I can manage that. Would you like something to drink?"

"No." After a moment she added, "Thanks."

I guessed it was not a word she had reason to use often. The kitchen reminded me of my family's when my two brothers had been home alone for a few hours. Spots of mysterious substances dotted the cracked green linoleum, dirty dishes filled the sink, paper torn from a coloring book and crayons covered the table. Four small handprints decorated the fresh sky-blue paint on the ceiling above the back door.

Finding the peanut butter and apple juice took no effort. The refrigerator held little else.

"My husband went to town to get groceries," Tammy Kay said from the doorway as I shut the refrigerator door.

Spreading the peanut butter, I concluded that Straw

Bulganov was a fool and a jerk. And broke. I could see him rustling a few cattle with his buddies, but not calculating the killing of Jesse Tornell or spontaneously garroting an experienced trooper. Mustn't jump to conclusions. I needed evidence. Obtained legally. *Scheisse*. With Annalynn's future at stake, I had to think like a goddam cop.

Tammy Kay sighed. "You know where Straw is, don't you?"

No point in lying. "Yes. I heard him make that idiotic nine-one-one call."

She didn't answer for perhaps half a minute. "Were they high?"

She had guessed high, not drunk. Was Straw back on meth? "They were pretty happy."

"Damn Tommy Ray! He promised me he'd keep Straw out of trouble."

The short, chubby guy matched short, chubby Tammy Kay. Twins, or at least brother and sister. "Straw told the nine-one-one operator he'd seen a deer at Six Six Two West Aldridge."

"Fuckin' idiot! That's Dad's house."

I rinsed out plastic glasses for the juice. "Where do you want the boys to eat?"

"There's a little table on the west side of the house."

The phone rang and she stepped back into the living room to answer it. A moment later, she said, "You goddam idiot. You go to the grocery store and then you come straight home. You hear me?" A long pause. "You come through the door with everything on my list by one o'clock or you can move in with Tommy Ray." She slammed down the receiver. "Sometimes he acts like he's no older than our kids."

I'd seen that for myself. "Men will be boys." I put the

twins' lunch on a greasy cookie sheet to carry outside. When I stepped into the living room, Tammy Kay was stretched out on the futon. "Would you like for me to stay with the boys while they eat?"

She shook her head. "I never worry when they have food in front of them."

I paused at the door. "Were you outside late Monday afternoon by any chance?"

"Nah. I was spackling the wall while Straw painted. Why?"

"The sheriff is hoping someone saw a strange car or pickup in the area sometime between four and seven."

Her eyes widened. "You mean when Jesse died. You think somebody killed him." She shivered. "We cooked hotdogs and ate outside around six. When I brought the drinks out, Straw was having a fit because somebody coming from that direction turned the corner real fast and the dust blew over onto our food."

"That could be important. The sheriff will want to know about that."

She looked away. "Straw didn't see who it was. Didn't even see the car."

He'd seen a car but wasn't about to tell a goddam cop. "If he remembers anything, have him call the sheriff." I'd bet he hadn't already told her.

The instant the boys saw the tray, they scampered away from the sprinkler and around the corner of the house to a red plastic play table.

"Ouch! This is hot," Willy said, hopping up from the bench.

"You got a hot butt," Wally laughed. A cushion protected his bare bottom.

I put down the tray, picked up a filthy towel covering a portable grill, and spread it over Willy's side of the bench.

He hoisted himself onto the towel. "I know your name. Your name is Fixit."

I laughed. "That's close. Do you eat dinner—supper—out here every night?"

"Jusch when we"—Wally swallowed—"make hotdogs or hamburgers."

"Your mother said it was dusty the last time you ate hotdogs."

Both nodded.

Too young to be witnesses, but not too young to yield information. "Let me guess. A big yellow bus made all that dust."

"Nah," Willy said. "Guess again."

"A purple car." Did they know their colors? "Purple like"—what was the name of that annoying dinosaur?—"purple like Barney?"

"Nah," Willy said. "It was a brown car. Brown like your pants."

I glanced down at my forest-green slacks and called off the interrogation.

SIXTEEN

THE BOYS WAVED goodbye as I backed out of their drive. Just beyond the gravel road that ran by the side of their house, I pulled over. Three aged pear trees stood between the dusty road and their yard, but Straw could have seen whoever raced around that corner.

Achilles at my heels, I got out and walked along the blacktop toward the side road's three shallow ruts to check for skid marks. Nothing. Monday night's rain had washed away any signs of a car sliding around the corner.

Wally jumped up and ran toward me shouting, "Wha-cha doin'?"

The threat sent Achilles back into the car.

"Looking for a doggie bathroom." I followed him into the car, backed up, and turned down the gravel road. A quarter of a mile away over a small rise, a track led into a soybean field. I pulled in to call Annalynn. No signal. I couldn't ask any of the Bulganovs to use their phone, so I drove on to the Tornells'. It was too hot to leave Achilles in the car, so I let him out to explore the yard before knocking on the back door.

"Come on in," called a tremulous male voice.

I walked into the kitchen. No one was there, but food—mostly pies and cakes—covered the table. Sympathy food.

"Leave it on the table or put it in the refrigerator," a young male voice called from upstairs.

Had to be Dorothy's son. "It's Phoenix Smith. May I use your phone, please?"

"Sure. Long as it's not long distance."

"It's not." I went into the empty living room, located the cordless phone, and took it outside to call Annalynn.

"Phoenix! Finally. I tried to call you."

"I'm at the Tornells'. Have you released Straw yet? He has some information."

"Let me check."

I heard a cat hiss and saw an orange streak leap up the trunk of an oak tree that shaded the house from the morning sun.

"Straw left a couple of minutes ago. What's the information?"

"He and his little boys saw a car, possibly green, skid around the corner by their house Monday evening. You can find Straw at a grocery store."

Annalynn sighed. "It wouldn't do any good. He's already said he saw no one pass his place."

I thought a moment. "His wife was afraid that he was on drugs last night. Maybe a search warrant—or the threat of one—would loosen his lips."

"I have to tread softly. His family has a lot of pull. Have you talked to his parents yet?"

"No. I'll go there from here."

"I have news, too. The medical examiner found a tiny fragment of something that didn't come from the antler in Tornell's wound. Would you mind telling Dorothy that we have proof her husband was murdered?"

An unpleasant assignment, one I couldn't refuse. "Of course. She's not here now, but I'll stop by again before I head back to Laycock."

I put the phone back in its cradle and, on my way out, called, "Please tell Dorothy I'll stop by later."

Heat buffeted me when I opened the car door. Achilles backed away. I turned on the engine and the air conditioning. It was only eleven thirty and the car thermometer said ninety-three degrees. I stepped back out so he could get in from my side. "Come on, boy. We'll head back to Annalynn's nice cool house soon."

He stalled by pretending to snap at gnats. Finally he got in.

The American flag hung limp as I turned into Straw's parents' blacktop driveway. It curved around a small stand of timber and ended in a well-shaded circular drive. In the center, large red-brown rocks encircled a four-foot-high metal fountain that could have come from a small Italian piazza. The one-story brick house sprawled between two magnificent—and now rare—elms that covered all but the center of the high-pitched roof. Those trees lowered the temperature about ten degrees. A broad brick walkway led to the front door. Low bushes lined the front of the house. Small rocks raked in patterns—reminiscent of a Japanese garden—filled the space between the bushes and the drive. Definitely not typical Missouri farmhouse landscaping.

The front door opened and a short, sandy-haired woman about my age came out wearing a loose purple top and slacks and a welcoming smile.

I stepped out of the car. "Good morning. Mrs. Bulganov?"

"Yes, and you must be the NutriDairy representative."

"No, I'm Phoenix Smith, part of the volunteer deer squad."

Welcome changed to wrath. "Your foolishness sent my boy to jail."

Achilles growled.

"No, Mrs. Bulganov. Your son's foolishness got him

arrested. Please lower your voice. You're upsetting my dog. Someone took a shot at him yesterday, and he's sensitive to negativity."

A man inside the house roared with laughter. "Bring her in, Nan. I gotta hear this. Leave the negative mutt in the car."

Vlad Bulganov wasn't laughing when I walked into what looked like the lounge at a dude ranch. Branding irons decorated the beams of a cathedral ceiling, and the chimney of a red-stone fireplace took up much of one interior wall. All the chairs were brown or burgundy leather. Oddly enough, Hummel figurines and lesser small collectibles covered most horizontal surfaces. The only sign of his Russian heritage was a battered nineteenth-century copper samovar.

A large, big-nosed man with a huge shock of white hair, Bulganov watched me from a giant recliner, his feet as high as his waist. He pointed with an arthritic hand to a glider directly across from him. The interrogation chair.

I sat down and made myself comfortable. The air was blessedly cool. "Thank you for seeing me, Mr. Bulganov."

"The charge against my boy will never stick. Tell the sheriff to drop it."

I considered pretending to be intimidated, but if you don't push back against powerful men, they consider it an invitation to roll over you. Besides, better for the refusal to come from me than Annalynn. "Your son behaved irresponsibly last night. He won't learn that's unacceptable if you get him off every time he messes up."

Nan Bulganov leaned against the back of her husband's chair. "He played a silly joke. Only an incompetent, insecure sheriff would have arrested the boy."

Bloody hell! No use trying to reason with a bully. I

had to scare her without seeming hostile. I chose my academic-paper presentation voice: "Sheriff Keyser caught a man on probation breaking the law. That illegal act threatens his probation and puts him under suspicion of having made a similar call earlier in the day, a call that lured the deer squad to Star Corner."

Vlad interrupted me. "That call was someone else's prank. You city slickers don't have any business going outside city limits. Some guy fired in the air to scare you."

"He certainly scared me," I said, "especially when one of his bullets knocked off Vernon Kann's cap. The charge will be attempted murder."

"The hell you say!" Bulganov slammed down the footrest and struggled to get out of the recliner. "I'll see what Vern has to say about that."

"Stay put," his wife said. "I'll bring you the phone."

Achilles howled, a sign of separation anxiety. Or maybe the heat.

I hurried toward the door. "I'm being paged."

Achilles shut up when he saw me. I opened the car door and he almost knocked me down trying to lick my face. "Down, Achilles. Sit. Sit. Sit!" When he obeyed, I knelt by him and went through a full regimen of stroking and soothing. What had upset him so? Had he heard the anger in the Bulganovs' voices?

"Too damn hot for him in that car," Vlad said from the doorway. "He needs water. Bring him around back to the patio. We got a faucet there." He pointed toward the north end of the house.

We walked around an attached two-car garage into the backyard. A green roll-out awning covered half of a huge flagstone patio sheltering three picnic tables and assorted chairs. At the patio's far edge, pink and white wave petunias spilled over the top of a planter resembling a sarcophagus. Red plastic hummingbird feeders hung on shepherd's crooks on either side of the flowers. Tall trees all around shaded most of the small lawn, including a swing set surrounded by sand. Obviously the Bulganovs didn't like to mow.

Nan came through a back door with a plastic bowl. She filled it at a faucet by the door and walked toward me without meeting my eyes. "Vern vouched for you."

The newsman had more influence than I'd expected. I took the bowl from Nan and put it down near the hummingbird feeder. "Drink, *Schatzi*. Everything's okay."

Vlad came out the door. He leaned heavily on a plain metal cane. "Had that fella a long time, Dr. Smith?"

"Call me Phoenix, please. Achilles has owned me about a month."

He chuckled as he eased into an Adirondack chair loaded with cushions and gave me an appraising look. "How much trouble is Straw in?"

"I have no idea." I walked over and stood in front of him. "I don't know whether making a false report is a misdemeanor or a felony."

Nan turned red, but she said, "Would you care for iced tea?"

So they had decided to play nice. "That would be lovely. Thank you."

She ambled back into the house.

I filled the silence. "I noticed the Russian samovar in your living room. Is that a family piece?"

"Yup. My great-grandfather's family came to Nebraska from Russia in the eighteen nineties. They moved to Missouri for a milder climate around nineteen hundred." He motioned to a chair. "Take a load off." He said nothing until I was seated. "Straw's given us plenty of headaches, but he's thoughtless and impulsive, not mean. He's settled down a lot since he became a father."

I said nothing, waiting for him to go on. Maybe I'd learn something.

The big man shifted in his chair and grimaced in pain. "He gets stupid when he drinks. I'd say his making that call at Harry's proves he didn't make the one about a rabid deer at Star Corner. And I'd swear on my mother's King James he wouldn't shoot anybody." He smiled ruefully. "If he tried, he'd miss. The Tornells can tell you that."

Nan came out and handed Vlad and me tall glasses of iced tea. "Straw got in with a bad crowd in Laycock," she said. "We moved him and his family—he has two darling little boys—to a house near here to get him away from bad influences."

My tea had no ice and no sweetening. Nan had made a subtle point of her antagonism in a way her husband wouldn't notice.

Vlad sipped his tea. "She spoils those little rascals."

"Straw's been doing really well," Nan added. "He helps Bob—Vlad's older son—with the milking in the morning and then does light construction and handyman work." She turned to go back into the house. "Excuse me. I hear a car. That must be the NutriDairy rep."

Vlad grinned. "A dietician for cows. You type in your production records for each cow into their software program and then test combinations of food supplements to see what works for each cow. NutriDairy claims the right balance of supplements will increase the average cow's milk production from six and a half to seven and a half or eight gallons a day. You believe that?"

I took my cue from him. "I've lived abroad for a long time, but I'm from Missouri. You have to show me when you make claims like that."

"That's what I say. We're considering a three-month trial."

My show-me credentials established, I got down to business. "Right now I'm concerned with deer rather than cattle, specifically a deer with one antler tip missing." I wiped sweat from my forehead with a tissue to give him a moment to realize what I was talking about. "You know this area. Where should I look for bucks?"

He studied me. "I hear there's a few over in the timber on Vanderhofen's place. A creek runs through there, so they have water." He stopped. "What are you really after? No deer killed Jesse. He would've shot a deer before it got close enough to gore him. You figure somebody found a broken antler and turned it into a weapon?"

I shrugged. "We don't know. Can you think of anybody who would have hated Jesse enough to do that?"

He sipped his tea, his expression and body language revealing nothing. "No. Must've been a stranger. I've heard rumors about small-time rustlers."

He'd come up with that idea pretty fast. "Dorothy said no cattle are missing."

"If I'd just stabbed somebody, I wouldn't hang around to load cattle. Jesse doesn't have a loading chute. Cattle don't hop into a truck or trailer, you know."

An interesting point. "Stealing cattle would be a two-man job?"

"I'd say so. I've loaded a cow or two by myself a few times, but believe me, it takes a whole lot of sweatin' and swearin'."

Two men could have carried Jessie's body to that blind

a lot easier than one. "Did any of your family see any unfamiliar trucks or cars go by late Monday afternoon?"

"We're too far back from the road."

Achilles rested his snout on my knee. He was ready to go, and so was I.

"Thanks for your help." I rose. "Please give my best to your wife."

He struggled to his feet. "Tell Sheriff Keyser to give me a call. We'd appreciate it if she would recommend community service instead of jail time."

Careful. No refusals, no promises. "I don't think that's up to her, but I'll tell her about your concerns"—I thought of Tammy Kay and the boys—"and about his family."

When I reached the front of the house, a freshly waxed dark-blue Dodge Ram pickup with a sparkling white over-the-cab camper was parked in front of me. Green block letters on the side of the camper declared this a NutriDairy vehicle.

Nose in the air, Achilles trotted to the back of the camper. He sneezed five times and went to sniff the back tire.

Afraid he'd lift a leg on a tire so clean it had to have been power-washed, I called him to come. He sneezed several more times as he trotted to me.

I sniffed as I went by the camper, and even my human nose could detect a mixture of disinfectant and deodorizer.

Garth Raymo opened the Bulganovs' front door. He wore a white polo shirt with a NutriDairy logo. "Hello, again, Phoenix. Would you like for me to move my camper?"

"No need, Garth. I have room to get out." I opened

the car door for Achilles. "Are you a part-time farmer or a part-time salesman?"

"More like full-time farmer and salesman. That's what a small farmer has to do to survive, or at least one who bought a farm with his dream house and it's turned into a nightmare." He yawned and rubbed eyes with dark circles under them. "I didn't have time to stop at Dorothy's. Have you heard when the funeral will be?"

"Not yet." I walked over to him. "Would you like for me to call you when I know?"

"You really are an angel." He took a business card from a leather case and handed it to me. "I'm headed to Arkansas to meet with clients. You can reach me on my cell."

Nan brushed past him, her face red. "I'd appreciate it if you leave Straw's family alone."

Tammy Kay must have called her mother-in-law, the wealthy woman who had let the young couple's refrigerator stand empty. "I'll leave them alone, but you shouldn't. She doesn't even have milk for those boys." Surprised at my anger and my failure to hide it, I jumped in the car and peeled out of there. I turned left to go to the Tornells' to talk to Dorothy.

The heat was getting to me. Not only the heat, I admitted. I'd recovered only half of my strength and endurance. And I'd let down my emotional guard. I had to adjust to my new limits. That included eating small meals. Maybe Dorothy would invite me to lunch. I pulled into the Tornells' drive and parked beside an old dark-blue Chevy Impala.

Dorothy stuck her head out the back door. "The sheriff called for you five minutes ago. She wants you to call her."

I fished some dog biscuits out of the trunk for Achilles before hurrying inside.

Dorothy, pale beneath her tan, met me on the porch with a cordless phone.

It rang four times before Annalynn picked up. "It's Phoenix. I'm with Dorothy."

"Stay there. I'll call you back."

"I'll be here." I hit the off button and handed the phone back to Dorothy.

"We can talk without being overheard here," she said softly. She led the way into the kitchen, cooled somewhat by a big floor fan. "Have something to eat. People brought lots of food." She fetched me a plate and utensils. "Have you found out anything yet?"

"Nothing officially. I may be able to tell you more when Annalynn calls back."

She gripped my shoulder. "The sheriff arrested Straw. Did he do it?"

I started to evade her question, but she had a right to the truth, at least when it didn't hurt her or the investigation. "From what I know so far, I don't think so."

She let go and slumped into a chair. "That's a relief. His wife called me this morning to give me her sympathy. She's the same age as Junior. He says she was a little wild but nice. Nan blamed her, not Straw, for the pregnancy, of course."

I helped myself to potato and kidney-bean salads, radishes, and a thin slice of ham. "I just met Nan. Garth Raymo was making a sales call."

"He asked yesterday how to get to the Bulganovs'. He's fixin' to sell them some of those fancy feed supplements." She smiled faintly. "Calls himself a bovine nutritionist." She tensed. "Have you checked Floyd Vanderhofen's alibi yet?"

Better to hold back the truth this time. "Annalynn is working on it. I'm going over to talk to him about a deer with a missing antler."

She drew in her breath. "You be careful. He's got a rotten temper."

I patted my gun and said, "I've got my Glock, and Achilles."

The phone rang. Dorothy handed it to me.

"Tornell residence."

"I don't want us to be overheard," Annalynn said.

I stepped onto the porch. "Go ahead."

"The pathologist says the cause of death was an unknown object slightly larger than the tip of the antler. Definitely not a knife. The killer pulled it out before inserting the antler. The foreign object is a tiny sliver of wood with a coating on part of it. It may be days before they can tell us what it's from."

"Any guesses?"

"No. But we're sure now he was murdered."

The deer hunt had become a manhunt.

SEVENTEEN

"I'VE CALLED A press conference at four to announce Tornell's death was a homicide," Annalynn said. "I don't want Dorothy to hear it on the radio. You'll have to tell her. Don't say anything to her, to anyone, about the wood fragment."

I glanced over my shoulder at Dorothy. She stood rigid with her fists clenched.

"When you've told her," Annalynn said, "come straight home."

An order with no "please" from my polite friend, her tone an echo of my mother's. "I haven't talked to Vanderhofen yet."

"I don't care. I want you out of there." She hung up.

Was she speaking for an audience? Or just worried that I'd confront a killer? I stepped back into the kitchen to face Dorothy. "As we suspected—death came from a human hand."

She didn't move.

I poured her a glass of iced tea from a pitcher on the table and pressed the cold glass into her right hand.

She jerked as though waking from a dream and fell back into a chair without spilling a drop. Raising the glass to her lips with both hands, she took a long drink. "They find fingerprints on the antler?"

"No."

"What about Straw?"

"They released him sometime this morning."

"I'm gonna go tell Junior." She put her glass on the table and hoisted herself out of the chair like an old woman. She went into the living room. A few seconds later *West Side Story* began to play—loudly.

Was she covering the sound of sobbing? Or her conversation with Junior? She hadn't come back by the time I rinsed off my plate. The clock on the wall said five to one. Annalynn wasn't expecting to hear from me for an hour or so. I had a few minutes to size up Vanderhofen before I reported in again. When I went outside, Achilles sprang up from his spot in the shade and trotted toward the car. I opened the door for him. He stuck his head inside and darted back into the shade. I groaned. If I cooled the car before we got in, he'd expect it all summer. What the hey. I hated the heat as much as he did. I turned on the air conditioner and joined him in the shade to wait for it to blow out the worst of the heat. Would I stay in Laycock all summer? New York City would be even hotter, and Achilles would find few shady spots there to nap in or hummingbird feeders to guard against cats. "Think about it tomorrow, Scarlett," I muttered as we got into the car.

I turned north at the crossroads and drove less than a quarter of a mile to Vanderhofen's place, a little beige manufactured home with forest-green window trim set amid towering hickory trees. My mouth watered at the memory of Christmas fudge made with the nuts gathered on my grandparents' farm. I parked in a shady spot behind a dark green pickup. The car thermometer read ninety-five degrees. To hell with the white blouse. Adults hardly seemed to notice my gun.

Achilles pressed himself to my left leg as I walked toward the three cement steps leading up to the door. Shrill yips inside the house announced our arrival.

I rang the bell and waited. No answer. I rang again.

"Just a minute," a man called.

Two minutes later he opened the door just enough to see through it with one eye. "Sorry. I was in the shower. Give me half a minute and then step in out of the heat. I'll get the flower money for you."

I didn't correct him. "May I bring my dog in?"

"Of course. It's brutally hot out there." He closed the door.

I timed the half minute on my watch and then opened the door.

A small, fuzzy white head peeked around the corner of a black faux-leather couch and then withdrew as Achilles extended his nose. The couch was one of three pieces of furniture in the living room, the other two being an old wood coffee table and a small television on a tray table. An excellent reproduction of an Audubon print hung on the wall opposite the couch. The place had the ambiance of a temporary home, or of one occupied by a newly divorced man. How could anyone live this way for three years?

A vain man, I thought, as he came out of a bedroom. He'd pulled on a pair of snug black jeans and a tight white T-shirt—apparently to show what good shape he was in. He'd also taken time to mold his elaborate comb-over.

I walked over to study the print. "Is this an original Audubon?"

"I wish," he said. He opened a billfold. "How much do you want? Ten? Fifteen?"

"I'm afraid you've mistaken me for someone else, Dr.

Vanderhofen." He didn't correct the unearned title. "I'm Phoenix Smith, a member of the volunteer deer squad."

He slipped the billfold in his back pocket. "You're doing a deer count? For which organization?"

"No count. You've heard that Jesse Tornell had an antler in his back?"

He frowned. "A bunch of nonsense. Deer pose no danger to humans."

"Apparently someone wanted to make it look like a deer gored Mr. Tornell. I'm trying to find out if someone shot a deer for that bit of antler."

"Good God! Some fascist killed a buck to frame it for murder?"

A skewed conclusion. "Do you know anyone who would do such a thing?"

"No one but Jesse Tornell. I'll bet he's killed six deer in the last year. I reported him to the sheriff, but the law cares nothing about animals." He pointed toward the bedroom, where a miniature gym was visible. "I marked the dates when I heard shots on my calendar. Once I caught him skinning a deer in the pasture next to mine. He said it was road kill."

He was either a great actor or obsessed with deer. "Isn't road kill always the excuse?"

His face went guarded. "Why are you wearing a pistol?"

"Scared of rattlers." I smiled. "You surely don't think I'd hunt deer with a pistol."

"No, no, of course not."

"I've heard that bucks live in your timber. Would you mind if I walk through and look for signs of a carcass? Or of a deer with a missing antler?"

He reached the door in two steps and flung it open. "No one who carries a gun is welcome on my property."

Achilles growled.

"Quiet, boy! Dr. Vanderhofen has every right to ask us to leave." And evidently a reason not to want me to search his property. I sent Achilles ahead and stopped on the front step. "I'm sorry if I offended you. Please check your property for a dead or wounded buck. If you find either, call the sheriff's office immediately."

"You can count on it." He slammed the door.

As soon as the car cooled enough to meet with Achilles' approval, I headed for Laycock.

A black Lincoln whipped around the corner at the crossroads and slid to a stop in front of me. I drew my gun, braked, and hit the button to lower my window.

Nan Bulganov jumped out of the car and ran toward me. "We need your help," she gasped as she reached me. "You and your dog. Straw's missing."

Missing? Unlikely. "He just got out of jail a couple of hours ago."

Hand over her heart, she took a deep breath. "He stopped at Bob's to pick up milk about twelve thirty. He never made it home. Tammy Kay called Bob to ask him to bring over some milk and they've both been looking for him. She's afraid whoever killed Jesse has hurt Straw. She's hysterical…"

As was his mother. "What do you want me to do, Mrs. Bulganov?"

"Track him, of course."

"Starting where? Achilles can track a man if he has his scent, but he can't track a car on a public road."

She glared at me. "Surely you can do something."

Obviously I had to do more than be logical. "We'll need a piece of Straw's clothing to give Achilles the scent."

That bit of inanity satisfied her. She ran to her car, reversed into the crossroads at about forty-five miles an hour, and took off at a speed I didn't care to equal. I used the three-minute drive to try to figure out what to do. Nothing reasonable came to mind.

Straw's driveway was filled with vehicles, so I turned left on the gravel road and pulled to the side a little way from the corner. When I let Achilles out of the car, he sniffed the air and stared out over the brush-filled unfenced field behind the house. He barked and trotted into the field.

My heart rate accelerated. He smelled something alarming. "Achilles!"

He paused, barked three times, and trotted on. He paused again and looked back to be sure I was following him. When I moved toward him, he trotted on.

Drawing my gun, I ran after him.

"The goddam cop drew her gun," one of the twins yelled.

Achilles wove around saplings and giant weeds but kept heading toward a decrepit unpainted shed. He went to a spot with a missing board and sat down to wait for me. His triumphant look told me he thought he'd performed a task well.

I brushed a spider web away from the hole to peer into the shed. A score of bare bulbs hung over a dozen two-foot-high green plastic pots holding leafy plants about six feet tall. Pots of pot. "Good boy, Achilles. Good boy." On the far side of the shed a door stood open. Through it I could see the bed of a pickup. But no Straw.

Had he gotten so stoned on his cash crop that he forgot to take food to his children? Gun at the ready and Achilles at my side, I walked around the edge of shed to the pickup, approaching it on the far side—the driver's side. The cab was empty. The keys were in the ignition. The passenger's seatbelt held in place two sacks of groceries and a glass jug of milk. The pickup bed was empty.

Someone big in a blue shirt was running toward me from the house.

I edged away from the truck toward the shed's open door. Achilles tried to block my way.

A big black running shoe protruded from between two pots.

"Oh, God. Not again. Stay, Achilles, stay." I crept through the door. Straw Bulganov lay sprawled face-down on the dirt floor.

EIGHTEEN

"STRAW!"

He didn't stir.

I holstered my gun and maneuvered between the big pots to kneel by his head. Scarlet blood covered the blond hair above his right ear. He didn't open his eyes when I pressed down on his carotid artery. I felt a pulse. Weak, but there.

"Call nine-one-one. He's unconscious," I yelled to whoever was running up to the shed. Some of the blood was still wet. He hadn't been here long.

"Call nine-one-one," Bob Bulganov bellowed, "and bring the Lincoln around."

Straw's skin was warm. I raised an eyelid. Dilated pupils. Drugs. "Bloody hell! I need help here!"

Bob charged through the shed door.

"Looks like a drug overdose," I said. "I can't tell whether he's breathing. Pull him out so we can check." I got out of the way.

Bob grabbed Straw's feet, pulled him out of the shed, and turned him onto his back. Bob put his cheek down by Straw's nostrils for several seconds. "Barely breathing." He began rescue breathing.

The Lincoln slid to a stop behind the pickup, Nan at the wheel and Vlad in the passenger seat.

Nan jumped out, leaving the motor running. "What happened? Is he hurt bad?"

I debated a moment: The pickup worked better if we had to do CPR, but we could make better time in the Lincoln. A couple of minutes could make the difference. If he needed CPR, we'd stop and put him on the ground. I opened the car's back door and said, "Vlad, you help load and hold Straw. Keep checking his heart while Bob works on the breathing. Nan, you call the paramedics and tell them to meet us on Route TT. We'll call nine-one-one to coordinate the meeting when we get close enough to Laycock that my cell works."

While they hoisted Straw into the back, I moved the front passenger seat as far forward as it would go to give Bob room to work. I motioned for Achilles to get in. Then I slipped behind the Lincoln's steering wheel and locked the front doors.

Nan tried to open the door. "What do you think you're doing?"

I rolled down the window just far enough to drop my keys on the ground. "Make sure nine-one-one knows this is *urgent* and we're on our way. Then follow in my car." I locked the back doors and handed my cell to her husband.

"Vlad?" She bent to look in the back seat. "Oh, God! Oh, God!"

I shifted into reverse. "Hold on, guys. Down, Achilles. On the floor."

Nan pounded on my door but stepped back when I gunned the motor.

I took out a small sapling as I backed the car around. By the time I reached the main road, I had the feel of the car. It responded beautifully when I pushed the accelerator to the floorboard. Blasting the horn every time we came near a corner or a driveway or another road, I took advantage of the Lincoln's power.

Five minutes on, Vlad said, "His heart is still going. You can slow down a little on the corners."

Slowing down struck me as a very bad idea, one they wouldn't have had if a man had been driving.

A couple minutes later, he said, "His eyes look funny. I suppose he's stoned. How in heck did you know to look for him in that shed?"

"I didn't. Achilles smelled the marijuana and led me there." Obviously he'd learned to identify narcotics before he flunked out of the DEA canine course.

We drove in silence for another five minutes.

I whipped around a tractor. "Vlad, if you can get a hand free, try my cell."

A few seconds later, he said, "It's ringing." A short pause. "This is Vladimir Bulganov. Where's the ambulance?" A long pause. "We're five—make that three—minutes from Roy Crawford's farm. He's got a wide driveway. We'll meet there to shift Straw to the ambulance. Tell 'em he's real bad."

I glanced at the clock. Just after two.

Two minutes later, Vlad said, "The farmhouse at the top of the hill. It's a gravel drive, so you're gonna have to slow down for it."

The ambulance siren sounded nearby as my tires skidded on the gravel. I turned the motor off, wriggled my tense shoulders, and put my head down on the wheel, relieved to relinquish responsibility.

Achilles licked my arm.

The ambulance pulled in beside me and two men and a woman jumped out. A moment later they were transferring the young man to a gurney. The woman said, "It looks like a massive overdose. Do you know what he took?"

I shook my head. I was betting he took nothing. Someone gave it to him.

Face pasty, Vlad climbed into the front seat of the ambulance.

I jumped out of the car. "My cell phone, please."

He handed it to me. "Thanks."

I dialed Annalynn's direct line and walked down the driveway. I got her voice mail. "Annalynn, I'm pretty sure somebody hit Straw Bulganov on the head and drugged him. I don't think he's going to make it. I'm following the ambulance to the hospital."

The ambulance pulled out, siren blaring.

"Let's go," Bob called, jumping into the back seat of the Lincoln.

Achilles hunkered down on the floorboard again. I backed out considerably more carefully than I had before but stepped on the gas to keep the ambulance in sight. "Bob, did Straw look high when he stopped for milk?"

"No. I saw him high on meth once. He didn't look anything like that."

I stayed several car lengths behind the ambulance. Bob seemed a straight shooter. "You did a great job."

"You almost stopped my heart on a couple of those corners. I suppose you learn that kind of driving in police training."

"I wouldn't know. I'm not a police officer." I gave my usual reason for my driving skills. "I took a defensive driving course that my company offered after September Eleven." I leaned on the horn and followed the ambulance through a stop sign.

Bob said nothing else until I stopped behind the ambulance at the emergency entrance. He jumped out. "Thanks for the lift."

"I'll bring the keys in when I've parked the car."

Naturally I had to park it in the blazing sun. Walking toward the emergency entrance with Achilles, I wilted under the heat's assault. A sign prohibiting dogs and guns stopped me at the door. I sat down on a bench in the shade of the portico and fanned myself with my hand while I tried to make sense of the attack on Straw.

Achilles joined me on the bench and put his head in my lap.

I had plenty of questions but no answers. Who could have hit him? A disgruntled customer? One of his stupid buddies? The same person who'd killed Jesse? Someone must have arranged to meet him at the shed. With his wife's ultimatum to motivate him to get home, Straw had to have a good reason to go to that shed before delivering the groceries. I tried to visualize how it could have happened: Straw greets someone and turns his back; the visitor slugs him, and injects something that causes respiratory failure.

That kind of killing took planning. And luck. Straw spent the night in jail. Who knew he was out? His family. Did one of them or his friends do this?

My Camry careened into the parking lot and screeched to a stop in front of me. Tammy Kay jumped out and ran inside. Nan unfastened the boys' seatbelts and took them by the hand as they scrambled out of the car.

"There's the goddam cop," Wally said. Like his brother, he wore blue shorts, a red T-shirt a size too small, and flip-flops.

"And the goddam police dog," Willy added. He

yanked away from Nan to stroke Achilles' back. "He found my daddy."

I handed Nan the keys to her car. "It's parked over there."

"I'm telling the county commissioners about you. Start looking for a new job." She grabbed Willy's hand. "Any word on how he's doing?"

"Maybe they've told your husband something by now." God, but I hated this. Straw was no prize, but he'd cooked hotdogs for his sons and remembered to stop for milk. He'd held them up so they could put their handprints on the ceiling.

Nan dragged the boys inside.

Achilles and I got into the car, which Nan had left running with the air conditioner blasting. I debated whether to go home. My phone rang.

"I heard you got him to the hospital alive," Annalynn said. "Are you okay?"

"Yes." I decided not to mention Nan's rage. "You need to send someone out to the shed behind Straw Bulganov's house fast."

"Hold on. I'm going to get Gillian and Spike on the line so you can fill us all in at once."

I turned the air conditioning down a smidgeon, drove out of the parking lot, and parked on the shady residential street across from the hospital.

"Go ahead, Phoenix," Annalynn said.

I gave them a quick, facts-only summary. No one interrupted me.

"Okay," Annalynn said, "now tell us what you *think* happened."

I visualized my first view of the shed. "I didn't see any footprints, not even Straw's, on that dirt floor before I went in. I also didn't see any sign of a vehicle other than his pickup. Best guess: Someone walked in through an untilled field north of the shed, whacked him hard enough to knock him out, and injected something."

I paused and when no one spoke, I said the—to me—obvious: "Looks like another attempt to obscure the cause of death." A standard tactic in intelligence operations, but this killer lacked the skill to deceive.

"An interesting point, but we shouldn't assume anything yet," Spike said, his tone that of the professional speaking to an amateur. "Did anybody see another vehicle?"

I'd been condescended to by much older and smarter men than Spike. I'd learned to get even without gloating. "Maybe his wife or boys did. They're in the hospital now."

Gillian spoke: "What do the doctors say?"

Now I felt like an amateur. "I don't know."

"Gillian, Spike," Annalynn said, "please go check the crime scene immediately. Spike, you question the neighbors before you come back in. Phoenix, you find out the victim's condition. Do you have that reserve officer ID with you?"

"Yes, but I don't have one for Achilles. I can't leave him in the car in this heat."

"Nobody's gonna question an officer with a dog," Spike said. "If they do, tell them he's a police dog."

Still a bit condescending, but he'd treated me as part of the team.

Annalynn said, "Do what you need to, Phoenix. I'll be there shortly."

Dreading to hear bad news, I stalled by pouring some water for Achilles and myself to drink. He lapped away, but my stomach turned after the first sip. I couldn't ignore my need to rest much longer, and I had to get out of the heat. I put Achilles' water bowl back in the car and took out his leash.

He trotted ahead of me sniffing the air until we reached the emergency room door. He stopped. "We have to do this," I told him, putting my hand on his head. "Come."

When we walked through the door, every head in the place turned toward us.

Willy jumped up from a table where he'd been coloring and came running. "Hi, Fixit. Hi, doggie."

A heavyset male security officer waddled toward me. "You can't bring that dog in here, ma'am."

I pulled out my ID card. "We're with the sheriff's department." I brushed my gun with the card before holding it up to him. "Official business."

Willy faced the guard. "He's a police dog. He can go anyplace he wants."

Bob walked over. "Take it easy, Marvin. She's an undercover officer."

So that's what his family, and probably many others, thought I was. Not the moment to deny it. "I'd appreciate your cooperation, Marvin."

"Sure." The guard went back to the chair where he'd been dozing.

Willy hugged Achilles from the left and Wally from the right.

I held my breath, afraid Achilles would either growl or run away.

Instead he trotted over to where the boys had been coloring and lay down by the table. They sat on the floor on each side of him and, to my surprise, stroked and patted him with a tolerable amount of childish roughness, competing for his licks on their faces. He was as sensitive to the boys' anxiety as he was to Annalynn's grief.

I motioned to Bob to join me by the door. "What do the doctors say?"

He stared out the door a long time. "No hope. Tammy insists they put him on life support at least a few hours. She's hoping for a miracle." He cleared his throat. "From what Dad heard the ambulance crew say, drugs are killing him, not the knock on the head." His eyes bored into mine. "But you already knew that."

I glanced at the boys. They were picking grass seeds out of Achilles' coat. "I'm so sorry." I could think of nothing else to say.

The big man leaned down. "He didn't do this to himself," he whispered. "He's been clean for six months. He was raising pot, but he wasn't smoking it. Nan makes him pee for a test at least once a week. Somebody came there to kill him."

I nodded. "Keep that to yourself for now. Any idea who it could have been?"

He shook his head.

"Did any of you see or hear another vehicle after he left your place?"

He shook his head again. "Tammy Kay said she and the boys were watching cartoons. They didn't hear Straw turn the corner and drive up to the shed."

Annalynn drove past the emergency room and pulled over nearby.

"That's Sheriff Keyser," I told Bob. "She's sent officers out to see if they can find anything in or around the shed. I'll watch the boys so she can talk to you in private."

We stood silent until Annalynn came in.

I decided to be formal. "Sheriff Keyser, this is Bob

Bulganov, Straw's brother. He'll tell you what happened."
I walked toward the boys.

Nan Bulganov erupted through double doors into the
waiting room. "Sheriff, arrest that woman." She pointed
at me. "She attacked my son."

NINETEEN

WILLY WAILED, AND Wally rushed at me with his arms flailing. Bob Bulganov swooped up Wally and held him close.

Horrified that the boys thought me a monster, I reined in my anger at my accuser and kept my voice cool: "Nan, you know that's impossible. Please calm down. Think of the boys."

She continued to point at me as though her arm had frozen in place. "I saw you run to the shed with your gun drawn. You hit him with it. I know you did."

Willy—sobbing as though his insides were being wrenched from his little body—stumbled to Bob and wrapped his arms around the tall man's left leg.

"She didn't hit your daddy," Bob said, bending and lifting Willy up with one arm. "Nan, I could see Straw was already down when she went into the shed."

"Then she ambushed him earlier," Nan insisted. "She couldn't have found him like that if she didn't already know where he was."

"My dog led me to the marijuana," I told her, aware the crowd was watching us as though we were zinging a ball at each other across a tennis net.

Nan Bulganov hesitated only a moment. "Straw had nothing to do with marijuana. You planted it on him."

I'd had enough. "Of course. I always carry a dozen

magic beans in my pocket. I throw them on the ground and they instantly grow five feet tall."

Willy stopped in mid howl. "Like Jack and the beanstalk?"

I'd stuck my foot in that one. "Exactly like Jack and the beanstalk. Jack's beans aren't real, and neither are mine. I'm not telling a story when I say I didn't hurt your daddy." What else could I say? Achilles pressed against me, teeth bared. I put my hand on his head. "That's the truth, so help me dog."

"Blasphemy," someone hissed.

Annalynn spoke close to my ear. "Phoenix, you're getting that gray look. Do you feel well enough to drive yourself home?"

"Certainly. Step outside a moment," I whispered back.

As soon as the door closed behind us, I said, "Bob says Straw will die as soon as they take him off life support. A drug overdose will be the cause of death. Talk to his doctor as soon as you can."

"Those poor kids." Annalynn turned her face away for several seconds. "Spike thinks a drug deal went sour."

I smiled grimly. "I hope he's not assuming anything."

She opened the door. "Drive carefully."

When she turned her back to me, I sank onto the bench and put my head down to fight wooziness. Achilles licked my neck.

"Fixit's goin' to frow up," Wally announced from inside the glass double doors.

"No I'm not." I stood up, afraid some nurse would rush out.

Willy joined him. "Don't worry. The doctor will make my daddy feel good."

I knew that wasn't so, and pity-induced nausea al-

most forced me back to the bench. "Thank you for telling
me. I feel better. Bye." I walked toward my car, afraid I
wouldn't be able to keep back tears—or lunch. Moving
helped. I stooped to pick up Achilles' dragging leash.
"We're going home."

He took the opportunity to lick my face.

A LONG SOAK in the tub gave me time to search my memory. Who could have gone to that shed? Almost anyone,
including Dorothy and Junior. Who knew Straw would
be there? Persons unknown. The combination of a marijuana crop and a drug overdose obviously pointed to a
drug deal gone bad. Too obviously.

The logical alternative: Straw had seen Tornell's killers drive by. He might not have known who he saw, but
his killer wouldn't know that. Annalynn hadn't yet announced that a deer didn't kill Tornell, just that she was
waiting for the autopsy results on Thursday—tomorrow.
Whoever showered Straw's hotdogs with dust must have
feared he would tell the police about the speeding vehicle. Even Straw's dumb buddies would know he would
trade the information to the police to get charges for the
9-1-1 call dropped. He posed a threat. He had an "accident."

Annalynn should question the buddies again.

I climbed out of the tub, dried off, put on a robe, and
stretched out on my bed for a restorative nap.

"Phoenix, are you awake? Phoenix?" Connie was calling me from downstairs.

I'd barely dozed off. "No. I won't wake up for two
hours."

"Annalynn's press conference is in two *minutes*." A

short silence. "I brought over a yellow cake to go with your strawberries."

Her typical pattern: She pestered but did something nice. I might as well go down to join her in admiring Annalynn on TV. "There's vanilla ice cream in the fridge."

"I know. I gave you a scoop. Hurry up before it melts."

Being undressed puts you at a disadvantage. I pulled on a white tank top and shorts and hurried down to the entertainment room.

Connie was flipping from channel to channel. "Here it is."

Annalynn stood in front of a lectern holding four mikes, a sign of increased media interest in rural crime—or in the sheriff dealing with it. The brick wall of the sheriff's department formed her backdrop. "Good afternoon." She paused. "It's anything but that. I have two pieces of bad news. First, the medical examiner's report has verified what we suspected: Jesse Tornell's death was at the hands of a person or persons unknown. A deer did *not* attack him. We ask the community to tell us about anything they saw at or near the Tornell farm between four and seven Monday afternoon. We also ask people in northern Missouri to notify us if they see a deer with approximately nine inches of antler missing."

Someone called out, "You arrested William Wallace Bulganov last night for making a false report about a rabid deer. Is he a suspect in the Tornell killing?"

"No." Annalynn gripped the lectern. "Mr. Bulganov is the subject of my second announcement. Early this afternoon his family found him unconscious. He was assaulted by an unknown person. His condition is critical."

Wow! Annalynn had implied Straw might survive to

identify his attacker. She could evade without lying as well as I could. She'd be a natural on Capitol Hill.

The reporters howled like hounds treeing a coon.

Annalynn held up both hands for quiet until they subsided. "Mr. Bulganov lives in the northeast corner of Vandiver County less than three miles from where Mr. Tornell died. We are asking residents of that area to report any unfamiliar vehicles or unusual activity between noon and two o'clock this afternoon. I'll take a few questions."

Three reporters spoke at once.

Annalynn held up a hand for quiet. When the voices died down, she said, "One at a time, or the press conference ends. We'll start with Mr. Kann of the *Laycock Daily Advertiser.*"

The camera panned to Vernon in his wheelchair. "Sheriff Keyser, are these two crimes related?"

The camera went back to Annalynn. "We're working to determine that. We have established no motive in either case, and the attackers used different weapons." She nodded to another reporter. "Arlen Jayson, KTVO."

"We know Mr. Tornell was stabbed with an antler. What was the weapon used against Mr. Bulganov?"

"A blunt object."

So she was withholding the information about the drugging.

Annalynn ignored two loud male voices. "Ronnie Walters, KOMU-TV."

"What leads do you have for each of these cases?"

Annalynn said nothing for a moment. "None that I can share with you without jeopardizing our investigation. M. L. Moniteau, KILC, you have the last question."

"Sheriff Keyser," said the bespectacled African-American kid from the local radio station, "someone killed a trooper on Highway 36 last Saturday. Is that killing related to the attacks in Vandiver County? Are you looking for a serial killer?"

I groaned. "*Scheisse.* He'll panic half the state."

"No," Annalynn said, firm but not dismissive. "We see no indication of a serial killer. They tend to strike randomly at victims with similar characteristics. These three attacks don't appear to be random, and the three victims have little in common."

Every reporter shouted a question.

Annalynn motioned for quiet. "I can tell you two things. One: The M-Squad—the regional major crime squad investigating Trooper Cansadi's death—has discounted any connection to Mr. Tornell's death. Two: Our preliminary findings suggest both Vandiver County victims knew their attackers."

The camera zoomed in for a close-up.

Annalynn gazed into the lens and into living rooms. "That said, we urge everyone to take reasonable precautions. Unlike during my childhood, we can no longer leave our front doors unlocked. Like during my childhood, we must be our neighbor's keeper."

Ignoring the reporters' cacophony of questions, she thanked them for coming, turned, and walked into the building.

"Bravo!" Connie said. "That last sounded like a campaign speech."

Exactly. And solving this case would jumpstart a campaign for a House seat.

The KTVO reporter's face filled the screen. "Sheriff Keyser certainly meant it when she said it's not a good day here. In the last two days this community has suffered a homicide, an attempted homicide, and an apparently random shooting at a volunteer deer squad member. Sources tell us that the latest victim, William Wallace Bulganov, was released from the Vandiver County Jail at eleven o'clock this morning, just three hours before his family called nine-one-one. We'll have more of this breaking story—"

Connie turned off the television. "Annalynn looked great, but she wasn't at her best explaining what happened to Straw Bulganov."

"Oh, yes she was. You have no idea what she managed *not* to say."

"Such as you being the one to find him?"

Annalynn must have sent her over to check on me. "Such as Straw Bulganov is as good as dead."

She sucked in her breath. "He's barely out of his teens."

"With twin boys and a baby on the way." Anger hit me so hard, I had to release it. I pounded on a cushion. Years of self-discipline kicked in and I shoved my emotions into my dark corner. "Do you mind if I play your grand piano while you're at choir rehearsal tonight? Beethoven helps relieve stress."

"Of course." Connie shook her finger at me. "Annalynn is right. You care about people."

The phone rang the double ring that indicated a call from the sheriff's department.

Connie collected our empty bowls. "That's for you."

I picked up the cordless phone beside the couch. "Keyser residence."

"How are you feeling?" Annalynn's tone told me this wasn't an idle question.

"Fine, now that I'm out of the heat. Great job at the press conference. Any news on what drug is killing Straw?"

"No. We may not know for weeks. I'm bringing in

those two young men who were with him last night for questioning."

She had a talent for the job. "You think they killed him?"

"I suspect they can guess who did. They and the killer all must have known Straw was growing marijuana in that shed."

My conclusion, too. "Who knew he'd been released from jail?"

"Everyone. The radio station announced his release on its eleven and twelve o'clock newscasts. Anyone could have called him. He had a cell phone in his pocket last night and in an ankle holster today. We're checking his call records now."

I puzzled over this. "Even if someone called him right after he got out of jail, that allows almost no time to prepare an injection, drive to his house, and sneak into that shed. This smells like a planned operation, not an impulse killing."

Annalynn said nothing for a half a minute. "They probably scheduled a rendezvous yesterday before the arrest. If Straw saw the killers' vehicle Monday evening, they may have seen him. They could have used the Web to find out who lived there, discovered his meth history, and contacted him either to sell or to buy."

Possible. "And you hope he told his buddies. They were celebrating last night."

"Yes. I'm going to talk to them separately. In my office, unofficially. I hope they'll tell me whatever they know." She paused. "I suspect they won't talk unless they're scared."

"So scare them."

"Their families forced their release last night. These

boys aren't afraid of me. One growl from Achilles, on the other hand, got their attention."

She had to be desperate to suggest something so out of character. I didn't like it, but I kept my voice neutral: "What do you have in mind?"

"A variation on good cop, bad cop. I'll do a straight informational interview—with my phone on speaker so you can listen in. Then I'll send the young man out through the garage to avoid the press."

"And Achilles and I will cut him off to have a little chat." Any coercion posed a high risk for Annalynn's potential political career. "If it backfires, you'll get hammered."

"You're too smart to let that happen. Tommy Ray is due in twenty minutes. You have nineteen to get in place. And bring Connie with you as backup." She hung up.

"Bloody hell!"

Connie appeared in the door. "What's the matter?"

"Annalynn has an errand for me, a damned chancy one. Where's Achilles?"

"Guarding the hummingbirds."

I should have guessed. "Could you bring him in while I change, please?" I'd take her along to please Annalynn, but damned if I'd tell Connie she was my backup. "And could I bum a ride to the jail? I'd rather people not see my car there."

"Certainly. I'll wait in the tavern next door and give you a ride home."

Perfect. Sitting in a bar worked much better than waiting in view of people and surveillance cameras. I remembered the tavern from going there with my ex-husband on a visit to Laycock soon after we were married. The back door opened to the alley next to the jail, an advantageous position. I ran upstairs to put on black slacks and an oversized black T-shirt with a no smoking symbol imposed over gray lungs, the closest thing I had to menacing. And loose enough to hide my holster.

Connie and Achilles waited for me at the front door.

Connie frowned. "Why on earth are you wearing black? It's a hundred out there."

I grimaced. "I know." I'd have to tell her a little bit. "I may need your help. I'm going to play bad cop to Annalynn's good cop."

"A natural division of labor. What's my role?"

"Bystander." Even as I said it, I realized that was the one role she never played.

TWENTY

I LAID OUT my sketchy plan as Connie drove us to the tavern. We parked around the corner a half block away and entered the tavern right on schedule. I paused and dialed Annalynn's direct line as my eyes adjusted to the darkness. High wood booths still lined the wall along the alley. To our right, the bar took up most of the front. The bartender wasn't in sight, which meant I didn't have to argue with anyone about bringing Achilles inside. Two gray-haired men on wood stools leaned against the bar, gazing up at a small television replaying a clip from Annalynn's press conference.

"I'm in place," I said when she answered her phone. "Leave at least fifteen minutes between—talks."

"Tommy Ray Conklin came with a lawyer. I'm going to put my phone on speaker." Pause. "Can you hear me?"

"Yes. Give me two minutes and bring them in." I muted my cell and handed Connie a twenty. "I'll find us a booth while you order. A beer for me."

I chose the booth by the back door and slid in so I faced the front door. The same spot I'd occupied with Russ so long ago. My ex's cheating heart evoked no pain and only a gram of anger. I couldn't see the entry to the garage from the booth, but I'd know when Tommy Ray Conklin left Annalynn's office in time to intercept him. Achilles settled down at my feet.

"Mr. Conklin, thank you for coming in at this difficult

time," Annalynn said. "I'm so sorry about your brother-in-law. How are you, Wendell?"

The only Wendell I knew was a former classmate who specialized in real estate law. Not exactly a high-powered defense attorney.

Connie slid into the booth and put a beer in front of me. She had a glass of white wine, something no tavern or bar in Laycock had served while I was growing up.

"I'll be brief," Annalynn said. "I know that you and Straw were close friends since grade school. Did he say anything to you about being in trouble?"

"No," Tommy Ray said, his voice strained. "Things were goin' good. We were celebrating last night because he just got a ginormous painting job. He was gonna get an advance today."

Hundred to one odds that advance was coming from a drug sale to the killer.

"Did he say who hired him?" Annalynn sounded concerned, nonaccusatory.

"Nah. Some dude who's fixing up an old farmhouse instead of paying rent."

Straw didn't have much imagination. He'd described his own situation to explain his windfall.

"Mr. Conklin," Annalynn said, "since Mr. Bulganov was attacked in a shed full of marijuana plants, that painting story is hard to believe. You'll save yourself a lot of trouble if you tell me everything you know about his marijuana business."

"Sheriff, I can't let you question the boy this way," Wendell said. "You've gone over the line and—"

Tommy Ray interrupted his lawyer: "I didn't know anything about the marijuana in the shed until Bob Bulganov told me! I swear to God! Besides, I know Straw hadn't smoked any weed in months. Tammy Kay and his mother both saw to that."

The denial sounded rehearsed. He knew something, and he was being careful. He'd specified he didn't know about marijuana in the shed. Was an outdoor crop hidden among the weeds and saplings?

"That's enough," Wendell said. A chair scraped. "We'll be going now."

"That's your right," Annalynn said, a touch of sadness in her voice. "I'm sure Tommy Ray wants to help us find out who attacked Straw."

"You mean who killed him," Tommy Ray said. He cleared his throat. "Straw's the same as dead. It will be, you know, official, as soon as my sister and his mother let the doctors turn off the machines."

"Then our investigation is urgent," Annalynn said. "Please answer one more question. Straw saw a speeding car turn the corner by his house Monday night around six. Did he describe that car to you, Tommy Ray?"

"He didn't say nothin' about a car." Silence. "He couldn't of seen a car at six. He called me at quarter to six to wake me up. We talked until the weather forecast came on. That's around six fifteen."

Maybe Tammy Kay had remembered the time wrong, an easy mistake.

Annalynn followed up. "He didn't mention a car throwing dust while he was cooking hotdogs?"

"Nah." Silence. "He was eating supper while we talked."

The timing fit.

"Thank you. That's helpful," Annalynn said. "If you remember anything that might lead us to the killer, call me. Please give my deepest sympathy to your sister. Oh,

Wendell, could I speak to you for a moment? Tommy Ray, if you'd like to avoid the press, my assistant will let you out through the garage."

Annalynn disconnected.

My turn. Tommy Ray had tried to help, and Tammy Kay had said he'd promised to steer Straw away from trouble. I opted for beer and sympathy rather than teeth and antipathy. "Achilles, stay with Connie." I handed her my cell and the end of the leash. "I need your help. If Annalynn calls before I come back, put it on mute and take notes."

"Okay." Her eyes widened. "What am I listening for?"

"Information on a small-time marijuana operation." Not dramatic enough. "And a murder."

I went out the back door, walked up the alley, and turned left to go past the tavern. I lingered in front of an auto parts store until I heard the jail's garage gate open. Then I sauntered back toward the tavern.

Tommy Ray stepped out of the garage driveway, looked around, and slouched toward me, his round face grim.

He passed me without a sign of recognition.

"Hi," I said. "Aren't you Tammy Kay's brother?"

He stopped and looked over his shoulder at me. "Yeah, what about it?"

"I'm terribly worried about her." I didn't need to pretend. "Grief could bring on a miscarriage, and whoever attacked Straw may go after her or even the boys."

His mouth fell open. "Who in hell are you?"

"Phoenix Smith. I'm the one who found Straw." I motioned toward the tavern. "Let me buy you a beer and explain why I'm worried."

He hung back. "You're a cop."

"No. I'm an economist and the sheriff's friend." I opened the tavern door. "Your sister needs help." I walked into the tavern and held the door open for him.

He cracked his knuckles and stared at me. "You're wearing a gun."

"I have a concealed weapon permit, like a lot of other people in Missouri." I called to the bartender, "Two Buds, please."

Tommy Ray came in. "Make mine a Coors."

Sure Connie had heard me order and would keep Achilles with her, I walked back and sat down so we had a booth between us.

Tommy Ray followed a minute later with our beers but didn't sit down. "You don't know what you're talking about, lady. My sister's not pregnant."

Had she been lying to me? Unlikely. "She was throwing up from morning sickness this morning." Why hadn't she told her brother? "Sometimes women don't tell anyone until they're far enough along they're unlikely to miscarry."

"She miscarried about a year ago." He dropped into the booth and slumped down. "Straw's been real worried about money lately. Could be because of a baby coming."

I nodded. "That explains why he took a chance on raising marijuana. He needed money for his family." I'd learned early on that giving people noble motives for bad behavior pleased them and their relatives.

"Yeah." Tommy Ray blinked away tears. "He fought his way off meth because he loved the boys so much. He swore he'd be a good father."

A selective memory. The boys had been toddlers by the time their loving father went to jail and then rehabilitation. "We both know he's not going to survive. You're going to have to take his place with the twins."

He squeezed his eyes shut. A tear ran down his right check into a heavy five o'clock shadow.

The kid cared. Good. "Tammy Kay told me you were trying to keep Straw out of trouble." I let her—and by extension my—vote of confidence sink in a moment. Then I scared him. "I'm afraid whoever killed Straw may think she or the boys can identify him and will come after her."

He half rose from his seat, panic on his face. "What'll we do?"

Excellent. We'd become allies. "For one thing, don't leave them alone." His presence in that isolated house afforded them no protection. "Ask Vlad and Nan to take them in until Sheriff Keyser catches the killer." Nan loved Willy and Wally but not Tammy Fay. "Even better, take them to stay with relatives in another state."

He sank into his seat again, relief on his face. "They'll be safe with ol' man Bulganov. He's got a fancy security system and a whole cabinet full of guns. I'll go talk to them right now."

"Good. I knew I could count on you." If saying that only made it so. "Maybe you can help find the killer, unofficially. You must have some idea who got Straw involved in this marijuana mess." This was like recruiting assets.

He slammed his fist on the table. "Jesus Christ! I bet Jericho talked him into it. I'll tear the bastard's balls off."

Jericho Kittle was Annalynn's second guest, and the sound of my cell phone ringing in the booth behind me told me he had arrived. "Could Jericho have killed Straw?"

"No way. They been best buds for five years."

Not proof positive. "Then as much as I approve of your idea of altering his anatomy, I think you should hide your suspicions. See if he'll confide in you, tell you something that might help identify Straw's killer."

He pointed at me, his pudgy finger inches from my nose. "You're the one with the narco dog."

"That's right. The sheriff and I have been best buds since we were born."

His hand fell to grip the beer bottle. "You want me to work undercover."

Oh, great. He was getting grandiose ideas. "You could call it that, but you must *never* take any chances. Whoever killed Straw is extremely dangerous."

He drank a third of his beer in one go. "Tammy Kay and the boys won't be safe until you catch him." His voice shook.

"I'm afraid not." A shiver went through me. I'd accidentally told the truth.

He stuck out his right hand. "Count me in. Just tell me what you want me to do."

Amazing how even losers will rise to the occasion. "Thank you. The big thing is to coax Jericho to confide in you. Any—uh—clue you get from him or anyone else, no matter how insignificant, call me or nine-one-one." I wrote my cell number on a napkin. "Be *very* careful. Don't tell *anyone* what you're doing."

"I'll do my damnedest." Halfway to the front door, he turned around and came back. "What did you say your name is?"

"Phoenix Smith." Asset recruited, for what little he was worth.

The second the door closed behind him, Connie pushed in beside me and held the phone so we both could listen.

"Mr. Kittle," Annalynn said, "this attitude will do you more harm than good. Surely you want to help us determine who assaulted your friend."

"I already told you I don't know anything about it." The young man spoke fast and breathlessly. "I spent the whole day painting my dad's garage. Just ask him."

He was much too eager to establish an alibi.

"I'm not accusing you of anything," Annalynn said, her voice calm. "Please answer my questions. Otherwise I'll have to bring you in for an official interrogation."

"I know my rights. You leave me alone or my father will sue you." A chair scraped. "I'm outta here." A door slammed.

"I'll intercept him," I said into the phone. I disconnected and tossed a ten on the table as Connie stood to let me out. I couldn't string this guy along the way I had Tammy Kay's brother. "Achilles, come."

I hurried to the front door with both Connie and Achilles right behind me. "You stay here, Connie. Achilles and I need to work alone."

She followed me out the door. "That guy sounded mean. I'm not letting you out of my sight."

"Okay, but stay out of *his* sight." I shaded my eyes against the sun and studied the cars parallel parked across the street. A red Nissan sports car had been parked at Harry's Hideaway the night before. If Jericho Kittle had been transporting marijuana, Achilles might be able to smell it.

"I'll be down the street," Connie said. "I can scream loud enough to be heard two blocks. We should have a signal."

She loved this. "If I put my hand on my holster, dial Annalynn's direct number." I started across the street.

Halfway across Achilles sniffed the air, veered right, and headed for the Nissan. He circled the car, sat down by the left rear tire, and looked at me for praise. That hubcap glistened. The one on the front wheel was dusty. "Good job, Achilles, good job. Good dog." I gave him a quick hug and rub.

Jericho Kittle, the tall curly-headed kid from Harry's, ran across the street from the sheriff department's parking lot. "Hey! Get that dog away from my car."

"Stay, Achilles." I leaned my back against the driver's door and held up my cell phone. "He's there because he smells drugs. Do you want me to call Sheriff Keyser to bring a search warrant, or do you want to tell me about the business you and Straw have been running?"

Kittle stopped dead. Then he advanced slowly, crouching slightly, his reedy but well-muscled body poised to attack.

Achilles growled and leapt to his feet.

"Come, Achilles." I grabbed his collar, afraid he'd go for the throat and I wouldn't be able to pull him off. I drew my gun to keep the cretin back. "The first shot turns you into a countertenor." Remember where you are. "A soprano. Then I'll shoot something larger and more vital."

He straightened and stepped back. "You can't make me tell you anything. That's illegal."

"Listen, pothead, I don't give a damn about your penny-ante drug operation. I want the monster who killed the father of two little boys. Who promised you two drug lords that big score you were celebrating last night?"

He gulped. "You think that guy hurt Straw?" Bravado gone, he stumbled to the car and leaned on the hood with both hands. "He might come after me."

I'd scared the self-centered jerk. Holstering my gun

but keeping my hand on it, I stepped back well beyond his reach and waited.

He stood there and stood there. Finally, his head still down, he said, "I don't know his name, and his number didn't come up. He called Straw on his cell about one yesterday. Said he wanted live plants to process himself." He raised his head but didn't look at me. "He offered Straw five grand for that crop in his shed." He covered his face with his hands. "God! I had no idea."

Stupid enough to be true. "He made an appointment to pick up the plants today?"

"Not right then. He called back today after Straw got out of jail."

Annalynn and Gillian came running across the street.

The young man glared at me. "You lied to me. You called her."

"No, I didn't."

Achilles trotted back to the tire and sat down, grinning at Annalynn.

She slowed to a walk. "Good job, Reserve Canine Officer Achilles. Gillian, our narco dog is telling us we have probable cause for a search."

A car drove by slowly, the older couple inside gawking.

I assessed Kittle. He had talked, he knew he was in big trouble, and he had names of customers to share. "Sheriff, I think it may be a good idea to conduct the search in the garage. And Mr. Kittle may feel safer in protective custody." Later the threat of release could be a lever to prompt him to talk. I faced him. "She's the law. I'm not. If you tell her what happened, you'll get better treatment than if you clam up and force me to tell her. But you have to talk *now*."

He shifted his eyes back and forth between Annalynn and me. "Okay. I want to find the guy who hurt Straw as much as you do. More than you do." He rubbed his eyes. "He's been my best friend since ninth grade."

I'd won this round, thanks to my long experience in dealing with liars and cheats in Eastern Europe. I hadn't expected to find so many of them, plus murderers, in lazy little Laycock.

My moment of triumph at getting Kittle to talk ended. We'd barely started our hunt for the killers.

TWENTY-ONE

I LEFT ANNALYNN and Gillian to handle the search of Jericho Kittle's car and walked back toward Connie's Bug, confident she and Achilles would follow me. Adrenaline had trumped fatigue through my encounter with the young drug dealer, but now exhaustion and heat pressed down on me so hard that I felt lightheaded. I summoned enough energy to reach the yellow Bug.

A few steps behind me, Connie beeped open the doors. "I've got to hand it to you, Phoenix. You really know how to terrify young men."

I ushered Achilles into the back and sank into my seat as Connie started the car.

"No comeback?" She poked my left arm. "My God! You look like something the cat refused to drag in. Are you okay? Should I take you to the emergency room?"

"No! I'm fine." An obvious lie. "Or I will be once I'm out of the heat. I'm not used to this steam-bath climate anymore."

Connie turned the air conditioning up full blast. "It's getting ready to storm. That will cool the air. You really should see a doctor. I've never known anyone to recover so slowly from gall bladder surgery."

"I'm much stronger than when I got here a month ago." Too exhausted to spar with Connie, I leaned back in the seat and closed my eyes.

After a couple of minutes, she said, "The way you

handled those two impressed the hell out of me. Anna-lynn wouldn't be able to function half as well as sheriff without you to back her up."

Connie had taken a big step toward smoothing over our rough spots. I responded in kind: "Thanks, and thanks for backing me up." I opened my eyes. "I give Anna-lynn a lot of credit for a surprising aptitude as sheriff."

"Do you think those two guys know something that will break the cases?"

The wooziness had passed. I tried to concentrate. "Tommy Ray knows more than he admitted about the marijuana, but I doubt either of them can tell Annalynn anything that will identify the killers."

Connie pulled into Annalynn's drive. "Do you still want to come over to play my piano this evening?"

"No, thanks. I'm too tired right now to do anything but sleep." I hesitated after I opened the car door. Connie had her own problems. Her teaching and singing engage-ments barely covered her expenses. I should put enough money in her pocket for that visit to her daughters. "I really miss my piano. I'll pay you a hundred dollars to find me a good one to buy or lease. Plus a hundred fifty to tune it once it's delivered to my house." A small start. I got out, Achilles on my heels. "And another hundred if you can do it tomorrow."

"That sounds like you're sticking around a while. I'll see what I can do." She backed out of the drive.

Time to reassess Connie. She still had the showbiz ego, but she'd sacrificed ambition to ease her mother's march toward death. What's more, she'd acted quickly and with good judgment today. My eyes fell on my ne-glected flowerbeds. The newly planted wave petunias drooped. Three still in pots were as wilted as I was. I walked across the adjoining driveways to the hose I'd left out two days ago. I turned on the faucet and soaked all the plants. A strong breeze sprang up and dark clouds approached from the west. My plants would get a long watering tonight. I hoped Spike and Gillian finished gathering evidence around the shed before the rain came.

ARTILLERY WOKE ME. I looked out my bedroom window to a dark sky. Lightning flashed and flashed again. Achilles stood up from his green blanket, put his nose on my bed, and whined. I reached out to pet him with one hand and turned on my bedside lamp with the other.

The grandfather clock chimed eight. I'd slept deeply, dreamlessly, for almost two hours. I felt revitalized.

Voices murmured downstairs. The front door opened and closed.

"Phoenix, I'm going to microwave the last of the casseroles," Annalynn called from the foot of the stairs. "Come eat with me."

The promise of food brought me to my feet. "Be there in a minute." I slipped into my sandals and went to wash the sleep out of my eyes—and to see how bad I looked. My color had returned. Unlike my first three weeks in Laycock, I no longer had to put on makeup to reassure Annalynn before I went downstairs.

Still in her uniform, she knelt by Achilles, stroking his head and telling him how wonderful he was. She rose. "We found five little bags of marijuana taped inside the hubcap. Unfortunately Jericho Kittle didn't give us any leads on who called the Bulganov boy. We checked his cell phone records, but we couldn't identify the caller."

"Why did he have a cell phone? They have no money and no service out there."

"I suspect he used it to talk drug deals with Jericho here in town or at some service point near his house."

"Did you get Jericho's customer list?"

"No." She headed for the kitchen. "We'll let him think about it overnight while Spike develops his own list. He'll use it when he questions Jericho in the morning." She took a casserole dish from atop the island, put it in the microwave, and punched in numbers. "I called the DEA's regional office. Their agents will check for information on Jericho's activities."

"Good. What did Spike and Gillian find at the shed?"

"Not much. Spike found a couple of dozen small plants among the brush and a broken branch the killer used to wipe out his footprints and tire tracks. He drove into that soybean field north of the shed and parked his vehicle—probably a pickup—in brush big enough to hide it."

"He?"

"Or she. One person. Gillian's certain only the driver exited the vehicle."

I filled Achilles' water dish and took silverware and plates from the dishwasher. "Any word on Straw?"

"Not yet. Phoenix, you couldn't have saved him no matter how fast you drove."

"I know." At least in my head. My heart hadn't accepted it yet.

"Did Tommy Ray tell you anything useful?"

"He blames Jericho for drawing Straw into dealing. Even so, I'd bet that Tommy Ray at least suspected Straw had some plants." And so did his sister. She hadn't wanted me to go out there looking for deer. I went into the dining room to set the table. "Anything else new?"

Annalynn didn't answer.

A bad sign. "What's wrong?"

She took glasses from the cupboard. "I'll tell you while we're eating."

She had mastered a public face in childhood. I studied her posture. She showed no tension, but obviously something had gone awry. "Who were you talking to a few minutes ago?"

"Give me five minutes, Phoenix. I need time to work some things out." She opened the microwave, checked the casserole, and closed the door again. "Before I forget, Strosmeyer's Hardware called. A crew is coming at eight tomorrow to install your replacement windows. I told them you would be there."

"Thanks." That meant no deer hunting tomorrow. A little respite. I reached down to stroke Achilles, who was pressed against me, shivering slightly. I wondered if the thunder reminded him of gunfire. I freshened his water bowl and gave him an extra treat.

Thunder rumbled in a baritone crescendo with lightning providing dramatic punctuation. A sharp crack from nature's percussion section made me jump, Achilles howl, and the lights go out. I stood still, hoping the lights would come back on.

"That hit a tree close by," Annalynn said. She opened a drawer and, a moment later, turned on a flashlight. "I'm afraid we'll have a candlelight dinner." She found two candles, placed them in her antique silver French holders, and lit them.

I went to the big window looking out onto the front porch and lawn.

"Phoenix! Please get away from the window. You know better than that."

My mother's words and intonation again. I replied as I had to her, "I want to see what's happening."

Annalynn laughed. "You'll never grow out of that. Come hold the flashlight, please, so I can bring in the casserole."

And get me away from the window. Where I couldn't see a thing except darkness. I went into the kitchen to hold the flashlight. "Should we call about the power failure?"

"No need. Several neighbors have the power company on speed dial."

We settled down to eat by the flickering light. After I'd eaten enough to satisfy my limited appetite, I broke the silence. "Your time is up. What's the matter?"

"A little complication," Annalynn said. "Our twenty-something prosecuting attorney came by with a list of ways that I'm 'jeopardizing justice.'"

"Such as?"

"Making you a reserve officer when you have no police training. 'Certain citizens' have complained about you drawing your gun to force Jericho Kittle to tell you that he had pot. The PA says that could result in evidence being thrown out of court."

Bloody hell! I'd really stepped in it this time. "I'm sorry, Annalynn."

"Good heavens, Phoenix, if I'd thought you'd done anything wrong, I would have said so. We're after a murderer, not petty drug sales. You did what you had to do."

She'd come a long way. Or a lack of sleep was affecting her attitude. Mine not to question why. I moved on. "What about Achilles' status as a reserve canine officer?"

"She didn't mention that." She smiled. "Until someone tells me otherwise, I'm assuming he had the state-required training."

Annalynn had definitely moved to my broader view.

"At least he learned to find narcotics. What else was on the PA's list?"

"She reminded me that I'm not a qualified police officer. She says I shouldn't leave the office." Annalynn spoke as though telling something a small child had said.

"And the solution is?"

"She's going to request the major crime squad take over both investigations. This time—the third?—Sam Gist may agree."

"The M-squad won't take over immediately. What do we do tomorrow as the county panics?"

The lights came on and went out again.

Annalynn picked up the flashlight and our empty plates and stood up. "What we've been doing. If I need to go into the field, I'll go. Every citizen has the right to report a crime and help *qualified* police officers find evidence."

"You're walking a thin line." One that could harm her chances for political office. "Be careful."

Annalynn peered at me through the dim light. "I can't believe you, of all people, are telling me to toe the line. I took an oath to protect and serve this county as sheriff for thirteen weeks, and no one is going to stop me from doing just that."

The lights came on.

TWENTY-TWO

I ADMIRED ANNALYNN'S determination to see through the investigation, but she had to consider what she risked. "I'll fix some tea while you change," I said. "We need to talk."

"Oh, Lord. What now? Did the CIA give you permission to go back to Vienna?" The faint lines in her forehead deepened.

I shook my head. "No, no. This is about you, not me." The New York offer would have to remain secret a little longer. "Black tea or herbal?"

"You're paying me back for making you wait, aren't you?" She handed me our dirty plates. "Very well. English Breakfast with lemon."

I considered how to bring up Vernon's proposition as I brewed tea in the Augarten teapot I'd given Annalynn and Boom for their twentieth wedding anniversary. I carried it and matching cups into the ladies' parlor on a silver tray that had been one of her mother's favorite pieces.

Achilles dragged his green blanket into the room. I took it from him, folded it into quarters, and placed it by my chair. He trotted out of the room and returned a moment later with his newest bone chew.

Annalynn came in wearing blue capri pants and a matching short-sleeved blouse that definitely hadn't come from a discount department store. She took her usual place on the loveseat. "The silver tray and the Augarten. This must be serious."

I reached for the teapot. "Shall I be mother?"

"Pardon?"

"That's something my British friends say. Shall I pour the tea?"

Annalynn smiled. "Mother would have loved to hear that in her parlor."

I laughed. "And Mom would have made me clean the bathroom for being pretentious." I poured the tea. "I talked to Vernon Kann this morning. He thinks you should run for the rest of Boom's term as sheriff and use that as a springboard to run for the House of Representatives next year." I watched her. "The incumbent is retiring."

Annalynn turned away, hiding her reaction. Finally, eyes bleak, she faced me. "Two months ago I would have been jubilant. Now I couldn't care less."

Although I knew she lost the battle with grief every night, I hadn't expected such despair. "Promise me you'll think about it. You've lost so much, but you're strong enough to endure. You mustn't ignore an opportunity to realize your dream."

She reacted no more than if I'd been reciting a recipe. I tried again. "Your present isn't your future. Think of—"

"Stop it. Please." She pressed her temples with both hands. "I can barely deal with the present. I can't contemplate anything past tomorrow morning. Change the subject."

What was safe? "The replacement windows for the house are coming just in time. And I'm getting a piano tomorrow."

She wriggled her shoulders as if sliding from under a

burden and smiled. "So you can play Mozart and figure out who done it?"

"And Scott Joplin. And Chopin. And Gershwin. And Beethoven. And Liszt—badly. Maybe a little Bach, in an emergency."

Distant thunder announced the storm's passing. Achilles dropped his chew toy, put his nose on my knee, and waited expectantly for me to stroke him.

Annalynn sighed. "Achilles and I both depend on you." She put down her cup. "Let's get to work. Any advice on questioning Straw Bulganov's wife about the marijuana?"

I pictured the young woman retching in her wretched house. "Don't. She's early in a pregnancy, and she miscarried once. Any threat of legal action that would take away her boys could make a horrible situation even worse."

"You find out a lot about people, don't you?" Annalynn sat back. "We have to talk to her. She may know something about her husband's big score that will lead us to his killer, and she must have known what was in that shed."

If Annalynn could prove that, she'd have to arrest the young woman, an emotional disaster for both. "Tammy Kay may not know anything about the marijuana. Remember he hadn't been home since he received the offer to sell his crop." Annalynn needed a credible reason not to threaten the young widow's freedom. I began with the truth and strayed: "Her brother and Straw's brother both told me she tried hard to keep Straw off drugs. Besides, she's afraid of spiders, and the shed has several webs. I doubt that she or the boys went out there at all."

Annalynn raised a questioning eyebrow. I kept my

mouth shut, neither acknowledging nor denying her un-spoken skepticism. I'd have to tip off Tammy Kay that spiders scared her.

"You obviously connected with her and the boys. Okay. I'll hold off, but you talk to her tomorrow and find out what she knows—all of it—or we'll have to question her officially."

I'd need Tommy Ray's help in evading Nan. "Of course. Meanwhile, check out Floyd Vanderhofen. He's hiding something on his farm. It could be marijuana."

Annalynn inhaled sharply and leaned forward. "Maybe Jesse Tornell planted some, too. Maybe that's what both these murders are about."

"The Tornells don't seem the type." Don't be naïve. "Desperation makes people act against type. They've been hanging onto the farm by their fingernails. Jericho Kittle could be a bigger buyer and supplier than I gave him credit for." I thought of the $1,500 in cash in the Tor-nells' flimsy safe. The money had looked like a payoff.

"Drug deals gone bad. That's Spike's theory," Anna-lynn said. "I hope he's right."

The phone gave two quick short rings. Annalynn rose and went around the screen to her desk to answer it. She listened a couple of minutes. "I know the name. He's represented several drug dealers in Boone County, so he knows what he's doing. Suspend the questioning of Kittle for tonight. We have enough evidence to compel the PA to file charges for possession. Before we talk to Kittle again, I want witnesses to verify his movements minute by minute since noon Monday." Pause. "Exactly. We need enough to hold him or to eliminate him as a sus-pect for both the murders." Pause. "No, we'll leave tracking the drug connections to the DEA. I'll ask them to do helicopter surveillance for marijuana all over that area." Pause. "The only help I can give you is Gillian. She's inexperienced, but she knows the cases." Pause. "Good. I appreciate your working the extra hours. Call me back when you've worked out your investigation plan—no matter how late it is. Bye."

The phone rang again the second she hung up. Her conversation consisted of little more than hello and goodbye.

She came back around the screen. "Dorothy Tornell called to let us know the funeral is Saturday at two at the Baptist church near their farm."

A funeral would reopen the gash in Annalynn's heart. "You don't have to go."

She went behind the screen. "I'm afraid I do." Her voice sounded choked.

To give her time to compose herself, I stood up and said, "I promised to call someone about the funeral. I'll do that while you call about the helicopter."

I went to the dining room and dialed Garth Raymo on my cell phone. He answered on the third ring.

"Garth, this is Phoenix Smith." I could hear the music and voices of a bar in the background. I upped my volume. "You asked me to let you know about Jesse Tornell's funeral. It's Saturday at two at a church near Vlad and Nan Bulganovs' farm."

"Thanks for letting me know. Could you hold on a moment?"

In a few seconds the background noise became faint.

"Sorry, Phoenix. I had to find a quieter place to talk. I heard the Bulganov boy overdosed. How's he doing?"

"He's in critical condition."

"Sorry to hear that. He's not much of a worker, but he seems like a nice enough young man."

An unexpected source of information. "You know him?"

"Barely. I hired him and a pal of his—Jerry something—to help me renovate my nightmare house last winter. They weren't up to the job, so I fired them. The only useful thing I got out of Straw was the suggestion to talk to his mother—I remember he said his mother, not his father—about improving milk production."

Connie had said something about Jericho coming by her house looking for work, but Raymo lived at least fifty miles away. "How did you happen to hire those two?"

"I saw an ad at a grocery store in Unionville, or maybe it was at a service station in Milan. I've seen the ads both places. My house—it's a beautiful but rundown Victorian—needs so much work, I can't do it all myself, and I can't afford contractors. Fortunately I complained about that to the Lapinskis and they suggested Jesse. He was a first-class carpenter with a tremendous work ethic. He came up and worked with me several times. We were about the same age, and his death hit me pretty hard."

Tornell definitely didn't sound like a marijuana grower. We needed to know more about him. "I never met him. How would you describe him?"

"Hmm. Well, a really serious guy. No interest in cars or sports or microbrews. He didn't know anything about movies or books or politics. The only thing we talked about was farming. He was obsessed with making extra money to meet his bills. Poor Dorothy will probably lose the place. It's too small to be economically viable."

"I'm afraid you're right." I remembered the books on the makeshift shelves in the living room and the music

Dorothy had played. Her interests were obviously broader than her husband's, but losing the farm would be a terrible blow to her. As hard as losing the castle would be for Annalynn? I could help Annalynn, but what could I do for Dorothy?

Raymo broke into my thoughts. "Will I see you at the funeral Saturday?"

"Yes, I'll go for Dorothy's sake."

"I look forward to seeing you there then."

Was he coming on to me? Did I care? Not much, but it never hurt to explore possibilities with a reasonably attractive man. "See you there."

I went back to the parlor to find Annalynn writing notes on a legal pad. "Good news, Annalynn. The DEA may be able to pinpoint Jericho Kittle's territory by where he's posted ads for handyman work, starting with grocery stores in Unionville and a gas station in Milan. Garth Raymo—he's Dorothy's parents' neighbor up in Putnam County—saw the ads, hired Jericho and Straw, and fired them for incompetence. The ads' real purpose may be to notify Jericho's clients he has merchandise."

She hesitated. "Wouldn't that bring in a lot of unwanted calls?"

"If it does, you give an outrageous price and get rid of them."

"Only a spy would think of that. I'll pass the tip on to the DEA." She made a note on her pad. "I have news, too. The Highway Patrol will fly over our crime scenes tomorrow while they're searching for leads on the killing of that trooper on Highway 36."

"Another rare murder in a rural area." I dropped into my chair. "Any likely connection besides proximity? Can we really discount the possibility of a serial killer?"

Annalynn rubbed her left temple. "We can't discount anything at this stage, but different MOs make a serial killer unlikely. We have a garroting on a highway, a stabbing in a field, and a drug overdose in a shed."

"And the garroting wasn't premeditated, as both Jesse and Straw's deaths were. Or as geographically close. My read: The same person or people committed both those murders, killing Straw because he saw the getaway car."

"I agree." She underlined something on her pad. "That indicates Straw knew the killer."

"We can count on that. A neighbor? A business associate? Maybe Straw and Jesse were raising marijuana for Jericho. Raymo said Jesse was desperate for money for the farm." Something I already knew from the financial records in his safe. "Maybe Jericho promised Jesse a bundle if he raised marijuana 'just this once.' Few people needing money can resist such offers."

Annalynn shook her head slowly. "You've lost your faith in innate goodness. I won't assume Jesse Tornell yielded to temptation. I need proof." She tapped her pencil on the pad. "I agree that the two Vandiver County murders seem linked, but I think we should remain open to two other lines of investigation."

"Of course," For the moment. "What are they?"

"One: The three murders are completely unrelated. The patrol officer died because he ran across the rustlers. Straw Bulganov died because he botched a drug deal. Jesse Tornell died because—I have no idea."

Neither did I. "The motive for Tornell's death could be key. What's your other option?"

Annalynn took a deep breath. "The domino effect. The first killing prompted the second, the second killing prompted the third."

I didn't buy it. "You think rustling a few calves led to three deaths?"

"Not necessarily rustling. The Highway Patrol *thinks* the trooper stopped a pickup carrying stolen cattle. What if it carried something else—drugs, stolen electronics, even contraband cigarettes? Missouri has one of the lowest cigarette taxes in the country."

I groaned. "Damn it! We just don't know enough yet."

"I don't have the resources to investigate one of these scenarios, let alone all of them. I have to start with the most likely. Which would you choose?"

I smiled. "I don't have to. You've already chosen by following the only solid lead you have, the marijuana trail. With luck, we'll know tomorrow whether it's a dead end."

My cell phone rang. Caller ID indicated the hospital. Puzzled, I answered it.

"Are you alone?" The male voice spoke barely above a whisper.

Tommy Ray. "No, but I can go upstairs and look the number up."

Annalynn cocked her head. She knew I never had to look up a number.

"Tammy Kay wants to talk to you. Just you. No one else. Don't tell your buddy."

TWENTY-THREE

ANNALYNN SCRIBBLED ON her pad and held it up. It said, "Who?"

I shook my head as I said into my phone, "Of course. I appreciate your call."

Annalynn's phone rang behind me, and she leapt up to answer it.

Tommy Ray said, "Hy-Vee parking lot in ten minutes. *Alone.*" He hung up.

"Thanks," Annalynn said. "Let all the staff know immediately." She hung up and said, "It's officially a homicide now. William Wallace Bulganov died ten minutes ago. Or had you already heard?"

"No. Nothing to worry about. I have to run that errand for you." It would puzzle her a little while, but she'd remember she'd asked me to talk to Tammy Kay. "I'll be back in an hour or so." Reinvigorated by anticipation of action, I rushed upstairs to strap on my gun under my black T-shirt.

When I got downstairs, Achilles and Annalynn stood by the front door.

She handed me his leash and an umbrella. "Punch in nine-one-one so you can call with one press of the button. Don't take any chances. I'll call you in half an hour."

"Okay." I checked my watch: nine thirty. Better use a code. "If I say not to wait up for me, I need help." She held her keys in her hand. "Where are you going?"

"To the office. I can't have my staff working overtime while I sit at home. I may not be able to go out to investigate, but I can certainly direct those who do."

"*Brava!*" I opened the door. The rain had dropped to a drizzle. Achilles and I trotted to my car without either of us damaging our hair.

I drove into the grocery store's block-square parking lot seven minutes later and, not knowing what car Tammy Kay would be in, looked for an isolated one. None. A dozen cars were parked in the rows nearest the doors. Not liking the surveillance cameras or the corners darkened by trees, I pulled in between two SUVs, turned off the motor, and rolled down the window to let in the muggy air. If she was here, she would come to me. Five minutes later I concluded that they—surely someone would be with her—either hadn't arrived from the hospital yet or were waiting to make sure I was alone.

Achilles was restless, and so was I. "Let's take a walk, boy." I opened the umbrella to hide my face and sauntered to the row of Bradford pears separating the parking lot from the street. I noted that cameras didn't cover the area there.

Achilles trotted from tree to tree, obscured by their shadows.

A car left, and a scooter pulled in. Thinking of the two-wheeled escape vehicle at Star Corner, I gripped the Glock. The heavyset helmeted rider rode slowly down the row of cars, paused a moment at my Toyota, and turned left and then right to go behind the Hy-Vee. Had to be Tommy Ray. Connie had said he worked here.

A car turned into the lot, the car Shelley Bulganov had driven to the Tornells' farm Monday night. I twirled the umbrella, and the driver turned toward me. He parked in the center of the camera's blind spot. Bob Bulganov got out. He opened his trunk and held up a new bone toy. "I'll watch your dog for you."

Achilles was at my side but not pressed against me. "Let me give it to him first."

He handed it to me. I removed it from the package and tossed it under a tree. When Achilles brought it back, I handed it to Bob.

He leaned down to murmur in my ear. "If Nan thinks Tammy Kay had anything to do with that stuff in the shed, she'll sue for custody of the twins."

I nodded. "Tammy Kay's too afraid of spiders to ever go near that shed."

"Bless you," he said. "I told Dad she's afraid of snakes."

I liked this guy. "I sympathize with her, but she needs to tell me the truth."

He opened the back door. "She's here to help you, Tammy Kay. Answer all her questions." He turned to me. "Make it quick, please."

I climbed into the car.

Tammy Kay was curled into a ball in the far corner, her face a white blur in the dim light.

My instinct was to reach out to offer comfort, but I guessed any physical expression of sympathy would unloose hysteria. "I'm so sorry, but the best way I can help you now is to find out who—did this awful thing."

She nodded but said nothing.

"Can you tell me something that will help us identify him?"

She shook her head no and took a series of short, deep breaths. "Please, please tell the sheriff I didn't do nothing wrong. Tell her—please, please tell her I'm a good mother. Please don't let anyone take my boys away."

"Annalynn Keyser is a compassionate woman, and a mother. She doesn't want to take your children away." I hated to put the squeeze on someone so vulnerable, but I saw no other way to help her. "The sheriff has to obey the law. If you help us find out who took Straw away from his family, it will be easier for her to help you."

She moaned.

Get answers now before she collapsed. "Do you have any idea who attacked your husband?"

She shook her head no.

"Do you think Jericho did it?"

Nothing for a long moment. Then she shook her head no again.

"You hesitated. Are you sure?"

"Yes. Jericho wouldn't hurt Straw," she choked out.

No one wanted to believe an old friend would betray them. "Did you know Jericho and Straw were selling marijuana?"

"No!" She extended her hands, pleading to be believed. "I knew Jericho used. He smoked it in front of the boys once, and I threw him out."

I believed her, partly because of what Bob had said about her. I also sensed she wouldn't volunteer information. I would have to ask the right questions. "Did you— did you *suspect* Straw was raising marijuana for Jericho?" No way she could admit she knew.

She curled tighter than a nine-month fetus. "I didn't know he had all those plants in the shed." Her voice, muffled by her knees, was barely audible.

A carefully phrased, rehearsed answer. She knew he'd planted pot somewhere or didn't know how much was in that shed. Maybe she felt guilty that she hadn't stopped it. I would push her no farther on that—at least for now.

What I guessed, I guessed. What I knew, I had to tell Annalynn. Charging the young mother as an accessory would be a lose-lose situation. "Do you suspect any of your neighbors of growing marijuana?"

She uncurled enough to look at me. "Who?"

"Anyone."

"Nah. I remember Jericho saying that most people around here don't even recognize marijuana. He told Straw to give Mother Nan a house plant."

A ring of truth in that. I was getting nowhere. "Straw's death may have nothing to do with drugs. We talked about his seeing a car skid around the corner Monday evening. Please try to remember anything he, or the boys, said about that."

She buried her face again. "I been thinkin' about it, but I can't remember nothing except his being mad about the dust. I'm pretty sure he didn't see the driver. The boys said it was a red truck, but I think that's because they like Grampa's red pickup."

They'd told me a brown car and pointed to my green slacks. The four-year-olds were unreliable witnesses.

Bob tossed the bone way down the line of trees. As Achilles ran to find it, Tommy Ray stepped out of the shadows to hand a plastic grocery bag and some change to Bob.

I let the silence go on for a couple of minutes. She said nothing. I tried another tack: "Was Straw doing handyman work with Jericho?"

"Straw couldn't work a screwdriver, but he helped Jericho paint houses."

That verified my suspicions that Kittle's bulletin-board ads weren't meant to get work. "Tommy Ray said Straw got a big paint job. Did Straw tell you about that?"

"No." She gasped for air. "I guess he didn't have a chance." Her voice broke and she sobbed, little animal noises coming from her throat. She curled up again.

I reached over and patted her hand. "I'm so sorry." She needed to grieve, not answer questions, but to catch the killer, we needed information. "If you think of anything that may help identify who hurt Straw, call me or Sheriff Keyser." I had to caution her. "You may not be in any danger, but play it safe. Don't stay in your house or anywhere else alone. Keep the boys inside, and go out only with people you trust."

She yelped and uncoiled. "Someone might hurt the boys?"

Damn! I'd terrified her. So use that fear to find out anything she'd withheld. "Until the killer's caught, and he will be, you need to be careful." I waited a moment for her to spill something, but she buried her face instead. "Where are Willy and Wally?"

"With Straw's parents. We're staying with them tonight, so we stopped to get the boys' favorite cereal and cookies." She threw open the car door. "Bob, we gotta go. I gotta get to my babies."

"Sure." He tossed the toy toward Achilles.

I rushed to intercept Bob. "I'm sorry to have scared her, but with a killer loose, it's a good idea to keep her and the boys out of sight or in crowds. If they were my family, I'd send them to relatives out of state."

"Tommy Ray is working on it." He leaned close. "You got any leads?"

"Nothing solid. Tammy Kay may remember something she saw or heard later. Or someone in your family may. Call me or the sheriff about anything—*anything*."

"We will." He jumped into the car and peeled away.

Annalynn called me a moment later. "Anything new, Phoenix?"

"No. Sorry. I'm fairly certain Tammy Kay doesn't know anything about the murders or the marijuana sales. Since I'm out, I'm going to pick up some groceries. Anything you want?"

"No. I won't be home for a couple of hours. See you at breakfast."

I left Achilles in my car and went in to locate Tommy Ray. I picked up some bananas and a box of shredded wheat before I found him stocking toilet paper. I paused in front of the paper towels. He didn't look up. Good for him. I dropped a two-roll pack in my cart and wheeled it around him and toward checkout. Like any asset, he was not to be trusted. He and Tammy Kay—and Bob—had set out to play me, to persuade me to call off the sheriff. An understandable but surprisingly shrewd move for three shocked, grieving people, particularly when two of them lived in the neighborhood of dumb.

Returning to my car, now in plain view of a camera, I put the groceries in the back seat and drove out of the lot. No one followed as I turned right and drove two blocks toward Annalynn's. I turned right and right again to reach Hy-Vee's back entrance. Parking on the street, I got out and let Achilles out.

"Stay with me, boy," I murmured as I opened the umbrella and walked into the employee parking area as though headed for the entrance. I'd almost reached the building when I spotted Tommy Ray's scooter between two pickups.

I'd seen no one, but a camera had seen a woman and her dog. "Okay, Achilles, do your stuff." What on earth was the command? "Search, boy. Find drugs. Please."

Nose in the air, he trotted down the line of vehicles away from the scooter.

Relieved that Tommy Ray carried no drugs, I dropped my umbrella as an excuse to inspect the scooter's tire tread. I shone my keychain flashlight on it and studied the pattern. Not the same as the fragment at Star Corner.

Achilles licked my cheek.

"You got me." I stood up and wiped my face. "Let's go home to bed before something else happens."

TWENTY-FOUR

ACHILLES AND I were almost home when Annalynn called and asked me to take him to Jericho Kittle's house. She had to give me directions because the street hadn't existed when I'd left Laycock in the 1970s.

A sheriff's car, a city police car, and an SUV sat in the driveway of a one-story house with beige vinyl siding. Lights shone from every room and the front stoop. Not wanting to advertise my presence to the neighbors, I drove around the corner to park in front of a dark house. The lawn's ankle-high grass was wet, so I kept Achilles beside me on the street until we reached the long cement walkway to the door. The flowerbeds in front of the house hosted nothing but four or five kinds of weeds, none of which looked like anything to roll into a cigarette and smoke. I pushed the doorbell but heard nothing, so I knocked.

Achilles raised his nose, and his shoulder muscles tensed under my hand.

The twenty-something black officer who had picked up the three stooges at Harry's Hideaway opened the door and ushered us in. He wore plastic gloves. "Thanks for bringing the dog, ma'am. He should save us time. I'm Michael Moniteau."

"I remember you from the arrest at Harry's." It struck me that he had the same last name and lean and hungry look as the teenage radio reporter. "Is M. L. your brother?"

Michael grimaced. "Yeah. Martin's always hounding me for news tips, but I don't tell him anything."

"Good." Down to business. "Find, please, Achilles," I said firmly, a needless command as he'd headed straight for a two-foot-high Christmas cactus on a small round table with a long plastic cloth draped over it.

"I'll be dawged," the officer said. "I already looked there."

Achilles sat waiting for praise.

"Good boy," I said, stepping over a pile of car magazines and past a sofa turned on its back. I pulled up the table's plastic cover.

Achilles barked and hit it with his paw, knocking it out of my hand.

"Don't touch anything, please, Dr. Smith."

"Sorry. Please call me Phoenix."

Achilles stared at the pot.

I stroked his head. "Good boy." I stepped back. "The pot is in the pot."

An unfamiliar voice in another room said, "Turn him loose in the garage."

A slender man in a faded blue T-shirt and threadbare jeans swiveled in a desk chair to hide his face—a sign that he was working undercover, probably for DEA—as Achilles and I followed the Laycock officer through a small dining room containing a littered computer desk.

Spike, standing before open cabinet doors in the kitchen, handed me a pair of plastic gloves. "Will the dog work for anyone besides you?"

"Maybe for Annalynn. Definitely not for a stranger."

Achilles pressed against me.

I stroked his head. "He's a little nervous tonight."

Spike grinned. "Probably that wild ride you gave him

this afternoon. Bob Bulganov told me you scared him—uh—silly."

"Out here, ma'am," Michael Moniteau said, holding a door open for me.

Jericho's sports car must have fit in the garage with just enough room to open the driver's door. Gardening tools, a gas push mower, and bags of potting soil and fertilizer took up much of one side. Paint cans and brushes and ladders of different heights and types took up most of the other side.

Achilles sniffed in the direction of the fertilizer but remained glued to me.

"Nothing here," I said. "I doubt there are drugs anywhere else in the house."

Michael nodded. "Then Jericho processed it somewhere else. Let's take a look out back. Maybe he's got a potting shed." He smiled at his pun and stepped back into the now empty kitchen. "How much did you find in the pot, Riley?"

"Only about ten grams."

Michael hit a switch to turn on the porch light as we went out the back door.

Achilles barked and raced into darkness.

Michael turned on his flashlight and ran after him yelling, "Pay day!"

I squished through the wet grass after them at a much more sedate pace, waiting for my eyes to adjust. Light rain was falling again.

Spike and Riley ran past me.

No need for me to get soaked, especially with my immune system still weak. I cut across the yard to my car to get the umbrella. As I opened the passenger door, a big, black Buick screeched around the corner and pulled over in front of my car. Two middle-aged men in white long-sleeved shirts jumped out.

Achilles barked excitedly deep in the yard, and one of the officers whooped.

"Oh, hell," one of the newcomers said. He ran into Jericho Kittle's backyard with the other man close behind.

A few seconds later the newcomers were yelling at the cops.

Achilles barked again, and this time I heard alarm.

"Achilles!" I grabbed the umbrella and a flashlight and ran into the yard.

Achilles growled at someone and sped toward me.

I stopped and waited. He whirled around in front of me and snarled at the men.

I knelt beside him and put my arms around his trembling body. "It's okay. I'm here. You're safe." I'd dropped the umbrella, but that didn't matter because the wet grass had soaked my slacks. I shone my flashlight toward the back of the deep but narrow yard where four men stood in hostile poses. Riley had slipped out of sight.

"Here's the search warrant, Mr. Kittle," Spike said, waving a paper. "I know you own the place, but Jericho is the one who lives here. We've found what we were searching for—processed marijuana in the house and seedlings behind the pole beans." He turned around and shone a light on plants growing between a lattice and the high board fence that bordered the back of the yard. "We're collecting evidence, so I'll have to ask you to leave."

"I'll escort you to your car, Mr. Kittle," Michael said, his voice deferential but firm. "You need to go, too, counselor."

"Come, Achilles." I wanted to get him out of there and

avoid confrontation. I picked up the umbrella and strode toward my car with my free hand on his collar.

He trotted alongside me until we reached the edge of the yard. Then he sprinted to the Buick and sat down by the left rear tire, the same place he'd found drugs in Jericho's car. And put there by the same hands, I was betting.

"Good boy. Good boy." I raised my voice. "Officers, we have another hit."

Michael reached me first. "Are you sure?" He kept his voice low. "Charles Kittle is president of the Chamber of Commerce and a deacon at the First Baptist Church. We can't afford to be wrong."

Annalynn would catch hell if we were, but not investigating would cause even more trouble. "Achilles seems sure," I whispered, and added, "Play it safe. Have the DEA agent handle it." Kittle couldn't pressure the Feds.

Michael nodded.

Kittle, breathing hard, lumbered up. "Get away from my car. You have no search warrant for that."

"We don't need it," Riley said from the darkness. "When a K-9 signals drugs, we have probable cause." He'd pulled his baseball cap so low over his face, little more than his chin showed. "Officer Moniteau, get another evidence kit."

Rain pelted us. In spite of the warm temperature, I shivered with cold. "If you don't need us, we'll be on our way."

"Sure," Riley said. "Thanks." He opened my car door for me.

Achilles leapt in and refused to spare my car upholstery by getting on the floor. Fair enough. I was as wet as he was. "This car is getting to be a mess," I told him as I backed to the corner and turned toward home. "I'm going to have to get one to drive whenever I have a human passenger." Not a bad idea. Something fast and fun.

During the drive to Annalynn's house I called to give her a heads up on Achilles' findings and the senior Kittle's anger. She brushed that concern aside.

As I unlocked the front door, Achilles gave a giant shake to get rid of the rain embedded in his coat. Thankful he had sprinkled the porch rather than Annalynn's antiques, I went straight to the kitchen for paper towels and rubbed him down. I praised him and gave him a biscuit and fresh water before going upstairs to shed my wet clothes.

I stood under a hot shower for several minutes before the shivering stopped. The sound of the special sheriff's department ring pulled me out of the shower. I wrapped myself in a towel and went to answer the phone.

"We got one more place to check tonight," Spike said. "I'll pick you up in fifteen minutes." He hung up.

TWENTY-FIVE

For a moment I rebelled at Spike's demand that I—no, not I but Deputy Dog's sidekick—go out again. The grandfather clock edged toward ten thirty. The day already had been unbelievably long. Spike was angry because I'd not told him about the shots at Star Corner, but he wouldn't call except on Annalynn's orders. I'd have to tough it out.

Not bothering to conceal my fatigue with makeup, I ran a brush through my hair and put on dry clothes, shoes, and my holster. Achilles hadn't appeared, so I went to find him. He slept by his water bowl, but he sprang to his feet as a car pulled into the drive.

"Take it easy. It's just Spike, and he can wait a minute." Just Spike. Why had he—not Annalynn—called me? Why didn't he ask me to meet him? Getting in a car with someone you don't know is risky. I gave Achilles a biscuit, put on the teakettle, and dialed Annalynn's direct number.

She answered on the fourth ring, and other voices almost drowned out hers.

"Spike called me about another drug check. Did you clear it?"

"Yes. I'd rather Achilles sniff around while Tammy Kay isn't home. Do you have reservations?"

"No. I just wanted to make sure Spike wasn't acting on his own." I'd been overly suspicious, a holdover from my undercover days. "See you in the morning."

The doorbell rang, and Achilles trotted over. He appeared unconcerned.

I checked to make sure it was Spike before I opened the door. "Come in. I'm fixing a cup of tea to take along. Do you want something to drink? Or to eat?"

He stepped in and glanced at the elegant dining room. The confident, aggressive officer turned into a shy boy. "No thanks, ma'am. I got a cup of coffee in the car." His stomach rumbled, and he blushed. "Well, maybe an apple. It's quite a ways out there."

I realized he probably had worked straight through since lunch. He was operating on adrenaline, and youth. "Come make yourself a sandwich while I find a travel cup." Not waiting for a reply, I went to the refrigerator and pulled out deli ham, lettuce, and sliced muenster cheese. I pointed to the breadbox on the kitchen counter. "Help yourself. Feel free to pile it on."

"Thanks," Spike said. "I didn't take time to eat. You gotta keep moving on a case like this, try to get there before people have time to hide the drugs."

Achilles whined. He loved ham. I distracted him with a chicken-based treat. "You didn't search Straw's house this afternoon?"

"No. It wasn't part of the crime scene, and we didn't have a warrant. We do now." His tone was defensive. He waited for my reaction and, getting none, took out three slices of bread and continued: "I figure your dog will save us a couple hours of hunting for illegal substances, and a lot of complaints about tearing up a victim's house."

"Right, no point in upsetting the family needlessly." Doubtless Annalynn, not Spike, had been the one to think of that. I poured tea into a St. Louis Cardinals travel mug. "What did you find in Charles Kittle's hubcap?"

"Ten packets ready for buyers." He layered ham and cheese and lettuce into a three-inch-high sandwich. "Mr. Chamber of Commerce was really steamed, but he didn't rat his boy out. Thing is, we got Jericho's calendar. He was taking his car in for service tomorrow morning, but he had an appointment in Chillicothe at nine." He grinned, more at ease on this topic. "I figure he planned to make his deliveries in his daddy's Buick instead of that flashy red sports car."

"Nice deduction." My voice conveyed admiration I didn't feel. If I had to go out in the rain with this young man, I better build rapport by showing respect. I squeezed some lemon in my tea and stirred in twice the usual amount of sugar. I needed the boost.

He put the fixings back in the refrigerator—something a lot of men forget—and bit into his sandwich.

"I'll grab a rain jacket from the hall closet," I said. "Achilles, get your leash."

I didn't need the jacket. The rain had stopped and the sky was clearing. Spike shoved the last of his sandwich in his mouth as we reached the car. I had to push Achilles into the back seat, where he sneezed repeatedly.

"Sorry, boy," I said.

He barked his "I found it" bark.

"He smells drugs," I told Spike.

"He's good. I carried those packets we took out of the hubcap tonight in an evidence bag inside a plastic bag."

"Good boy, Achilles." I reached back to stroke his head.

Spike kept the speed down through Laycock's empty streets and accelerated when we hit the county road. "I've always heard how K-9s bond with their officers," he said, tension in his voice contrasting with the bland statement.

"I figure you were pretty upset when somebody tried to shoot your dog yesterday."

Yesterday? It seemed days ago. A light dawned. Spike was working up to asking me why I hadn't told him about the rifleman. "Upset—that's putting it mildly. I'm used to analyzing figures, not dodging bullets. I couldn't quite believe it had really happened."

"You should have told me," he said, his tone both accusing and hurt.

Time to repair relations. Annalynn had to count on him. "Yes, Annalynn made that clear. I'm sorry." I couldn't say I didn't trust him. What was believable? "You don't know me, so I wasn't sure you'd believe such an unlikely story. Besides, Vernon needed to go to the hospital and I needed to stay to show Gillian where to gather evidence."

After a moment, he said, "You violated basic police procedures, ma'am."

I couldn't argue with that one, but I couldn't let it hang either. "I acted as a confused civilian in a shocking situation, not a trained police officer."

"You reacted like an officer," he shot back. "You took Mr. Kann's rifle and fired back."

No dolt this one. "Pure instinct."

"Most women—most *citizens*—would have hunkered down screaming for help." He paused. "I've heard talk that you used to be an FBI agent."

"That's ridiculous," I snapped. Nothing irritates a CIA operative like being confused with some self-righteous FBI agent. I recycled an old lie. "My company gave all its American and British staff training in basic self-defense, including target shooting, after the attacks on the World Trade Center and the Pentagon."

Achilles stuck his head over the seat. I reached up to scratch behind his ears. "Get down, boy. Take a nap."

I wanted to take one myself, but I needed to salvage the fragment of rapport Spike and I had experienced in the kitchen. "That shooting at Star Corner and these two murders make no sense to me. Do you think they're related?"

"Probably. The killings for sure. A couple miles and a couple of days apart—they got to be. We'll keep gathering evidence until we can tie them together. Then we'll know who did it and why."

This time, I judged, he was giving his own conclusions. "You sound pretty confident you'll solve the murders. Any theories?"

He slid around a corner. "In police work you got to be really careful not to jump to conclusions before you get the facts." After a few seconds, he added, "Almost all the crime around here goes back to drugs. Or money. Really, drugs *and* money. That's why we called in the DEA."

The royal *we*. Annalynn had won his allegiance. "Did Jesse Tornell have any arrests for drugs?" I knew he hadn't, but I wanted the deputy's reaction.

"No, but he needed money real bad. You can make a lot more money on marijuana than corn and beans. Did Sheriff Keyser tell you we've got a helicopter checking for marijuana all over the area tomorrow?"

"She mentioned it." We slid around another corner on the wet blacktop. "What if it doesn't find anything? Where would you go from there?"

"Damned if I know, but we'll figure it out. Don't worry about that."

"You're very reassuring." He obviously didn't buy the serial killer or the rustler theories. I leaned against the door. "I'm sorry, but I'm exhausted. If you don't mind, I'll nap until we get there."

A fifteen-minute doze refreshed me enough to worry about what we might find when we reached Straw and Tammy Kay's house. It stood dark.

"You wait here until I check it out," Spike said. The headlights shone on the front door as he walked to it. He knocked several times and then tried to turn the knob. He backed up.

I jumped out, afraid he'd kick the door in. "You try the windows while I see if the back door is unlocked." I opened the car door for Achilles.

"Okay." Spike pulled a flashlight off his belt and shone it on the living room windows.

I hurried to the back of the house with a pick on my keychain ready. The yard was so dark that I could barely see the door, but I didn't need a light to pick the lock in a second. "This door's open," I called.

He ran around the corner of the house with his gun in one hand and the flashlight in the other. "Police. We have a search warrant." He handed me the flashlight, pulled on a pair of gloves, and pushed the door open. "Is anyone here?" He waited a moment and switched on the kitchen light. "Wait until I give the all clear." He moved on into the living room.

Achilles relieved himself on a small tree.

I relaxed. He would have smelled pot by now.

"Bring Achilles in, ma'am. Don't touch anything."

"Come, Achilles." The kitchen looked as it had during my earlier visit. Toys littered the futon. I guessed that Tammy Kay had grabbed some of the boys' favorites to take to their grandparents' house. I didn't want to see more of this pathetic little private world. I went back into the kitchen. "Search, Achilles. Find. Please."

An unexpected sense of bereavement swept over me as I studied the handprints on the ceiling. Achilles licked my hand.

"No drugs, but I need to check for weapons, cash, records of drug deals, stuff like that," Spike said. "You look beat. Why don't you and Achilles wait in the car?"

"We'll do that." Halfway back to the patrol car I saw headlights approaching.

A pickup swung into the drive. Bob Bulganov jumped out with a rifle in his hands. "What are you doing here?"

"Achilles checked the house for drugs. He didn't find any. A deputy is inside with a search warrant."

Bob looked from me to the house. "I should go in."

Spike opened the front door. "Hi, Bob. Did Straw have a gun?"

"No. They were afraid the boys would get to it."

"Good. You go on home. I'll lock up when I'm finished." Spike closed the door.

Bob turned back toward the pickup and stopped. "You had a chance to talk to the sheriff about Tammy Kay yet?"

"No, but I will. Tell her not to worry."

"Thanks." He stretched. "Three o'clock is going to come mighty early. Good night." He left.

Three o'clock. Straw had started his shift at the dairy barn at four. Each of the two daily milkings constituted almost a day's work. Who helped Bob with the afternoon milking? His wife? His kids? A tough life, especially when the price of milk fell.

I adjusted the car seat for snoozing. Achilles refused

to get into the back seat, so I let him wander, sure he wouldn't go far from me.

He woke me with a bark.

Spike opened the car door and handed me a paper evidence bag. "Set that on the floor, please."

I sensed he was eager to tell me what was in it. "What did you find?"

"Hundred-dollar bills hidden in the ceiling over the hall closet. Fifteen of them."

"Good work." And maybe a major break. I'd found the same thing in Jesse Tornell's little safe. *Verdammt!* I couldn't tell Spike or even Annalynn about my ill-gotten information. The illegal search would render the bills useless as evidence. What's more, I couldn't be positive they were evidence. If only I'd had time to check the serial numbers. I wouldn't make the same mistake twice. I had to see these serial numbers.

I searched for a ruse as I ushered Achilles into the back seat. Send Spike back to the house to check the locks while I went through the money? Too risky. Better to play it straight. "I don't know much about police work, Spike, but I know about money—what the serial numbers signify, how to spot counterfeit. I might be able to save the department some valuable time if I inspect the bills."

"Great! Everything we send off to experts takes forever. I'll get you some gloves from the trunk."

I pulled on the gloves Spike handed to me and opened the bag. Even in the dim light I could see that some of the bills were wrinkled and some fresh. "I'd guess these come from more than one payment. You may be able to trace the new ones to an area bank and find out whether Jericho Kittle or any other suspects withdrew cash in hundred-dollar bills." I lifted the money out. "If you'll shine your flashlight on the bills, I'll go through them."

Three bills were the new design. None of Jesse's were. "The new one shouldn't be too hard to trace," I said. The others were the old design and came from six different series. Knowing the process of printing serial numbers, cutting sheets, and distributing bundles of bills to banks, I could tell this was a mixed bunch. Tracing them would be a waste of time. I tilted the "100" in the upper corner of each bill to make sure it was a hologram that changed color. No counterfeit. By the time I dropped the cash back in the evidence bag, I'd memorized every serial number. Next step: Check to see if some bills came from the same print run as those in Jesse Tornell's envelope.

"A good night's work," Spike said as he backed out of the driveway. "Do the bills give you any idea how many different payments there were?"

"Not really. The three new bills came from the same source, which could mean five three-hundred-dollar payments." I thought about Straw's character. "Probably not that many. I doubt that Straw could hold on to cash long."

Spike stepped on the gas. "Everything in his house is junk, and so is his pickup. I figure he must have been new at this. Even with the lights in the shed, it would have been too cold for the plants in there until around three months ago, say late March."

Good. He was analyzing what he saw. "That's about the time his wife found out she's pregnant." I pictured the tall plants. "Those plants seem awfully big to have been planted that late. Jericho must have a winter nursery somewhere."

"I reckon so." He yawned as we sped by Bob Bulganov's dark house. "The sheriff asked me to find out if ol' man Kittle owns any farmland. If he does, the helicopter will check it out tomorrow, too."

His tone told me Annalynn had gained his respect, maybe even some loyalty.

Right after we passed the crossroads near the Tornells' house, three deer darted across the road ahead of us.

Spike braked hard, and Achilles yelped as he slid off the seat and onto the floor.

"Sorry, ma'am," Spike said. "The damned deer are a menace to motorists. I wish the hunting season lasted all year long."

I unfastened my seat belt to reach back to check Achilles. He hopped back onto the seat and barked three times in Spike's ear.

Spike laughed. "I think he's criticizing my driving."

"He's okay. Go ahead."

Instead Spike peered over the steering wheel. "What in hell is that?"

A dog-sized animal was twirling around in the road two hundred feet or so ahead of us. The headlights caught the distinctive profile of a fox.

Spike honked the horn. Achilles growled.

The fox raced toward the car.

"Gotta be rabid. I'll have to shoot him," Spike said. He put the car in reverse and backed down the road at a good clip. "I need to get far enough from him to get out of the car and get a shot." He stopped the car and sprang out. He fired five quick shots without touching the racing animal. "Shit!" He switched to a two-hand grip.

Enough fooling around. I opened my door, jumped out, and fired twice. One bullet went between the whites of the wild eyes.

The fox staggered but kept coming for another ten feet or so.

"Finish him off," I said, kneeling to pick up my casings. I wanted to be able to say Spike had killed the animal rather than explain my skill with a gun.

He edged toward the fox. "Wow! What a shot!" He took careful aim from six feet away. This time he hit the mark. "It's got a little foam around the mouth. I'll put it in a garbage bag and take it in for testing. We'll have to alert everybody to be watching for rabid foxes, and skunks and raccoons, too."

I groaned. "We'll be back to nuts shooting at mad deer."

TWENTY-SIX

WE PULLED INTO Annalynn's driveway at half past two.

Spike smothered a yawn. "You mind giving the sheriff a report on the fox?"

"I'll be glad to." Achilles and I got out. "Good night, Spike."

"See you tomorrow, Phoenix."

I smiled as I walked up the porch steps. Shooting that fox had turned me from a ma'am into a peer and, I hoped, strengthened Annalynn's hand.

Achilles and I dragged ourselves upstairs.

Annalynn's bedroom door stood open and her bedside lamp threw light on her sleeping face. She was stretched out atop her lace bedspread with a folder beside her.

I tiptoed in and turned out the light before going to my own bed across the hall. By the time I had set my alarm for seven thirty, pulled back my spread, and kicked off my shoes, Achilles had fallen asleep. I followed his example.

The alarm went off soon after, or so I thought until I opened my eyes to daylight. Achilles stood up, yawned and stretched, and dropped back down on his green blanket.

Annalynn tapped on my open door. "You have just enough time to eat breakfast with me before your window people come." She turned and headed downstairs.

For an instant I allowed myself to think this could be a normal day. Then I remembered the fox and the money and the helicopter. I jumped up to put on my standard beige shorts and green tank top and run a brush through my hair before hurrying downstairs.

Annalynn sat with a bowl of oatmeal in front of her and a folder on the table beside her. "I got Spike's message on the search. Anything else I need to know?"

"We shot a rabid fox about a mile this side of the Tornells' house." I scooped some dried cranberries into my oatmeal. "Spike brought it in to send to a lab."

Annalynn closed her eyes and took a deep breath. "One more complication. I think another department is responsible for finding the den and checking the area, but we'll have to issue a warning." She rubbed her forehead. "People will be bringing in dead squirrels and rabbits and Lord knows what else."

More deer, I thought. "Anything new on your end? What about Jericho's father?"

"We released him. It's obvious Jericho put the pot in Charles' car." She pushed back her chair. "I have to get to the office. What are your plans for the afternoon?"

"Play my new piano, take a nice long nap." Check the serial numbers on the bills in the Tornells' safe.

She frowned. "Why don't I believe you?" She walked toward the front door. "Please don't go anywhere without telling me. I may need you."

She read me too well. "I'll call you if I decide to go out." I waved goodbye.

I finished breakfast and cleaned up the dishes before strapping on my gun and going next door to unlock my house. The window crew—a young white crew chief and three middle-aged Hispanics—pulled into my drive right at eight. I greeted them, retrieved my trowel, and finished planting the wave petunias I'd been working on when Annalynn interrupted me Monday evening.

The sound of Achilles' frantic barking sent me running back to her house. He leapt up on me when I opened the door, ecstatic to see me.

"Down, boy, down." I warded off his doggy kisses and knelt beside him to stroke and calm him. "I'm right here." I stayed with him while he ate his breakfast and then took him out the front door with me and led him between my house and garage into my backyard. He immediately ran into Annalynn's much bigger backyard to say good morning to the hummingbirds.

I put my gardening stuff in my garage and was closing the door when Connie drove her yellow VW into Annalynn's drive.

She hopped out, a flash of yellow and red. "Good news, Phoenix. I can have a wonderful piano delivered at eleven today."

"Great! Where did you find it?"

She smiled, but she didn't meet my eyes. "In my living room."

That instrument was her most treasured possession. "I can't take your grand piano. What would you do without it?"

"One of my most untalented former piano students has a good console. I'm buying that." She walked over to examine my petunias.

She needed money. Her baby grand was worth at least $5,000 more than the console. That meant little to me but a lot to her. I couldn't let her sacrifice her treasure. "Let's have a glass of lemonade on the porch and talk about it."

She shook her head and walked back to the car. "There's nothing to talk about."

"Yes, there is. You didn't need money so badly yesterday. What's happened?"

She got into her car. "It's not your problem."

I leaned down and put my hand on her steering wheel. "Annalynn isn't your problem either, but you spend a lot of time helping her. You and I aren't as close as you and Annalynn"—a giant understatement—"but we're old friends, renewed friends. Come on, Connie. Tell me what's wrong."

She averted her eyes.

When we were in high school, I'd scrambled to earn money for clothes and school activities. Annalynn and Connie had never worried about money. Giving either financial help now required both tact and subterfuge. "Connie, do you want to worry Annalynn with a problem we can handle?"

"Of course not." She stared at the keys in her hand. "You'll think it's silly."

Probably. "Connie, the first half of my life I never had enough money. I haven't forgotten what it feels like."

She met my eyes. "You're a real smart-ass, Phoenix Smith, but you're a hard person to dislike. Bring on the lemonade."

She said nothing else until we had settled into rocking chairs on Annalynn's porch with our glasses and a pitcher of lemonade on the wrought-iron table between us.

"Okay, Connie. What happened last night?"

She stared at her hands, folded in her lap. "Dick, my ex, called to invite me to his wedding. Our girls want me to be there. I said I'd come."

Dick, the other half of a supposedly amicable divorce. "Jeez, if Russ had invited me to his wedding, I'd have time-bombed the wedding cake."

"Russ was a cheating jerk. I would have helped you set the timer. It's different with Dick and me. We've been friends since we were eighteen. We married at nineteen. By the time we were twenty-five, we realized that we wanted different things from life. We compromised to stay together and make a good home for the girls."

Compromise had meant settling for local theater rather than making the push for a real stage or film career. "Do you regret your choices?"

"No. I adore my girls." She blinked away tears. "I don't want them to see me as a failure—living in my mother's house, driving an old car, running from wedding to funeral to music lessons and barely making enough to live on."

"They won't see you as a failure unless you do." I couldn't believe that bull had come out of my mouth. Think, Phoenix. "Nothing says success like a designer dress. You'll want to fly out to Oregon with a stunning wardrobe for the wedding. And have a performance or two to brag about."

Her eyes widened in surprise. "You got it!"

"The clothes are the easy part."

"Says the woman in Count Cheapo couture."

A solution to two problems hit me. "You can change that. I'm desperate for some 'grown-up' clothes. You can go on a buying trip—St. Louis or Kansas City—for both of us. Find what I need for business meetings and social events and I'll pay you by buying what you need for the wedding."

"You mean be your personal shopper?"

"Yes. Think of it as choosing a wardrobe for a character in a play."

Connie jumped up to pace. "I can do that. I could drive to Kansas City Monday. I'll need your sizes. And your measurements." She spun around. "You'll need shoes, too."

"Complete outfits, including jewelry and a smashing briefcase."

Connie resumed her pacing, but now she was almost dancing. "Annalynn says you have a fabulous wardrobe in Vienna. What designers do you buy?"

"None, really. My seamstress has been making suits and dresses for me for years. She shows me a selection of designs and cloth and I choose." I put in the secret pockets myself.

"Your personal designer, in other words. I shouldn't be surprised. Your mother made you lovely one-of-a-kind clothes. I'll never forget how I envied that pale green dress you wore to the junior prom."

News to me. I'd been embarrassed that my mother made so many of my clothes. "That was a *Vogue* pattern that she modified."

"I'll pick up some fashion magazines and catalogs and we'll go over them together this weekend." She dropped into her chair, her face sober. "Any ideas on how I can get an impressive gig before Labor Day?"

"No." Gigs were out of my orbit. "Do you have a business plan?"

"I don't even know what one is."

"Basically a strategy for growing your business, in your case for getting better gigs and charging more for the ones you're already doing."

Connie bounced out of her chair. "Of course. What I

need is a business manager, someone to write a business plan and negotiate contracts for me." She grinned. "You."

What could it hurt? She had nothing to negotiate. "Fine. We'll work it out after we wrap up the murder investigations."

"What can I do to help?"

Nothing. "We need to know everything we can about Jericho Kittle—who his friends are, how he explains the money he spends, his relationship with his parents."

Connie nodded. "I have a voice student who may know. What about the piano?"

"Deliver the console to my house, and add on a ten percent finder's fee for yourself. How much does everything come to?"

"Eleven hundred."

"I'll get you the cash." I went upstairs to the old safe in the judge's office and counted out eleven hundred-dollar bills. Crooks weren't the only ones who used them, I reflected. I flipped through the bills to check the serial numbers. Five I'd received at a local bank came from the same bundle as the three new ones in Straw's packet.

The phone rang the double ring. I answered, "Keyser residence, Phoenix Smith speaking."

"This is Dorothy Tornell. I've been listening to the news about Straw being killed. Does his death have anything to do with Jesse's?" Her voice verged on hysteria. "Please tell me what's going on."

My chance had come. "The sheriff is following some leads. She expects to receive some important information this morning. If it's convenient for you, I'll come out this afternoon between two and three to discuss everything with you."

"Thank you. Thank you so much."

"Did you hear that a deputy killed a rabid fox near your farm?"

"Yes. It was on the eight o'clock news. I just told an officer that I'm pretty sure there's a den on Floyd Vanderhofen's farm. We saw a vixen with a couple of pups come from his timber a couple weeks ago. We'll keep an eye out, and a pitchfork handy."

"Good. I'll see you after lunch." I hung up and hurried downstairs.

Connie held up her cell phone. "I called the mover. The piano will be here in half an hour." She accepted the bills from me and stuffed them into a small yellow cloth purse. "Do you think the Kittle kid committed those two murders?"

If I said no, how would I justify asking her to find out about him? I fudged. "I haven't seen anything yet to convince me he's guilty or innocent of either murder."

She tilted her head and raised a skeptical eyebrow. "No gut feeling? No hunch?"

Damn but she had good instincts. "He knows something."

"Annalynn will get it out of him. She's a natural. Talk to you later."

I went to my house to check on the progress. The men had installed the living and dining room windows, leaving bits of dust and debris scattered around the hardwood floor. I inspected the work, found it good, and swept the dirt into a corner to leave a clean space for the piano. Then I went down the hall to the bedrooms. Two men were working on the window in my two brothers' old room and two on the windows in my old corner bedroom.

"We'll finish before lunch," the crew chief assured

me. "Everything's a perfect fit. You'll need to do some replastering before you paint, of course."

Of course. The house wouldn't be ready to show for weeks.

A knock on the front door signaled the arrival of my piano. One of the window guys helped two muscular young black men wearing Laycock Community College T-shirts get the piano up the two low front steps and into the house.

The moment the movers rolled it into place against the dining room wall, I lifted the lid and played an arpeggio the length of the keyboard. An excellent tone and firm keys. One of the movers grabbed the old piano bench from the corner and put it in place. "Give it a real test."

I couldn't resist. I handed him a twenty as a tip and sat down to play Scott Joplin's "Maple Leaf Rag." Connie was right—an outstanding console.

The movers applauded when I finished.

"You're really good. You oughta play out at Harry's," one said. "I'll tell him to give you a call." He and his colleague left.

I played part of a Mozart piano concerto and schemed to convince Dorothy to show me the money. Nothing occurred to me, so I left my noisy house and went back to Annalynn's and to my laptop. The Adderly intranet reported that Gunther was handling the Szabo project.

Curiosity compelled me to type "Mario Marrone" into Google. My former *amore* had his own website, mostly photos of him in operatic costumes. No mention that his real last name was Brown. I clicked on a link to a profile. It included a photo of him being made up for a performance. Seeing his wrinkles and receding hairline cheered me. I'd weathered the years much better than he had. Or did I not see the signs of my own years? I checked in the mirror. Not one gray hair amid the black.

Annalynn's call interrupted my self-appraisal. The helicopter hadn't spotted any marijuana plants, but a trooper thought Floyd Vanderhofen might have dug some up in a clearing in the last day or two. The Highway Patrol would email digital photos of the area to her later that day.

"Another dead end," I said, let down at the news.

"Not quite," but her voice revealed how discouraged she was. "The DEA has some leads on Jericho's drug deals. Any other ideas?"

"No, but Dorothy Tornell called to ask what's happening. I'm heading out there after lunch. Maybe she'll remember something else."

"Be careful," Annalynn urged. "Please, Phoenix, don't do anything risky."

I REACHED THE Tornells' place a little after two. A pitchfork leaned against the house by the porch steps.

A gangly teenager with strawberry-blond hair and dark circles under his blue eyes stepped out of the porch door with his hand extended. "Hi, Dr. Smith. I'm Junior Tornell. Thanks for staying with my mother that—that first night."

"I'm so sorry for your loss. Please let me know if there's anything I can do."

He snorted, a bitter sound. "You're a financial expert. Convince her to sell this rathole and escape. Both of them worked fourteen hours a day, and they still couldn't get out of debt." His voice broke. He rubbed his eyes with his fists. "I won't stay here. I won't be trapped the way she's been."

He was pleading for his life, and for hers. "I understand. I'll be glad to go over the farm's books and give her my opinion on its viability." And check those serial numbers.

"Thanks," he choked out. He sniffed. "She's picking the last pint of strawberries. Follow the path along the garden fence and go behind that old brooder house."

I went where he pointed. When Achilles and I came around the corner of the building, Dorothy was squatting between rows, her back to me. She sprang up and grabbed a bow and arrow, fitting the arrow as she rose.

"It's Phoenix," I hastened to assure her. "Sorry to startle you."

She lowered the four-foot-long wooden bow. "Between the murders and that rabid fox, I'm pretty jumpy. I brought Junior's bow just in case."

I remembered seeing the bow and arrows the night I slept in Junior's room. "Could you hit an animal with that?"

"Sure. I've been the 4-H Club's project leader for archery for years. I could kill a fox with this easy. With the right arrows, I could bring down a deer. I feel safe with this."

I didn't. I knew now what had killed Jesse Tornell.

TWENTY-SEVEN

DOROTHY TORNELL'S PROWESS with the bow meant we couldn't dismiss her as a suspect. I kept my tone casual: "Have you hunted deer with a bow?"

"I went with Junior once when he was fourteen. He wounded a buck, and I had to finish it off. Never again." Shaking her head as though to blur an unpleasant image, she handed me the bow and arrows and picked up two small baskets full of strawberries. "You look like you need to get in the shade."

A thick coat of lacquer covered the arrows I held. Could lacquer have been the substance on the sliver found in Jesse? "I'm not used to this heat. Summers in Vienna are much cooler."

She led the way toward the house. "You goin' back there?"

"No. The job bored me." Until I said it, I hadn't admitted how unsatisfying the work had become.

She glanced at the plants we were passing. "Time to stake the late tomatoes."

Tomatoes filled a third of her large garden. They must be her cash crop. I scanned the plants, looking for marijuana seedlings, but saw none.

"It's hot in the house," she said, moving on. "We got a couple of chairs under the maple. You go on around and I'll bring us some iced tea."

That left me a long way from her safe, but I had no

choice. Achilles and I walked past the back steps to the front lawn and to two white plastic chairs. The aging tree's deep shade and a soft breeze made the spot comfortable. Waiting for Dorothy, I fought sleep.

She joined me with a large thermal glass in each hand. She'd changed from her grubby pink tank top into a clean white T-shirt, but her hands still bore strawberry stains. She handed me a glass. "You said the sheriff found out something this morning."

"Yes, but it didn't help as much as we hoped." I shifted my chair so we were facing each other. "I have to ask you to keep what I tell you to yourself."

She nodded, and the knuckles of her hand holding the glass turned white.

"The truth is, we still don't know who killed your husband or why."

She waited for me to go on. Dorothy Tornell was no dummy.

I prolonged the silence with a sip of brutally cold tea. "The sheriff has several possible theories. The most likely one is that the same person killed Jesse and the Bulganov boy. My personal opinion is that Straw saw the killer drive past but didn't know it mattered. The killer was afraid that once the sheriff announced a human rather than a deer killed Jesse, Straw would come forward and identify him."

Dorothy frowned. "The radio report sounded like a drug dealer killed Straw."

"That's a possibility. Certainly whoever did it knew Straw was raising marijuana." I remembered that Dorothy had left me in the kitchen with music playing about the time Straw was killed. Could she have sneaked out and gone over to kill him? Would the music have covered up the sound of a car? Where would she get a syringe and drugs? Easy. She'd have a syringe and possibly drugs for medicating animals, and any idiot could make meth. Unlikely as the scenario seemed, I couldn't completely discount Dorothy for one or both murders yet.

She broke the long silence. "I wouldn't recognize marijuana if I saw it. We've never had anything to do with any illegal drugs. Why would a drug dealer kill Jesse?"

"The same reason someone killed Straw—he saw something. Can you think of Jesse mentioning anything—*anything* unusual in the last week or so?"

"Nothing." She blinked away tears. "I've thought a lot about that. He hardly talked at all Sunday. He'd get quiet when he was worried about something."

So Jesse had anticipated trouble. That cast a new light on his death. "Dorothy, I had assumed he took the rifle because he planned to shoot a deer. Maybe he took it to the pond for protection instead."

She straightened in her chair, eyes wide. "That could be. We have plenty of venison in the freezer." She choked back a sob. "I knew he wasn't telling me something. But what could it be?"

I shivered as a chilling thought ran through me. If the killer thought Dorothy knew whatever Jesse knew, she'd be on his list.

"What's the matter? You've got goose pimples."

I covered. "Europeans don't ice their drinks. I've lost the habit."

She reached for my glass. "I'll bring you—"

"No, thank you. I like it. I'm extra sensitive to heat and cold because I'm so tired. Achilles and I spent half the night looking for drugs."

Achilles trotted over from a honey locust he'd been

marking. I stroked his head, and he plopped down with his nose on my feet and closed his eyes.

I forced myself to banish my drowsiness. "You said Straw was angry because Jesse got him fired earlier this spring. Had they had any contact lately?"

"No. Jesse never had any reason to see Straw. Didn't like him. His mother spoiled him as a kid and then couldn't rein him in when he grew up. He was nothing like Bob—his stepbrother. Bob threw a fit when his folks made him hire Straw at the dairy. Bob can tell you all about Straw."

I was getting nowhere with this. "What else could have been worrying Jesse?"

She took a long drink of iced tea. "Floyd Vanderhofen's small-claims suit. Did you check him out?"

"We're still working on it."

"He came over this morning to tell me he was dropping the suit. I told him to get his cattle out of our pasture or I'd send them to market with ours." She rubbed away a tear. "I'm selling six head next week to pay for Jesse's funeral and the July mortgage."

She'd just given me an opening. "You mentioned that Jesse did carpentry to earn some extra money. Could he have been worried because someone didn't pay him?"

She shook her head. "He'd been too busy farming to work for anyone lately. The last job he did was for Garth Raymo, the man who drove my parents down. He gave Jesse a check that day and asked him to spend a weekend working on his fancy staircase as soon as he had time." She teared up again. "Garth told Dad Jesse was a great carpenter."

So the hundred-dollar bills didn't come from Garth Raymo. Maybe from the Bulganovs. I couldn't ask straight out. "I'm paying for the repairs on my house with credit cards, but I guess you don't operate a part-time business that way."

"No. I don't even take checks at the farmers' market, not since one bounced. Jesse accepts checks, of course. No one keeps much money around these days."

"Not even the Bulganovs? Someone said they have a fancy security system."

Dorothy shrugged. "I got no idea. I know Nan pays everything by check at the end of the month. Jesse did all our bookkeeping, such as it is." She squirmed in her chair. "Junior looked you up on the computer. He said you're a financial expert. Sometime when you're not busy, would you mind going over our records and telling me"—she cleared her throat—"how bad things are?" She lurched to her feet and stumbled over to the tree trunk. She leaned her forehead against the rough bark and her shoulders shook. After a moment, she regained control, but she continued to lean on the tree. "I don't know anything but farming. I don't want to lose this place."

I hesitated a moment, careful not to seem eager. "I could take a look at your books and your tax records right now."

She pushed away from the tree, her expression uncertain. "Would it be confidential? Like if you tell a lawyer something?"

I smiled. "No, but no one will know if neither one of us tells anybody." I extended my hand.

She smiled back and shook. "What worries me is—well, I don't keep any records of what I make at the farmers' market. I spend that money on groceries and don't declare it on my taxes. Jesse didn't declare all his car-

pentry work either." Her smile faded. "You won't tell
the sheriff."

"No, she doesn't care about your taxes." Careful.
Leave some slack. "Of course, we'll tell her if we run
across something that would help identify Jesse's killer."

"Yes, of course." She started for the house. "I'll spread
the stuff out on my bed. I don't want Junior to know what
we're doing. He wants me to sell the farm."

Dorothy stopped at the porch steps. "We better bring
your dog in. If he should go after a rabid animal, you'd
lose him."

"Thank you." Distraught as she was, she'd thought
about Achilles. Surely this woman couldn't be a killer.

We didn't see anyone as we went up the stairs to Dorothy's bedroom. She pulled back faded red drapes from
the east and south windows to encourage air circulation,
but the room was uncomfortably warm. I sipped on my
tea, now watery from the melted ice.

She squatted in the closet, opened the safe, and
brought out the papers I'd skimmed Tuesday morning,
but not the envelope with the money. I went through the
papers and put key figures down on a pad. "According to your tax returns and your bills, you don't break
even. Your farmers' market income and Jesse's pocket-
to-pocket carpentry jobs have been keeping you going.
Can you possibly pay living expenses with your income
from the farmers' market?"

"No." Her robust body seemed to shrivel. "Not that
I don't do pretty good, better than I let Jesse know. I
charge top prices because I mix my own stuff and don't
use commercial pesticides." She studied the figures I'd
jotted down. "I sell free-range turkeys for Thanksgiv-

ing, too. People pay twice as much for them as they do frozen turkeys."

Probably a few hundred dollars when she needed several thousand. "I'm sorry, Dorothy, but I don't see how you can make a living if you continue to farm this way." Her despair pushed me to suggest something to give her hope. I was way out of my comfort zone, but basic business principles applied. "You have a small farm. You need to make the most of what you have." What on earth could she do? "Change your product line—raise more free-range turkeys, build greenhouses and sell organic vegetables year-round, switch from cattle to goats." I'd run out of questionable ideas. "I can help you with the numbers, but you need a farm expert to give you viable options—good ideas."

"I can't do anything that takes a lot of money up front. I won't be able to get a loan." She rubbed tears from her eyes. "Junior wrote a paper about organic gardening for one of his classes. That might work. I don't know anything about goats. I'll ask the extension agent to give me some advice. Thank you, Phoenix."

I patted her hand. "I'll be glad to help with evaluating markets and estimating costs." I still hadn't reached my objective, checking the serial numbers. "Don't you have any other records? I saw nothing about the cost of maintenance of equipment, a deductible expense. You may have overpaid your taxes."

"I think everything else in the safe is old bills." She went to the closet, emptied the safe, and dumped all the papers on the bed. She picked one up. "Here's a note about the work on the Family Baptist Church. He did that for half price." She picked up the envelope that held the bills. "My God! Money. A lot of money."

If she wasn't surprised, she deserved an Oscar. "You can certainly use that."

She counted it out bill by bill, her face puzzled but growing more and more pleased with each bill. "It's like a gift," she said. "I can't imagine how he earned it."

Unfortunately, neither could I. "Maybe he did some work he didn't tell you about and planned to surprise you on your birthday."

"Jesse never gave me birthday gifts."

No wonder she hid part of her earnings from him. My eyes ached to see those numbers. "Are you sure it's real? Not counterfeit?"

She held up a wrinkled bill. "I've never seen a hundred. It sure looks real to me."

"I can tell. Bring them over by the window." I checked each bill. Only one came from a series found in Straw's house. No statistical significance. The bills were the kind of random, hard-to-trace selection I would have used to pay off an asset. Tornell wouldn't have earned that much as a nonunion carpenter in a week. If he hadn't been wielding a hammer or dealing drugs, where did he get the money?

Dorothy needed the cash desperately. That meant I faced another dilemma: What in hell was I going to tell Annalynn about that $1,500?

TWENTY-EIGHT

I HANDED THE last of the bills back to Dorothy. "I'd put the money back in the safe until you need it."

She smoothed the bills and tucked them back in the envelope. "A gift," she said softly, placing it in the safe. "Jesse's gift."

The phone rang.

"Junior can get it," she said, gathering up the papers.

"Dr. Smith," Junior called a moment later, "an emergency call for you."

I picked up the phone receiver on the bedside table. "Phoenix Smith."

"Thank God you're still there," a man said, his voice blasting in my ear. "A fox has my dog cornered in the backyard. The sheriff's office said you'd come shoot him."

"Who is this?"

"Floyd Vanderhofen. You came here yesterday."

"I'll be there in two minutes." I hung up and ran, Achilles right beside me. "A rabid fox is at Vanderhofen's. Tell the sheriff I'm going there," I called over my shoulder as I scooted down the stairs. Achilles pushed past me to jump in as I opened my car door. I slid under the wheel, gunned the car out of the drive, accelerated to the cross-roads, and slid around the corner. When I whipped into Vanderhofen's drive, I adjusted the windows so Achilles could get air but not leap out. "Stay, Achilles, stay."

He tried to squeeze out the door before I closed it, but I shoved him back. "Stay."

He barked in protest as I ran past Vanderhofen's pickup toward the sound of a dog yipping frantically.

"Over here," Vanderhofen called from an unpainted, waist-high board fence to the left of his house. His comb-over hung down the back of his head. "I wounded him, but I ran out of arrows."

Another archer for the suspect list. I ran up to him. His little white dog had flattened himself out on a green plastic table in a small grape arbor some twenty yards away. An overturned matching chair lay on the ground next to the table. A fox with froth-edged jaws circled the chair. An arrow protruding from its left rear haunch impeded its movement. The fox leapt at the table, not reaching the dog but causing its perch to rock.

"Wait until Snowball's out of the line of fire," Vanderhofen said.

The fox threw itself against a table leg, toppling the table.

I fired one shot behind the fox's right ear as the dog slid off the table. The fox thrashed around for a few seconds and lay still. The dog, which had landed like a cat, raced toward us. Vanderhofen leaned over the fence to scoop him up.

I looked for other movement in the yard, bounded in the back by a row of old-fashioned white roses. "Have you seen the pups?"

"Two men came out this morning and found them at the den. The mother wasn't there." He held the quaking dog in his left arm and ran his right hand up its leg with the other. "I'm almost sure the fox didn't get close enough to bite him."

A fond owner's delusion. "Put him in a cage or a box and take him right to a vet. And be sure he doesn't bite you."

"Of course." He stuck out his right hand. "Thanks. You saved his life with that shot. I'm sorry if I overreacted yesterday. I thought that talk about a rabid deer was a ruse to search without a warrant."

I shook his hand. "Think nothing of it. As soon as you secure your dog, could you get me a garbage bag for the fox, please?" I trotted back toward the car and the steady barking coming from it. "I have to see to my own animal."

Pain blasted along the bottom of my rib cage. For an awful moment I thought I'd been shot again, but it was a flare-up of my wound, the worst in two weeks. I leaned on the car door, determined to stay conscious. Achilles struggled to squeeze through the window to me.

"Down, boy." I gathered my strength to open the door and crawl in. I leaned back in my seat while he whined and licked my hands and face. The pain receded, leaving a residue of nausea and dizziness.

"Are you okay?" Vanderhofen touched my arm through the window.

"I will be in a couple of minutes." I kept my eyes closed. "I'm recovering from a post-op infection. I guess I overdid it in this heat."

"I'll bring you a bottle of water."

By the time he came back with the water, I felt okay but weak. Sweat covered every centimeter of my body. He stood by while I drank most of the water and used the rest to wash Achilles' kisses off my face. "I'm okay now," I assured Vanderhofen. "I'd appreciate your help getting the fox in the bag."

"Why don't you rest in the house where it's cool while I take care of that?"

I resisted temptation. I had to make sure that arrow went into the bag with the fox. "Thanks, but it will be easier with two of us." I looked at Achilles. "Stay. Down. Stay."

He frowned and positioned himself to leap out the door when I opened it.

Vanderhofen laughed. "Give up. That magnificent animal is not going to let you out of his sight. Do you have a leash?"

"Yes." Vanderhofen read animals better than people. "Leash, Achilles."

He didn't move.

Vanderhofen laughed again, but this time his eyes didn't crinkle. "Spouses desert you in a crisis, but your dog won't."

The man had issues. I could use that. Later. "The leash is on the floor on the other side of the car. Would you mind getting it for me?"

He retrieved the leash and brought it back around the car to me.

I snapped it on Achilles' collar before getting out of the car. "Dorothy Tornell told me you dropped the small-claims suit. That was good of you."

He shrugged. "She's a nice woman. She's going to have a rough time without that muleheaded husband to help with the work." He led the way back up his drive. "Her boy hates farming. I had him in one of my classes. He's a very bright kid."

"Have you had a chance to drive your cattle out of her pasture?"

"I don't know what she's talking about. I came back

after I talked to her and counted my herd." He lifted a big black garbage bag off the yard gate and pushed it open. "None of my cattle are missing, and there's no break in the fence between our properties. Apparently she doesn't know how many cattle they have."

Something really wrong here. With finances so tight, Dorothy would know exactly how many cattle belonged in that pasture. I'd have to ask her to count again. At least she might have more cattle to sell than she thought.

Once in the yard, Achilles tried to block my way.

"It's okay, boy. It's dead." I'd been so focused on the fox earlier that I hadn't paid attention to Vanderhofen's arrows. Three protruded from the ground in front of the table. Two more were embedded in the soil well to the left of the table. Bad shooting, or perhaps he'd aimed low to avoid hitting Snowball.

Vanderhofen held back. "Are you sure it's dead?"

"Pretty sure." We would have seen a lot more blood if the heart hadn't stopped. I handed him Achilles' leash. "Keep a tight grip." I drew my gun and approached cautiously. The bullet had hit the brain. Not a twitch. Eyes getting that unseeing look. Definitely dead. I holstered my gun, took back the leash, and looped the end around a tree. Achilles whined. I stroked him until he quieted.

Vanderhofen crept up to the fox, pulled out a wood arrow, and placed it on the ground. "If you hold the bag open, I'll hoist the fox by its back legs and dump it in."

After we executed the awkward maneuver, I said, "Put the arrow in the bag, too. The point is contaminated."

He dropped it in and took the heavy bag from me. "Your dog isn't going to like having this in the car."

I untied Achilles' leash. "I'll get rid of it as soon as I can. Would you please call the sheriff's department and tell them I'm bringing it in? And let the Tornells know, too."

"Certainly."

We walked to my car in silence, Vanderhofen holding the heavy bag as far away from him as he could. When I opened the trunk, he swung the bag up and in.

He started to shake my hand and then drew his hand back. "I better wash before I touch anything. Tell the sheriff I'm taking Snowball to a vet right now. Again, thanks."

Achilles pulled on the leash. He wanted out of there. So did I. As soon as we were in the car, I turned up the air conditioner and headed for town. When we reached the driveway where we'd met the ambulance the day before, I pulled in to call Annalynn on my cell. I had to wait on hold five minutes before she came on the line.

"Sorry to make you wait," she said barely above a whisper. "I'm in a meeting."

She had an audience. Maybe both of us did. "I shot another rabid fox. More important, I'm ninety percent certain I know what killed Jesse Tornell."

"Thank you," Annalynn said. "Hold on a moment." Voices sounded in the background. A door closed. "Meet me at home in half an hour. I'm ninety percent certain I know *why* he was killed."

TWENTY-NINE

If ANNALYNN KNEW the motive for Jesse Tornell's murder, we were halfway home. I sped toward town, eager to fit together our pieces of the puzzle. In spite of, or perhaps because of, the great differences in our personalities, we'd always been a great team. I'd missed that a lot when, at eighteen, we'd left home to attend different colleges. I exulted in reinstating that connection after so many years.

A mile from Laycock a squad car pulled out of a gravel side road behind me and hit the siren.

Verdammt! I slowed from the sixty-five I'd been driving on the now-familiar route and pulled over as far as the shoulderless road allowed.

Spike pulled up behind me and jumped out of the car. "You know what the speed limit on this road is?" He scowled as he walked up and then grinned, improving his rugged face a hundred percent. "Dispatch told me you shot another fox. I know the drill now. I'll take it to the vet for you."

"Achilles and I both thank you." I popped open my trunk. Why would the young deputy go to the trouble of meeting me? To tell me something he'd accomplished. I got out of the car to make it easier to talk. "Anything new on Jericho Kittle today?"

Spike beamed. "Yeah. I figure we got enough to convict him for distribution. He couldn't have committed any of the three homicides, though. Not unless he hired someone." He lifted the heavy bag out of the trunk as though it were a sack of bread. "You were right about the money. A teller at First National says Jericho brought in a lot of tens and twenties every couple of weeks and changed them for fifties and hundreds, most likely including those three new ones hidden in Straw Bulganov's ceiling."

"Good work." Receive information, give information, receive more information. "I have a theory on what killed Tornell. I'd like to run it by you before I tell the sheriff."

He put on his neutral cop face, but he stretched another inch taller and his eyes gleamed. "Sure, Phoenix."

"When I got to Vanderhofen's place, he was shooting at the fox with a bow and arrow." Leave Dorothy out of it. "A wood arrow could have made the kind of wound Jesse Tornell had before someone forced that deer antler in."

He whooped like a kid who'd just won a video game. "That's gotta be it!" He sobered. "You think Vanderhofen killed Tornell?"

"I doubt it. He's a lousy archer." Could he have been faking with those errant arrows? No way. "One of his arrows is in the bag with the fox. The lab can see if it matches that sliver in Tornell's chest."

"Good." Spike untied the garbage bag and looked in. "He looked in the clear, but we'll recheck his alibi." He grinned. "One shot to the brain?"

"No need to waste ammunition." His respect for me added to my respect for him. "How many people around here could kill someone with an arrow?"

"A helluva lot," he said, closing the bag and putting it in the trunk of his car. "How far do you figure the killer was from the victim?"

I pictured the way the track turned to run past the pond to the pasture gate. "No more than thirty-five feet, and it could have been half that. And he had to get off his shot fast. Tornell had a rifle." Spike knew that. I mustn't condescend. "What do you think?"

Spike stared into the fields. "The guy probably used a recurve bow, sorta like the ones you see in western movies. You can fit an arrow and shoot fairly accurately in a second." He mimicked the motion of fitting and shooting an arrow. "We better go through the deer hunting licenses first. This county has one of the highest archery kill rates in the state." He brightened. "But we may see some names on that list to give priority. I'll see what Sheriff Keyser says. I'm going in to give her my full report—stuff I couldn't radio in—after I drop off the fox and the arrow." He closed the trunk.

"I'm meeting her at home in five minutes. I'll tell her." I opened my car door.

"Were you with ATF, Phoenix?"

"Never." Cops are suspicious people, and observant. I'd have to be careful.

"Secret Service?"

I laughed. "No." His next guess could be the right one. "You don't have to be in law enforcement or the military to be a good shot. Look me up online. You'll see that I write esoteric economic papers and advise companies and entrepreneurs on what start-up companies to invest in or to avoid. See you later."

The stop made me a little late. Annalynn's SUV was parked in her driveway when I pulled into mine. I let myself into the castle and didn't see or hear her.

Achilles trotted into the kitchen where we kept his water bowl and gave a short bark to remind me of my duty.

"Phoenix," Annalynn called from the basement, "I'm in Boom's office."

That surprised me. She avoided going there. I filled the water bowl before going downstairs, through the judge's woodshop, and into the passageway—part of a 1960s bomb shelter—that ran between our basements. Boom had converted a section into a home office. I suspected it had served mostly as a place for him to play video games.

Annalynn sat in the big ergonomic chair at the glass computer desk. "This monitor is better than the one upstairs," she said. "Please look at the photos taken from the helicopter." She clicked to set the photos up as a series of slides and yielded the chair to me.

"What am I looking for?"

"The reason Jesse Tornell was killed. Something Captain Gist didn't see when we met this afternoon." Her cell phone rang. "I'll take this upstairs where the reception is better."

Okay. So these photos contained something that told Annalynn—but not Gist—why Tornell died. And it wasn't marijuana. Intrigued, I glanced over sixty or so slide-sized photos. They looked much alike, a lot of green interspersed occasionally with buildings and some black dots that must be livestock.

I expanded each photo to full screen in quick succession to get an overview. I didn't recognize the places in the first or last shots, but the Tornells' pond and Bob Bulganov's rambling white barn identified those in the middle. Even I could tell from the land's contour and cultivation that the Bulganovs owned the best farmland in the area. I spotted two large dairy herds on nearby side roads I hadn't traveled. No wonder Bob and his family were milking twelve hours a day.

Half of the Tornell place was cultivated. One hilly part served as a grazing area for thirty milk cows and three calves. The hilliest pasture, behind the pond, was less than half the size but fed eighteen black Angus. Hadn't Dorothy said they had twelve head? I zoomed in. Twelve of them were cows or heifers. Maybe she hadn't counted the spring calves. No, she said he'd sold the calves. Something yellow was on one ear of several of the mature animals but none of the calves. Had to be an ID.

Vanderhofen's herd of about thirty grazed in the brushy, hilly neighboring field. It was twice the size of the Tornells' two pastures. I zoomed in. What the hell? Not a black Angus in Vanderhofen's herd. All were Herefords, stocky animals with curly red hair and white faces. Surely Dorothy knew those black calves in her pasture weren't Vanderhofen's. Maybe he had another herd and had shifted them around. I searched the photos of Vanderhofen's farm. I saw freshly dug earth among some brush, doubtless where police suspected marijuana plants had been growing. Vanderhofen had no other herd. His only crop was hay. He farmed as a hobby, not a business. I zoomed in on his cattle. All had yellow ear tags.

Could the extra Angus cattle have come from someone else's farm? I found two other small Angus herds among the photos, but none in pastures bordering the Tornells' place. Unable to believe my own conclusion, I ran through all the photos again, zooming in on all of those with livestock.

Annalynn came in and watched over my shoulder. "See anything interesting?"

I continued to click through the photos. "Jesse Tornell should never have grazed that many cattle in that pasture. No one else has that low a ratio of animal to acreage for beef cattle. Or even for dairy cattle, who get extra feed when they're milked."

"Which means?"

I swung around to face her. "Dorothy told me several of those animals aren't hers. Vanderhofen says he has all of his. Besides, he owns a different breed. So where did the extra cattle—more precisely, the extra calves—come from?"

She subdued a smile. "And your answer is?"

"Rustling. Maybe even the cattle in that pickup the murdered trooper stopped. Tornell was involved in the rustling."

She lifted her eyes and put her hands together in a gesture of thanks. "Now I know I'm right. Sam Gist said I was jumping to unsubstantiated conclusions."

"Then we'll have to substantiate them." I clicked back to the photo of the cattle. "We need the rustled calves' IDs, ear tags or brands or whatever."

"They had none. As I understand it, you don't need them until you sell an animal or it reaches a certain age."

"Smart to steal the babies. One black calf looks pretty much like another." I peered at the yellow specks. Plastic? "I wonder how hard it is to forge an ear tag."

"Difficult but not impossible. The Missouri Cattle Theft Task Force hasn't found a record of any of the rustled cattle being sold. Typically rustlers steal a truck or livestock trailer and take stolen cattle straight to an auction barn. We know the license on the pickup the trooper's killer was driving was stolen."

"So these rustlers follow part, but not all, of the pattern. Either they've been able to forge tags and papers or are holding the cattle. Fattening up the calves and taking them to market weeks or months later."

"Or building up a herd. Some of the stolen calves have good bloodlines."

I brought up the photos of the Tornell farm. "The Tornells don't have enough land for that. Besides, if Dorothy were involved, she would never have said anything about the extra calves. She worked in the garden; he took care of the beef herd."

"She must have suspected something. Husbands can't hide illegal income from wives all that easily."

Annalynn's had, and I'd buried his secrets. I shut off the monitor and moved toward the hall. "I'm parched. Let's go into our how-and-why theories upstairs over cold drinks."

She turned off the office light. "I squeezed some lemons and made lemonade. I know you hate the frozen concentrates."

"Thanks." Typical Annalynn. "Jesse Tornell doesn't seem like a rustler, but he was desperate for money." I worded my next sentence carefully. "He left a few hundred dollars in the house that Dorothy didn't know about."

Annalynn grabbed my shoulder. "Tell me you know this legally."

"Yes, but she told me in confidence. She needs that money to survive. Please don't go after it unless it becomes essential to the case."

She didn't loosen her grip. "I know you, Phoenix. You have a photographic memory for numbers. You checked the money Spike found for 'counterfeit bills' and you probably pulled the same thing on Dorothy. Did the bills come from the same source?"

Annalynn became more like a cop every day. "Not as far as I could tell."

She dropped her hand. "I wish I could trust you not to withhold information."

"I'll tell you anything you need to know. I swear."

She scowled. "It's your interpretation of what I 'need to know' that bothers me. You're not a spy anymore. Don't act like one." She charged ahead of me.

Chastened by her well-placed criticism, I followed her up the basement stairs and into the kitchen.

She rested her forehead on the refrigerator door. "I'm sorry, Phoenix. Everything is so overwhelming. You go off in your own secretive world sometimes. When we were kids, I knew what you were thinking and feeling. I don't anymore."

"It's okay. We're doing fine. You're reading my mind all too well." I smiled to reassure her as she turned to look at me. "You're handling this case amazingly well. That trooper may be giving you grief, but Spike respects you, and that's a major accomplishment. Which reminds me, he wants to report personally."

"He's on his way over." She took out a pitcher of lemonade. "You haven't told me how Jesse was killed."

"Let's finish with the why first, what you think those photos indicate." I took glasses from the cupboard.

She hesitated. "It's only a theory. When I thought of it, it seemed so logical. Now I'm not sure."

"Spill it!"

"I don't think Jesse Tornell was a rustler. I think he was receiving stolen property, feeding the calves to take to market later when they would bring more and be harder to identify."

"You're brilliant! He may not even have known they were stolen."

Annalynn's smile returned. "But he must have suspected. And at Harry's Monday afternoon, people were talking about rustlers killing the trooper."

I added my nugget: "Dorothy said they had enough

venison. He didn't go to the pond to shoot a deer. He must have been afraid he would be arrested as an accomplice to the trooper's murder. Maybe he called the rustlers to come get the calves and took the rifle to protect himself."

Annalynn poured the lemonade. "But the rifle didn't protect him. Why not?"

Now I was on the spot. "I don't know, but I'm betting the weapon that killed him was a bow and arrow. Dorothy runs a 4-H archery project, so she and practically everyone else out there know how to shoot a bow. Spike says Vandiver County is known for its bow hunters." I constructed a big ham sandwich. Spike was sure to be hungry. "Jesse was standing at the gate when he was shot. How do you sneak up on anyone with a bow four feet long?"

"Perhaps one person talked to him, held his attention, and another shot the arrow."

We took the food and drink to the entertainment room and put it on the petrified wood coffee table in front of the couch.

I took a long drink of lemonade. Delicious. "Another thing: How did he—or more likely they—move the body from the gate to the pond bank without leaving a trail of blood?"

We sat glumly, our exuberance at our findings dampened by the unanswered questions. It was like walking up a mountain in scree; with every step forward, you slid half a step back.

The doorbell rang. Annalynn went to answer it.

When she ushered Spike in, I handed him a glass of lemonade and the sandwich.

"Thanks," he said. "I missed lunch."

Annalynn lingered at the door. "I appreciate the extra

hours you've been putting in. I'm afraid I have to ask you for more."

He nodded. "Sure. I reckon I can hang in there. You can't afford to stop when you're working a big case like this."

"Phoenix, please tell him our latest theory while I make a call."

I summarized the photos and our extrapolation from them while he ate in huge bites, his expression becoming more and more guarded.

When I finished, he swallowed the last bit but remained silent for a long time. Finally he said, "I gotta agree with Captain Gist: The widow miscounted the herd." He shifted uneasily. "Or pretended she did to throw you off."

He thought we were fanciful amateurs. Unfortunately, we needed him. "I respect your skepticism, but you're wrong about Dorothy Tornell. If you'll keep an open mind and work with us, we'll prove it."

He ducked his head.

Annalynn rejoined us. "Spike, you've been tracing Jericho's drug operation. Do you think he, Straw, and Jesse Tornell could be the rustlers?"

"It would make the case a lot simpler if they were. Jericho's the only one still alive, so he would be the murderer. The thing is, he doesn't have any history of violence." Spike brushed some crumbs off his shirt into his hand, deposited them on his plate, and squared his shoulders. "Sheriff, we've got no evidence linking Straw and Jericho to the rustling or the farmer to the marijuana." He stopped again, his forehead knotted. "We gotta keep investigating. Wish we had a couple more people to work on this."

"Amen." Annalynn sat down on the couch. "Both the rustling and the drugs are relatively small-scale operations. From what we've learned, neither would gross more than seventy-five thousand dollars a year. You wouldn't expect either operation to lead to murder."

So she didn't always think like a cop. Spike ducked his head again. Apparently he also found her remark naïve. Or maybe he was just thinking. His brain worked in slow motion.

He raised his head and faced me: "That first murder wasn't premeditated, but the guy Trooper Cansadi stopped knew how to kill, and he didn't stop to think before he did it. I reckon he had a lot more at stake than being caught with five calves." He switched back to Annalynn. "The M-squad guys say he's had special training, like law enforcement, the military, or private security. The way he killed so fast, he's probably got a record."

He'd shared inside information, a sign of loyalty to Annalynn. I went fishing for more. "I've never understood how the M-squad tied the trooper's death to a string of cattle thefts."

Spike smiled. "We got lucky with something left behind."

Annalynn and I both stared at him, waiting.

When he remained silent, she said, "I know your work with the M-squad is confidential, Spike, but two murders took place in our jurisdiction. We need every bit of information available."

He ducked his head a long moment. "Are you ordering me to tell you, Sheriff?"

"Yes. I'll take responsibility."

"Thanks." He leaned forward. "They found a tire track from a pickup and some bits of a special feed blend at a couple of places the rustlers hit, and one or the other at a few others." He straightened to deliver his big clue: "They found the same tire print at the edge of the road where Trooper Cansadi was killed."

Annalynn nodded. "That certainly establishes rustlers killed Trooper Cansadi, but that murder wasn't premeditated. The other two were." She rose and walked to gaze out the French doors into her backyard. "He went to considerable trouble to set those two up, and took huge risks. If someone had driven by…"

"Right," I agreed. "A real risk-taker. He's either an egomaniac or desperate to eliminate anyone who could expose him." Who was that desperate? And that capable? "Jericho is an arrogant bully, but I doubt he has either the skills or the nerve for these killings."

"I'm with you on Jericho," Spike said eagerly. "His daddy has been keeping him out of jail since he was in high school. The DEA says he's set up a penny-ante distribution network for pot at LCC and in a few small towns—Chillicothe, Milan, Trenton, Princeton, Unionville."

I nodded encouragement to keep the flow of information coming.

"I talked to the Putnam County sheriff's department. In early January they picked up him and Straw after a one-car accident on a country road near Unionville. A deputy smelled pot on their clothes but didn't find anything in the car. No charges filed. That's the only report connecting Straw to marijuana in the last four years."

Since the twins were born. "Whoever set Straw up knew he was raising marijuana. He also knew Jesse Tornell was deep in debt. We have to figure out how their lives intersect. And how either one of them intersects with the rustlers. Any suggestions, Spike?"

He blew out his cheeks and fidgeted. "I'll reread my reports on the rustling. It may be something really simple, obvious when we find it. Truth is, a lot of rustlers get away with it."

Something else gnawed at me. "We also need to determine how the shooting at Star Corner relates to the murders."

"Someone was playing with us," Annalynn said, no doubt in her voice.

Spike grinned. "His mistake. He didn't know you were sending Deadeye out there to check that rabid deer story."

I remembered the sound of the bullets. I'd heard them before the shots. That meant a rifle powerful enough to shoot a bullet faster than sound and big enough to be hard to swing and aim through a telescopic sight. Yet the shooter hadn't used a tripod. "I couldn't have hit Vernon's cap at that distance only a fraction of a second after firing at Achilles." Could anyone else? "The shooter could be the one we're after, a marksman with a rifle and a bow. A person who will use whatever is at hand as a weapon. I agree with the M-squad: We're looking for a trained killer."

THIRTY

SPIKE HAD TOLD us what he didn't want to put in writing, so he left for the station to prepare his official report. An hour later he emailed Annalynn his notes on the dates and places of the rustling and of Jericho's sales. The lists had nothing in common.

When I thought Dorothy had finished the milking and eaten supper, I called her and asked for a list of any places her husband had gone in the last six months. His longest trips were to Putnam County to work on Garth Raymo's house, and only once was he gone overnight, staying at her parents' home. She finally dredged up a memory of his having attended a one-day Rural Electric Cooperative meeting. She couldn't think of any new acquaintances during the last year.

"Nothing from Dorothy," I reported to Annalynn, who was working at her computer. Did she need to know that Dorothy found $1,500? I estimated the sales value of the calves in the Tornells' pasture at $2,500 to $3,000. If he were merely feeding them for a rustler, his cut would be maybe a fourth to a half of that. So check the numbers. "Dorothy said Jesse sold their calves weeks ago. We need to know how many he sold in the last two years, when, for how much, and whether he deposited the money."

She swiveled to face me. "You mean find out if he sold stolen calves as his own?"

"Yes. It's worth checking. If he sold a few head more

than usual at the local sale barn, who would pay any attention? He's the ideal fence."

She dialed Spike and asked him to request the information from the Cattle Theft Task Force.

I checked her screen: a list of people who had applied for archery deer hunting permits in Vandiver County in the last two years. When she hung up, I asked, "Any familiar names?"

"Dozens, but not because of this case."

"Any Bulganovs on the list?"

"No, but people don't need permits if they hunt on their own land." She closed the file. "I called the head of the local National Guard to ask if he has any Special Forces veterans. The only one he knows was in Vietnam in the 1960s." She stood up. "I need to think about something else. Tell me about your morning."

I described my new piano and mentioned Connie's upcoming trip to her ex's wedding. I ended with, "Connie will shop for me when she buys clothes for her trip."

"Good. Choosing clothes will give you two an opportunity to bond."

Achilles yawned, and we did the same. It was barely dark, but we all went to bed.

I WOKE UP the next morning to a rare sound—Annalynn's laughter. Pulling on my robe, I hurried downstairs.

Annalynn, a big smile on her face, sat at the dining room table holding the *Laycock Daily Advertiser*.

"What's so funny?"

She handed the paper to me.

The front page featured a large photo of me at fifteen holding a .22 rifle in one hand and a frozen turkey in the other. Two fingers formed a V, representing Satan's horns, behind my head. My younger brother, Quintin, had never been able to resist that joke. Had I really been that young and full of myself? Definitely. The caption read, "Always a sharpshooter, Phoenix Smith used the same deadly aim to win rifle competitions as a teenager and to kill a rabid fox yesterday."

I skimmed the accompanying article, headlined: "Deer Squad Volunteer Shoots Rabid Fox." Vernon told Floyd Vanderhofen's version of how I had rushed over from visiting family friend Dorothy Tornell to save Snowball.

"Your father was so proud when you beat him and all the men." Annalynn pushed back her chair. "I have to get to the office and organize the troops."

"Would you like for me to take a look at the Tornells' cattle?"

"No. I'm going to request a search warrant, but I'm not going to serve it until we have a way to identify the rustled cattle. I don't want to tip off the rustlers." She picked up her holster from a chair and strapped it on. "I'd rather you stay clear of the Tornells and the Bulganovs today and work on that shooting at Star Corner." She walked toward the front door. "Don't go anywhere without telling me."

Another direct order from super-polite Annalynn. "I'll be good." She was afraid I'd muck up the case by doing something illegal, like break into safes or pick locks. No. She was afraid I'd get hurt.

Achilles dropped his leash in my lap to give me notice that he was ready for his morning run. He obviously couldn't tell pajamas from street attire.

"Five minutes," I told him, heading back upstairs to put on my running shoes, shorts, and a T-shirt long enough to cover my holster. The grandfather clock struck seven as I went back downstairs. We had an hour or so before the temperature topped eighty degrees.

I warmed up with a brisk walk while Achilles, unleashed, ran back and forth in front of me. If anyone approached, he rushed to my side. His alertness left me free to be inattentive and rack my brain for a way to carry out my assignment. Coming up blank, I headed toward Vernon Kann's house. As I'd hoped, he was sitting on his front porch reading a newspaper. I strolled up the short semicircular drive, giving myself time to cool down.

"Morning, Vernon. How's the ankle?"

He looked up and smiled. "Better. I'm walking with a cane." He tossed his newspaper onto the table beside him and motioned me to a chair. "I know what you want: twenty-five copies of the paper to send to all your relatives. No need. They can read it on our website."

"They'll react the same way Annalynn did. I haven't heard her laugh like that for a long time." I accepted the chair. "Where did you get that ancient photo?"

He chuckled. "I promised to protect my source."

Had to be Connie. "I just hope my boss in Vienna doesn't see the story."

He ran his hand over his silver hair. "Are you afraid your boss will call you back from medical leave if he knows you're running around the county hunting murderers?"

"Something like that."

"If I promise not to quote you, will you join me for breakfast? Waffles with fresh strawberries and the best coffee in town."

"An offer I can't refuse."

"You hear that, Patty?"

"I heard," a woman answered from inside the front door. "Breakfast will be ready in five minutes."

Vern held a finger to his lips for half a minute or so. He leaned forward. "She eavesdrops." He spoke barely above a whisper. "What are the chances Annalynn is going to solve these two murders?"

"Good. Very good." I trusted reporters as much as I had KGB operatives.

He waited expectantly until he knew I'd say no more. "This kills me, but whatever you tell me about the investigation is off the record."

I hesitated. Every instinct said to keep quiet, but this man could help Annalynn get elected to Congress. "You don't print it. You don't breathe a word of it. Agreed?"

"Agreed." He sighed dramatically.

"We know how and why Tornell was killed. The who we don't know." I stopped.

"I already know it's not Jericho Kittle. I already know young Bulganov saw the killer drive by his house."

Maybe he knew something I didn't. I took a chance. "Annalynn has uncovered information that ties Tornell's death to the murder of the trooper last Saturday."

He kept a poker face but his eyes glittered. "Tornell was involved in rustling?"

He'd confirmed that the reason for the trooper's death had leaked. "We think so. It's going to take a lot of leg-work to prove it. Have you heard anything?"

"Nothing." He leaned back, his face thoughtful. "I'll put both ears to the ground. Don't worry. I won't let drop what I'm looking for."

A well-rounded woman with salt-and-pepper hair and granny glasses hustled out the front door carrying a tray with two plates of waffles, two giant ceramic mugs, a bowl of strawberries, and a small ceramic pitcher. "Morning, Phoenix. Remember me? Patty Wilcox. My Fred was one of the men you outshot for that turkey. I never let him forget it."

Funny what people remember. "I still remind Ulysses, my big brother, occasionally. He came in third."

Achilles bounded onto the porch.

Patty put the tray on the table and reached out to stroke him. "Are you hungry, too, Achilles?"

Apparently Deputy Dog was Celebrity Dog. "He had breakfast with Annalynn." I inhaled the odor of the coffee. "A French morning blend?"

"You have a good nose." Vernon handed me the bowl of strawberries. "Patty, would you please clean up my bedroom right away? It needs vacuuming."

"Sure, Vern." She patted me on the shoulder as she went by on her way inside.

He obviously wanted to give us privacy, but a vacuum running in the bedroom didn't mean Patty would stay there with it. I ladled a mound of strawberries on my oversized waffle and poured hot milk into my coffee. I sipped it. "Excellent."

We ate in silence until we heard the vacuum cleaner at the back of the house.

Vernon leaned close. "Have you talked to Annalynn about running for office?"

"I tried to. She refused to even think about it until she locks up the killers." How much should I say about the depth of her despair? "Maintaining control, that public face, is all she can handle at the moment."

"I can understand that. When my wife died, I… I know how hard it is." He moved his shoulders as though shifting a burden. "This is confidential: I've drafted an editorial urging the county commissioners to extend her temporary appointment from September until the elections in November." He grinned. "As a cost-saving measure."

"Doesn't Missouri law restrict the appointment to thirteen weeks?"

"The lawyers can surely find a way around that, particularly if she solves these murder cases. I need to advance the idea soon to give them time to get a waiver."

"That's a great idea." Annalynn had to know about this. "You have to tell her."

"*I?* Not you?"

"She needs to understand how much others value her."

He nodded. "I trust your judgment on this."

Having the press on your side could be extremely useful. I had an idea. "Could I now become a 'reliable source'?"

He put down his coffee and opened his omnipresent laptop. "Certainly."

"The car that skidded around the corner by Straw Bulganov's house threw up so much dust that he couldn't see the car or the driver."

He studied me. "Is that true?"

If I lied and he caught me, Annalynn would suffer for it. "It could be. No one had a chance to ask him about it." I loaded a strawberry on a bite of waffle. "What's important is that the killer doesn't think Tammy Kay or the kids can ID the driver."

"My God!" He ran his hand back over his silver hair. "I'll work it in with what I got from other sources and put it on the paper's website as breaking news this morning. It'll run on the front page tomorrow."

"Thanks. Have you come up with any theory about the shots fired at Star Corner?"

"No, but they must be connected to the murders." He started to type. "Forgive me, Phoenix, but I have to write this while the lead is in my head."

I finished my waffle as he typed. He barely looked up when I pushed back my chair and said goodbye.

When I reached Annalynn's house a little before nine, Connie's car sat in the driveway.

She met me at the front door, her normally sunny face grim. "You had an urgent phone call." She held a pad of paper in one hand and a measuring tape in the other.

"From whom?"

"Reginald. He had to run to catch a plane so I took a message."

He must have said something about the New York job offer. "Thanks." I waited, but she stared at me without saying anything. A silent Connie spelled trouble. "What's the message?"

"He's flying to New York Monday for meetings on organizing the new branch. He's made plane and hotel reservations for you. You 'simply must' meet him for breakfast Tuesday and talk over your new duties."

"Bloody hell!" With everything that had been going on, I'd not given Reg's offer serious thought. A rationalization. I'd not wanted to think about my future.

She put her hands on her hips and glared at me. "Why didn't you tell me about this yesterday when you asked me to shop for you?"

"I didn't know about these meetings." Holding back now would make it worse. "He called three days ago and offered me a job in New York starting in September. He asked for my decision by next Friday."

She turned and walked down the hallway to the window seat. Her back to me, she said, "What did Annalynn say?"

"I didn't tell her."

"Coward," she spat out. "Were you planning to walk out and leave her a note?"

I wanted to slap her. "You know I would never do that to Annalynn. Calm down so we can talk about this like reasonable people."

"Reasonable? Like you?" She whirled around to face me. "Annalynn pretends she's fine, but she's as breakable as her antique Wedgwood. She relies on you, and I don't mean for these awful murder investigations."

Her assumption of my callousness infuriated me. "I know better than you how fragile she is. That's one reason I didn't tell her about the job. It's a unique opportunity, for your information, and I won't get another like it. I have to consider what's best for both of us." My anger cooled, but I struck out anyway. "Maybe she would like to move to New York with me."

Connie shook her head so hard her blond curls appeared ready to fly off. "She would never leave Laycock, never leave this house."

True. "In any case, I won't upset her by discussing my future while she's putting every ounce of her energy into being sheriff. I want your promise that you won't either."

She sat down on the window seat. "Today's Friday. You leave Monday morning. Can the Great Phoenix fix the world by then? Catch the murderers? Demolish Annalynn's inner demons? Find something besides a tank top to wear?"

The re-emergence of her sense of humor told me she

was coming out of her funk. "The Great Phoenix could use your help."

She glared rather than smiled. "This is no joking matter."

"I'm not joking. For Annalynn's sake—for all our sakes—we have to work together." I perched on the window seat beside Connie. "If I can't get out of going to New York Monday, I'll tell Annalynn about the job offer and ask her to help me decide what to do."

Connie jumped up and walked toward the front door. "You know damned well she'll tell you to do whatever you want to do."

"You're right." Thoughts that had been swimming around in my subconscious surfaced. I couldn't bring myself to lay them out before Connie, but I said, "I'll turn down the job if Annalynn decides to run."

Connie hesitated, hand on the doorknob. "Annalynn refuses to look beyond this murder investigation."

"She can't focus on more than one day at a time. She functions because of her sense of duty." I had Connie's attention. "She's doing a great job. She figured out why Jesse Tornell died."

Connie raised a skeptical eyebrow. "You want her to run for sheriff."

"No, for Congress."

Connie's mouth dropped open. For once, her tongue didn't move. She walked toward me slowly. "You'll risk your sure thing in New York for Annalynn's long-shot chance at Washington?"

"Yes. If that's still her dream and she's willing to go for it."

Connie held out her right hand and let the cloth tape

measure in it unroll to its full five feet. "First, we'll measure you for some big-shot clothes. Second, we'll crack the case."

THIRTY-ONE

THE BODY MEASUREMENTS took ten minutes, with most of that spent arguing over whether I should shed my shorts and T-shirt for greater accuracy. I wasn't modest. I couldn't chance Connie realizing the web of scars beneath my ribs didn't come from gall bladder surgery.

"I can't possibly find all those clothes," Connie said after I'd spelled out what I needed. "I sing at weddings tonight and tomorrow and a wedding anniversary Sunday."

"We have no choice. I have *nothing* I can wear to business meetings or evening social events. Come on. Be creative. What would you do if your stage wardrobe burned up the day before you opened? You have an unlimited budget."

She snapped her fingers. "Got it! We order everything you need on the Web from top boutiques. They'll do quick alterations and deliver the clothes to your hotel."

"Great solution. Thanks." I relaxed. "Start with Saks. I bought a cocktail gown there a couple of years ago and it may still be in their records. We'll order three sizes of each piece to increase the odds of a good fit. How about you shop on Annalynn's computer while I use my laptop to see if my office emailed me any details."

I went to my bedroom to go online. Sitting on the bed and propping the laptop on my legs, I skimmed a long email and an even longer attachment. I'd hoped to discover Reg didn't need me for the meetings any more than he had for the Szabo account. That hope vanished when I studied the agenda. Regardless of whether I accepted the job, I owed it to my employer to advise on two major issues. I emailed that I'd be there.

Connie bustled in. "I can solve your tank-top problem. Can you solve the murders?"

"No, but maybe Annalynn can." Letting Connie in on it now would save nagging later. "Strictly between us: If she's right, the rustlers—the ones who killed that trooper—hired Jesse Tornell to feed stolen calves and then killed him to keep him quiet."

"Geez, Phoenix, that sounds really far-fetched." Connie leaned over to see my screen. She wrinkled her nose at the sight of the spreadsheet there. "I need more details on what you like, your credit card number, and the name of the hotel."

"I don't know the hotel yet." I downloaded the material and shut off the computer. "Annalynn asked me to work on the Star Corner shooting. I need to drive out there to look around again before the sun gets any hotter."

"I'll come with you. We can talk about your wardrobe and the case in the car."

"Okay." No escaping it. "Would you please grab some bottled water from the refrigerator and call Achilles while I put on hunting clothes?" When she left, I changed into jeans and a white top and strapped on my holster. What I really needed was a hunting rifle that approximated the shooter's weapon. I dialed Annalynn's direct number and asked for what the department might have: a 270 with a 4X scope and forty rounds of ammunition.

"I'll have everything waiting for *Reserve Deputy* Smith in the public area in ten minutes," she said. "Hold on a moment." She came back on the line in a couple minutes. "Jesse Tornell sold six calves at a livestock auction in Chillicothe in late April for seventeen hundred dollars and fifteen calves and heifers at the Macon County sale barn in late May for six thousand, six hundred dollars. We won't be able to trace the money until at least Monday. The Cattle Theft investigator is contacting area sale barns to see what other sales Tornell has made over the last two years. What do you think?"

"That we're on the right track." Odds were that Jesse Tornell received $100 for each of fifteen stolen animals he sold in May. I might have to tell Annalynn Dorothy had found $1,500, but not yet. "We need to know how much, if any, of each payment he deposited. The higher his percentage, the likelier it is he took part in the actual rustling."

Someone spoke in the background, and Annalynn said, "We're doing the paperwork now. I have to go. Call me when you get back from Star Corner."

I pocketed my card identifying me as a reserve officer and went down to meet Connie and Achilles.

DURING THE DRIVE to Star Corner, Connie kept me occupied answering questions about the image I wanted to project, the other cast members, and the probable sets and lighting.

The sight of black Angus grazing on a hillside brought me back to the present. I pulled over to the side of the road halfway down a long hill. "Connie, would you please get the binoculars out of my glove compartment."

"Don't tell me you see a deranged deer in the field."

"No, targets for rustlers." Using the binoculars, I counted twenty calves among about fifty heifers and cows, just the right mix for the rustlers. "If you wanted to steal half of those calves, how would you do it?"

"I'd back a truck up to the fence, cut the wire, run a ramp from the field into the truck bed, and make a trail of whatever calves love to eat."

Not a bad guess. "Close. Rustlers hope the owner won't discover cattle are missing for a few days—until after they're sold. If you cut the fence, the owner would notice right away and start counting." I looked for a gate but saw none. "If you can find a gate, you can drive in, load up, and leave with no one the wiser."

"Annalynn said rustlers haven't stolen cattle in this county."

"So far as the police know." I handed her the binoculars and pulled back out into the road. "Maybe other places they've hit are getting too risky. Besides, Missouri is second only to Texas in the number of cattle. Plenty of choices."

Connie raised the binoculars. "I don't see any other roads. Didn't you tell me that the rustling and the murders took place near crossroads?"

"We're close to Star Corner." My mind raced. "That call about the rabid deer came in approximately four hours after Annalynn's press conference announcing the deer squad. The shooter had to already know Star Corner would be a good place to shoot and run. It's a good bet he'd scouted it for rustling."

Connie reached between the seats to pet Achilles. "He was on TV standing guard over Annalynn. If he'd been killed, she'd have switched her focus to that."

And so would I. "The problem with that theory is that no one knew Achilles would be here." I remembered

Spike's characterization of the person who garroted the trooper: "He didn't plan to kill but didn't hesitate to do it."

We topped the long hill leading down to Star Corner.

Connie raised the binoculars. "More of those black cattle. A lot of calves. And a gate halfway down the hill."

I pulled over by it. Padlocked. No problem for a thief.

Connie surveyed the landscape. "There's a track into the pasture and a fence—a corral—by the creek." She handed me the glasses. "Here, eagle eye."

I refocused the binoculars. "A corral with a loading chute. Rustlers' heaven."

"Are *you* going to crawl through the fence and hike over there to look at it?"

"No need. I can see enough from here. I came out here to duplicate the shooter's shots. That will indicate how good a marksman he is and whether he intended to kill Vernon." I drove on and turned left onto the road running up to the shooter's post.

Agitated, Achilles barked in my right ear.

I put my hand back to scratch under his snout. "It's okay, boy. No bad guys here today."

Connie scanned the fields by the gravel road. "You don't know that."

Ignoring her, I parked next to the open gate. "He shot from that grove. Want to come?"

"No, but I want to stay here alone even less." She opened her car door. "Really, Phoenix, you've got to teach me how to use a gun."

I said nothing.

Achilles propelled himself over the front seat to follow her out of the car. He ran into the pasture and sniffed the air. Satisfied, he trotted back to the car.

The rifle case was disconcertingly heavy. I wouldn't

have noticed the weight before my surgery, but lifting it from the trunk reminded me that I was far from healed.

"I'll take the gun. You take the binoculars." Connie exchanged burdens with me. "Three months after your gall bladder surgery and you're still wincing whenever you lift anything heavier than a gallon of milk. Why won't you go to a doctor?"

"I'm healing right on schedule." Ahead of what the doctors had expected, considering the severity of my injury.

We walked to the grove and the fallen tree where the shooter had rested his rifle. The shade offered welcome relief from the sun now overhead.

I'd seen no one on the roads or in the fields Tuesday, and I saw no one today. I removed the rifle from its case, loaded it, and crouched behind the trunk. With my naked eye I could see where Achilles had dropped. With the scope, I spotted where Gillian had dug out the bullet.

I found two pairs of earplugs in the case and handed one to Connie. "This is going to be loud, and the shell casings are going to fly. You and Achilles need to be ten feet away. He'll be farther away than that after the first shot."

"What are you going to shoot? I'll watch the target through the binoculars."

"Leaves on that little tree by the creek." The bullets would lodge in the roadside bank by the culvert.

I took aim and fired five shots before I got the feel of the gun and conditions and hit my tiny target. Shooting off an antler wouldn't be terribly difficult with a weapon like this. The shooter and Tornell's murderer could well be the same man.

"I don't understand why you're shooting an innocent tree," Connie said.

"I'm seeing how far the bullet drops at that distance before I aim at the shooter's targets. I may be able to tell whether he hit Vernon's cap because of marksmanship or luck." I turned the rifle to the spot where Achilles had stood and then swung it uphill to the left to where I estimated Vernon had been. A tricky shot. The shooter's second bullet had hit more than fifteen feet away and eight feet higher. I chose a tall weed near that spot as my second target.

"Connie, sometime in the next thirty seconds, say, 'Now.'"

I'd barely got my first target in my sight when she gave me the signal. I fired at the two targets as fast as I could. I added a hole just above where Achilles had stood. The weed stood untouched. "Again."

I tried three times. The weed still waved. Then I aimed only at the weed. Clipped it off in one shot. Hitting Vernon's cap required luck as well as skill. "Vernon wasn't a serious target. But the shooter certainly intended to kill Achilles."

"Perhaps, Sherlock," Connie said with a British accent, "the killer was afraid Achilles would sniff him out."

I considered that. "The wind was blowing the wrong way."

"I mean from when he tracked Jesse Tornell. Achilles must have picked up the killer's scent, too."

I flashed back to the murder scene. "I asked Achilles to follow Tornell's trail—only Tornell's. Achilles must have noticed another scent, but I didn't ask him to follow it. I doubt he would recognize it a day later. Even if he did, he wouldn't know it was the killer's scent. Or be able to tell us if he did."

Connie shrugged. "Too bad the killer didn't know that."

THIRTY-TWO

WHEN WE GOT back to town, Connie hurried off to give a voice lesson and I left Annalynn a message with my—and Connie's—conclusions and then dug into updating information for the meetings in New York. About four o'clock a combination of fatigue and boredom put me to sleep. The sound of the front door closing woke me a little after six. Recognizing Annalynn's step, I washed the sleep from my eyes and went downstairs.

She was in the kitchen making tossed salad to go with a take-out Canadian bacon pizza, a food she'd loved as a kid and refused to eat as an adult.

"Smells good," I said, taking out plates and bowls. "Any new developments?"

Her face tired but relaxed, she said, "Jesse Tornell sold four bull calves a year ago May and six heifers last August. His sales were about the same the year before." She filled our salad bowls. "The Cattle Theft Task Force investigator agrees with us that Tornell's murder, and Straw Bulganov's, may be related to the trooper's murder and is tracing the animals and the money."

She acted casual, but her voice held triumph.

"Congratulations," I said. "You'll wrap this up in a few days." Preferably before I left for New York on Monday.

"It may take weeks, but we'll find the evidence." She put pizza on our plates. "I'll be working with a team going through information tonight and all day tomorrow. I'm going back to the office in a few minutes." She picked up the plates. "Would you mind representing the department at the Tornell funeral tomorrow afternoon?"

I followed her into the dining room with the salads. "Of course I'll go." A good place to pick up more neighbors' ideas about both killings.

"I'd like for you to go out early and check the cemetery for any sign of rabid animals." She smiled. "That gives you a reason to carry your gun." She pointed to a file on the table. "I brought home a duplicate folder on the rustling for you to look at tonight. Or do you have something else to do?"

I had to tell her about the trip. "A little work from the office. Reg emailed me some files today. He's coming to New York for meetings next week and needs my input." I took a big bite of pizza and chewed it thoroughly.

Annalynn asked absently, "You're writing a briefing for him?"

Get it over with. "I'm afraid it's not that easy." I met her eyes, making every effort to look matter of fact. "I have to fly to New York Monday." I saw her shoulders pull back, a sign of tension. "Sorry to leave while you're wrapping up the case, but I'm still officially on the payroll, and I owe it to Reg and the company."

She sat completely still for several seconds. "When will you be back?"

"I'm not sure. Wednesday night or Thursday afternoon."

She relaxed and took a bite of salad.

Achilles trotted in from the kitchen and stood at the corner of the table between us, his eyes going back and forth and his good ear on the alert.

He was going to be a problem. "I'll ask Connie to check on Achilles a couple of times a day while I'm gone."

"No, he'll be too upset to stay here alone. I'll take him to the office with me."

Good. They would support each other. He was amazingly attuned to her moods. "I'll call during breaks. It will help for him to hear my voice."

She cut off a bit of pizza. "It's only a couple of days. He'll be fine without you."

We both knew she was speaking of herself as well as Achilles.

THE FOLDER YIELDED little new information on the cattle thefts that law enforcement officers in Kansas, Iowa, Illinois, and Missouri had tied together. I flipped through it and then picked up the *Laycock Daily Advertiser* and skimmed its twelve pages. Jesse Tornell's obituary caught my eye. His only sibling was an older brother living in Unionville. He and his two sons from Chicago were serving as pallbearers. The other three were neighbors, the only one I knew being Bob Bulganov. The rustlers had to be people the victim knew, so I googled the pallbearers.

Only Bob's name popped up: "Bulganov Addresses Cattlemen's Meeting in St. Joseph." A short article in a farm magazine from last October reported he spoke on computer tracking of feed and production for dairy cows. Beside it was a photo of Bob towering over a man in the front row: Garth Raymo. I'd had the impression that Garth knew none of the Bulganovs except Straw. Nan definitely hadn't known Garth, and Dorothy had said he'd asked her where the Bulganovs lived. I studied the picture. Both men were frowning as though they'd locked horns. I doubted that Nan had solicited Bob's opinion before she decided to test the NutriDairy product on their herds. No wonder he sided with Tammy Kay.

I needed a break. Maybe a little Mozart. I glanced out the window and reconsidered. Still enough light for a game of catch. Achilles was napping with his nose on my left foot. He'd shown signs of insecurity since the Star Corner shooting. I needed to reassure him that I wasn't going to desert him—before I deserted him.

"Achilles, get your ball," I said. "Let's play."

He jumped up and darted away. A moment later he raced back with a yellow tennis ball in his mouth.

We went out to the backyard through the French doors. Dark clouds were rolling in, and the air was so thick with moisture that I couldn't get any distance on my throws. We played the mindless game until the first distant rumble. Achilles raced into the house.

I'd barely locked the doors when my cell phone rang. Tommy Ray.

"I know you told the newspaper that stuff about the dust making the car invisible to protect Tammy Kay and the boys," he said when I answered. "Thank you."

"They still need to be very careful."

"I know. I got a big tip, but you got to swear you won't say I told you."

Better to swear than to pay for information. "I swear."

"I heard—I can't say where—the car was an old green Corolla, a rental car. The driver wore a baseball cap and sunglasses." He hung up.

My pulse raced. My asset had come through with a real lead. All Annalynn had to do was check rental agencies to see who had rented an old Corolla. I started to dial her and stopped. Rental companies carry new models, not old ones. Not always. Connie and I had rented an older model from a used car dealer when we'd gone undercover in May. We'd had to. No place within seventy miles had a car rental agency. And you had to pay with a credit card. This guy was too smart to leave a paper trail. I'd bet he hadn't. But how would he avoid it? The same way I would. I dialed Annalynn's direct number. It rang five times.

"Hi, Phoenix," Spike said. "Annalynn asked me to take a message."

I hesitated. I wanted her to have full credit for the lead, but it couldn't wait. "Could you please check to see if Clunkers on Call reported the theft of an old green Corolla sometime Monday?"

A long pause. "Does this have something to do with Tornell's death?"

"Yes. Don't say anything to anyone until you've checked."

Another long pause. "Right. I'll call you back in five."

I paced as I waited. If the killer was local, he might have talked to Tornell at Harry's Hideaway early that afternoon. We'd need to check the list of people who had seen Tornell in the sports bar again.

The telephone rang the double ring. "Touchdown!" Spike shouted. "Clunkers reported a green 2003 Corolla missing at seven Monday evening. The student who rented it for the weekend claimed he left it on the street outside the dealership about two o'clock. He put the keys under the seat." Spike took a deep breath. "Get this: Michael Moniteau cruised the area. He found the car parked a block over. They figured the kid just parked it in the wrong place."

We had him! "Tornell's killer drove that car. Let's hope he left his prints on it."

THIRTY-THREE

"I FIGURE THIS guy's too smart to leave prints in the car," Spike said. "What did Tammy Kay tell you about the people in the car?"

I smiled. He wanted me to reveal my informant. "I can't name my source, but it wasn't Tammy Kay. The driver was alone. He wore a baseball cap and sunglasses." I thought a moment. "Even if he managed to wipe away all his fingerprints, he might have missed cleaning up some blood from the weapon or his clothes."

"Right. I'll tell Sheriff Keyser." He hung up.

The doorbell rang, and when I went into the hall, Achilles sat posed to shake hands. He did that only for Connie. I opened the door.

She thrust a big plastic bag at me. "I found you a funeral outfit at a consignment shop in Moberly."

"Thank you. I hadn't thought about what I'd wear to that." I looked in the bag at a gauzy calf-length Indian skirt, black with green tendrils sprouting small peach-colored blossoms, and a peach-colored short-sleeved cotton blouse with black trim around the boat neck. I hadn't worn anything like that since my teens.

"It suits you," Connie said. "You'll see when you put it on. Anything new?"

"Yes, we got a big lead." Telling her about it would delay my modeling the outfit. Maybe forever. I led her into the entertainment room and told her about my anonymous tip.

Connie fingered a turquoise earring that matched her snug spaghetti-strap dress. "Amazing what you can get for a bottle of Coors."

Her perception surprised me. "A bottle of Coors had nothing to do with it."

"Then you won't mind if I tell Trudy it was Tommy Ray."

Trapped. "Keep your guesses to yourself, please."

She grinned. "For a bottle of a good French wine, I won't even tell Annalynn."

"Deal."

She sobered. "I can see how the car can be valuable evidence when you catch the guy, but I don't see how it's going to lead Annalynn to him." She removed her earrings. "Last time we solved a murder we made out a timeline. Why don't we try that again?"

"Not a timeline, but organizing some facts may help. I'll get my laptop."

"Put on the new outfit first. I'm going to raid the kitchen."

I took the clothes upstairs, slipped them on, and inspected myself in the closet's full-length mirror. I looked good. Not appropriate for New York, but fine for a funeral at a country church. Connie had a good eye. I changed back into my shorts and tank top, grabbed everything I needed, and returned to the entertainment room.

Connie had cleared the coffee table of everything but a plate with Camembert, little crackers, and carrot and celery sticks.

I handed her a couple of hundreds. "The outfit works—

not too simple, not too fancy. Here's some cash for it and anything else you may see."

"Thanks." She kicked off her stiletto heels. "What are we looking for?"

"Something to tie together the rustlers, Jesse Tornell, and Straw and Jericho's drug business. Let's set up a file in four columns. I'll get the case folders."

As I retrieved the folders from Annalynn's desk, the phone rang twice.

Annalynn, and she wasted no time: "Phoenix, how did you identify the car?"

A slight echo told me she was on a speakerphone. The team was listening. "An anonymous caller told me what Straw saw. I rented a similar model from Clunkers on Call, which puts its logo on a magnetic sticker on the back bumper. The odds favored the killer stealing it the way he stole a scooter to use at Star Corner."

"We need the caller's name," Annalynn persisted. "Was it Tammy Kay Bulganov?"

"No. The caller didn't give a name." Completely true. "Forget the tipster and check the tip. Test the car and make sure it's the right one."

"Dr. Smith," Spike said, "as a reserve officer it's your duty to name your source."

Which might endanger Tommy Ray and definitely would discourage him from telling me anything else. "I've told you everything I can." I hung up. "*Scheisse!*"

Connie appeared at the door. "What's wrong?"

"I refused to tell Annalynn's colleagues who tipped me off. I'm afraid they'll think it was Tammy Kay and bring her in for questioning. That could give her mother-in-law an excuse to claim the twins."

"Don't worry. Annalynn will protect Tammy Kay

from the wicked grandmother." Connie smiled. "You're a nut with a hard shell and a marshmallow filling."

My business associates would deny that. "Let's get started."

We settled down in the entertainment room. I opened the folder on the rustlers and flipped through the printouts. "They linked certain cattle thefts—always calves—early this spring, but the rustling started last September, probably earlier."

"If the thefts took place in different states, how did the cops connect them and the trooper's murder?"

"Primarily the tire tread and the feed used as a lure. Crossing county and state lines to sell rustled cattle has become so common that jurisdictions are sharing information." I kept reading. "A Kansas sheriff captured the tire tread, a deputy in Illinois tested the grain, and an Iowa sheriff found the grain and the tread in the same place. The Highway Patrol found the tread on the shoulder by the trooper's body." I read off the dates of the thefts' discovery, which often came days after the thefts. Only the last three, March 10, May 16, and June 22, could relate to Jesse Tornell's cattle sales and murder. Connie put those in both his and the rustlers' columns. Then we put the dates and places Tornell had sold animals in his column.

I opened the marijuana folder. "If we can find the link between the rustlers and Jericho's pot operation, we'll know where to look for the killer." Arrests for drunken driving and minor drug possession went back to Jericho and Straw's high school years. Jericho had never served time. Straw had served a short sentence and mandatory rehabilitation for meth possession and distribution. Tommy Ray had been arrested with them once five years ago for smoking pot but served no time.

I focused on the reports for the last year, noting particularly the places where Jericho had advertised his "handyman services."

"Dozens of people knew Jericho was selling pot," Connie said as she typed those towns into our chart. "He probably bragged that he and Straw were growing it."

"Even if we get names, we can't check all the buyers out." I skimmed the Putnam County sheriff's accident report that Spike had mentioned. "Put down 'suspicion of using pot, January ninth, near Unionville.' Nothing hints they were rustlers."

Connie got up to pace back and forth, pirouetting each time she reached the end of the room. "You keep saying rustlers, but one person shot at you and one person drove the rental car past the Bulganovs."

A valid point. "I assumed it took two to move Jesse Tornell's body and to load those skittish calves."

"He didn't need to load the whole herd. Just the ones he could catch fast. Maybe he put the body in a wheelbarrow." She rubbed her neck with her right hand. "Sorry, but I'm beat. You don't look so great yourself. Could we order the clothes early tomorrow?"

"Sure. Breakfast at seven thirty." Connie could serve as a buffer if Annalynn was angry about me not naming my source.

After I let Connie out, I went back to the laptop to copy what we had to another file and add Jesse Tornell's off-the-book payments. I arranged them in chronological order with the calf sales hoping the figures would tell me something.

1/14:	Garth Raymo	$175
3/10:	First Baptist	$75
4/16:	V. Bulganov	$1050
4/20:	calves-Chillicothe	$1700
5/16:	Harry's Hideaway	$200
5/24:	calves-MaconCty.	$6,600—source of $1,500?
6/4:	Garth Raymo	?

Tornell had left the amount off the last note. Raymo had mentioned Tornell had worked for him in June. Dorothy hadn't. Garth had first hired Jesse January fourteenth after Jericho and Straw had done a lousy job a few days earlier. Perhaps smoking marijuana on their way to Raymo's farm accounted for their bad work. Or not. Dorothy had said Straw didn't show up to work on his father's barn, and Tammy Kay said he hadn't mastered a screwdriver.

Achilles dropped his ball on my delete key.

"It's dark and wet outside," I protested as I hit Undo. He whined and put his nose on my knee.

"Okay. You've been a very good dog." I saved the file. "We'll play fetch in the basement for a few minutes."

Annalynn never played fetch. Would she toss a saliva-saturated tennis ball for him while I talked about venture capital in New York?

ANNALYNN DIDN'T WAKE me when she came home. I woke to the smell of coffee at seven the next morning. Saturday. Wearing my last clean tank top and shorts, I went downstairs to the kitchen.

"Bowl, Achilles," Annalynn said. "Please put your ball in the bowl."

He looked at the red plastic bowl she held in front of him and then at her.

I took the ball from him and dropped it in the bowl. "Ball in bowl," I said. "Please." I took it out of the bowl, gave it back to him, and repeated the command. The third time around he figured out the new game.

Annalynn and I both lavished praise on him, but when she put the bowl with the ball on the floor by his water dish, he grabbed the ball and trotted away.

Annalynn laughed. "He's as independent as you are. What's the real reason you wouldn't admit Tammy Kay told you about the car?"

I washed the drool off my hands in the sink. "Because she didn't."

"Then she told Bob Bulganov."

"Good guess, but wrong. I suspect the information originated with Jericho Kittle. He wants the killer caught to avenge Straw and to protect himself."

"Okay." Annalynn sipped her coffee, her eyes on my face. "I called Tammy Kay to express my sympathy. She claimed she didn't know anything about the marijuana. She didn't go out to the shed because she's afraid of snakes and spiders."

"That sounds credible." When Annalynn cocked her head skeptically, I added, "Do you really want to challenge her?"

"You know I don't, but I need the facts. You understand 'need to know.'"

Point taken. "You need to know she was against him using. She's scared, for herself and her boys. She'd have told me if she knew anything else that would help identify who killed Straw." I opened the refrigerator. "Connie's coming for breakfast in about five minutes. I'm going to make a giant western omelet." I extracted eggs, ham, green peppers, onions, milk. "Did you find prints or blood in the car?"

"Only an employee's prints on the steering wheel and front door. The magic spray showed flecks of blood in the trunk. We won't be able to verify it was Jesse Tornell's blood for ages, if ever." She took plates from the cupboard. "We've asked for all records of car rentals for the last two years. Whoever stole the Corolla knows how the place operates."

"Yes, but he couldn't have known someone would leave a car on the street that afternoon." I thought of a time when I'd been desperate for a car. "How difficult would it be to hotwire one of the clunkers and drive it away without being seen?"

"I have no idea. Is that what you would have done?"

"In an emergency. I prefer renting, using a disguise and a false identity, but that takes time to set up. You can steal most cars in a minute or two." I chopped up the pepper and onion. "Does the dealer keep his clunkers parked on the street?"

"Yes." She pressed her lips together, her face disconsolate. "They all have that gaudy Clunkers on Call sign on the bumper. Anyone driving by could have seen it."

The doorbell rang and she went to open the door. She and Connie chatted about Connie's weekend engagements as I prepared and served the omelet. Annalynn laughed as Connie told of a sixtieth wedding anniversary party at which the groom repeatedly asked her to sing "Jeanie with the Light Brown Hair." She didn't have the music, so she turned him down each time. At the end of the evening, his wife slipped her an extra five dollars. A woman watching whispered to Connie that the wife's name was Mabel.

Connie went from one story to another, and we listened, laughed, and ate. A momentary return to normality.

A vehicle parked out front. Achilles barked and ran to the dining room window.

"FedEx," Annalynn said. "That must be your airplane ticket, Phoenix." She began to clear the table.

I answered the door and signed for a surprisingly thick envelope. I ripped it open as I walked back to the table and extracted two airplane tickets. Reg had expected Annalynn to come with me and decorate the dinner table, where I was often the only woman. "Anyone want to go to New York Monday?"

"You already know I can't," Annalynn said from the kitchen.

Connie reached for a ticket. "For real?"

"Of course. You could shop for me and for your wedding outfit."

Connie gasped. "Phoenix, these are first-class seats."

"Tax deductible," I pointed out. "The company will list you as my personal assistant."

Connie pressed the ticket to her heart. "What's our hotel?"

I looked at the schedule. "The Plaza." Not my favorite, but a good location.

"Wow!" Connie pirouetted around the dining room. "I always wanted to stay at the Plaza. I'll send my girls postcards from there. From a trip with my new business manager." She danced into the kitchen. "We can turn in this first-class ticket for two coach tickets. Won't you please come, Annalynn?"

Annalynn smiled. "Another time."

"Of course," Connie said. "If Phoenix takes the job, you'll be going to New York to see her all the time."

Annalynn drew back, her face pinched. "What job?"

Connie whirled to face me. "You said you'd told her."

"About the trip, not the job offer." I hadn't prepared for this. "Come sit down. Both of you. We have to talk."

Annalynn, the most graceful of women, walked to her chair like a battery-operated mannequin. She wasn't ready to solo yet.

I took her left hand in both of mine. "This is a planning meeting for a new branch the company is opening in New York this fall. Reg has offered me a senior position there. He gave me until Friday to give him my decision."

Connie sat across from me, huddled in her chair. "She hasn't decided, Annalynn."

Public face now in place, Annalynn said, "They value you, Phoenix. They'll give you everything you want. Congratulations."

If only I'd had time to select the right words. "You know that's never true. We never get everything we want. What's crucial is knowing what we value most."

Connie bounced in her chair. "You sound like a fortune cookie."

Annalynn pulled her hand free. "Get to the point, Phoenix. I'm already late."

"Here it is. My life has had some big holes in it, but I turned my dream into reality. I need something new to want. You've raised two great kids and made Laycock a better place to live, but you haven't achieved your dream."

Connie threw her hands in the air. "Oh, for God's sake, Phoenix. You're not Chekhov." She leaned toward Annalynn. "If you'll run for Congress, Phoenix will stay here and help us run the campaign. What do you say?"

Annalynn pushed back her chair and stood. "I liked it better when you two didn't gang up on me."

THIRTY-FOUR

"SHE WON'T LET you 'sacrifice' for her," Connie said when Annalynn left. "You blew it big. What do we do now?"

At least she said "we," not "you." I reflected only a second: "Bring in reinforcements—namely Vernon." I handed Connie the packet. "Go through the schedule to see if I need anything we didn't talk about while I call him. Please." I went to the hall phone without waiting for an answer.

The phone rang as I reached for it. "Keyser residence."

"Good morning, Phoenix," Vernon said. "Could I speak to the sheriff?"

"She left for the office a couple of minutes ago."

"You'll do. I called to verify that Jesse Tornell's killer stole one of Clunkers on Call's cars."

Vernon knew his trade. "I doubt *anyone* can verify that." Enough information. "I was just about to dial your number. I'm going to New York on a short business trip Monday. It may be a good time for you to discuss politics with Annalynn."

"I'll do that." He paused. "I hope this trip is a one-time thing."

Never give a reporter anything concrete if you can avoid it. But she needed his help. I settled for, "If she decides to run, I'll be delighted to work on the campaign."

"Good. Call me before you leave. Bye."

Achilles nudged me with his ball. I took it and called, "Connie, I have to take Achilles out for a few minutes."

She didn't look up from the schedule. "Okay, but make it fast. You need as many wardrobe changes as the lead in a three-act play. We have to get right on it."

Achilles led the way to the backyard. The grass was soaking wet, and the cloudy sky promised more rain.

After twenty minutes of playing fetch and his version of hide and seek (he always found me much quicker than I found him), I went back inside to see what clothes Connie recommended. By the time she left to sing at a wedding, we'd ordered ten suits and dresses to be delivered to the Plaza Monday. I expected to find at least three acceptable ones among these.

Once alone, I emailed an old CIA friend to send to the Plaza a small disassembled pistol, a lipstick camera, and a ballpoint dagger. Whether in New York, Washington, or Laycock, I wanted the tools of my trade.

I wished I had them after lunch as I put the Glock 27 in my leather purse. A holster didn't go with my vintage outfit or with a funeral. The rain hadn't yet arrived, but the humidity reminded me of what I liked about Vienna's summers. I groused as I put on hose and heels for the first time in weeks. After decades of dressing for success in my day job and obscurity in my spy work, Laycock had been a wardrobe vacation.

The front door opened. "Phoenix," Annalynn called, "where are you?"

"In my room." I rolled up a pair of jeans and a T-shirt and stuck them in a plastic bag with socks and running shoes. If I had to chase a rabid animal through the fields, I wanted suitable attire.

"You look nice," Annalynn said from my bedroom

door. "More than that, you look—young. Investigating agrees with you."

"And you." Less tension along her jaw, less pain in her eyes. "Did you come to pick up Achilles?"

"Yes, and to leave you my SUV. You need a radio. Besides, I want to talk to you." She leaned against the doorframe. "Much as I want you to stay in Laycock, I won't let you push me into running for sheriff or Congress."

She was reprimanding me. For a moment I was hurt. Then I realized that she'd declared her independence and liberated me. I smiled. "Good for you. No one but you should make your decisions." I sobered. "Are you saying you won't run?"

"No." She stared at the grandfather clock against the far wall of the bedroom. "I'm saying that I have to decide what's best for me, and you have to decide what's best for you." Her eyes bored into mine. "If you don't know whether you want that high-powered job in New York, don't use helping me as an excuse to turn it down."

"*Touché.*" I'd always been a decisive person, but in this instance I'd procrastinated, avoided thinking about the pros and cons of the job and concentrated on the murder case and Annalynn's future. "We both have a decision to make."

ON THE WAY out of town, I bought a miniature red rose bush that Dorothy could keep in the house or plant outside and signed my and Annalynn's names to a pedestrian sympathy card.

Driving the familiar road, I thought about earlier trips on it. Monday evening, only five days ago, Annalynn and I had arrived around nine, less than five hours after the killer had jammed an antler in an arrow's path and driven away in a stolen car. If we were right, a cattle thief had garroted a state trooper Saturday night and then killed Jesse two days later because he might figure out the thief had turned killer.

What we didn't know was how an honest, hardworking farmer became mixed up in rustling. Or how the killer had managed to move the body from the gate to the pond bank without leaving blood or drag marks. I could guess why now. Finding Jesse at the gate to the pasture might have drawn our attention to the livestock. Figuring out whether a mad deer caused his death slowed— and could have stopped—our investigation and diverted us from the cattle.

The shooting at Star Corner had been another tactic to distract us. That had been Tuesday's big event, if you didn't count my breaking into the Tornells' safe and Annalynn arresting Straw, Jericho, and Tommy Ray for their drunken 9-1-1 call.

I slowed at a crossroads and glanced at the empty seat beside me. Achilles was an ideal companion in some ways. Unquestioning loyalty and affection, few arguments, simple demands. Besides, he always had my back. If I took the job in New York, I'd have to buy a place with a big yard out in Connecticut. He'd be alone twelve hours or more a day, not to mention during business trips.

Annalynn's warning not to make her an excuse for turning down the job came back to me. The same applied to Achilles. If I wanted the job, I'd find a way to keep Achilles and to continue to support Annalynn.

Back to the case. The killer had to know both local victims. Consider family and neighbors first. When I'd gone to check out Straw's family Wednesday morning, Tammy Kay's situation—the morning sickness, the wild but appealing little boys, the empty refrigerator—had aroused my sympathy. Was it clouding my judgment? My experience with deceitful informants, entrepreneurs, and bankers had made me cynical about people. Had I overcompensated and discounted her responsibility for the marijuana too quickly?

Maybe, but what she knew about the marijuana didn't matter. The young widow had nothing to do with the murders. If the law came after her for raising marijuana, she would lose her kids, her life. Would she have the internal or external resources to recover? I doubted it. I didn't want that on my, or Annalynn's, head.

Much more to the point: Could the man speeding away from Jesse Tornell's murder have seen Straw's plants growing in the brush behind the shed? Not from what I had seen in the aerial photos. The brush could have hidden the young plants from a bird's-eye view. Half-brother Bob could have seen the plants in the field on his way to one of his dairy barns and checked the shed. Getting rid of Straw would leave Bob the sole heir to Bulganov Farms.

I'd seen no indication of greed or meanness in the dairy farmer. Nor any hint of animosity toward the Tornells.

Who else? I doubted that either Vlad or Nan Bulganov had the strength to kill Jesse, and they certainly didn't kill their son.

Dorothy Tornell had the skill and the time to kill her husband. She could have gone with him to the pond and walked back through the fields before calling the sheriff. No, she wasn't that good an actor. She could have spotted the marijuana earlier and driven over to take revenge on Straw for killing Jesse while I ate in her kitchen. But she wouldn't have pointed out the extra cattle, and killing Straw virtually under my nose defied reason. Not guilty.

Dorothy's other suspect was Floyd Vanderhofen. Something definitely out of line there, but nothing connected him to Tornell's murder. Besides, if Vanderhofen were a marksman with a bow or rifle, he'd have shot the mad fox to save his dog.

The killer had to come from the periphery, close enough to know both the Tornells and Bulganovs but outside the circle Annalynn and I had identified. Person or persons unknown. No: persons unidentified.

I passed the Tornell farmhouse. Several cars were parked in the drive and barnyard. Doubtless family members had gathered to break bread before the funeral. A four-wheeled trailer with high sideboards sat near the barn. Dorothy must use that to take produce to the farmers' market.

I slowed at the corner where we'd entered the field and found Jesse Tornell's body. Dorothy had put a shiny new padlock on the gate. Ironic that she had locked the gate on stolen cattle. Trees and brush blocked my view of them.

As I turned off the blacktop onto the gravel road leading to the church, I glanced up at the dark clouds coasting toward me. The SUV's clock said one thirty. We'd be lucky to complete the burial before the rain came.

Two old Chevys and Garth's BMW were parked on the edge of the road in front of the church, apparently leaving the small parking lot free for the family. I turned around and parked behind the BMW. Garth had added a makeshift trailer hitch. Why would a man who had a super-clean pickup do that? I smiled as I thought how the BMW's new appendage would offend one of my Austrian friends.

Carrying my miniature rose bush in both hands, I walked toward the open double doors of the classic white-frame country church with a stubby—and empty—bell tower. Someone had opened the big side windows. That meant no air conditioning. Inside, worn pine pews filled all but the front and back. In the front, on a low stage, flower arrangements on stands and plants in pots graced each side of the lectern/pulpit. A stand awaited the casket. Near the open back door stood an upright piano with a round swivel stool. Two ceiling fans kept the moist air moving.

I found a spot for the rose and went to the back door to look out. A green canopy in a back corner of the cemetery marked Jesse Tornell's final resting place. The tombstones, some tall and narrow and some short and rectangular, told me this was an old cemetery. About thirty feet to the left a blue tarp lay on the ground. Covering the grave awaiting William Wallace Bulganov? I hoped the twins wouldn't see their father's body descend into that darkness.

I walked along the edge of the cemetery toward the canopy looking for any signs of mad wildlife. A man in a short-sleeved white shirt sat hunched over in one of the folding chairs by Tornell's grave. His hands covered his face. I started to turn away rather than intrude on his distress when he dropped his hands. Garth Raymo. Despite what he'd said about Jesse having no small talk, they must have become friends while working on Garth's house. Maybe I should have asked him more about their relationship.

He rose. Darkness surrounded bloodshot eyes. "Hello, angel of mercy."

"Would you like to be alone?" He looked ten years

older than he had the morning he dropped off Dorothy's parents.

"No, no. Please sit down. It's cooler out here than in the church."

Not an ideal setting for an interrogation, but people are less guarded in such places, and when they're distraught. I took a seat two chairs away from him. "You and Jesse must have connected."

He sat down and stared at the bronze frame on which the casket would rest before being lowered. "We had a lot in common. We both grew up on farms where our fathers worked us to death. We both joined the army to get away, and we both came back to the farm. He loved that pitiful piece of land, loved the work. He knew if he lost it, he'd have to start from scratch in something he hated." Garth cleared his throat. "He died for it. He didn't deserve that."

"No one deserves a violent death." His intensity puzzled me. He cared much more about Jesse's death than the neighbors did. Was Garth alarmed about his own mortality? Did he, like Jesse, fear losing his farm? Another possibility hit me: Could he be involved in the rustling that had prompted Jesse's murder?

He stood and smiled wanly. "Please excuse me. I'm exhausted. I had to haul a load of a special feed supplement to Bartlesville, Oklahoma, yesterday so I slept in my camper. I got up early this morning to get home in time to bring the Lapinskis down for the funeral."

"That was very kind of you." One bad night hadn't made his eyes that bloodshot.

"It was the least I could do." He tightened his black tie. "I heard on the radio that whoever killed Jesse stole a car in Laycock. Did the police find the bastard's fingerprints?"

A lot of people would be asking me that. A simple answer worked best. "I don't know."

He cocked his head, disbelief on his face. "You know what's going on. Do you think the sheriff will track down Jesse's killer?"

I could give only one answer: "I expect an arrest soon."

He raised his eyes to study the darkening sky. "Mrs. Lapinski said the sheriff called in the DEA. Do you suppose the drug dealers who killed that worthless Bulganov kid murdered Jesse by mistake?"

"That possibility hadn't occurred to me." He felt as negative toward Straw as he did positive toward Jesse. I detected movement in the tall grass of the field next to the cemetery. I slid my hand into the gun pocket in my purse in case the grass hid a rabid fox. "Do you know the Bulganovs well?"

"No. I met his parents for the first time Wednesday morning."

No mention of Bob. The animal was moving toward the cemetery. Hand on my Glock, I rose and strolled toward the waving grass. A large orange tomcat emerged from the field and sauntered over, seeking affection. He wove around my legs once and moved on. Achilles would have a fit.

"I'm going to get some water. See you later." Garth walked toward the church. He passed Bob Bulganov, and the two men nodded. Neither smiled.

Bob came toward me. "What's that huckster doing here?"

The antagonism visible in the photo obviously remained. "He gave Dorothy's parents a ride. He bought a farm next door to them a little over a year ago. I take it you don't like his product."

He snorted. "I rate pushing cattle feed with chemical additives up there with pushing drugs to kids." He strode toward the blue tarp. "It's going to storm soon. I don't want rain to get into Straw's grave."

I trailed behind him, debating whether I should say anything about Nan's meeting with Garth. No. The family had enough problems already.

He checked a stake holding down one corner of the tarp. "Looks secure. Nothing penetrates these tarps."

Nothing. Not even blood. Could the killer have wrapped Jesse's body in a tarp to keep from leaving a trail of blood? I thought of Spike carrying Vernon up the roadside bank in a firefighter's carry. One strong man could have transported the body onto the pond bank that way.

Bob checked another stake. "Some fool almost dammed up a creek by throwing a tarp like this off a bridge on that road that runs past Straw's house. The tarp caught on a log and stopped the flow. I had to wade in water above my knees to pull the tarp loose."

His jeans had been wet when I gave him the strawberries. The morning after Jesse Tornell's killer drove that road. Maybe the killer hadn't been so careful about fingerprints this time. I kept my voice casual. "What did you do with that tarp?"

"I brought it along in case I needed another one to cover the grave." He stared at a gravestone, his mother's. "Why do you ask?"

I couldn't think of a credible excuse, so I gave a transparent one. "I heard someone lost a tarp Monday evening. I'd like to see it, if you don't mind."

"Monday evening." He turned to stare at me. Then his eyes went to the canopy.

He'd made the connection to Jesse's death. I might as well be blunt. "Did you notice any stains?"

"You mean blood?" He clutched his stomach as if an ulcer had kicked in. "I don't think so. I washed the dirt off it with a high-powered hose. Damn! It never occurred to me it could have anything to do with Jesse. Are you sure?"

"No," I admitted, "but I'd better take it in for testing anyway. Does the sheriff have your prints on file?"

"No. The National Guard may. I was in the reserves for four years after I got out of the army."

Where he'd learned to kill. Holy hell, I hoped I hadn't been wrong. "Let's transfer the tarp to my vehicle before the crowd gets here."

Too late. The crowd had already arrived. Cars lined the road. Little groups of men, women, and children stood talking in front of the church. When Bob dropped the tarp into a garbage bag I'd taken from the evidence box, they all watched.

A hearse turned off the blacktop road onto the gravel road and led five cars into the parking lot. The people lingering in front of the church went inside. Bob Bulganov joined two other pallbearers.

I stayed by the SUV, planning to radio Annalynn about the tarp while the pallbearers carried the casket into the church.

Dorothy got out of a car and motioned to me. I stepped over the shallow ditch to join her.

"My mother says you play the piano." Dorothy thrust a piece of paper at me. "Nan Bulganov couldn't come today. Could you please play these hymns?"

I read three titles from my childhood: "I'll be glad to."

"I'd like for you to play 'The Old Rugged Cross' while they carry in the casket."

"Certainly."

"I can't thank you enough for all your help." She leaned close. "The cattle are all ours after all. I found the papers and some ear tags in a box in the barn. Jesse took the calves as pay for carpentry work one weekend. I called Floyd to apologize." She glanced at her family. "Please join us in the church basement after the service."

So the rustler provided fake documents. Did she realize that? She had to know the animals would sell for about ten times as much as Jesse made for two days of work.

Wasn't anybody innocent anymore?

THIRTY-FIVE

WHILE THE PALLBEARERS discussed who would stand where to carry the casket, I jumped into the SUV and flipped on the radio transmitter. "PDS reporting." I thought a moment. I didn't want to tell the world what I'd found out. "The widow has papers for the surplus animals. A neighbor found an abandoned tarp. More later."

I hurried into the church and up the side aisle to the piano. I located "The Old Rugged Cross" in the hymnal and played a pianissimo arpeggio to test the old upright's keys. Approximately in tune. I glanced over my shoulder. The family waited outside the front door. I started the hymn, and they moved forward to take their places in the two empty front pews. Men in sensible short-sleeved dress shirts and women in their Sunday best—probably not purchased in Laycock—filled the pews behind them and the standing room at the back.

As I finished the chorus, Junior stepped up beside the piano and faced the mourners. He nodded to me, and I played the verse again. To my surprise, he had a beautiful, albeit untrained, tenor voice, and he knew every word of all four verses. By the third verse, the pallbearers had placed the casket on the stand and taken their seats.

I stayed at the piano, thankful a rising wind blowing through the back door provided some relief from the heat. My seat offered another advantage: I could see every person—squirming children, nodding elders, serious middle-aged couples. Only the women in the family wiped away tears. Only Dorothy muffled sobs.

Bob was the lone Bulganov present. I recognized no one else except Floyd Vanderhofen and Harry of Harry's Hideaway, both of whom stood expressionless against the back wall. I scanned a second time, looking for Garth Raymo. Not there. Odd.

The rotund minister, the only man wearing his suit jacket, talked about the joys of heaven for several minutes and signaled for me to play "Blessed Assurance." Junior stepped up to sing. The boy was disciplined, in shock, or unmoved by his father's death.

After a brief recitation of Jesse's good qualities and Junior's performance of "In the Garden," the sweat-drenched minister stepped down, opened the casket, and invited the mourners to file by. Dorothy hadn't requested music for this. I knew part of Mozart's "Requiem" by heart, so I played that as the mourners passed by and left the church. I thought about Garth mourning at the grave, Bob finding the tarp, Dorothy claiming the cattle. My chart of the dates of the rustling and the payments to Jesse flashed through my mind. So did the image of Achilles sniffing at a camper with new tires. Crucial pieces of the puzzle slid into place. I had to tell Annalynn.

Decorum dictated that I continue to play the piano until the family, the last to leave, followed the pallbearers and casket out the front door. As soon as they cleared the steps, I hurried to the SUV. As I'd expected, Garth Raymo's BMW was gone. I flipped on the transmitter and said, "I have to talk to the sheriff."

To my surprise, Annalynn's voice sounded through the static in seconds: "What is it? Are you okay?"

"I'm fine." I hesitated. "Is this channel secure?"

"No. Is this urgent?"

Scheisse. "It could be. I have a name for you to check."
Wary of broadcasting accusations, I thought of the Tornells' empty house. "I'm leaving the church. I'll call you
in five minutes." I turned off the transmitter and pulled
out.

As my wheels hit the blacktop, dark sheets of rain
streaked the distant sky. I accelerated and then slowed
for the corner.

The padlock no longer hung on the gate leading to
the Tornells' pond.

I drove on down the road the equivalent of two blocks
and pulled over to the side in a dip in the road. What a
perfect time to take the rustled cattle and wipe out any
evidence of Jesse Tornell's connection to rustling. Garth
Raymo had left as the funeral started, about thirty minutes ago. He couldn't put the cattle in the BMW. He had
to steal or retrieve a trailer. Like the one in the Tornells'
barnyard. He could still be rounding up the calves.

And monitoring the sheriff department's transmis-
sions. I tried my cell. No signal. Time was passing. If I
didn't call in ten minutes, Annalynn would send out the
cavalry—a half-hour drive. I had to make sure the rustler
was there and, if so, get photographic evidence. I reached
for my change of clothes. A minute later I wore my jeans,
T-shirt, running shoes, and holster. I took a police waist
pack to hold the camera and an umbrella with a camouflage pattern from the cooler. Too bad Annalynn didn't
carry a shotgun or a rifle.

Glock in one hand and the umbrella in the other, I visualized the area beyond the gate—the noisy gate. The
dirt road ran through grass and weeds no more than forty
yards toward the pond past one big tree and three little

ones and then turned right toward the second gate. The pasture behind the pond and the lot with the water tank sloped down steeply. If Raymo was near the pasture gate, he would spot me on the dirt road. My best bet was to go through the soybean field and use the pond bank as a shield and vantage point.

The soybeans would hide me only if I crawled between rows on my stomach. No way my still-tender wound would tolerate that. I opted to hunch over in the low roadside ditch and trot toward the corner with the open umbrella in front of me. A steady rumble of distant thunder and the mooing of cows drowned out any noise I made. When I drew close to the road gate, I closed the umbrella and crawled between the strands of barbed-wire fence into the field. I couldn't see the cow pasture, but the grass and brush might not hide me completely as I headed for the pond bank's protection. I took several deep breaths and ran like hell between two rows of soybeans until I reached a point behind the pond.

The sprint drained my lungs of air and awoke my wound, but I exulted at my successful effort and welcomed the familiar rush that came from confronting danger. I ducked between strands of barbed wire into the high grass growing on the pond bank, here about waist high. I'd have to crawl—no other way—to stay out of sight while going to where I could see. I abandoned the umbrella and, gun in my right hand, crawled on elbows and knees along the bottom of the high bank on the side away from the road.

A whip cracked and cattle bellowed in the pasture. I dropped and hugged the ground. I stayed there a minute listening to cows running and Garth Raymo swearing. Sure I hadn't been spotted, I crawled forward until

I judged the pasture would be in sight. I took the camera out of the waist pack, set it on telephoto, and raised my head to peek through the top of the grass.

He'd backed the Tornells' old trailer up to the gate of the pipe fence around the water tank. Five calves stood in the trailer, their heads down to feed. He'd evidently used fear and feed—must be a veritable catnip for cows—to lure the calves into the lot and then into the trailer. I searched for Raymo. He stood a couple of hundred yards down the hill, his back to me. He'd changed into a pair of jeans and a black T-shirt. He held out a plastic bucket to the last calf. A cow moved restlessly nearby, her head stretched toward the calf.

A high-powered rifle hung by a strap from Raymo's shoulder. At that distance he had a lot better chance of a fatal shot with his rifle than I did with my Glock.

I photographed the BMW and trailer and waited a tense minute for Raymo to turn enough that I could get his profile. Then I dropped flat to put away the camera. Giant sprinkles landed on me. In seconds they turned into a soft rain. Good sense said to get out of the rain and the line of fire. I stuck my head up again to monitor Raymo's progress and estimate the odds of taking him by surprise as he loaded the calf. Better a bird in hand than on the run.

Something moved in the grass behind me. I rolled onto my back ready to fire.

Achilles crept toward me, a doggie grin on his face.

"Down, quiet!" I whispered, my heart in my mouth. He thought we were playing hide and seek.

With all the noise of the storm and the cattle, I hadn't heard a car, but Achilles wouldn't be there without Annalynn. Frantic to find her before Garth spotted her, I crawled back around the pond bank with Achilles scooting along beside me. Annalynn was running through the soybeans with a rifle in her hands. I motioned for her to hurry and made a shhh sign.

When she reached us, I stuck my Glock in my holster, took the rifle, and helped hold the strands of wire apart for her to come through.

She huddled beside me on the pond bank. "The rustlers?"

"One rustler, well armed. He's still trying to coax the last calf to a trailer. How did you get here so fast?"

"When you sent word Dorothy had papers for the cattle, we decided to serve the search warrant. I came out ahead of the others to tell her what's happening. Achilles tracked you from the SUV." She took a couple of deep breaths and wiped rain—now pelting us—from her face. "How do we go about taking him in?"

I motioned for quiet and listened. The cattle still bawled and moved around, typical behavior before a storm. They'd hide the sound of our movement. The pond's inner bank on the pasture side offered us the best available protection and a good spot to fire from. "We'll crawl over the bank here and keep low. I'll go around the water on the side next to the road. You go the other way. We'll get the drop on him without exposing ourselves."

I checked the rifle. It was loaded and ready to fire.

"Phoenix, who are we arresting?"

"Garth Raymo."

She frowned. "I've heard the name, but he's not on anybody's suspect list."

"He went on mine this afternoon. He knew Tornell was desperate for cash, and he knew Straw and Jericho had a marijuana operation. I'm almost certain he committed all three murders. I'll explain later. You go over the bank first." I pointed to the lowest spot.

She gazed at it a moment, drew her gun from her holster, flattened herself against the bank, and slithered over the top.

"Guard Annalynn, Achilles. Stay down. Quiet."

He didn't move.

"Please." I began my crawl over the bank, confident he would follow.

Annalynn crouched below me as I topped the bank. She nodded and crept around the edge of the water toward the opposite side of the pond.

Achilles stared at the rifle a moment and then followed Annalynn.

I chose a spot about twenty feet from the blind where we'd found Jesse's body, signaled to Annalynn, and we both peeked over the bank through the grass.

Thunder boomed, and the cow and calf stampeded down the hill. Cursing, Raymo looked at his watch. He jogged toward the car, still holding the bucket.

I cleared a peephole through the grass with the rifle barrel and signaled Annalynn with my hand.

"Police," she shouted. "Drop your weapon and spread eagle on the ground."

He tossed the bucket aside and broke into a run.

I sent a bullet past his ear and yelled, "Drop or die."

Pulling the rifle from his shoulder, he dropped and rolled.

I put a bullet through his shoulder.

He screamed and let go of the rifle.

"Roll away from the gun and spread eagle," I ordered.

He didn't move.

I put a bullet between him and the rifle.

He rolled away.

"Keep down," I cautioned Annalynn. "He's sure to have other weapons on him. I'll watch him while you radio for backup."

"I called for it when Achilles started tracking you in the ditch. Spike and the Cattle Theft officer are on the way. They should be here in fifteen minutes."

"Good. We'll wait." I bounced a bullet off of Raymo's rifle to show him I was watching.

Achilles trotted down to the pond and lapped up some water.

"Fill me in," Annalynn said. "Who is this man and how did you know he's our rustler?"

"He's the Lapinskis' neighbor, the one who hired Jesse Tornell to work on his house. He's also a regional sales-man for NutriDairy, a feeding program for dairy cattle. That may be one reason he stole only beef animals. I'm betting NutriDairy's records will show he was visiting clients every time cattle disappeared. He travels part of the time in a pickup with a camper—big enough to haul stolen calves and unlikely to attract suspicion. That's why the trooper mentioned the smell of cattle."

"Could Raymo have set up Straw Bulganov?"

"Yes. He and Jericho had been smoking pot the day they worked for him. Besides—"

"I remember now," Annalynn said. "Raymo is the one who told you Jericho posted those ads for handyman jobs—the ones signaling he had marijuana to sell."

Raymo groaned and yelled. "Help me. I'm bleeding to death."

"So sorry," I called, not moving. To Annalynn I said, "From what he told me, he's in over his head financially. He probably stole more cattle than he could sell or graze and recruited Jesse because he was desperate for money, too. Raymo's financial records should lead you to other evidence. He may even have some of the stolen cattle on his farm. I saw new tires on his camper at the Bulganovs' Wednesday, so he's ditched the ones that left the tread marks."

"We can hold him on the rustling charge while we gather evidence on the murders." Annalynn stood up. "I'm the sheriff, Phoenix. I can't let a bleeding prisoner lie there in the rain while I wait for a deputy to come."

Rain pounded my face. If it picked up any more, Raymo would be hard to see. "Okay, but we have to be careful. Keep our distance and approach him from different angles." I studied the area. The car and trailer would block our view of him as we went through the gate into the pasture. We didn't dare let him out of sight for a nanosecond. "You and Achilles go first while I cover you. Stay about thirty feet away from him until I get there. Shoot him in the chest if he moves."

The wind picked up. The rain would be coming in horizontal sheets soon.

"Come, Achilles." Annalynn ran along the water's edge behind me and up and over the bank with Achilles at her side.

I wanted to wipe the water off my face, but I didn't dare do anything but a rapid blink.

A few seconds later she stood in place, her service revolver in her hands, a snarling Achilles at her side. I'd never imagined I'd see such a sight. I took one hand off the rifle long enough to retrieve the camera and record the moment.

Now came the dangerous time: the moment Raymo

and Annalynn would be out of my sight. "Achilles," I shouted. "Go around to his other side. Watch."

"Go, Achilles," Annalynn said. "Watch, please!"

Figuring Achilles' movements would hold Raymo's attention for a few seconds, I hustled over the bank and sprinted through the gate and past the blind spot.

Achilles barked furiously as I passed Raymo's BMW.

Three deer bounded over the fence and darted between Annalynn and Raymo.

"Drop!" I yelled, anticipating him pulling a handgun. Falling to my knees, I fired toward Garth without aiming.

Two other shots sounded simultaneously.

Annalynn lay flat on the ground ahead of me.

The deer turned and raced back in a bunch, blocking my view of Raymo. I jettisoned the heavy rifle and rolled to my left, pulling out the Glock with my right hand.

Raymo screamed as the last deer's hooves dug into his back.

As I aimed for Raymo's brain, Annalynn fired, hitting him in the left shoulder.

He dropped the pistol in his left hand and lay still.

"Phoenix?" She didn't take her eyes off him.

"I'm fine. You?"

"Fine. Cover me, please." She pushed herself up and wiped a clump of dried cow patty off the knee of her uniform. "I hope you're satisfied. I'm as filthy as you are."

THIRTY-SIX

ACHILLES GROWLED AT the inert man from the right and Annalynn knelt with her gun pointed at his head from the left while I frisked him. He had a knife in a sheath just above his left ankle and a grenade in a cell phone pouch on his belt.

The blood flowed freely from the back of his right shoulder where my bullet had gone through and near the socket of his left shoulder where Annalynn had shot him. He breathed shallowly with occasional gasps. Unsure whether he was unconscious or playing possum, I cut a six-inch strip from his shirt, pulled together his limp hands, and tied his wrists above his head. Buckets of wind-driven rain washed the blood into the grass around him.

"I'll radio for the ambulance and bring the first-aid kit," Annalynn said. She ran toward the road.

"Here, Achilles. Watch, please," I said, placing him directly in front of Raymo. I straddled his hips and cut more strips to bind the wounds. My efforts did little good, and when Annalynn drove the SUV up by us and brought out big gauze pads and tape, I threw the bloody strips away.

By the time we'd applied the bandages, we were soaked with rain and coated with blood and mud. The rain settled down to a gentle patter that wet but didn't wash us.

"We can't wait for the ambulance," Annalynn said. "He really might bleed to death."

I nodded. "The problem is getting him into the SUV."

A pickup with a covered bed turned off the road and roared into the pasture, a white metal livestock trailer bouncing behind it. Spike jumped out of the passenger seat and ran to us. "My God! Were you hit?"

"The blood is all his," I said. "Can you two lift him into the pickup bed?"

"Sure. We'll roll him onto a blanket and use that as a stretcher."

The driver, a short man dressed like a cowboy, unhitched the trailer and helped us get Raymo into the pickup bed and strapped down.

"Watch him every second," Annalynn warned Spike. "He's still dangerous. Phoenix will drive and fill you in. Make sure she gets out of those wet clothes as soon as possible. Her immune system is still weak." She waited until he nodded. "Go! We'll finish up here."

Nothing could make me any wetter, but exertion had kept me warm. I pulled out and, more concerned about getting a cold than saving Raymo, accelerated to a moderate speed.

Spike had opened the window to the pickup bed. He kept his eyes on the prisoner and his service weapon in his hand. "Is this the guy you wanted us to check?"

"Yes. Garth Raymo, a farmer and traveling salesman from Putnam County. I put together the pieces this afternoon." I turned on the radio so Raymo couldn't hear me and explained how I'd linked him to the murders and the rustling.

Spike didn't say anything for a little while. "Why

would he risk stealing back the calves? Somebody was sure to see him before he got far."

I put myself in Raymo's situation. "He didn't need to take the calves far. All the neighbors went to the funeral. Raymo could cart the calves a few miles away and turn them loose in an Angus herd. I remember seeing two nearby in the aerial photographs. Most people don't notice a few extras right away, and most don't notify police when they do. He could ditch the trailer in some timber or an abandoned farm building. He's been around here enough to have figured out his spot."

"We got him on rustling," Spike said softly, "but we need proof that he killed at least one of the victims."

Finding proof was his job. "That shouldn't be too hard. Check his cell phone for calls to Straw, and to nine-one-one. Gillian can test to see whether the bullet at Star Corner came from the rifle Raymo was carrying." I went into a corner without slowing down.

Spike braked and braced himself with his free hand but didn't stop watching Raymo. "We'll need a lot more than that to take to court. Too bad he doesn't live in this county. I'll ask Captain Gist to let me go with the M-squad to search Raymo's place. Maybe we can find the bow and arrow he used to kill Tornell, or the tires that were on his pickup when he killed the trooper."

"He probably burned or buried or drowned that stuff. I'd follow the money—bank accounts under false names, bills of sale for the cattle he sold, that kind of thing."

"The M-squad can take care of the paper trail." He stuck his head through the window for a closer look at Raymo. "He's still breathing. Damn! Wish I'd been there when Sheriff Keyser arrested him. Tell me exactly—exactly—what happened."

Knowing he'd spread the story, at least among the law enforcement community, I emphasized how Annalynn had saved both our lives—possibly the truth—when the deer had interrupted the arrest and Raymo had pulled a concealed pistol.

I figured the tale of the acting sheriff bringing in a vicious killer would turn her into a celebrity and launch her bid for Congress.

If she chose to run.

AT THE HOSPITAL, Spike called a nurse's attention to my miserable state. She gave me a towel, a cup of hot coffee, a set of scrubs to replace my filthy clothes, and a blanket to wrap around me. As soon as I stopped shivering, Spike paid me the compliment of trusting me to guard Raymo and rushed off to join the search of his farm.

Raymo remained silent and still, but movement under his closed eyelids convinced me he was feigning unconsciousness. I watched him with my Glock ready until the staff put him under for surgery.

The minute I put my gun away, a nurse led a limping Vernon and M. L. Moniteau, the kid from the radio station, to me. "I'm not a police officer. I can't tell you anything," I said as they both turned on tape recorders. "You'll have to talk to Sheriff Keyser."

"But you shot the prisoner," the teenager protested. "Everybody knows that."

Vernon touched the kid's arm in gentle warning. "Annalynn's office says she can't meet with us tonight. She said to get the facts from you."

I didn't doubt him, but I had no intention of taking any of Annalynn's thunder. I made a zipping motion across my mouth.

Vernon stepped back a few feet and talked to young Moniteau. As they came back toward me, a man in the Highway Patrol's blue-gray uniform and broad-brimmed hat followed them.

"Okay, Phoenix," Vernon said, "we have to—*have to*—report this story, and we want to get it right. You give us the details on background so we can eliminate rumors, and we won't quote you."

The trooper—a tall, thin man with an expressionless face—nodded. "Best offer you're likely to get, ma'am. I'll stop you if you start to go over the line."

Vernon stuck out his hand. "Thank you, Sam. Go ahead, Phoenix."

I managed a welcoming smile. This had to be Captain Gist, the condescending trooper Annalynn had called the night we found Tornell. "Okay. Short and sweet. The night we found Tornell's body, Annalynn speculated that his death could be connected to the trooper's murder two nights before." Might as well rub that in. "Dorothy Tornell told us there were too many cattle in the field. She thought they belonged to her neighbor. So Annalynn's investigators followed the standard procedures—looking at friends and family." I looked straight at Gist, who'd advised Annalynn to take that route, but his face remained immobile. "Annalynn changed the course of the investigation when she tied Straw Bulganov's death to his having seen the murderer drive past his house in a car stolen from Clunkers on Call. Obviously Straw died because he could have recognized Jesse's killer."

Vernon stopped me. "You have evidence Raymo stole the car?"

"No, or at least not to my knowledge. I'm not involved in that. The key thing is that while investigating Straw's murder, Annalynn figured out Jesse Tornell had been grazing and selling stolen cattle. The Cattle Theft Task Force confirmed this."

The captain cleared his throat. "Confirmed is too strong a word. They're investigating the possibility."

I shrugged. "So Sheriff Keyser worked to find the links between the rustling and the murders. She knew the murderer had to be someone who knew both Jesse and Straw well enough to lure them into traps and had a motive to kill both."

Impatience replaced neutrality on Captain Gist's face. "But she didn't identify the alleged murderer until you two stumbled across him loading the calves he'd left with Tornell."

The teenage reporter cleared his throat. "You can't see that field from the road, sir. I know. I went out there to look around after the murder." He turned to me. "How did you know the killer was there?"

I smiled. M. L. Moniteau had a future. "Raymo took the padlock off the gate and didn't put it back on. When I drove by, I—umm—deduced that he had left the funeral early to remove evidence." I chose my words carefully. "Annalynn drove out to serve a warrant to seize the rustled calves. She knew who was loading cattle in that field before she saw him." Because I'd told her.

Vernon smiled and hid it immediately. "He was shot twice. Tell us what happened."

I gave them a full account from the time Annalynn and Achilles arrived. All three listened intently, their eyes widening when I told how the deer had bounded between Annalynn and Raymo.

The nurse who had given me the scrubs bustled up.

"For God's sake, Sam, get someone in here to relieve her. Can't you see she's exhausted and in pain?"

Captain Gist flushed. "Sorry. I'll take over myself. You go on home."

The radio reporter shot forward. "I'll give you a ride, Dr. Smith."

"Phoenix can take my car," Annalynn said, coming down the hall with Achilles at her side. She'd changed into a clean uniform. She felt my forehead. "If she feels like driving."

I didn't, but that was a much better alternative than being trapped in a car with a sharp young reporter. "I'm fine." Muscles all over my body aching, I forced myself to walk briskly to the exit with Achilles glued to my leg. Once outside I looked up to a star-studded sky. I'd missed that while I lived in Vienna. City lights conceal the earth's ceiling.

Annalynn's house was dark as I pulled into her drive. I put her SUV in the garage and walked toward the front porch.

Achilles, trotting ahead of me, raised his nose for a big sniff. I reached for the Glock, but he seemed interested rather than concerned about something on the porch. Even so, I took my time going up the steps.

A white box about three feet long and two feet wide blocked the entry. Achilles sniffed and sneezed and whined for me to open the door and give him his evening treat. As I stooped at one end of the box, I smelled roses. Beware of unexpected gifts. I let Achilles in and turned on the porch and hall lights. The box was from a local florist, and the slip on it had my name. Still on the alert, I brought a yardstick from the hall closet and pried up the lid to reveal two dozen long-stemmed dark-pink roses.

Achilles poked his nose into the blossoms and then trotted off.

He didn't know everything. Holding the box as far away from me as I could, I took it into the kitchen and put it on the island. I gave Achilles his snack before reaching into the envelope attached to the stems and pulling out the card. It read, "My fervent wishes for the return of your health. Your Eliza."

Odd phrasing. Like a message from my CIA days. I searched my mind for anyone called or code-named Eliza and came up blank. Too late to call the local florist who had delivered them, and probably pointless anyway. I turned the card over. On the back it said, "I never forget a voice or a kindness."

I still didn't get it. I ran water over the flowers and checked each with gloved hands before trimming the stems and arranging the roses in a big Lenox glass vase. Hoping my subconscious would solve the mystery, I headed upstairs for a soothing hot soak and a sound sleep.

THIRTY-SEVEN

I DIDN'T HEAR Annalynn come home that night, and she was gone when I woke up a little after six. She'd left a note on my bedside table: "Raymo will recover. He asked for a public defender. Apparently crime doesn't pay very well. The M-squad is searching his farm inch by inch. I'm coordinating the investigation in Vandiver County. Let's celebrate tonight."

Achilles licked my hand as I put the note back on the table.

"Good morning, Deputy Dog. Ready to go out?" I grabbed my robe and went downstairs to let him into the backyard before going upstairs to dress. A day of leisure stretched before me—except for laundry and packing and catching up on Eastern Europe financial news germane to the meetings in New York.

With no clean clothes, I gave laundry first priority. I'd just taken my clothes out of the dryer when the phone rang.

"Good morning, Phoenix," Vernon said. "Have you read my editorial yet?"

"No. Annalynn left before the paper came, and I haven't gone out to get it."

"Please read it and let me know what you think." He hung up.

I went onto the porch to pick up the paper. A banner headline read: "Sheriff Keyser Captures Suspected

Killer." I skimmed the accurate article, which included quotes from Annalynn, Spike, Dorothy, Vlad, a doctor who'd operated on Raymo, and—my favorite—Captain Gist. He said Sheriff Keyser had conducted an outstanding investigation.

The editorial's headline read: "Extend Sheriff Keyser's Appointment." Vernon got right to the point. "Acting Sheriff Annalynn Carr Keyser displayed great courage and skill in a gun battle with an alleged rustler and murderer yesterday. Thanks to the investigation she led, this man will be charged with three murders.

"Let's save the county some badly needed funds by canceling the special election (no candidates have come forward) and extending her appointment until the regularly scheduled election in November."

I smiled. The county commissioners would look like idiots if they didn't extend Annalynn's appointment, and Annalynn would feel it her duty to accept. I called Vern and told him that the editorial was brilliant but not to push her any farther, to give her time to decide what she wanted to do on her own.

When I took my clothes upstairs, I remembered that I still had the department's camera. I downloaded the photos I'd taken to my laptop and emailed them to Annalynn. Then I emailed the one of Annalynn holding the gun on Raymo to Vernon with a note: "Open the attached photo only if you're willing to keep it off the record until the police release it or she's a candidate."

For me, the case was over. The M-squad would take care of gathering the evidence that would convict Garth Raymo of triple homicide. I felt the familiar letdown that came after a mission high. The meetings in New York would be an intellectual and tactical challenge, but they wouldn't speed the adrenaline flow.

Neither would the prestigious job that Reg had offered me. I'd spend my days in meetings and my nights reading reports and analyzing figures. Since resigning my job as a covert operative, I'd countered my boredom at Adderly International by performing CIA missions as an independent contractor. That door had closed forever when I'd been shot in Istanbul.

I went to the window overlooking the backyard and watched Achilles drive off a cat creeping toward the hummingbird feeder, a task he'd assigned himself a day or two after I'd brought him home. "Deputy Dog, defender of birds and other vulnerable creatures. You've found your new niche. Where's mine?"

Not as a manager behind a desk in New York. Not as a permanent houseguest in Laycock. Not as a spectator anywhere. "I'm almost well, I've got more money than twenty sensible people could spend in a lifetime, and I'm not wired to live a dull, useless life."

Achilles looked up at me from the hummingbird feeder, barked twice, and ran to pick up his tennis ball.

My future could wait a week or two. In this moment, life was good. I hurried downstairs to play with my dog.

NEITHER ANNALYNN NOR I had eaten a decent dinner all week. With nothing urgent on my schedule, I planned a menu of my favorite European and American dishes for our celebratory meal. Then, admitting that Connie would add to the fun, I called and asked her to bake the lemon cake her mother had served after our annual piano recitals.

I ducked into the Hy-Vee for ten minutes to pick up

the ingredients and ended up spending an hour as person after person stopped me to get the inside scoop on how Annalynn had tracked down and trapped the killer. All endorsed Vernon's suggestion to extend her appointment.

I told Connie about their reactions when she joined me in the kitchen about five thirty to complete preparations.

She dipped a finger into one of the three sauces I'd prepared to go with beef fondue. "I can't get over how modest you are these days. When you were in high school, you would have made sure everybody knew *you* broke the case and *you* brought in the bad guy. What's happened to the egomaniac we all knew and didn't love?"

"I grew up. Don't you think it's time you did?"

"Maybe after we get back from New York."

I laughed. "Good timing. Remember that when Reg insists on going to a karaoke bar." He'd love singing with her, a plus I hadn't thought about.

"At least I'll be able to say I sang in a New York night-spot." She buried her nose in the roses. "Did you get these for Annalynn?"

"No. Someone named Eliza sent them to me yesterday." I sliced half a loaf of Italian bread. "Do you know an Eliza?"

"Only Eliza Doolittle." She began to hum "I could have danced all night" and whirl around the kitchen. "Let me see the note."

I pointed to a drawer in the island and started buttering the bread.

"Hmm. Not just Eliza but 'Your Eliza.' This 'fervent wishes' doesn't sound very American. She must be one of your European friends." She tore off a piece of tinfoil to wrap around the bread. "The only other Eliza I can think of is the one who leapt from one piece of ice to another to cross the Ohio River and escape Simon Legree and slavery. Dark pink stands for gratitude. Someone is thanking you for helping her escape."

"Of course!" Relief swept over me. The flowers came from Klara Szabo—now living in Ohio—as thanks for getting her across the Hungarian border. Her husband had taped our telephone "business" conversation, and her musician's ear had recognized my voice despite the years. I smiled, confident now that the Szabos would keep our secret. "You deduced it, Connie. Very clever. Thanks."

"Really? What's *Uncle Tom's Cabin* got to do with these flowers?"

The front door opened and Annalynn called, "I'm starving. When do we eat?"

I stuck the bread in the oven to warm. "You have just enough time to have half a glass of red wine."

Annalynn leaned against the doorframe, lines of exhaustion around her mouth and circles under her eyes but a genuine smile on her face. "No wine. I have to go back to the office."

"A spritzer, then," I said, "half wine and half soda water."

"Yes, I remember having that in Vienna. Try one, Connie."

Connie reached for wine glasses. "Tell us what happened today while you make your wonderful oil and balsamic vinegar salad dressing."

"The only cooking skill I learned from my mother," Annalynn said. "First I'm going to wash my face and see if I can unpack the bags under my eyes."

I fixed the drinks and Connie took Annalynn's up to her. Connie and I worked together to get the meal on the table: the small chunks of raw steak marinated in wine, olive oil, and Italian spices; curry, mustard, and hot sauces; Mom's potato salad made with mashed potatoes; fresh green beans cooked with bits of bacon; a tossed salad loaded with green peppers, Roma tomatoes, and red onions; the warm bread.

Connie put out the ingredients for the salad dressing while I heated vegetable oil in the copper fondue pot I'd given Annalynn years ago. When the oil was hot, I took the pot to the table and lit the Sterno under it.

"Dinner is served," I called to Annalynn.

"With raw meat," Connie added.

I pointed to the long narrow two-tined forks by our plates. "You cook each bite to taste in the hot oil. It's a Swiss dish, *fondue bourguignonne*."

"You'll love it, Connie," Annalynn said. She went straight to the kitchen and made the dressing in half a minute. Bringing it to the table, she said, "Tell me about your plans for the trip, and then I'll tell all."

Connie entertained us with kooky schemes to get on camera during the *Today Show*. She finished with, "Your turn, Annalynn."

She speared two pieces of meat on her fork and put the fork into the oil. "We have enough evidence to charge Garth Raymo with Trooper Cansadi's and Jesse Tornell's murders. When we know what drugs killed Straw Bulganov, we'll track down the evidence to charge Raymo with that murder, too."

"Fantastic job of getting the goods, Annalynn," Connie said.

Annalynn turned to me and smirked, a rare expression for an aristocratic Carr. "Phoenix, your fan Spike wanted me to tell you he dove into Raymo's pond in the buff ten times before he found the pickup tires."

Connie raised an eyebrow. "Phoenix! You told Sergeant Stud to skinny dip?"

I laughed even as I enjoyed the image of Spike diving. "I suggested Raymo may have submerged evidence. Did they find a bow and arrows?"

"No," Annalynn said, "but they found a barrel where Raymo burned trash. They hope the Highway Patrol's lab will find fragments of the weapon in that." She pulled her meat from the pot. "He has a herd of forty-six Angus, half of them heifers and calves. The Cattle Theft investigator thinks he can identify a young pedigree bull stolen last fall through DNA. He hopes to prove the calves at the Tornell farm were the ones stolen last Saturday."

I donned my economist hat. "Raymo stole to build a herd and to generate income. His bank accounts will probably show that his job with NutriDairy didn't produce the operating capital required for the farm he'd just bought. He and Jesse had debt in common."

"Thank you, Dr. Smith," Connie said.

"Sorry. I've been preparing for my meetings in New York." I shifted gears. "Anything to connect Raymo to the stolen clunker yet, Annalynn?"

"Maybe." Annalynn's face lit up. "I don't do field work, of course, but I took a nice long walk this morning by Clunkers on Call. Barb Sidwell, the manager of the convenience store a block over, saw a black BMW parked in her lot Monday afternoon. It sat there so long that she wondered if some kids had taken it for a joyride and then abandoned it."

"So did she write down the license number?" Connie prompted.

"No, she photographed it with her iPhone. She's also

volunteered to ask everyone who comes in the store if they saw the driver in the area."

Connie and I applauded.

Annalynn bowed her head in acknowledgment. "That's all we have for now. Bank and phone records require several days." She turned to me. "You're next. Tell me what you're going to do about clothes for your meetings."

I deferred to Connie. "Ask my personal assistant."

"I've ordered thousands of dollars worth of stuff for her to choose from," Connie said. She described the dresses, shoes, and accessories being delivered to the hotel.

When she paused to breathe, Annalynn focused on me, her eyes no longer smiling, her posture no longer relaxed. "Are you shopping for a full business wardrobe?"

The moment of truth. Literally. "Only what I need for these meetings—plus some clothes to wear here." I had to be sure she understood. "Annalynn, I don't want that job in New York."

Her shoulders relaxed. "Maybe you two should stay in New York an extra day."

"Great idea!" Connie said. "But why?"

Annalynn's neck went pink. "To shop for clothes for a political campaign."

"Hallelujah!" Connie raised her glass. "To friendship!"

"To the future," Annalynn said.

What could I add? "To realizing our dreams."

* * * * *

ABOUT THE AUTHOR

CAROLYN MULFORD STARTED writing while growing up on a farm in northeast Missouri. After earning degrees in English and journalism, she served as a Peace Corps Volunteer in Ethiopia. There she became fascinated by other cultures. She has followed those interests by traveling in seventy countries and by editing a United Nations magazine in Vienna, Austria, and a national service-learning magazine in Washington, DC. As a freelancer, she wrote hundreds of articles and five nonfiction books. She now lives in Missouri and focuses on fiction. Her first novel, *The Feedsack Dress,* became Missouri's Great Read at the 2009 National Book Festival. In her first mystery, *Show Me the Murder,* she introduced three old friends coping with crime and personal crises. For more information, visit http://CarolynMulford.com.

REQUEST YOUR FREE BOOKS!
2 FREE NOVELS PLUS 2 FREE GIFTS!

Ⓗ HARLEQUIN®

INTRIGUE

BREATHTAKING ROMANTIC SUSPENSE

YES! Please send me 2 FREE Harlequin® Intrigue novels and my 2 FREE gifts (gifts are worth about $10). After receiving them, if I don't wish to receive any more books, I can return the shipping statement marked "cancel." If I don't cancel, I will receive 6 brand-new novels every month and be billed just $4.74 per book in the U.S. or $5.49 per book in Canada. That's a savings of at least 12% off the cover price! It's quite a bargain! Shipping and handling is just 50¢ per book in the U.S. and 75¢ per book in Canada.* I understand that accepting the 2 free books and gifts places me under no obligation to buy anything. I can always return a shipment and cancel at any time. Even if I never buy another book, the two free books and gifts are mine to keep forever.

182/382 HDN GH3D

Name _____ (PLEASE PRINT)

Address _____ Apt. #

City _____ State/Prov. _____ Zip/Postal Code

Signature (if under 18, a parent or guardian must sign)

Mail to the **Reader Service:**
IN U.S.A.: P.O. Box 1867, Buffalo, NY 14240-1867
IN CANADA: P.O. Box 609, Fort Erie, Ontario L2A 5X3

**Are you a subscriber to Harlequin® Intrigue books
and want to receive the larger-print edition?
Call 1-800-873-8635 or visit www.ReaderService.com.**

* Terms and prices subject to change without notice. Prices do not include applicable taxes. Sales tax applicable in N.Y. Canadian residents will be charged applicable taxes. Offer not valid in Quebec. This offer is limited to one order per household. Not valid for current subscribers to Harlequin Intrigue books. All orders subject to credit approval. Credit or debit balances in a customer's account(s) may be offset by any other outstanding balance owed by or to the customer. Please allow 4 to 6 weeks for delivery. Offer available while quantities last.

Your Privacy—The Reader Service is committed to protecting your privacy. Our Privacy Policy is available online at www.ReaderService.com or upon request from the Reader Service.

We make a portion of our mailing list available to reputable third parties that offer products we believe may interest you. If you prefer that we not exchange your name with third parties, or if you wish to clarify or modify your communication preferences, please visit us at www.ReaderService.com/consumerschoice or write to us at Reader Service Preference Service, P.O. Box 9062, Buffalo, NY 14240-9062. Include your complete name and address.

HI15

REQUEST YOUR FREE BOOKS!

2 FREE NOVELS PLUS 2 FREE GIFTS!

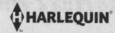

ROMANTIC suspense

Sparked by danger, fueled by passion

YES! Please send me 2 FREE Harlequin® Romantic Suspense novels and my 2 FREE gifts (gifts are worth about $10). After receiving them, if I don't wish to receive any more books, I can return the shipping statement marked "cancel." If I don't cancel, I will receive 4 brand-new novels every month and be billed just $4.74 per book in the U.S. or $5.49 per book in Canada. That's a savings of at least 12% off the cover price! It's quite a bargain! Shipping and handling is just 50¢ per book in the U.S. and 75¢ per book in Canada.* I understand that accepting the 2 free books and gifts places me under no obligation to buy anything. I can always return a shipment and cancel at any time. Even if I never buy another book, the two free books and gifts are mine to keep forever.

240/340 HDN GH3P

Name _____ (PLEASE PRINT) _____

Address _____ Apt. # _____

City _____ State/Prov. _____ Zip/Postal Code _____

Signature (if under 18, a parent or guardian must sign)

Mail to the **Reader Service:**
IN U.S.A.: P.O. Box 1867, Buffalo, NY 14240-1867
IN CANADA: P.O. Box 609, Fort Erie, Ontario L2A 5X3

**Want to try two free books from another line?
Call 1-800-873-8635 or visit www.ReaderService.com.**

* Terms and prices subject to change without notice. Prices do not include applicable taxes. Sales tax applicable in N.Y. Canadian residents will be charged applicable taxes. Offer not valid in Quebec. This offer is limited to one order per household. Not valid for current subscribers to Harlequin Romantic Suspense books. All orders subject to credit approval. Credit or debit balances in a customer's account(s) may be offset by any other outstanding balance owed by or to the customer. Please allow 4 to 6 weeks for delivery. Offer available while quantities last.

Your Privacy—The Reader Service is committed to protecting your privacy. Our Privacy Policy is available online at www.ReaderService.com or upon request from the Reader Service.

We make a portion of our mailing list available to reputable third parties that offer products we believe may interest you. If you prefer that we not exchange your name with third parties, or if you wish to clarify or modify your communication preferences, please visit us at www.ReaderService.com/consumerschoice or write to us at Reader Service Preference Service, P.O. Box 9062, Buffalo, NY 14240-9062. Include your complete name and address.

HRS15

REQUEST YOUR FREE BOOKS!

2 FREE NOVELS
FROM THE SUSPENSE COLLECTION
PLUS 2 FREE GIFTS!

YES! Please send me 2 FREE novels from the Suspense Collection and my 2 FREE gifts (gifts are worth about $10). After receiving them, if I don't wish to receive any more books, I can return the shipping statement marked "cancel." If I don't cancel, I will receive 4 brand-new novels every month and be billed just $6.49 per book in the U.S. or $6.99 per book in Canada. That's a savings of at least 19% off the cover price. It's quite a bargain! Shipping and handling is just 50¢ per book in the U.S. and 75¢ per book in Canada.* I understand that accepting the 2 free books and gifts places me under no obligation to buy anything. I can always return a shipment and cancel at any time. Even if I never buy another book, the two free books and gifts are mine to keep forever.

191/391 MDN GH4Z

Name	(PLEASE PRINT)	
Address		Apt. #
City	State/Prov.	Zip/Postal Code

Signature (if under 18, a parent or guardian must sign)

Mail to the **Reader Service:**
IN U.S.A.: P.O. Box 1867, Buffalo, NY 14240-1867
IN CANADA: P.O. Box 609, Fort Erie, Ontario L2A 5X3

Want to try two free books from another line?
Call 1-800-873-8635 or visit www.ReaderService.com.

* Terms and prices subject to change without notice. Prices do not include applicable taxes. Sales tax applicable in N.Y. Canadian residents will be charged applicable taxes. Offer not valid in Quebec. This offer is limited to one order per household. Not valid for current subscribers to the Suspense Collection or the Romance/Suspense Collection. All orders subject to credit approval. Credit or debit balances in a customer's account(s) may be offset by any other outstanding balance owed by or to the customer. Please allow 4 to 6 weeks for delivery. Offer available while quantities last.